CAPTURING
Love

ALSO BY ANN PENNY

Capturing Love

Finding Beauty

Saving Soul

CAPTURING
Love

ANN PENNY

Arndell

Arndell

This edition is published by Arndell, an imprint of Keeperton in 2026
Dharawal Country, 1 / 18 Manning Street, Kiama, NSW, Australia, 2533
CAPTURING LOVE
Copyright © Ann Penny 2019
EXCLUSIVE PAPERBACK CONTENT
Copyright © Ann Penny 2026

10 9 8 7 6 5 4 3 2 1

ISBN 978-1-923232-11-2 (paperback)

Excerpt from Finding Beauty Copyright © Ann Penny 2021

The moral right of the author has been asserted

This novel is a work of fiction. Any reference to names, characters, businesses, places, events and incidents are products of the author's imagination or are used in a fictitious manner. Any resemblance to real persons, living or dead, is entirely coincidental.

All rights are reserved. No part of this book may be reproduced or transmitted in any form or by any means, graphic, electronic, or mechanical, including photocopying, recording, taping, or by any information storage retrieval system such as AI, without the express written permission of the Publisher.

Edited by Heather Bosevski Editing Services & Jenn Lockwood Editing
Formatted by Kirby Jones
Cover Design by Christabelle Designs

Printed and bound by CPI Group (UK) Ltd, Croydon, CR0 4YY

Sydney | Washington D.C. | London
www.keeperton.com/arndell

*For my husband. Who doesn't read my books,
but supports my writing dreams anyway.*

Chapter 1

I fucking hate hen's nights. *Cocks, Cocktails and Cock straws.* Argh, don't get me started. Masses of women assembled in one place to celebrate anything, from my experience, was never a good thing. It always led to excessive squealing, hugging and crying. Way too many emotions flying around for my liking, so this was my worst nightmare, and I didn't even know the bride-to-be.

I was hired to take photos and write an article on the upcoming nuptials of Melanie Warren, renowned Californian socialite. Luckily my job ended about five minutes ago, when she rolled up a hundred-dollar bill and began snorting cocaine off a compact mirror. For some bizarre reason she didn't want that part documented.

Although my abrupt dismissal was unexpected, I secretly rejoiced. I got a free trip to Las Vegas and now had the rest of the night to explore. *Yeefuckinghaa!*

Sliding through the masses of sweaty bodies, bumping and grinding against each other, I finally located the bar. I exhaled in relief and threw the company credit card on the counter, shouting my order to the first barman who looked my way.

The shot of tequila barely had a second to settle on the counter before I scooped it up and threw it back, welcoming the burn that hit my throat. Needing to escape the torture of the relentless, pulsing beat penetrating my skull, I stormed towards the exit and out of the club.

Cheers erupted from the huge queue waiting outside and the bouncer let just one overly enthusiastic girl inside to take my place. *Lucky her.*

Rolling my eyes, I turned my gaze to the unfamiliar interior of the MGM Grand Casino. Overwhelmed by the lights, the sounds and all the glitz, I picked a direction and started walking, determined to find my way to the Strip.

An exit sign materialised ahead and my heart fluttered as I approached. Reaching into the back pocket of my skinny jeans, I slid out the napkin I'd quickly scrawled my to-do list on during the flight over and took a deep breath. *Here we go!*

It was daytime when I flew into the city and I hadn't left the casino since I arrived. Night had fallen, and the city lights were breath-taking. As I absorbed my surroundings, my shoulders relaxed and my smile grew. I'd never been to Las Vegas before and I had ten hours left to make the most of it.

I was born and raised in Australia, but was one of the lucky few blessed with a dual passport. My dad grew up in New Jersey, but moved to Australia to be with my mum almost thirty years ago, giving me the best of both worlds.

Manhattan had been my home for the past six years and I was loving it. I didn't belong there, but fuck, I was trying. When my parents died, I decided I wasn't going to fester around suburbia, waiting for a life to find me. I needed to find a life. My own life. Away from the shadow of my parent's untimely death and the pitiful stares of all who remained.

Every cent of my inheritance was spent on a kick arse apartment in Greenwich Village, and I was working my butt off to earn just enough money to pay my bills, not starve to death, and put a little away each month towards my trip around the world.

I never set out to be a writer, but when our company laid off half its staff, I had to learn quick. I was a photographer primarily, but now I was required to write all the adjoining stories which doubled my workload, but unfortunately, not my pay.

With my camera hanging loosely around my neck, I strolled down the main drag until I reached the second item on my list. The Bellagio Fountain. Although it was already close to 10pm, there were people everywhere waiting for the next show.

I didn't push through to the front with the others. I hung back on the outskirts, searching for the perfect position. Music filled the air, and my heart picked up its pace as the water began jumping around in formation. Momentarily mesmerised by the lights and colours, my gaze drifted to the onlookers. Their delighted faces mirrored my own.

Scooping my long hair up into a messy bun, I brought the camera to my face and made every effort to look inconspicuous as I spied the crowd closely through the lens. I had no intention of taking photos of the show, but instead, I aimed to capture people's emotions as they experienced it. I had always been captivated by the way faces change when they saw and experienced beautiful moments, and I made it my life ambition to travel the world doing just that.

So while everyone was taking photos of the Bellagio Fountain, I was taking photos of them. It was a little weird, but I never imagined the pictures would see the light of day. It was just something I did. And apparently, I did it well.

As I scanned through the bodies pressed up against the barrier, I paused on a man not much older than myself. He leant over the railing, vacantly staring at the dancing water. *Snap*. His eyes were glazed and he appeared lost in thought. *Snap*. He ran his hand through his scruffy brown hair and breathed a heavy sigh. His shoulders relaxed but his face remained laced with tension. *Snap*.

I zoomed in a little closer, hoping to catch a glimpse of his eyes. Eye colour had always fascinated me, and I wondered which particular shade he was blessed with. Moving up his well-built body, I paused on his flawless face. *Snap. Snap*. My heart quickened as I examined his defined jawline, tempting lips and sparkling eyes. Eyes that were…looking directly at me. *Fuck*.

My trigger finger trembled as I casually swung the camera back towards the show, hoping he hadn't noticed. I didn't dare uncover my face, and pretended to take photos of nothing until the pounding in my chest eased. I'd been doing this for years and never been caught out.

After a long moment, I panned the camera back through the crowd and sure enough, he was still there. But he wasn't watching the show anymore. Instead, he waved in my direction with a playful smirk on his lips. *Hmm. Cocky.*

I pursed my lips behind the camera, and he tilted his head, clearly trying to see my reaction. *Stay cool, Josie.*

My cheeks grew warm and I slowly backed up until I disappeared into the crowd. I shoved my camera back in its case, and groaned in frustration as I let my hair loose from the pile on my head. The perfect photo opportunity had been ruined.

As my gaze settled on a burger joint across the road, my stomach let out an embarrassing cry. I hadn't consumed anything since this morning and I was starving. Apparently socialites don't eat, because I hadn't seen an ounce of food all day. Unless cocaine was somewhere on the food pyramid. *Fruit and Veg, perhaps?*

I waited by the roadside, trying to figure out how to cross without killing myself. Fancy cars sped by, followed by a limo with people popping their heads in and out of the open sunroof. It reminded me of an arcade game I used to play with Dad. If only I had a mallet.

Throwing my head to the sky in frustration, I found myself staring at an overpass leading directly to my desired destination. *Hallefuckingluiah!*

I bounded up the stairs and across the bridge, eager to cheer up my belly. Ambling into the diner, I glanced around the popular restaurant for an empty booth. Unfortunately, the only one left was behind a group of rowdy and obviously drunk men, in the back corner of the restaurant.

I cringed as I passed them, copping a few wolf whistles and muffled comments as I slid into the booth. Keeping my back turned, I hoped to discourage any further interaction. It didn't work.

"Hey there, beautiful. You should sit with us if you're all alone," a male voice said from behind me.

My shoulders instantly tensed. "No, that's fine. I'm actually waiting for someone."

He seemed to take the hint when I didn't turn around. "Lucky man," he muttered, returning to his jeering friends.

I picked up the menu and prayed they'd leave before they caught on to my lie.

As I carefully considered all my burger options, one by one, I flinched when I felt my hair move. Hoping it was an accident, I decided to ignore it. It wasn't until the movement turned into a little tug that my blood began to boil.

This was the reason I only had underlights. I loved having rainbow coloured hair, but I sometimes hated the attention it brought, so I hid it under my long auburn waves. At a distance you would assume I was a plain jane, but if I let you close enough, you'd find the real me hiding underneath.

"You've got a little rainbow under there," the man behind me slurred. "It makes me wonder what's down below."

I shifted across the seat and glared at him. "Don't touch me."

The man laughed and turned to his friends. "Feisty one, isn't she?"

Refocusing on the menu, I tried to ignore the grown men snicker.

They were obviously on a buck's night, going by the half-naked man lying next to them with a penis drawn on his face.

Another man from their table decided to join mine, and I cringed. I smelt the stale beer on his breath before he even spoke. "It doesn't look like your friend is going to show, perhaps *I* could keep you company tonight."

I shifted uncomfortably in my seat. "No, I'm fi—"

"Hey, Hun, sorry I'm late." A new voice glided past me, announcing the arrival of a broad-shouldered man who loomed over my unwanted guest.

Raising his hands in defeat, the drunk man sheepishly slid out of the booth, much to the enjoyment of his company.

My eyes grew wide as the man, who busted me taking his photo earlier, eased into the seat opposite me.

"Hazel," I murmured, staring into his alluring eyes. *Or are they green?*

"Pardon?" He chuckled as his brow rose.

I cleared my throat. "I mean, thank you."

His eyes lit up with his warm smile. "Would you like me to stay here until they leave?"

I exhaled in relief. "If it's not too much bother."

"Not at all." He held out his hand. "Grayson."

Smiling back, I shook it and my heart raced when he didn't break eye contact. "Josie."

"Pleased to meet you, Josie." The corner of his mouth lifted. "Bachelorette party?"

Such an easy assumption in Las Vegas. "How do you know I'm not a local?"

"Well apart from the accent, your accessories give you away." He glanced down at my chest and I awkwardly followed his gaze. I let out a small laugh at the discovery of the penis candy necklace, that Melanie had insisted I wear, still sitting around my neck. My cheeks warmed as I pulled it over my head and wrapped it in a serviette.

"Whoa, wait! Don't just throw it away. Those actually taste pretty great."

"What?" I laughed. This guy was weird. *Good weird, I hope.*

He held out his hand, palm up. "I'm not kidding, it's my favourite type of candy."

I tilted my head and narrowed my eyes before slowly handing it over. "Penis candy?"

"It comes in other shapes too."

I couldn't help but smirk. "Sure it does."

"Don't knock it till you try it." Breaking one off into his mouth, he let out a delighted moan and leant back in his chair. *Wow. That was something.*

I watched him chew, and found it strangely arousing. "Alright, give me one."

Grayson held the necklace to his chest. "No way. You were going to throw them away."

"Give me a little penis," I insisted sternly, holding out my palm.

Suddenly the waitress was standing by our table, blinking rapidly. My cheeks burned and Grayson's eyes grew large as he held on to his laughter. She took my order and moved her impatient gaze to Grayson. He looked over my shoulder at the neighbouring table and back to me quizzically, clearly unsure of what to do.

"Let me buy you a burger as a thank you," I said, hoping he would stay. I felt much safer with him there, and his company was proving to be entertaining.

A look of surprise passed over his face.

"Come on, I have an expense card. Help me abuse it." I grinned.

He chortled and shrugged indifferently, ordering the same as me. As the waitress walked away, Grayson handed back my necklace and I popped a tiny penis in my mouth. He was right. It was tasty.

"So...buck's night?" I asked, intrigued to learn more about him.

He ran his hand through his already dishevelled hair and leant forward to close the gap between us. "How do you know *I'm* not a local?"

I smiled and pointed out the lipstick smear on his face. He rubbed his thumb over his cheek and scowled when the pink mark transferred onto it.

"Not your scene?" I asked, hopeful he wasn't just like the men behind me.

He shook his head. "Nope."

I glanced around the restaurant at the other patrons. "Yeah, me neither."

"So, what's with the fancy camera? I wouldn't have thought anyone would want their last night of freedom recorded."

I chuckled. "You're right there. As soon as they pulled out the cocaine, I was sent on my way."

Grayson frowned. "What? Your friends ditched you?"

"Oh no, it's not like that, I'm actually here on a job. I was hired to document the 'civilised' part of the day. Like all the primping and pampering stuff. Not so much the debauchery."

I handed the necklace back to him and he bit off another penis.

"So, you're a photographer?" he asked, mid-chew.

I thought about it for a moment. "Partly. I don't really know what I'm classified as anymore."

"Is that what you want to be?"

He passed the necklace back and I slid the little penises up and down the elastic as I pondered my answer. "Yeah, I guess… one day."

"Is that what you were doing outside?"

Heat rose up my neck. *Dammit! He recognised me.* "Yeah, you totally busted me. Normally people don't notice what I'm doing."

"I noticed you."

Our eyes collided and I sucked in my breath. *Argh. Connection. There it is.* I shook off the unexpected flutter in my stomach. *I have a boyfriend, for Christ's sake. And as much as I'm unsure of my relationship with him, I'm not a cheater.*

Clearing my throat, I lowered my gaze to where my camera bag lay beside me. "I like to take action photos. Unsuspecting people, moments, stuff like that." I slipped the camera out and turned it on, flicking through the images I took just moments before. "Can I show you something?" I asked, meeting his curious gaze.

With his nod, I jumped out of my seat and slid in beside him. He was momentarily surprised until I held up the camera's viewing screen, eager to show him an example of my work.

As his eyes tried to adjust, he sighed. "Hang on." He slid a pair of reading glasses out of his side pocket, and perched them on his nose.

I gazed up at him and giggled. "I thought only old people carried around reading glasses."

"They make me look serious though, right?" he asked, holding back a smile.

"I don't think that's possible."

"How's that?"

I grinned. "You're eating penis candy."

Chuckling, he lifted the camera out of my hands. "So, what am I looking at?" He blinked a few times and fell silent for a moment as the image became clearer to him.

I winced, not sure how he would take my 'art'.

It was a photo of him watching the fountain. Leaning up against the barrier, surrounded by people, yet totally alone. The light reflected off his eyes, making him look both sad and peaceful at the same time.

My heart lurched. "I'm sorry. I know it's a little strange. I'll delete it if you want."

Grayson shook his head. "No, no, don't apologise. It's... *wow*. You actually captured a rare moment for me. As much as *you* don't think I'm a serious guy, I definitely don't get a chance to relax often." He looked back at me. "Can you show me more?"

My heart leapt and I nodded, taking the camera back to find him another image. Careful not to breach my non-disclosure agreement, I discreetly scrolled past the images of Melanie Warren until I found some of my personal favourites.

He relaxed back into the seat. "These are amazing, Josie. What do you do with them all?"

I laughed and leant back with him. "Some are for work, but as for my favourites, nothing really."

"Nothing at all?" His brow furrowed as he turned to me.

I shrugged. "Sometimes I print them and hang them up at home, but that's about it."

Grayson shook his head. "You're really talented. You should be having exhibitions."

"I'm not *that* good," I said with a snort.

He handed back my camera and I returned to my side of the booth to slip it back in its case.

"My fiancé takes me to tons of them. You're definitely *that* good."

Momentarily pausing on the zipper at the mention of his wife-to-be, my heart dipped. *Why do you care, Josie? You only just met this guy, like, five minutes ago.*

I lifted my gaze to his. "Well, thank you. That's kind of you to say, but I don't think I'm ready for anything like that."

Grayson's disbelieving stare was only broken by the food arriving at our table. I pushed his plate towards him and brought mine closer, already salivating over the promise of greasy goodness. He appeared to be as starving as I was, and we both hoed in.

"Oh my god, this burger is amaaazing," I mumbled through my full mouth.

Grayson wiped some ketchup from his lip. "Surely you've had one of Joe's famous burgers before? I get one every time I'm here."

I swallowed my food and took a sip of my cola. "This is my first trip to Vegas."

"What? Really?"

I shrugged. "*And* it's a work trip, so I'm leaving early in the morning."

A deep line formed between his eyebrows. "But have you had any time to check out the sights?"

"Does a VIP suite at the MGM Grand count? Oh, and some swanky club where I appeared to be undressed—well, *overdressed*." My eyes bulged at the memory. "You should've seen how fucking short their skirts were. And no underwear! Like, nothing. Nada!"

Grayson burst out laughing and it was a divine sight. "This really is your first trip here, isn't it?"

"It's my first trip anywhere in a long time," I uttered, with a sad smile.

His mouth dropped. "How long is long?"

"Six years. When I moved to the States."

"Are you joking?" He pondered me for a moment before taking off his glasses. "Finish your burger. I'm going to take you on an express tour."

"What?" I laughed. Surely he was joking.

"I've been here a million times. I know all the best places and know all the right people."

I narrowed my eyes at him. "Why would you do that? You don't even know me."

He shrugged. "Well, for one, you've made my night a lot more interesting. And two, I can't go back to my hotel until morning."

"What? Why not?"

"Because I'll never hear the end of it. My friends are relentless."

I nodded with a strained laugh, not really understanding. "Riiight."

We ate the rest of our burgers in a comfortable silence, which was odd considering he was a total stranger. I called for the bill and Grayson watched me hand over my company credit card with the strangest expression. Like he'd never been bought dinner before.

As we both stood to leave, I almost collided with one of the drunk men from earlier. Without hesitation, Grayson slipped his arm around my shoulders and ushered me out onto the Strip, holding me tightly against his side until we were out of sight. Once we were safe from detection, he gave me a little squeeze before dropping his arm, leaving a current of electricity flowing through my body, which was unexpectedly exhilarating. *This is not good.*

Chapter 2

"So, where do your friends think you are right now?" I asked curiously, as we headed back towards the overpass.

Grayson sniggered. "In a strip club, getting a private show."

My mouth fell open and my eyes lit up in amusement. "That's a long and expensive lap dance."

He chuckled. "I told the staff if they keep the guys distracted, I'll give them a big tip in the morning. Hopefully with all the free-flowing booze, they won't even notice I'm gone."

I stopped suddenly and turned to him. "Wait, is this *your* buck's night?"

He grimaced and nodded.

"You're kidding?" I gasped as my eyes went round.

Grayson shook his head. "Well, it's kind of a joint bachelor night with a friend of mine."

I chuckled and continued walking up the stairs. "Why on earth are you having your buck's in Vegas if you're not into it?"

"It was a surprise trip," he said, shoving his hands in his pockets. "I didn't know where I was going until this morning. I personally think it's just an excuse for our friends to escape their boring married lives."

I laughed. "Ah, so you're the last of the unmarried, hey?"

Grayson's jaw twitched. "Much to my father's disappointment."

"Well he must be happy now. When's the wedding?" I glanced up at him when he didn't respond straight away.

He cleared his throat and focused on the pavement as he walked. "Two weeks," he replied, deadpan.

"You sound…excited." I crinkled my nose. "What is it? An arranged marriage?"

He lifted his brow and laughed. "No, not intentionally. We've known each other since we were kids. Our families are close, so we're a good fit."

"A good fit? Sounds *romantic*."

"We've been together for eleven years. We're past that stage."

"Aren't you supposed to be married for fifty years before you say that shit? You should be head over heels in love right now. That's how I want to feel before I ever get married."

He shot me a sideways glance. "You're a romantic?"

I shrugged. "Perhaps not in the obvious way."

We silently made our way back to the fountain, where we first unofficially met.

"Don't get me wrong, I love her. I do," Grayson continued as he leant his back against the guardrail.

I paused in front of him, remembering a job I did a few months ago. "Wait a sec." I grabbed my camera and brought it up to my eye, watching him through the lens.

He shifted uncomfortably. "What are you doing?"

"Tell me about your fiancé."

"What, why?" he asked, scrunching up his nose.

I smiled at him as I focused in on his eyes. "Just tell me what you love about her."

He folded his arms across his chest. "Well, she's sweet and attractive." *Snap*.

"Go on."

He sighed and looked away. *Snap*. "We've had similar upbringings, so she understands me, and my parents adore her, which makes my life a hell of a lot easier." *Snap*.

I studied the photos on my camera and moved my finger over the delete button, hesitant to show him what was lacking while he described his soon-to-be wife.

"What is it?" he asked, stepping forward.

I lifted my gaze. "A few months ago, I interviewed this guy about his wife. They'd been together since they were teenagers and I took photos of him while he answered that same question."

I flicked through the old images and held my camera out to show him.

Grayson cautiously took it, shooting me a peculiar look. Sliding his glasses back on, he peered down at my photograph. "It's a beautiful picture, but I'm not sure what you mean."

"Check out his eyes...they lit up when he talked about her." I took my camera out of his hands and pressed a few buttons before passing it back. "*This* is you."

He blinked a few times, and went quiet, falling back onto the guardrail. "Are you always this good at reading people?"

I offered him a sad smile. "Through a lens, maybe."

He handed back the camera and turned, focusing his attention on the fountain as it started to dance.

"So, what is it? The eleven-year itch?" I asked hesitantly, hoping I hadn't offended him.

He snorted. "I've been feeling the itch for a while now," he said, loosening his collar.

My mouth dropped, but I scooped it back up. "Does your fiancé feel the same?"

"I suspect so. We were both so reluctant to set a date, our families called an intervention and forced us to."

"*Oh.* So you're one of those couples with the epically long engagement?"

He chuckled. "Yeah, you could say that."

I brought the camera back to my face and panned through the crowd, sensing Grayson watching me.

"So, what about you? Are you seeing anyone?"

I cleared my throat. "Um, yeah."

Something flashed across his expression before he nodded. "And is he *the one?*"

I laughed without meaning to and covered my mouth in embarrassment.

Grayson's eyes widened as a smirk formed on his lips. "I'll take that as a *hell no.*"

I sighed, annoyed at myself. "He is...lovely. *Super* lovely."

"*But...?*"

I dropped the camera back into its case. "Argh, I don't know."

"How long have you been together?"

I thought for a moment, trying to figure out just how long it had been. "Um, almost two years...I think."

"Marriage on the cards?"

I breathed in deeply. "He keeps hinting at it."

Grayson appeared entirely fascinated. "And you?"

"I keep changing the subject."

"Right." He chuckled, clearly amused. "Well, it looks like we both need to blow off a little steam tonight. What do you want to do first?"

"Well..." I pulled the torn napkin out of my pocket.

Grayson moved closer. "What's that?"

"My to-do list," I replied, straightening my posture. "I wrote it on the plane, hence the lack of real paper."

He smirked and squinted down at the ratty napkin with great interest. "Only six things? That should be easy."

"Five, actually," I muttered, quickly folding it back up.

Grayson shrugged nonchalantly. "Alright, so what's number one?"

I shook my head. "Number one isn't possible. We'll have to skip it."

"Hang on, what is it?" He reached for my list, but I snatched it back.

"It doesn't matter." But it really did. I'd wanted to see the Grand Canyon my entire life and I was so damn close.

Grayson's expression softened. "Well, what's number two then?"

"The Bellagio Fountain." I grinned.

He smiled and raised his index finger. "Check. Except you seemed to have more interest in the crowd than you did the show."

I shrugged happily. "It still counts."

"Okay, so what's next?"

"Number three. Play legit poker."

Grayson raised one eyebrow. "Legit?"

I nodded eagerly. "When in Rome, right?" I chuckled. "One problem though. I have no idea *how* to play poker."

Grayson grimaced. "Well this isn't exactly the place to learn. Unless you're a secret millionaire and can afford to lose a couple of grand."

My face fell. "I guess the slot machines will do."

"No, no." He shook his head. "You want to play poker, let's play poker."

"It's okay." I waved him off. "I have no money anyway."

Grayson placed his hand over my elbow and led me off in a new direction. "Come on, you won't need any."

I tried to think of a game of poker that didn't require money and my eyes grew wide. "I'm not playing strip poker!"

He laughed wholeheartedly and I resisted the urge to take a photo of the exquisite sight. "As much as I would like to see that, no, your clothing will remain on." His cheeks turned pink when he realised what he said.

Following Grayson up the Strip, we reached Caesar's Palace. As we walked through the breath-taking casino, all the staff appeared to acknowledge him with a nod. It only took a whisper into an employee's ear before we were ushered to a room full of serious gamblers.

"I told you, I can't play," I murmured as we approached a large table surrounded by extremely well-dressed players and onlookers.

He leant down to my ear. "But *they* don't know that," he whispered, guiding me into the empty chair beside him. "Bluffing is everything."

Grayson nodded to the dealer and he slid over a pile of poker chips.

"What are you doing?" I gasped. "How much is there? Like a hundred bucks?"

He chuckled. "Yeah, something like that." Grayson grabbed a handful and placed them on the table in front of us. He continued to whisper the rules as the dealer shuffled the cards. His warm breath on my neck distracted me from his words, leaving me just as clueless about poker as I was when we started.

We played as a team and lost terribly. Grayson didn't seem too upset, so I figured he must have exaggerated how much the chips were worth.

As we sauntered out of the casino, I paused at the slot machines, fishing in my pocket for the quarter I was supposed to throw in the fountain earlier. I pulled it out and held it up triumphantly.

"Last chance," I said with a grin, and pulled down the lever.

To my delighted surprise, I won a ton of free spins and *at least* a hundred dollars. I couldn't believe my luck. Grayson crossed his arms and shook his head with a chuckle.

"Here," I said, handing him the overflowing bucket of coins. "This should cover my poker debt."

Grayson held up his hands and stepped away. "You don't have to repay me."

I forced the bucket into his chest. "Yes, I do."

Lowering his eyes, he slowly lifted his hands to cradle the container. "Thanks." He hesitantly turned around and handed it over to an employee, who was hovering nearby.

"What are you doing?" I gasped, pulling his arm back.

"It's okay." He chuckled. "I'm staying at this hotel. He'll just put it on my account."

"Oh. I guess that explains why everyone seems to know you."

He smiled tightly and quickly changed the subject. "So, what's number four?"

"Gondola ride at The Venetian."

"Of course," he muttered, rolling his eyes.

I dropped my gaze as my cheeks heated. "Well, I'd prefer to go to Venice, but I need to save a shit load more money first."

"I'm sorry, that was rude of me. If you want to go on a gondola ride, I'll take you. In fact, it's not too far from here."

The corner of my mouth quirked up. "Will you pretend to be my lover and serenade me with Italian love songs?"

He shook his head with a laugh before taking off down the Strip. We crossed the road again and headed directly to The Venetian, but when I saw the length of the queue for the ride, I groaned. "Shit," I mumbled under my breath.

Grayson didn't seem deterred at all. He marched straight past the waiting customers and spoke to the man at the front taking tickets. I was about to tell him not to worry, when the same man escorted us onto our own private gondola.

"What did you say to that guy?" I asked, glancing back at the disgruntled customers glaring at us from the water's edge.

He shrugged. "I just paid him for the small favour."

"You didn't have to do that."

Grayson climbed into the boat and held out his hand. As he guided me down, he whispered, "We just need to pretend like we're newlyweds."

I let out an embarrassing snort and Grayson quickly hushed me. He sunk into the seat and lifted his arm, inviting me in, so without hesitation, I slotted myself into his side. His expensive cologne ignited my senses, and I found myself leaning in for more. Grayson's jaw twitched and I quickly redirected my attention to the water as our gondola began to move.

"Does this mean you'll be serenading me now?" I asked, hiding the obvious heat in my cheeks.

Grayson laughed and wiped his hand down his face. "Trust me, you do not want to hear me sing."

As we floated through the amazing shopping mall, Grayson asked about the next item on my list.

I shifted out from under his arm and faced him with a smile. "The Stratosphere."

"The *Stratosphere*?" he moaned. "What exactly do you want to do there?"

"Enjoy the amazing lookout over the city, of course."

Grayson looked relieved.

I grinned cheekily. "And the Sky Jump?"

His face dropped and turned a shade of grey. "*No*. Really?"

"Don't like heights?"

"No, not exactly," he uttered, pretending to watch the scenery glide by.

I nudged him playfully. "Come on, do it with me. It'll be fun."

He spun back with round eyes. "That is not what I call fun."

"Hmm, figures." I folded my arms across my chest.

Grayson tapered his gaze. "What does?"

"You don't seem like the type to leave your comfort zone."

"My comfort zone?" He snorted. "You don't even know me."

"You're right. It's a bit of an assumption on my part, but you don't seem to be much of a risk taker." I tried to hide my smirk as I messed with him.

"Ha-ha, I see what you're doing," he said, with a return nudge. "I'm just not one to jump into the unknown. Plus, it's not that I don't *like* heights…I'm *petrified* of them."

"Really? I never would have guessed," I said, studying him curiously.

"I've become quite proficient at hiding my weaknesses."

I pondered him for a moment. "How many people know this about you?"

He leant back into the padded seat and closed his eyes. "One."

"Your fiancé?"

His left eye opened. "You."

My heart skipped. "Oh."

Grayson let out a long sigh. "Look, I'll take you up there, but I'm staying at the bar."

As much as I resisted, Grayson used his generous wallet to get us to the front of another queue at the famous Stratosphere Sky Jump. Lucky he did, because I was already chickening out with a mere glimpse out the window at the city below.

Sweat beads rolled down my neck at the realisation of what I was about to do. Jump off the 108th floor of the tallest tower in Las Vegas. *What am I thinking!?*

My heart started to pound as I pulled on the jumpsuit.

"Are you okay? You look green." Grayson stood in front of me, analysing my expression as I sank into an empty chair, feeling defeated.

I swallowed down the lump in my throat. "Um, no…" *Soooo no.*

He pinched the bridge of his nose. "Is this the first time you've been up this high?"

"No," I said, shaking my head. "I've been this high before."

Grayson rested his hands on his hips and narrowed his eyes. "When?"

My shoulders dropped. "On the plane coming here."

"Ooookay," he replied, suppressing his laughter.

I glanced out the window at the sea of sparkling lights. "I just didn't think it would be so…so…"

"Far down?" Grayson didn't follow my gaze. He kept his eyes fixed on mine.

Panic flooded my body. "The old me would've been fine with this, but the new me…well, I don't take many risks these days." *I can't afford to.*

"You'll be fine," he said, resting his hand on my shoulder. "You've come this far. Don't you want to cross it off your list?"

Tears welled as I realised this may be my only chance.

Grayson clenched his jaw. "I'll do it, if you do it," he blurted.

My mouth fell open. "What?"

He lifted his serious gaze to meet mine. "It's a one-time offer."

"You would really do that for me? A total stranger?" My eyes glazed over with emotion.

"Let's just say, there's something about you that makes me feel invincible." He pulled me onto my feet by the front of my jumpsuit until we were standing face to face, just inches apart.

My breathing shallowed. "Thank you, Grayson, for everything."

He grinned, but his face was paling. "Don't talk like we're not going to survive this."

"Well if I don't, at least I've had one of the most amazing nights of my life."

As colour returned to Grayson's stunned face, I stepped away from him and towards the platform to await my final instructions.

Then, I jumped into the unknown.

Chapter 3

As I fell to my almost certain death, all the air sucked out of my lungs, hindering my scream. The target below grew closer but I didn't want it to end, because the feeling was like nothing I'd ever experienced.

My feet hit the ground, but I was still on a high. I couldn't keep still until I saw Grayson leap from the tower above. He zoomed down the cable at speed, looking as exhilarated as I felt. A moment later, he landed, hanging his head back with laughter as the employee detached him.

He panned his gaze to where I stood and my stomach somersaulted. His euphoric smile caught my breath, and I blinked as if I was taking a mental photograph.

Our excess adrenaline had us jogging towards each other before I launched myself into his arms, giggling as he spun me in circles. My feet found the ground, but neither of us stepped away.

Grayson's heart pounded through his chest as he ran his hand down my cheek. "That was…"

"Amazing?" I gushed.

His gaze burned into mine, but his smile faltered. Quickly stepping back, he let out an awkward laugh. "Yes, amazing."

"So, have we cured your fear of heights?" I asked, wanting to diffuse the obvious tension.

He peeked up at the next jumper and winced. "I don't know about that. But I haven't done something like that since I was a kid."

"You should do it more. It suits you." I smiled.

Grayson's cheeks turned pink. "We'll see. Depends on what's next on your list."

I unzipped my jumpsuit and pulled out the napkin, reading the fifth item in my head. "Well, the last one's pretty lame compared to that. Perhaps we should go on the High Roller instead?" I pointed up to the roller coaster that wrapped around the Stratosphere tower and my heart quickened.

"Oh my god, check that out!" Grayson hollered, pointing over my shoulder.

Whirling towards his line of sight, I felt a light tug on my fingers as he snatched the list from my grip. I turned back and narrowed my eyes. "That was cruel," I said, trying to snatch it back, but he shrugged me off with a chuckle.

Grayson brought the list to his nose and squinted. "Number five. Go dancing at a fancy nightclub." He dropped his gaze to mine. "That's it?"

"Well, yeah," I shrugged. "But not that house techno soulless crap. I want to dance to real music."

He pursed his lips. "I know what you mean. My fiancé loves that shit and it drives me nuts."

"Well, that's a deal breaker right there," I blurted, and my eyes grew wide. "I mean for me, that would be a deal breaker for me. I'm sure your fiancé has a ton of better traits to make up for her bad taste in music." Palm meet face.

He laughed and slipped the list into his back pocket. "Come on, I know the perfect place."

As I followed Grayson's lead, I wondered who he was. The way people treated him, I half expected to find out he was some sort of celebrity. He certainly had the looks of a movie star, but no one approached him for an autograph or selfie, so it couldn't be that. His clothing, his confidence, and his ability to get whatever he wanted definitely screamed money. The type of money I could only dream about.

"So, what do you do for a living?" I asked, curiously.

Grayson took his time formulating his answer. "I work for the family business."

He didn't elaborate on the type of business, so I tried not to pry. "Where are you based?"

"LA for now, but who knows where my father will ship me next."

I nodded, but kept my thoughts to myself.

Grayson turned to me as we strolled down the Strip. "And you? When you're not taking photos of strangers, what do you do?"

"I work for a little magazine in New York."

He arched his brow, clearly interested. "Really? In Manhattan?"

I nodded proudly. "It's just an indie publication, but we have a strong fan base."

"What's it called? I might know it."

I snorted. "I just binge-watched *You* on Netflix, so it's probably best I don't elaborate until I'm sure you're not a psycho."

He chuckled and shoved his hands in his pockets. "Smart girl."

"Plus, even if you wanted to stalk me, there's a high chance I won't be working there for much longer anyway."

"Why is that?"

I sighed. "The management are totally old school and don't want to move to an online platform like all the mainstream mags. It is going to kill us eventually. We've already lost some big advertising accounts because we don't have a digital presence." My face fell at the thought. I didn't know what I was going to do without that job.

"Wow, yeah, you're right. You won't survive on print alone."

"That's what I keep telling them," I groaned. "But what would a twenty-seven-year-old photographer from Australia know about business?"

Grayson nodded slowly. "I know the feeling. I have ideas to grow our company and my father just laughs them off."

"Really? But won't you be taking over someday, if it's a family business?"

"I've yet to prove myself in his eyes. That role is currently reserved for my older brother. He who can do no wrong." He ran his fingers through his hair and returned them to his pockets.

Pressing my lips together, I offered him a sad smile. It was obviously a sore point.

"I've always wanted a sibling," I said, after a moment of reflection.

"They're overrated."

My heart ached. "I don't think so."

Grayson tilted his head and caught my eye. "You don't seem like an only child. Your parents didn't spoil you growing up?"

I looked away as my breathing shallowed. "Not with material things, but they were always there for me."

"They sound great," he responded in a haze, deep in his own thoughts.

"You know what?" I stopped walking and turned to him with my hands on my hips. "I think we both need a drink."

As we reached a famous nightclub, notorious for its celebrity VIPs, my heart sank; the line outside was twice the size as the one at the club I left earlier. "Perhaps something a little less busy?"

Grayson chuckled and kept walking past the line towards the two huge burly men blocking the entrance. *Again?!*

I jogged up behind him. "Grayson, no. I can't let you hand over any more money."

"Don't worry," he chortled. "I won't have to here. I know the owner."

Security merely nodded their heads before lifting the red barrier for us. Grayson didn't even have to speak. I wanted to ask him more questions, but the bass became too loud to talk at a normal level and we had to resort to sign language. I motioned towards the ladies' room and left him at the bar to order our drinks.

Instantly intimidated as I pushed through the crowd of beautiful people, I glanced down at my outfit and grimaced. *I don't fit in here.*

Hiding away in the first available cubical, I ran my fingers through my tousled hair, adjusted my bra, and loosened my shirt until my dismal cleavage peeked out. All while listening to the constant chatter of drunken women as they primped themselves in front of the mirror.

"Oh my god, do you really think that's William Harlow?" one woman said.

"He looks just like his brother. It has to be, right?" her friend gushed.

"I don't know. I heard he's not into the party scene, and that clearly isn't his fiancé."

"You're right, maybe it's not him. Fucking hot though…"

As their conversation faded away, I realised the whole place must've been rolling in celebs and socialites. It was wasted on me though because I had no interest in them. I had better shit to do with my time.

Washing my hands, my eyes grew wide at the array of fragrances on offer. I lifted a few to my nose and breathed them in. Settling on a zesty citron and floral aroma, I applied it to my neck and wrists, hoping to freshen myself up before hitting the dance floor.

When I returned, Grayson was sitting in a private booth, not far from the dance floor, sipping a drink. I eyed the bottle of champagne on the table, next to the reserved sign, and shook my head with a laugh. This guy had some sweet connections, and I didn't even care to know why. I wasn't going to see him again, so why not enjoy the perks?

"You wanna dance?" he yelled over the music that was already triggering my body to move to the beat.

"Um…yeah, yes!" I stammered, blinking multiple times in surprise. Pete never danced with me.

I quickly sculled down my drink before Grayson grabbed my hand and pulled me onto the crowded dance floor.

Stumbling out of the club well into the early morning, I laughed hysterically as Grayson impersonated the dance moves of the fifty-something-year-old man who had been trying to hit on me for the past hour.

I hadn't had that much fun with someone in years. Perhaps it was because we both had partners and lived on opposite sides of the country, but it made it easier to relax. It was freeing not to have expectations on each other. It was just what I needed, and what I preferred.

"What time is it?" I asked, glancing around at all the people still wandering the street.

Grayson lifted his sleeve to reveal a super flashy watch. He held it ridiculously close to his face so he could read it without his glasses and I giggled.

"Three am." He peered back at me. "Tired yet?"

Adrenaline was still pumping through my veins. "No, you?"

He shook his head. "Nope."

We looked at each other and smiled bashfully, and I felt oddly relieved our night wasn't over just yet.

"So, what's next on the list?" Grayson reached into his back pocket, but came up with nothing.

I held the napkin in my hand and waved it triumphantly. I had managed to steal it back mid-move on the dance floor. "I'm like a dancing ninja!" I held up my arms in a karate pose and robot danced them away.

Grayson burst out laughing. "You're such a dork. Come on, show me what's next."

"Nope, that's it! It's all done. Thanks to you I've completed my top five, well, minus the Grand Canyon that is."

"Wait, was that number one?" he asked, narrowing his eyes. "The Grand Canyon?"

"Yeah, I told you it was impossible."

"Difficult, yes, impossible, no. You should have told me."

"What were you going to do? Hire a helicopter in the middle of the night to fly us out there?"

He shrugged. "Well, yeah."

I scrunched up my face before bursting out into laughter. "You're hilarious. I almost believed you for a second."

Grayson looked away with pursed lips. "We don't have enough time now."

"It's fine, Gray. I'll do it when I come back." *In fifty years.*

Grayson stared at the list in my hands, like he was trying to figure something out. "Are you sure there wasn't another item on there? I may have shitty eyesight, but I definitely counted six."

My eyes grew large. "Nope, that's all of them."

Grayson moved towards me and pointed. "No, there is another one. I just need my glasses to read the ridiculously small handwriting."

I stepped backwards and hid the list behind me, cheeks heating up.

"Look, there's no judgement here. We barely know each other and we're unlikely to meet again, so come on, hand it over." He held out his hand, palm up.

I grimaced and shook my head.

His eyes lit up. "It must be something sinful," he said, tapering his gaze. "Is it drugs?"

I scoffed. "No! I'm not stupid."

"So it must be...sex? You want to sleep with a prostitute? Become a stripper?"

"*What?!* No!" I laughed.

Grayson chortled. "Not sure how you'd go as a stripper though, now that I've seen your dance moves."

My mouth flew open and he seized the opportunity to snatch the list out of my hand.

"Argh, you're so sneaky!" I shoved his arm and frowned. "And my dance moves are awesome."

Grayson grinned as he slipped his glasses back on.

I exhaled in defeat as he read my scrawl. "It's just a silly bonus one."

He chuckled quietly and cleared his throat to read it aloud. "Meet a devilishly handsome man and get married by Elvis in a Las Vegas chapel."

"It was meant to be a joke," I muttered, rolling my eyes.

He rested his hands on his hips and sighed. "I don't think I'll be able to help with that one."

I nudged him away. "Well, of course you can't," I agreed with a smirk. "You're not devilishly handsome."

"Oh, buuurn." He clutched his chest. "Well, it sounds better than what I have planned in a couple of weeks."

My heart dipped. Why did the thought of him getting married bother me so much? I had only known him for a few hours. *A few amazing hours.*

"Big wedding?" I asked, not really wanting to know any more about his relationship.

He snorted and dropped his gaze to the ground. "Just four hundred of our *closest friends*."

"Holy shit!" My eyes almost popped out of their sockets. "How on earth do you even know that many people?"

"I don't. They're mostly friends of my parents, business associates, that kind of thing."

My eyes narrowed. "Is that what you and your fiancé want?"

"It's what's expected," he said, with a shrug.

I raised my brow and nodded, but I didn't understand. "We come from different worlds, you and I."

Grayson shuffled his foot over some loose gravel. "Your parents don't have expectations on you?"

I shook my head and smiled tightly. *Here comes the pity stare.* "My parents are dead."

His eyes shot up and blinked twice. "Fuck, Josie. I'm sorry."

"No, no. It's fine. It was a long time ago," I said, desperately wanting to change the subject. "Hey, you wanna go for a swim? My hotel has the most amazing pool, and I'm going to miss out if I don't take a dip tonight."

His eyes were laced with sadness as he pondered me, but his mouth slowly curved into a smile. "Sounds like an excellent idea."

We made our way back to my hotel. The fanciest place I'd ever stayed in my life, and it wasn't even the flashiest hotel in Vegas. As we reached the massive pool that had been on my mind all day, my face fell.

"Oh no, it's closed!" I cried, running my hands down my face. "I haven't been swimming in years."

Grayson frowned. "Years?"

I rolled my eyes. "I'm a starving artist in New York. I'm not around fancy pools all that often."

Grayson scanned the grounds until he spotted one of the night security guards, and turned back to me. "Go to your room and change into your swimsuit. I'll meet you back here in five minutes."

"What are you up to?" I asked, narrowing my gaze.

He smirked. "Have I disappointed you yet?"

With a quick shake of my head, I grinned and bolted for the elevator.

I returned to find him wearing hotel branded board shorts beside a pile of towels, with yet another bottle of champagne sitting in an ice bucket. Just as I went to grill him about who exactly he was, he bombed into the pool.

With a laugh, I followed his lead, jumping in after him. I waded lazily around the pool while Grayson swam laps. His parents must've spent a ton of money on swimming lessons, because his strokes were flawless. My expertise consisted of doggy paddle and floating.

Grayson shook the water from his hair as he found his feet. "So, have you had a good night?" His eyes sparkled under the moonlight, and I found myself edging closer to glimpse his eye colour. They had been changing all night.

"I've had an amazing night. Thanks to you." I grinned back at him. "Your fiancé is one lucky lady."

The reminder seemed to cut the tension and Grayson fell into the water, propelling himself backwards. "So, do you think you'll say yes when your boyfriend finally pops the question?" he asked, floating like a starfish.

"I don't know," I groaned. "He's a really good guy..."

His head popped up. "But...?"

"I...I feel like I'm settling."

Grayson remained silent and waded towards me.

"How did you know your fiancé was the one?" I asked, meeting his eyes. Wanting to see truth in them.

He lowered his gaze and ran his hands over the water between us. "I never really had a choice."

My eyes were drawn to the shimmering ripples. "And if you did?"

Our gazes lifted together and my heart fluttered. *I'm in trouble here.*

Grayson's now green eyes burned into mine as he stepped closer. The beads of water rolling down his hard chest mesmerised me and my body temperature rose.

"How's about we...err...crack open that champagne," I stammered, stepping backwards, ignoring the ache below. We were in very dangerous territory.

Grayson dipped back under the water and popped up at the edge of the pool. His gaze trailed after me as I slipped out and tiptoed to the sun lounge. As I picked up a towel from the pile and wrapped it around my waist, my sideways glance caught his eyes moving over my body.

"Are you coming out?" I asked, hiding my blushing cheeks as I dried my hair.

"Just a sec," he rasped after a moment of hesitation. He disappeared under the water again and proceeded to swim four solid laps of the pool.

Instead of watching temptation pass by my eyes every few seconds, I distracted myself by opening the champagne and filling two glasses.

Grayson finally rose at the edge, still looking reluctant to leave the water. "Can you pass me a towel?"

With a shrug, I grabbed one from the pile beside me and threw it over. He wrapped it around his waist as he exited the pool, while discreetly adjusting himself. *Well, at least I'm not the only one affected.*

The double sun lounge dipped as he lowered himself beside me. I offered him a glass and he took it with a lazy grin and leant back.

"To conquering my top five in six hours." I smiled, leaning back with him.

"Almost."

I clinked his glass. "Close enough."

We lay side by side, quietly watching the sky change colour as the sun rose behind the hotel buildings.

"Your boyfriend is the lucky one," Grayson said, after a long sigh.

"I don't think so," I muttered.

He nudged my side. "If he sees you the way I do, he is."

My cheeks warmed at his compliment, but I shook my head with a sigh. "I'm going to break his heart."

Grayson turned to me with a raised brow. "Why do you think that?"

"I'm just not great at relationships. I have…walls."

"Walls worth climbing over I bet."

I laughed and punched his arm. "Oh my god, can you stop?"

"What?" He chuckled, rubbing his arm like I actually hurt him.

"Flirting with me!"

He smirked. "I can't seem to control my mouth around you."

I looked down at his lips and unconsciously licked my own.

"Josie…" he warned in a deep voice.

My eyes quickly shot back to his and I jumped off the sun lounge. "I should go," I said, rewrapping the towel around my waist.

Grayson lowered his gaze and turned back to the pool. "You probably should."

I tucked my wet hair behind my ear and swallowed. "Well, thank you for spending the night with me. I mean…argh." I threw my hands in the air. "You know what I mean!"

He smirked, but remained staring at the water in a daze. "I know what you mean."

I pressed my lips together, not knowing how to say goodbye. "Well, you have a nice life, Gray." I spun on my foot and headed towards the gate.

"Josie…"

I froze and hesitantly turned back to him.

He peered up at me with tired eyes. "If he doesn't light you up, let him go."

"Says you," I whispered, feeling an unusual surge of emotion as I watched him fold his arms behind his head, and close his eyes.

He breathed out a long sigh. "It's too late for me."

I smiled sadly at the perfect specimen, who would be very much married in two weeks, knowing I'd never see him again. Drawing in a deep breath, and ignoring the twinge in my heart, I turned and walked away. Ending what was the best night of my life.

Chapter 4

As I lugged my suitcase up two flights of stairs to my apartment, I couldn't help but think of the man I spent the previous night with. *Innocently, of course.* Heat travelled through my body as his colour changing eyes flashed through my mind. *Hmm, perhaps not so innocently.*

I had never experienced a connection with someone so quickly before. Perhaps knowing we would never see each other again tore down certain boundaries that would normally inhibit such feelings. Especially for me. I rarely let anyone in.

When I unlocked my front door and pushed it open, I discovered something red, torn up and scattered all over the floor.

"Luuuci," I groaned. "What have you got into now?" I knelt down and picked up a piece to decipher what it had once belonged to. *Please not another pair of my shoes!*

My Irish Wolfhound cross demon, came bounding over. He launched himself onto my shoulders almost knocking me down. Steadying myself as I laughed, I tried to push him away as he attempted to kiss my face. "Serves me right for going away. How's my gorgeous boy?" I muttered, scratching his head before he galloped away.

I looked down at the velvety object in my hands. It wasn't what I thought. In fact, it was much, *much* worse.

It was a rose petal.

Dragging my gaze across the floor, I followed the trail to my bedroom. The door was slightly ajar and soft music played within. My heart stopped and I struggled to move my feet.

The line of petals was like blood leading me to a murder scene. My gasp filled the room as I pushed open the door. The bedroom was bursting with roses and balloons...and Pete, my boyfriend, kneeling on one knee, holding out a little box. *Noooo. No no no no no.*

At the sight of the diamond ring, nausea set in and my hands flew over my mouth as I sprinted to the bathroom to vomit. Slumped by the toilet bowl, I tried to catch my breath and process what was going on.

After washing my face, I slowly exited, gnashing my teeth, to find Pete sitting on the edge of my bed with his head in his hands. *Shit.*

Wincing as I moved closer, he raised his despondent gaze to meet mine. "Not exactly the reaction I was hoping for," he said, standing back up.

I grimaced. "I'm so sorry. I haven't had much sleep and I'm a little stunned by all of this."

He ran his hand through his deep chestnut hair. "That's okay. I wanted to surprise you, and I guess I achieved that." He laughed, but the humour didn't reach his eyes.

I chuckled uneasily. "Well, I'm definitely surprised."

Pete's smile morphed into something more serious as he stepped towards me. "Josie, will yo—"

"Please don't," I blurted, jumping backwards.

He blinked rapidly. "But I—"

"You can't ask me. *Please* don't ask me." He took another step forward, and I slammed into the wall behind me. "I won't say yes."

His shoulders slumped and he looked away, slowly exhaling. "Ever?"

"I don't think so, no."

He turned to face me, but kept his eyes lowered. "You don't love me, do you?"

"I...I...*care* about you..."

Pete cackled and shook his head. "I can't believe this. After two years, you're telling me this now?"

"I'm sorry, Pete, I don't want to lie to you. I thought my feelings would grow into something more, but..." I trailed off, not knowing how to make this easier on him.

"I thought when you gave me your keys, it meant you were ready to take our relationship to the next level."

I winced. "I asked if you could feed and walk Luci, I didn't mean to blur the lines. I would've asked my neighbour to do it, but he's away at some tech conference."

Pete ran both hands through his hair and groaned. "I'm such an idiot."

"No, you're not, I'm the idiot," I said quickly. "You're an amazing guy and you deserve so much more than what I can give you."

"I'm totally fine with what I'm getting from you," he said quietly, lifting his eyes to meet mine. "If you need more time, I can give you time."

I held his gaze as Grayson's voice played in my mind. *If he doesn't light you up, let him go.* "I think I've wasted enough of your time, Pete."

He pursed his lips, but I could see the anger building behind his eyes. "So, this is it then? You're breaking up with me on our two-year anniversary?"

My eyes widened. *Fuck.*

He almost laughed. "You didn't even know, did you?"

"I'm sorry." I cringed, wanting to slam my head against the wall.

Pete shoved the little box into his back pocket. "I should go."

I took a step towards him, but he held out his hand to stop me. "I'm fine. I'll see you at work."

Before I could find my voice, he stormed out of the bedroom and slammed the front door behind him.

Falling back onto the bed, I lay motionless amongst the sea of rose petals. I knew I'd done the right thing, but fuck, I felt bad. Pete was a great guy. He just wasn't the guy for me.

"Trust me to mess everything up," I murmured before my dog blasted into the room, preparing his attack on the heart-shaped balloons. "It's what we do best, hey, Luc?"

My mouth curved into a smile when Luci growled at his floating tormentors, threatening their demise. As he leapt into the air for his first kill, I let out a small giggle. And when the balloon popped, sending him sprinting from the room with a whimper, I burst out laughing. Because just like Luci, I always took off when the shit got too real.

Dating a co-worker turned out to be one of the worst ideas I've ever had. Pete walked around the office in a heartbroken daze and everyone knew I was to blame.

Amy bounded into my office, quietly closed the door and squealed in delight. "About freakin' time!" She clapped, then proceeded to perform a happy dance in front of my desk.

I hushed her. "Sit down. It's bad. Everyone thinks I'm an evil bitch."

A serious expression fell over her face and she dropped into the visitor's chair. I loved how her moods were so flighty. Some people found her too erratic, but I thought she was fascinating.

"No one thinks that. Except maybe Janice in accounting, but she hates everyone."

I laughed and rubbed my temples. I had a ton of work to do and all the drama in the office was hindering my productivity.

She leant over my desk and took my hand. Turning it palm up, she analysed all the lines and creases until a small smile played on her lips. "He wasn't the one, never was."

I was used to this sort of thing from our resident psychic. "I thought you loved Pete," I said, narrowing my eyes.

She shrugged casually. "I do. I just love you more, and he wasn't right for you. There was no spark."

"Ah, the mythical spark," I muttered with a chuckle. I had my doubts whether it even existed until I met Grayson. But what good was a spark if it didn't ignite anything?

"So, how was Vegas?" Amy asked, smiling like she knew something.

"It was fine, and speaking of which, I need to write my article. Marlene's rushing this one." I raised my brow and waited for her to take the hint.

"Alright." She stood up with a grunt. "You can tell me more on Friday. You're coming to drinks, right?"

I smiled tightly. "Right." *Not if Pete is going to be there.*

Amy narrowed her eyes, before returning to her office across the hall.

Turning back to my laptop, I opened the file of images from my whirlwind trip to Vegas. I flicked through them until the bachelorette's pretty face filled my screen. All I knew about Melanie Warren was that *Maude* was one of her favourite magazines. For some reason, celebrities and socialites loved our little publication, and in particular, my feature *Capturing Love*.

It was a unique idea that had become, to my surprise, one of *Maude's* most popular segments. Normally I would interview and photograph ordinary couples and write about their journey together, but lately I'd been forced to spotlight *celebrity* couples. *Ick*.

The lives of the rich and famous really weren't my thing, and I wasn't a born wordsmith, so every article was a struggle to pull together. Getting up close and personal with Melanie Warren was a rare opportunity to try and get a real story and an honest photograph. The Warren family had paid a large sum of money to have her wedding and the lead up featured over the next two editions. Usually we didn't accept payment for exclusives, but we needed the money to stay in business, so the deal was made.

I didn't know the first thing about Melanie and preferred it that way. Having no pre-conceived idea about the person she was made it much easier to interview and photograph her. It also kept me from becoming a bumbling mess.

She seemed nice enough, but unfortunately possessed all the princess traits you would expect from an only daughter in a massively rich family. I had no complaints though. I was treated exceptionally, from the moment I arrived at her hotel suite, right up until I was politely asked to leave by her so-called-friends who wanted to really 'get the party started'.

Melanie loved being the centre of attention and was ecstatic to find out she'd be starring in a special feature of *Capturing Love*. She was under the impression we asked her family, but it was actually her parents who approached us to do the piece. A 'secret wedding gift' they called it. Even her husband-to-be was unaware of the plan.

As I studied the photographs on my computer screen, I noticed something unusual about the images I took while she described her fiancé. The light in her eyes dulled. I compared them with the photos of her raving about her wedding dress and decided to use these for the article instead. There was something missing, and it left me wondering who exactly she was marrying. Opening my web browser, I typed in 'Melanie Warren's fiancé' into the search field, but a light tap on my open door distracted me before I could hit enter.

Glancing up, I found my boss striding into my office. I fumbled over the keyboard, frantically trying to close the screen displaying the blatant admission I hadn't been prepared for my interview with Melanie. In my defence, I'd only had a day's notice.

I smiled tightly. "Marlene, hi! I'll have that article to you by the end of the day, I promise."

The editor and owner of *Maude* slumped into the chair in front of my desk with a dramatic sigh. "Oh, don't bother."

"What? Why?" Worry lines consumed my forehead.

"They called off the wedding."

My blood ran cold. "*What?!*" I knew how much we needed that job.

"They just released a statement ten minutes ago. It's apparently 'postponed', but you know what that means. My sources say William Harlow grew cold feet." *Why does that name sound so familiar?*

I grabbed the world globe stress ball off my desk and squeezed it tightly. "Oh my god, I could kill him. Who does that so close to their wedding day?"

Marleen smirked. "At least *you* did it right before the proposal."

"Wow, Pete really told everyone, didn't he?" I asked, rolling my eyes as my fingers almost split the stress ball in two.

Marleen let out a little chuckle. "Well, not everyone. I heard from Linda, who heard from Trudi, who heard it from that bitter woman in accounting."

I groaned and leant back into my chair, more concerned about my job. "So, what are we going to do now?"

She stood up and walked towards the door. "Just put together a fluff piece. I'm starting to think this magazine is doomed."

I shuddered. "Me too," I whispered. *Me fucking too.*

Word that our company was in trouble spread quicker than my breakup with Pete. We all spent the next three weeks walking on eggshells, while discreetly checking job advertisements online. I had no idea what I was going to do. Jobs like mine were hard to come by and I didn't have enough money saved to travel, so I had a lot to think and stress about.

"I need you to cover a wedding," Marlene said, barely looking up as she typed away on her computer. She hit enter and leant back in her chair, entwining her fingers as she peered up at me. "I wouldn't normally take a job like this, but in all honesty, we need the money. And after losing Melanie Warren's wedding, this is the next best thing."

I nodded. "So, what's the problem?"

"The bride-to-be is Sabrina Lowman. Frenemy of Melanie Warren."

I gasped. "What a bitch."

"Oh, you know what these people are like. Besties one-minute, arch enemies the next. Who knows what's real? I wouldn't normally partake in such petty behaviour, but she's paying an obscene amount of money to hijack her feature, and I'm in no position to refuse it."

I grimaced. "Melanie won't be at this wedding, will she?"

"Oh, god no. The groom is good friends with William Harlow, and according to social media, Melanie's in Mexico slamming down tequilas and pretending the break up was all her idea."

"Phew," I breathed, relieved I wouldn't have to bear witness to their inevitable catfight.

"They've also generously offered to place you at a table, so you can enjoy the festivities once your work is done."

"Lucky me," I murmured.

"My advice...just photograph as much as you can and get the hell out of there. These people aren't like us mere mortals." She handed over a wedding invitation and expense card. "And buy yourself a pretty dress. The wedding's this Saturday."

The end of the week couldn't come fast enough. Even though I had an early start the next day, I decided to join my colleagues for a much-needed drink. I knew Pete would be there, but my need for wine overpowered my empathy. He'd just have to deal with my presence.

Our local bar, The Edge, was just around the corner from our building in East Village, and most of us met up there at the end of the week to debrief. And ever since the first job cuts, it had become our refuge.

"So, did you go back and buy that dress you tried on over lunch break?" Amy asked, when I arrived a little later than everyone else.

I grinned and lifted up the bag that held the latest addition to my wardrobe, causing Amy to clap her hands enthusiastically.

"What's in the bag that's so exciting?" Pete chimed in. His eyes were glazed, meaning I was about four beers behind him.

Amy bounced on her toes. "Josie just bought a new dress, and it's hot, hot, *hot*!"

My eyes bulged at her, willing her to shut up. It was hard to judge where Pete's head was at. Some days he struggled to be in the same room as me, but other days he acted like we were still friends. And I really hoped we were.

Pete cleared his throat. "You've got a date?"

Amy pressed her lips together and slowly backed away from us, clearly realising her mistake.

I groaned inwardly. "No, no date. I'm photographing a wedding tomorrow."

"So, why did you have to buy a new dress? Couldn't you just wear something you already own?"

I chuckled. "Not to a wedding like this. No."

"Who's wedding is it?"

"Sabrina Lowman and Hank somebody," I said, but he didn't seem to know them either. "Apparently friends of the Harlow family."

Pete rolled his eyes. "Ah, the Harlows. Watch out for them."

"What? Why?" I glanced up at him curiously.

"Well, Adam Harlow is a notorious playboy, and his brother was recently seen getting cosy with a mysterious woman in Vegas just weeks before his wedding."

That's it! Vegas! The ladies in the nightclub bathroom were talking about him.

"Don't worry, if William Harlow comes near me, I'll kick him in the balls. Not just for cheating on his fiancé and cancelling the wedding, but for placing all our jobs in jeopardy in the process."

Pete's mouth curved upwards as he took a sip of his beer.

I stayed for a little while longer, chatting to colleagues, before finally heading home. My apartment was an easy half hour walk across to the west side of town, quicker if I cut through Washington Square Park, but I would never risk it at night. Plus, if I did, I'd be bypassing Lenny's Pizzeria, and that wasn't an option.

When I arrived from Australia, Lenny, an old friend of my father's, was the first person to offer me a job. He knew it would only be temporary, but hired me regardless. Lenny offered me a place to stay too, but I was so hell bent on supporting myself that I declined the offer, but not the job.

Since I started working at *Maude* five years ago, I promised Lenny I'd check in every Friday so he knew I was doing okay. Even though we weren't blood related, he was the closest thing I had to family, so I always made the effort.

After devouring my pizza on the living room floor, I crawled over to my dad's record collection and ran my finger over the spines. With a long sigh, I checked the time and decided to head to bed instead of my usual routine of listening to music all night. I needed to be on my game the following day, and resist every urge to tell William Harlow what I really thought about him.

Chapter 5

"Move, Luci!" I pushed my giant dog out of the way so I could review my reflection in the mirror. I opted for a traditionally inappropriate little black dress, which hugged my slim frame and gave me some unexpected, but welcomed, cleavage. The colourless number brought out my rainbow underlights, which interwove through my purposely messy bun.

After adding a little more eyeshadow to highlight my coffee coloured eyes, and the tiniest amount of blush along my high cheekbones, I gave myself one last glance. I looked pretty damn nice until I added all my camera gear. *Urgh*.

A private car picked me up and drove me to the reception venue, where the wedding party were staying. As it pulled up in front of the Plaza Hotel, my mouth gaped in awe. *Kevin McCallister has nothing on me.*

The wedding planner met me in the foyer and escorted me to the bride's suite. I manoeuvred through the room of bustling women in teal gowns, until I found the bride fussing over her bright red hair in front of the mirror.

"This isn't anything like the picture," she whined, examining the hair piled on top of her head.

As the hairdresser's lower lip began to quiver, I grabbed the reference photo out of her hand and stood next to Sabrina, facing her reflection.

"You're right," I said. She looked down at me with a gasp, but I smiled back at her. "It's so much better." She really did look amazing.

Sabrina blinked back tears and smiled. "And you are?"

"Josie Spencer. I'm here to cover your wedding for *Maude*."

Her eyes glimmered with excitement and something else. *Revenge?* "Wonderful," she said, and her hair was forgotten.

The hairdresser clutched her chest and smiled in relief, mouthing the words 'thank you' as I followed the bride to the chaise lounge.

I hated staged photos, but she obviously had her heart set on the arrangement so I went with it. Asking Sabrina questions about her future husband deemed to be a waste of time, because all her answers circled back to herself, making it difficult to take a sincere photograph.

With a sigh, I left the bridal party and headed across the road to Central Park where the ceremony would be held, eager to capture the excitement of the waiting guests and groom.

Knowing Sabrina planned to be fashionably late, I took my time watching the anticipation grow. I focused in on the groom, capturing all the emotions on his face as he waited patiently for his bride. *Snap.* It was magical. I loved weddings for this reason alone.

Sabrina finally arrived, exactly one hour past start time, looking gorgeous in a dress that was worth more than my apartment. *Snap.* She made her way down the carpeted aisle to her love. *Snap.* The groom's eyes sparkled, not entirely from love, but from the alcohol I'd seen him consume beforehand. *Snap.* At least it made for a good picture.

After the ceremony, I shadowed the happy couple until the reception began, careful not to get in the way of their official photographer. I was hoping to seize an intimate moment between the two of them, but it never came. Everything was so contrived; I could have vomited.

Knowing I had enough material for my article, I called it quits to enjoy the rest of the evening. Ambling through the magnificent Plaza foyer, I headed to the Grand Ballroom, stopping at the table listing to find my name. I cringed. 'Josephine Spencer—Table 6'. *Argh! Why does everyone assume my real name is Josephine?!*

Supposing I would be seated towards the back of the room, I automatically made my way through the sea of white floral arrangements. As I scanned the surrounding tables, I found most of the numbers were well into the thirties. I walked through the twenties, and finally located table six, right next to the dance floor. These tables were normally reserved for close family and friends. *Why on earth would I be placed here?*

I moseyed around the table, reading the names of who I was stuck with for the next few hours. All appeared to be male names, except one. Mine. I mentally face palmed. I'd been placed on the singles table. *Well at least I'm getting a free meal.*

Finding my place card, I leant to my left to see who was next to me. *Craig Lauder.* Then I checked the one on my right. *No. Fucking. Way.* The douche himself, *William Harlow.*

"Let me."

I startled at a man's voice and whirled around to find a stocky—and very sure of himself—man pulling out my chair for me.

"Thank you," I replied and sat down. I placed my bags under the table, but kept my camera hanging around my neck just in case the married couple surprised me with something more… authentic.

He slid into the chair next to me. "So, you must be…" He picked up my place card and grinned. "Josephine."

"It's Josie, actually. And you must be Craig." I held my hand out to shake his, but he turned it over and kissed it. *Ick.*

His gaze moved to my chest and I wasn't sure if he was eyeing my camera or my breasts. "Nice…camera," he said, with a slight slur. He must've started drinking well before the bar opened.

"Leave the poor girl alone, Lauder," a voice said from behind me.

Craig glanced up in surprise and his eyes widened. "Harlow!" He dropped my hand and stood to greet his friend.

Not sure if I was ready to face the man who unknowingly caused me so much grief, I quickly grabbed the menu and studied it.

"Never thought I'd see *you* on the singles table," said Craig.

"Neither did I, but here I am," he replied, nonchalantly.

"Were you at the ceremony? I didn't see you."

"No, I missed my flight. I doubt Hank noticed."

Craig chuckled. "Well, loosen your tie, bro, you're here for the best part. And the talent here tonight is…"

I cringed. He didn't say the next word, so I could only guess he was making some sort of hand gesture to fill the gap.

William chuckled. "Well, good luck with that."

While I was trying to figure out what the hell a fizzled carrot was, Craig placed his hand on my shoulder. "Speaking of which, let me introduce this lovely lady." He gave me a little squeeze. "This is Josephine."

Argh. I hate being called that. I turned in my chair and lifted my gaze to Craig. "It's Jo—"

"Josie?"

My eyes shot across to the man standing next to him and I blinked rapidly. "Grayson?"

Grayson stood before me, mouth open, and as wide-eyed as I was.

Craig slowly motioned between us. "You guys know each other?"

My heart summersaulted as I stared speechlessly into his warm hazel eyes.

He cleared his throat, not deviating his gaze. "Um, yeah. We met a little while ago."

"Hi." My mouth curved into a smile that matched his.

His eyes sparkled back. "Hi."

Craig groaned. "I need another drink," he muttered and wandered away.

Grayson slid into the seat to my right, and sudden confusion clouded my mind.

"Wait, why did he call you Harlow?" I asked in a panic. "Are you somehow related to William Harlow?" *Another brother?*

He ran his hand over his face. "I *am* William Harlow. William *Grayson* Harlow."

I furrowed my brow. "But you…we were…" My brain was having a complete meltdown. I let my forehead fall into my hands and left it there. *Oh my god.*

Grayson leant forward, peeking under the multi-coloured strands that had fallen over my face. "My friends call me Grayson."

I groaned. "So *you're* the arsehole who ruined my article?"

"What?" He chuckled uneasily.

I lifted my head. "That's why I was in Vegas. I was doing a feature on Melanie's bachelorette party."

His eyes went wide and he muffled his laughter with his hand. "No shit?"

"It's not funny. I was supposed to cover your wedding too. It was going to save our company."

His smile faded. "I'm sorry, Josie. I had no idea."

I looked him up and down, and frowned. "Apparently, neither did I."

"I really am sorry. Melanie's family planned the whole wedding, so I had no idea what was going on most of the time. I was just expected to show up."

I snorted. "Well, you buggered that up."

Grayson burst out laughing and nodded. "Yeah, I guess I did."

"So now I'm here covering *this* wedding, because Sabrina is paying a shit load of money to steal your fiancé's thunder."

"Ex-fiancé."

I waved him off. "Whatever."

Grayson smirked at the empty bridal table, clearly amused. "She never did like Mel. They've been rivals since college."

I lowered my eyes and fiddled with my camera. "So, are the rumours true?" I asked, peeking up to see his reaction.

He chortled. "Which one? I've heard a fair few."

"Were you really with another woman in Vegas?"

"Yes," he answered, blatantly.

My heart sank. I thought he was a better man than that. "Was it at that club we went to?"

Grayson leant back into his chair, crossed his arms, and nodded.

My nose crinkled. "Hang on, how did you manage to…I mean, weren't you with me the whole night? When did you…" My mouth fell open. "Oh no."

He smirked as he watched me piece everything together.

I swallowed down the lump forming in my throat. "I'm her, aren't I?"

"You mean...the other woman? The home wrecker?" He laughed, clearly unfazed by the gossip.

"Oh my god, please stop." I squeezed my eyes shut.

Grayson laid his arm across the back of my chair. "Come on, it's no big deal. Nothing happened and we both know it."

We stared at each other for a moment, silently challenging whether or not that was the real truth.

I pulled my gaze away from his, needing to change the subject. "So, how do you know Hank and Sabrina?"

"Hank and I went to high school together. College too. That's where he met Sabrina."

"Wait a minute, you said it was a joint bachelor party. Was he the other one?"

He nodded with a chuckle. "I got back to my hotel the next morning and found the poor guy passed out naked in the elevator, sporting a fresh tattoo on his right butt cheek."

I gasped. "What happened?"

Grayson shifted his chair closer and whispered. "Well, you know how I left them at the strip club that night? Well, one of the girls was *extra attentive*, and after she slipped a little something in his drink, he was convinced he was in love with her."

"Oh no."

"Oh yeah. When he couldn't convince her to marry him that very night, he made his way to the nearest tattoo parlour to *prove* his love."

My eyes widened. "What did he get?"

"A whip wielding, semi-naked woman with hundred-dollar bills hanging from her thong."

I burst out laughing.

Grayson hushed me and grinned. "I had to take him back to the tattoo parlour to change her blonde hair to red, so she looked like Sabrina."

"How did Sabrina take it?" I asked, between chortles. "Was she furious?"

He nodded. "At first, but not for long. Apparently she went and bought a whip for the honeymoon."

I covered my mouth, cackling with laughter. "Oh, too much information."

Grayson placed his elbow on the table and leant into his palm, watching me with the most peculiar expression.

"What?" I uttered, nervous I had something on my face or in my teeth.

"I just can't believe I'm seeing you again."

"And *I* can't believe you're William fucking Harlow."

He burst out laughing and I smiled at the sight, lifting the camera to my eye. *Snap.*

"So, how did the two of you meet?" Craig asked, slamming back yet another whiskey as our table began to fill.

I swallowed nervously. "Um, at a diner in Vegas."

"In Vegas? What? Waaait." His eyes tapered in on Grayson. "Is this the girl who…"

I glanced back at Grayson who was now red and silently motioning for Craig to shut up.

"Who what?" I asked, narrowing my eyes at him.

Craig sniggered and leant back in his chair looking smug.

Grayson took a sip of his beer. "Who made me reconsider a few things in my life, that's all."

"Oh," I said, shifting uncomfortably in my seat.

Craig lowered his eyes to my chest. "I bet," he grunted.

Grayson watched Craig with a clenched jaw. "Let's go find some more of that whiskey, shall we?" He sounded jovial, but his eyes were dead serious. He stood up and left the table with Craig under his arm, glancing back at me apologetically.

Before I had a chance to process the underlying tension, another man from our table struck up a conversation with me. I'd been so entranced by Grayson I hadn't even noticed him sit down.

"Scott," he said, reaching over the table.

I shook his hand and smiled. "Josie."

"Do I detect an Australian accent?"

I nodded. "I moved here about six years ago."

"Do you like living in New York?"

"I love it." *So much*.

He smiled knowingly. "Yeah, me too."

"Oh, I assumed most of the guests flew over from the west coast for the wedding."

He smiled tightly, breaking eye contact. "I'm originally from there, but moved here after high school."

We continued to chat about what we loved about New York and I found him to be much more down-to-earth than most of the other people I'd met that day. Scott glanced upwards just as Grayson returned, and sighed.

Grayson narrowed his eyes. "Scott Blackwood."

Scott swallowed and offered a reluctant nod. "Grayson."

"It's been a long time," Grayson followed, expressionless.

"It has."

They exchanged a look I couldn't decipher, but didn't speak another word.

Applause filled the room and glasses began to clink as the newly married couple made their grand entrance. *Snap*. We quietly watched and listened to all the formalities, but Grayson kept distracting me.

"Will you stop staring?" I whispered as the bride and groom walked onto the dance floor for their first dance. I struggled to focus my camera, so I turned and took a photo of him instead.

He grinned. "I can't help it. I never thought I'd see you again." *Snap*.

I blushed. I knew exactly how he felt.

After Hank and Sabrina did their customary dip and kiss, everyone was asked to join them on the dance floor.

Grayson turned to me. "Before all these vultures descend on you, will you dance with me?"

I lifted my eyes to his, but he was staring at my legs. My dress was hitched dangerously high, and my cheeks grew red.

"Your legs look fucking amazing," he whispered as he stood up.

I sucked in a breath as an unmistakable tingle travelled straight to my core. Glancing over at the filling dance floor, I was about to decline when he took my hand and pulled me onto my feet.

"I guess I don't have a choice," I said, stumbling along after him. I wasn't planning to dance tonight, so my shoe choice was much more daring than what I was used to. I didn't regret wearing them though. Grayson was so damn tall, I'd wear stilts to get closer to those eyes.

He pulled me into the middle of the floor. "Your eyes said yes."

I fit perfectly into his large muscular frame, and we began to sway. All I wanted to do was nestle my face into his neck and inhale his earthy scent, but my camera lay awkwardly between us.

His hot breath grazed my ear. "So, tell me, how's that boyfriend of yours?"

"What boyfriend?" I asked, holding back a smile.

He chuckled and pulled me closer, nudging the camera out of the way. "Best. Answer. Ever."

My heart pounded against his chest as I breathed him in.

"What happened?" he asked.

I blushed and looked away. "He proposed."

"The nerve," he uttered sarcastically, shaking his head.

"It's your fault, you know," I added, playfully narrowing my eyes.

He raised his brow. "How so?"

I shrugged. "Just something you said."

"Obviously the smartest thing I've *ever* said." He offered me a cheeky grin and I giggled. *Yep, just like a little school girl.*

Grayson spun me around and brought me back in. "So what's the problem?"

"We work together." I groaned.

"Oh…" He nodded slowly. "Well, you know what they say. You should never mix business with pleasure. It's a Harlow rule."

I wrapped my arms around his neck, falling silent as I enjoyed our gentle rhythm. His chin grazed the top of my head and I closed my eyes. "What did I say in Vegas that made you change your mind about Melanie?"

He lifted my chin with his finger and tucked a loose wave behind my ear. "It wasn't just something you said." His throat bobbed up and down as he swallowed. "It was you."

I sucked in my breath and held it.

His twinkling eyes penetrated mine. "I've never met anyone like you, Josie."

"You…you barely know me," I rasped, heart racing.

He lowered his head until his warm breath caressed my shoulder, causing each hair on my body to stand on end. "That's what scares me," he whispered.

Pure desire paralysed me. "I think we should leave," I blurted, unfazed by my unusual forwardness and the fact dinner had yet to be served.

His mouth moved dangerously close to mine. "Meet me in the foyer in five."

We quickly parted and went our separate ways. I rummaged up my gear, while Grayson disappeared into the foyer to wait for me. On my way out, I made a detour to the restroom only to find a few women already waiting impatiently in line.

I briefly considered ignoring my bladder, until I glanced across the hall where the men's restroom door was sitting slightly ajar. Tilting my head, I pricked up my ears and moved closer. When it became evident no one was in there, I slid in using my ninja stealth, and raced into the nearest cubicle.

Bubbling with excitement, I hurriedly washed my hands and fixed my hair in the mirror. Leaving with Grayson was totally out of character for me, but I didn't care. He set my body on fire and there was only one way to settle the flames.

As I attempted to leave, approaching male voices drove me straight back into the cubicle. My heart hammered in my chest as I leant against the stall door, hoping their visit would be a short one.

"Jesus, no wonder Grayson didn't come back to the hotel that night. If a girl like that wants to fuck you, you let her."

My heart dropped. *What the hell did he tell them?*

Craig's distinct laughter bounced off the tiled walls. "I still don't understand why he called off his wedding. Mel never would've found out."

"He's too fucking honest, that's why. It's not like he's the first person to fuck someone else on their stag night. It happens."

Excuse me? I didn't know what shocked me more. The fact they thought I'd slept with Grayson, or the way they condoned cheating.

"You would know," Craig sniggered.

"Shut-up, man. I just got married, remember?" *Hank?*

"Like that will stop you."

"It's all about discretion, and I have it down to a fine art."

"Like your tattoo?"

"Shut the fuck up," Hank snapped. "The bitch drugged me."

"Speaking of which, is this a white wedding or did I just follow you in here for a chat?"

"Yeah, yeah, here, take this."

There was a moment's silence before they began inhaling whatever Hank offered him.

"Do you think he'll get back together with Mel?" Craig asked, between sniffs.

"I have no doubt."

"You sure? He seems pretty keen on that girl out there."

"That girl just gave his dick a big wakeup call. Grayson will crawl back to Melanie once he's done sowing his oats. Just like last time."

Craig hummed. "Perhaps he'll give me her number when he's done with her."

"Perhaps he'll keep her number. There's no reason why he should stop tapping that hot ass."

I felt each bubble of excitement pop as the realisation of what I was to Grayson sunk in. Pressing my lips together, I flushed the toilet and as anticipated, the room fell deathly silent.

"Fuck," Hank whispered.

I casually opened the door and ambled over to the sink to wash my hands. Their eyes grew wide in my peripheral vision.

"What are you doing in here?" Hank's entire body went rigid.

"The ladies' was full, so I thought I'd sneak in." I chuckled in disbelief and shook my head as the water ran through my fingers. "And I'm so, *so* glad I did."

Hank cleared his throat. "I'm assuming you heard all that."

I lifted my gaze to the reflection of both men and smirked. "It was very…eye-opening."

Moving towards the door, Hank grasped my bag, making me stumbled backwards. "None of this is on the record," he rumbled over my shoulder.

"Don't sweat it. Our magazine doesn't print trash."

"No, they just employ it."

My head snapped back to Hank. "Just for the record, I never fucked your friend…and now you can explain to him why I never will." My smile tightened as I suppressed the ache in my chest. *What a fucking disappointment.*

Storming out the door and through the foyer, I almost forgot Grayson was waiting for me until he caught my arm. "Hey, Josie…wait up."

I spun around and slapped his hand away, tears stinging my eyes. Marlene was right. These people were not like us. They were arrogant, entitled, cheating fuckers, and I wanted nothing to do with any of them.

His eyebrows drew together when he met my angry gaze. "What's wrong? What just happened?"

I shoved him hard and he held up his hands in complete surprise. "Why did you tell your friends we slept together in Vegas?"

"I…I didn't—"

I held up my hand with a growl. "You know what? It doesn't even matter. I don't know you, and you certainly don't know me." I pushed past him, needing to get the hell out of there.

"I don't know what you've heard, but I think you're mistaken," he said, catching up to me in a few short strides.

"I heard enough to kno—argh!" My heel snapped off as I whirled around to face Grayson. *Fuck.* I kicked off both shoes and picked them up with a scowl. "I heard enough to know you're definitely not the person I thought you were," I continued, pointing my broken shoe at him.

Craig and Hank materialised behind him, and bile crept up my throat. He followed my fiery gaze to his friends and his shoulders fell. "What the fuck did you guys say to her?"

They shrugged innocently, making me hate them even more.

Grayson's eyes darted back to me and he stepped closer. "Josie, please…"

My fight or flight reflex kicked in, and the broken shoe shot from my hand, colliding with Grayson's shoulder. My eyes bulged.

"Fuck," Hank gasped.

"Crazy bitch." Craig chuckled under his breath.

Grayson stood motionless, clearly in as much shock as I was.

My face burned red. "Just stay away from me. Best this ends now." I spun around on my bare foot and ran, until the fire inside my body turned to ice.

Chapter 6

Still reeling, I marched up the stairs to my apartment and slammed the door behind me. Luci trotted over at the vibration in the floor and I threw my lone shoe to him, which he happily took back to his bed to eat.

I dumped my bags on the couch and stormed into the kitchen to cook some mac and cheese. I needed comfort food; stat. Especially as I missed out on experiencing all the exotic-to-me dishes on the menu.

As my meal cooked, I ripped off my dress and threw on my pyjamas and my original Australian sheepskin boots, before shuffling back into the kitchen.

Nursing a bowl of cheesy goodness, I relaxed into my shabby little couch, and turned on the television. The video clip of Easton Blue's *In Time* appeared and I almost threw the remote through the screen. *Fucking love songs*.

I flipped through the channels until I found the perfect movie to match my shitty mood. *Friday the 13th Part XIII: Jason Takes Manhattan*. It was fucking ridiculous, but I loved it.

As Grayson nuzzled into my neck, I giggled. His body was warm against mine, and so, so…furry. My eyes sprung open and Luci was smothering my face with his stinky breath and wet kisses.

"Yuck!" I cried, pushing him away the best I could. As much as I adored my beast, I was not the dog kissing type, even if Luci was insistent on getting to first base.

The old couch creaked as I stretched out, trying to ease the ache in my back from sleeping in an awkward position all night. I groaned as I pushed myself upright and rubbed my neck. *This must be what old feels like.*

I let Luci out onto the terrace and dragged myself to the shower, wincing as the memories of the night before came flooding back. *What a shit storm.*

Deciding to put the ugly event behind me, I overturned my Sunday pyjama rule, and took Luci to the park to enjoy the morning doing what I loved most; watching life go by and capturing moments with my camera. The rest of the day was reserved for leftover pizza and b-grade horror movies. *Because that's how I roll.*

I spent the following week working on my article. For the first time, the words came before the images because I couldn't bring myself to look over the photos that taunted me from my camera.

It was Friday, and Marlene wanted the draft by the end of the day, leaving me no choice but to finally upload the pictures onto my computer. They bounced onto my screen like an explosion of memories—unwelcomed memories—that I was happy to keep repressing.

Skipping over the man with the beautiful colour-changing eyes, I searched for the perfect photograph of the bride and groom, but there weren't any. It didn't help that I disliked both of them. It was always harder to see beauty when you couldn't feel it.

I printed off a contact sheet with the best images I had, and planned to ask Amy her opinion. I couldn't risk screwing it up. Marlene was keeping quiet about the future of the business and it made me nervous. She had been in and out of meetings all week with the blinds closed, which was always a bad sign. The last time that happened, our staff list was cut in half.

"Oh my god..." Amy moaned as she sauntered into my office.

"Jesus, Ames, you look mid-way through an orgasm."

"I think I am." She sunk into the chair opposite my desk, her pixie hair cut looking a little spikier than normal. "Did you see him?" she asked, gazing lovingly towards the hallway.

I frowned. "See who?"

"Mr. Perfect. I'm surprised you didn't notice him."

"As you can see, I'm a little pre-occupied." I motioned to the pile of notes and photos covering my desk.

She narrowed her eyes. "He walked straight past your door. I'm pretty sure he was checking you out."

I scoffed. "Are you fucking with me?" *I don't have time for this.*

"I fuck you not. He just came out of a top-secret meeting with Marlene, and when he saw you, he slowed his pace."

Amy's office was opposite mine, with the same glass facade and no privacy. I found the constant movement in the hallway distracting, so I filled my window with enough indoor 'screening' plants to supply enough oxygen to the whole floor.

I rolled my eyes. "I think you're reading too much into it, Ames."

"His energy was…" She shuddered. "Electric."

I laughed and shook my head. "Well, if Mr. Perfect ever decides to come back, chances are I won't be here. I haven't picked out any photos and my article is due this afternoon."

Amy seemed to ignore the urgency in my voice. "You never did tell me what happened at that wedding *or in Vegas*."

"Best just to forget," I said, lowering my eyes to the contact sheet on my desk.

She picked it up and squinted at the tiny images.

"I was going to ask which one you would choose…"

"Who's this?" Amy interrupted, narrowing in on the one image I was trying to avoid. I didn't even realise I had included it.

I groaned. "*That* is William Harlow. Total douchebag."

She leant back into the chair and stared out my door, deep in thought. "Hmm…"

"What is it?"

Looking back at me and then at the photo, Amy repeated the action a few times before speaking. "Oh, nothing," she said, slowly rising from the chair. "I'll let you get back to work." Placing the sheet of images back on my desk, she pointed to the photograph of Hank and Sabrina holding hands in Central Park. "This one." And then to the newlyweds on the dance floor. "And this one."

"Thanks, Ames." I smiled, and circled them with my pen. It was handy having a friend who could quite literally read my mind.

"But this one is my favourite." She pointed to the last photo I took that night.

I peered down at the image of Grayson staring straight into my camera lens. His eyes picked up the light in such a beautiful way, he looked awestruck. Warmth flooded my body and I quickly looked away, but there was no hiding from Amy.

"Total douchebag, hey?" She chortled.

I sighed. "Let's not talk about it."

Amy shrugged, but her know-it-all smirk remained. "Okay…"

I waved her out of my office. "Go read someone else's aura for once, will you?"

She laughed and paused momentarily at the door. "But yours is so fascinating. It just keeps changing colour…green…hazel…green…hazel…"

My eyes widened in shock. *Now she's messing with me.* I picked up my stress ball and threw it at her, missing by far. She giggled loudly and raced back into her office before I had a chance to throw something else.

Turning back to my computer, I dragged the contact sheet across my desk for a closer look. I tried to concentrate on the circled images, but Grayson's eyes kept pulling me in. As much as he was a douchebag, I really didn't mind seeing his handsome face on my desk.

A message popped up on my screen.

A. Mitchell: **He has pretty eyes.**

I swivelled around in my chair to find Amy sniggering in her office, spying on me through my personal forest.

J. Spencer: **I have work to do!**

A. Mitchell: **Okay, okay!**

A. Mitchell: **Drinks after work?**

J. Spencer: **One drink.**

A. Mitchell: ***sad face* We'll see about that. *beer glass* *wine glass* *dancing girl***

I laughed and closed the little screen that was bound to get me fired one day.

The weekend was a write off after my 'one drink' at The Edge turned into too many. I made my deadline, I always did. But the stress of the unknown state of my job was taking its toll, and the only people who understood were my workmates. They had become my family over the past five years and I adored them all. *Even Janice.*

Pete shared a cab home with me as he lived close by, and helped me up to my apartment. As I said goodbye, he habitually leant in for a kiss.

I pressed my hand against his chest and gently pushed him away, shaking my head. "I'm sorry, Pete."

He nodded sadly and didn't say a word. Just turned and slowly made his way down the stairs, clearly waiting for me to call him back. I didn't.

I closed the door and leant my head against it. *Why can't I just make it work with him?*

Missing my usual Friday night pizza, I whipped up another batch of mac and cheese, and repeated my steps from the weekend prior. Carrying the bowl over to my dad's old record player, I sat cross-legged in front of it, like it was an altar, because in some ways it was. Closing my eyes, I randomly picked out a record from my huge collection and hoped the lyrics would speak to me and offer the guidance I craved.

My dad loved music and used to constantly quote song lyrics. He said there was a song for every occasion and believed if you listened hard enough, you could find the answers to all of life's problems.

Running my hand over the mystery record, I tried to guess by the feel. When I obviously couldn't, I opened my eyes and smiled, but it was laced with sadness. Fleetwood Mac's white album was one of Mum's favourite records. I flipped it over and loaded side two into the record player. Laying back on my timber floorboards alongside Luci, I waited for Mum's beloved track to play. The beautiful melody of *Landslide* filled the room, and I closed my welling eyes and drifted off to sleep.

A dozen roses awaited my arrival to work on Monday morning. I grimaced as I picked the card out of the scarlet blooms, praying I wouldn't see Pete's name within. After making sure my ex-boyfriend wasn't spying on my adverse reaction through my office window, I opened the card.

I would much prefer to apologise in person. Call me (323) 302 9917 ~ G.

My eyes almost popped out of their sockets. *Grayson?*

As if I would call him just because he sent flowers. I didn't even like roses. I mean, I could admit they were lovely, just not my thing. I dropped the card back into the long stems and pushed them to the edge of my desk.

Pete stopped buying me flowers early in our relationship because I told him to. I hated the thought of cutting a life short, just to have it brighten a room for a few days.

When my parents died, my whole house was full of flowers. Bunches and bunches of roses, lilies and orchids were delivered, and then, days later, they died...just like my parents. A painful reminder that their lives were also cut too short.

Later that day, Pete slowly ambled past my office like he always did, waiting for an invitation to talk to me.

"Didn't take you long," he muttered, pausing at my open door.

I followed his gaze to the roses on my desk and rolled my eyes.

"They're from a friend," I said as he sauntered closer.

"A friend?" He picked up the note that I should've thrown away, and pursed his lips. "Who's 'G'?"

"Pete..." I warned, now wishing the roses hadn't been de-thorned. He deserved a prick for invading my privacy.

Pete folded his arms. "You told me you hated flowers."

"I don't *hate* flowers, I just don't like receiving them as a gesture," I replied shortly.

"Alright, well...good luck to your *friend*," he uttered and stormed out of my office.

The next day I received more flowers. This time, oriental lilies. I hesitantly picked out the card.

You're not a rose girl, are you? Call me (323) 302 9917 ~ G

Nope. Not even close.

―――

Wednesday brought Tulips. I scoffed. *Really?*

The florist said white tulips symbolise forgiveness. Please forgive and call me. (323) 302 9917 ~ G

―――

Thursday brought something quite unexpected. Hydrangeas. *Dammit.* They were my favourite and to make matters worse, it wasn't just a bunch of flowers…it was a plant. My fingers trembled as I opened the adjoining card.

Embarrassed yet? Please call me (323) 302 9917 ~ G.

Unfortunately, he was right. I *was* embarrassed. Everyone in the office was talking about me—and not in a positive manner. After questioning Amy about why everyone was giving me the cold-shoulder, she admitted to overhearing whispers that I was flaunting a new relationship in Pete's face. That not only had I broken his heart, I was trampling all over it. It had to stop.

―――

On the last day of the week, I braced myself for another delivery and the office gossip that would follow. I wanted to set everyone straight, but I also couldn't bring myself to explain why I was getting them, or who I was getting them from. It would only create more controversy and that was something I usually steered clear of.

In lieu of flowers, I received a mysterious package. Half expecting to find Gwyneth Paltrow's severed head (*yes, I watch too many movies*), I reluctantly opened the box.

Curiously pulling back the tissue paper, I revealed what was inside and burst out laughing. The shoe I'd thrown at Grayson lay beneath and my cheeks instantly reddened. Not only had he kept it, he'd had it professionally repaired. I pulled out the small note underneath and chuckled.

Cinderella. Please call me (323) 302 9917 ~ G

I picked up my phone and leant back into the chair, swivelling around and around, trying to figure out what to do.

"I haven't seen those dimples in a while," Amy said, pausing in the doorway as she walked past my office.

My blush deepened. I didn't even realise I was smiling.

She grinned and rested her shoulder on the doorframe. "So, are you going to call him?"

"Who?" I placed my cell back onto the desk and began aimlessly rustling around some papers to avoid her stare.

"You know who."

I hadn't even told Amy about Grayson, but I never really had to tell her anything. She just knew. Glancing at my cell, I chewed the side of my thumbnail.

"Well, just sex—I mean *text* him," she blurted.

I glared at her.

Amy held her hands in the air. "Sorry! But your aura is as bright as your hair right now."

I groaned as my eyes rolled. "Ames…"

"I just tell it like I see it." She smirked and continued on to her office. "Text him!"

For the one millionth time that afternoon, I picked up my phone, typed a message, then deleted it. I wasn't sure what I wanted to say, or if I wanted to say anything. I didn't want anything to do with him…*did I?* But there was no harm in a simple thank you text…*was there?*

Me: **Thanks for returning my shoe. J.**

I barely blinked before the three little dots appeared, and my heart raced.

Grayson: **I wanted to keep it. But it wasn't my size.**

I tried my hardest not to smile.

Me: ***rolling eyes***

Grayson: **I never told my friends we slept together. But I never said we didn't either, for that I'm sorry.**

Me: **What did you tell them?**

Grayson: **That I spent the night with an amazing girl.**

Me: **You're an idiot. *face palm***

Grayson: **I realise.**

Grayson: **I'm only in NYC for a few more days. Can I see you?**

This was what I was dreading. He wanted to meet up.

Grayson: **Dinner?**

No way. Way too intimate.

Me: **Sorry. Busy.**

Grayson: **I didn't say when...**

Fuck.

Grayson: **What about lunch?**

Me: **Nope.**

Grayson: **Coffee? *praying***

Me: **You're impossible.**

Grayson: **I'm persistent.**

With a sigh, I tried to think of a place where we could meet, that was public and gave me the ability to escape at any moment.

Me: **I'm taking photos in Washington Square Park in the morning. If you bring me a coffee and a donut from Rosie's, I may even talk to you. You'll find me at the fountain at 8am.**

Grayson: **8am? *wide eyed* You do realise it's Saturday, right?**

Grayson: **I'm joking...I'll see you then.**

Me: **Latte please.**

Me. **Whole milk. Not that skim shit.**

Grayson: **Rebel *wink face***

Chapter 7

I spent way too much time preparing myself for a guy I had no interest in pursuing. He lived in Los Angeles for starters and I didn't believe in long distance relationships. I tried it once when I moved from Australia to the States, not long after my folks died. But with no intention of moving back and the fact that my now-ex-boyfriend was sleeping with my best friend, it made no sense to keep pursuing—or to ever return.

My favourite yellow dress, that fell softly over my small frame, was perfect for the warm spring day predicted. I slipped on some sandals, and tied my hair up into a messy bun. I didn't want to look like I was making too much of an effort. Plus, I couldn't find my brush.

Grabbing my keys from the kitchen bench, Luci's ears pricked up and I winced. "Sorry, Luci, I'll take you to the park later." I knelt down to his gorgeous scruffy face, and tickled his chin. "Promise me you'll behave while I'm gone." He licked my hand, sending me back to the bathroom to wash off the residual slime.

Grabbing my bag and camera, I slid out the front door while Luci was running around, distracted by his new chew toy: my long-lost shoe.

It was a stunning morning and the park was only a ten-minute walk away, so I took my time ambling through the streets of Greenwich Village on my way there. Even after six years, I still couldn't believe New York was my home. I loved growing up in Australia, but there was too much heartache there now. This was my fresh start, and so far, it was the best idea I had ever followed through with.

The fountain was the heart of the park and the most public place I could think of. As I sat on the steps by the water, it reminded me of the night we first met. Grayson was kind, charming and funny, not at all like his friends. But surely they knew him better than I did.

To ease my nerves, I lifted the camera and scanned through the crowd. Unsuspecting people went about their daily lives, while I patiently waited to capture their emotion. The mother's smile as she watched her children splash around in the water. *Snap*. The teenage boy timidly reaching for his date's hand. *Snap*. And the elderly man, sitting alone on a park bench, rotating his wedding band as tears welled in his eyes. *Snap*.

"Have you ever thought about becoming a private investigator?"

I jumped so high I almost dropped my camera. Spinning around, I found Grayson smiling from ear to ear, with a coffee tray in one hand and a brown paper bag in the other.

"Hi," I said, nervously, eyeing his casual attire and the backpack resting on his shoulder. He wore designer jeans, a plain black shirt, a baseball hat and dark sunglasses. "Have *you* ever thought of becoming a private investigator?"

He glanced down at his outfit and smirked. "Well, I think I'd be pretty good at it, considering I was just watching you for the last ten minutes without you realising."

My mouth fell open.

"Joke, Josie." He chuckled, taking off his sunglasses. "It was only five."

I narrowed my eyes, trying to see if Grayson was serious, but he distracted me with donuts.

"You didn't tell me which flavour, so I bought them all," he said, holding up the paper bag with Rosie's stamped on the side.

My eyes widened and my mouth curved into a smile. *Marry me.* "I guess this means I have to hear you out now," I said with a smirk. Grabbing the bag from his hand, I made a beeline to the nearest empty bench, glancing back to hurry him along.

Grayson sat beside me, watching curiously as I tore at the paper. I grabbed the first donut I came in contact with and tore it in half, offering him the other.

His eyebrows rose.

"Well, don't you want to taste them all?" I asked in disbelief. I hadn't met anyone who didn't love Rosie's donuts. But then, he wasn't from New York.

He smiled and hesitantly took it out of my fingers, then threw his share into his mouth. Grayson's eyes glazed over as he chewed.

"Amazing, right?" I mumbled with a mouth full.

He nodded approvingly. "Amazing."

We were halfway through the bag, when Grayson cleared his throat. "I really am sorry for misleading my friends like that."

I finished off the rest of my coffee and nodded, but kept my eyes lowered.

"Honestly, I never thought I'd see you again, and it was easier for them to believe there was someone else, rather than the truth."

"What's the truth?" I asked, picking at the lid of my empty coffee cup.

"That I wasn't in love with Mel…I'm not sure I ever was."

I breathed in deeply and met his eyes, smiling sadly. "Thank you for your honesty."

Blush rose into Grayson's cheeks.

I chuckled. "You don't apologise much, do you?"

"I've never really had to." He reached out and brushed some sugar off my nose, but when he pulled away, I noticed his grazed knuckles.

Taking his hand in mine, I grimaced. "What happened?"

"It doesn't sit well with me when the girl I like is called a crazy bitch."

"Oh." I drew in a shaky breath as my face warmed. "Well I did throw a shoe at you. That's a little crazy…even for me."

He shook his head with a chuckle. "You didn't mean to throw the shoe, did you?"

"No!" I laughed as my blush deepened. "It just slipped out of my hand in the moment!"

Grayson smiled. "I thought so. You looked as surprised as I was."

I winced. "I'm sorry…for the shoe…and for the hand."

"You have nothing to be sorry for. I deserved the shoe and Craig deserved the split lip."

"Did he retaliate?"

Grayson chuckled. "He wouldn't dare. He works for my father."

"So…that makes you…untouchable?"

"Something like that."

Curiosity got the better of me. "Just how well-known is your family, anyway?"

"You've really never heard of us?" he asked, clearly amused.

I screwed up my nose. "Did your grandfather invent Post-it's or something?"

Grayson laughed. "No, nothing that exciting."

"All I know is that your real name is William, you're from LA, and you have a bizarre affection towards penis shaped candy." I peeked up at him with a cheeky grin.

His eyes sparkled back. "You didn't look me up on the internet?"

I burst out laughing. "Are you serious? Did you look me up?"

He fell silent and ran his hand through his hair.

My voice softened. "I generally try to stay away from all that bullshit. I'm not even on social media."

"I noticed," he uttered, clearing his throat.

My cheeks warmed. He *did* look me up.

Grayson slipped on his sunglasses and stood, before taking our rubbish to the nearest bin. He returned a moment later, reaching for my hand. "Come on, let's walk off those donuts."

His fingers entwined with mine as we strolled along the tree-lined pathways from one side of the park to the other. "How did your article go?" he asked.

"To be honest, it was a struggle."

"I'm sure Sabrina will love it."

I cringed. "And how will Melanie take it?"

"Oh." He chuckled. "Mel is going to lose her shit when she finds out."

I peered up at him, dreading the answer to my next question. "She won't try to sue us, will she?"

"I wouldn't let her, even if she tried."

My heart dipped. "So, you still keep in touch?"

He glanced my way, but I pretended to be interested in the passing scenery. "Yeah, I speak to her occasionally, mostly to keep my parents happy. They're holding on to the hope that I'll change my mind. They think not marrying her is some belated act of rebellion."

"They do realise you're not fifteen anymore, right?"

He chuckled. "I actually think my father is angrier than Mel. That's why I'm still in New York. He can't even meet my eye right now."

"That's a bit harsh, isn't it?"

"You don't know my dad."

My brow arched, but I didn't comment. "So, what have you been doing since Hank and Sabrina's wedding?"

"Trying to get back on my father's good side," he said, with a sigh. "He wants a bigger east coast portfolio, so I'm here to find some new business prospects. His arch nemesis just jumped above our family on America's most wealthy list, and he can't handle it. Had I married Mel, our rank would have sky-rocketed."

I grimaced. "I guess that's what happens when you have too much money." I stopped walking and turned to him with a smile. "It's just like that Bruce Springsteen song."

The corner of his mouth turned up. "You like Springsteen?"

"Who fucking doesn't?"

He chuckled and nodded. "Go on."

"You know the song *Badlands*?" I started humming the tune and singing the lyrics about how having too much money only makes you crave power.

"That's actually pretty spot on."

"Bruce is always on point," I said proudly. My dad was a huge fan, as was I.

With a deep-chested laugh, Grayson nodded in agreement and we continued walking.

While elaborating on my love of music, I spotted two elderly men heckling each other as they played chess. There was a gleam in one man's eye, so I glanced down at the chessboard. Anticipating his next move, I brought the camera to my face and angled it towards Grayson who stood in front of them.

"Smile," I said, and Grayson hesitantly obliged. Only the photo wasn't of him. I moved the camera angle ever so slightly and zoomed in on the old man as he took out his friend's king then erupted into a fit of laughter. *Snap.*

Grayson rubbed the back of his neck. "That wasn't even of me, was it?"

I shook my head and winced. "I'm sorry. I needed the cover to get the shot."

He followed my gaze to the chess game, that had evolved into a heated argument, and turned back to me. Glancing down at the camera, he held out his hand. "Can I see?"

I stepped closer until our toes were almost touching, and lifted the camera to his eyes. "Do you need your glasses?"

He wiggled his sunglasses. "Prescription."

Grayson took the camera from my hands and stared into the display screen. "Wow, this is so great, Josie. Anytime you need a cover, I'm your man."

My body filled with warmth as he passed the camera back. "Thank you," I said, meeting his eyes through the dark shades.

"How do you read people's emotions so quickly? I barely even noticed the chess game before you had your camera pointed their way. Mind you, I *have* been a little distracted." He grinned.

I playfully rolled my eyes. "I've always been an observer, picking up on subtle clues. It's not always about a person's smile, or their tears, it's everything leading up to them. The glistening eyes, the trembling lip, the clenched jaw...they all show something deeper. *That* is where the beauty lies."

His gaze remained on mine for a moment longer before breaking away. His cheeks grew pink as he diverted his attention to the old men setting up their next game.

"You're afraid I'm reading you right now, aren't you?"

The corner of his mouth quirked up and he let out a nervous chuckle as he turned back. "Should I b—"

Snap.

We spent the next couple of hours walking around the park talking about photography until my stomach let out an embarrassing cry.

Grayson smirked. "I know you said no to lunch, but I may or may not have a backpack full of food if you would like to join me for a picnic?"

I crossed my arms, trying my hardest to contain a smile. "Were you planning on having a picnic for one, or are you really that smug?"

His grin grew bigger as I stared longingly at his bag full of edible promise. "Perhaps a dash of smug, and a ton of wishful thinking?"

I barely heard him over my growling belly. "What exactly have you got in there?"

"Just a few things I had whipped up in The Plaza kitchen."

My mouth dropped open and I quickly closed it before I drooled.

"Come on," he said, pulling me towards a patch of grass, away from the masses.

"But I haven't even said yes yet."

He chuckled. "Well your eyes clearly decide before your head, because those pretty browns just hollered a big *hell yes*."

With a laugh, I grabbed the backpack from his shoulder and sank to the ground. Grayson followed my lead and stretched out his legs, watching in amusement as I rummaged through the bag, pulling out all the goodies.

"If you don't mind me asking, why did you end things with Melanie so close to the wedding day? I only met her briefly, but it must've been quite a shock for her." I took a large bite of a club sandwich, and watched his reaction closely as I chewed.

Grayson's jaw tightened and he looked up at the clear sky. "Yeah. My timing was definitely shitty. But it was the right thing to do. I refuse to end up like my parents."

"Did she feel the same way?"

He sighed. "She will...eventually. It was almost a business arrangement between our parents and we just got caught up in it all. She'll realise that one day."

I nodded, but remained silent.

"She was actually more upset I cancelled the wedding, than when I broke it off with her completely. It made me realise just how fucked up our whole relationship was. We weren't in it for the right reasons. Well, not the reason I want anyway."

"What reason is that?"

Grayson blushed and his smile grew as he nudged my side with his elbow. "You know."

His gentle tap made my heart flutter. "Oh, so you *are* a romantic?"

Sparks were definitely flying again, and I feared what would happen if one hit me.

"I guess I've had fresh perspective on things lately." He looked up and grinned, sneaking in a mischievous wink.

Zap.

Another few hours passed and I lay quietly on the grass, beside a man I barely knew, feeling completely at ease. In the occasional lulls in conversation, I sat and watched the world go by and Grayson appeared content to do the same.

Long after we'd finished devouring all the delicious treats courtesy of Grayson's hotel, I showed him some of my favourite photos on my camera and told him the stories behind them all. He appeared fascinated; I never had anyone pay so much attention like he did.

Grayson shook his head. "I still can't believe you've never had an exhibition. You obviously have enough work for your own show…What are you waiting for?"

I shrugged and leant back onto my elbows. "I just don't feel like I've seen enough yet. All my camera has witnessed is six years in New York and twenty-four hours in Vegas."

A deep line formed between Grayson's eyebrows.

"It's okay though," I added quickly. "I've been saving up to see the rest of it."

"America?" he asked.

I grinned. "The world."

The sun dipping below the trees was a gentle reminder of how long we had been lying there, talking about everything and nothing at all. I didn't want it to end.

I let out a long sigh. "Look, I know I originally said no to dinner, but do you want to get some pizza or something?"

Grayson smirked. "I thought you said you were busy."

"Oh yeah, I forgot. I better go." I attempted to stand, but Grayson laughed and pulled me down into his lap.

He cupped my cheek with one hand, and pushed my hair behind my ear with the other. "Something."

My voice caught in my throat as my heart hammered. We were so close.

"You said 'pizza or *something*'," he clarified.

A shiver of anticipation ran through my body before he leant in, moving closer to my lips.

Suddenly, his forehead slammed against mine with a thud, and we both jerked back in surprise. A soccer ball landed between us, and a sheepish child appeared at our side.

"I'm really sorry. May I have my ball back?"

I shifted myself off Grayson, embarrassed to be so intimate with a child present.

Grayson rubbed his head and threw back the ball with a smile. "With a kick like that, you'll be the next Ronaldo."

The kid's eyes went round and a huge grin took over his face. "Wow, thanks! I sure hope so!"

I quickly texted Reed from my apartment building, and asked if he could check on Luci. For an old dog, he still possessed all the puppy traits that drove me mad and would've surely torn the place apart by now.

A few minutes later, he sent back a message stating he found a deceased pair of shoes, and asked if he could take him back to his apartment to hang out. Reed was a professional gamer and didn't get out much, making Luci the perfect companion. I told him to keep Luci overnight as I didn't know when I'd be coming home. Sometimes I thought Reed loved my dog more than I did.

I stood up and held my hand out to Grayson. "Come on, I'm going to shout you the best pizza in New York."

"That's a very big call."

I shrugged. "Trust me. It's the main reason I moved into this neighbourhood."

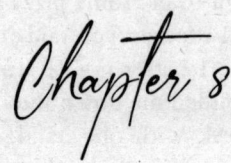

Chapter 8

As we walked through the front door of Lenny's Pizzeria, a bell chimed out the back.

"Josie girl!" Lenny hollered through the serving window.

"Lenny!" I smiled and waved.

"Take a seat. I'll be out in a minute."

I turned to Grayson, but he had already wandered over to Lenny's hall of fame. It was primarily photographs of celebrities who had eaten there, but also incorporated some of my original work.

As he was about to comment on one of my images, I ushered him to my usual table by the front window. "This is the best seat in the house. You can sit here and watch strangers walk by, and make judgement calls about their lives until your pizza is ready."

He laughed. "I gather you come here often."

"Yeah, it's pretty much the only take-out I get. I feel like I'm cheating on Lenny if I go anywhere else. Plus, he always slips me a free garlic bread." I grinned.

Grayson chuckled as he sat down.

Lenny came waltzing out of the kitchen dressed in his apron and high chef hat, reminding me of the chef from the muppets.

He pulled me into a hug. "I haven't seen you in two weeks. I've been worried."

Grayson watched our interaction curiously.

"Sorry, I had a crazy week at work and last Friday I was filling my belly with whisky and wine instead of pizza."

"You work too hard. I wish you'd take a holiday."

I scoffed. "Careful what you wish for, I might be on a permanent holiday soon."

"Don't say these things. You'll be just fine. Plus, there's always a job here if you need."

I smiled warmly. He always had my back. "I know. Thanks, Len."

Lenny looked across at Grayson. "And who is this young gentleman?"

"Lenny, this is Grayson. Grayson, Lenny."

Grayson stood up and reached out to shake his hand, but Lenny pulled him in for a hug. Grayson's eyes bulged as Lenny whispered something into his ear. His alarmed gaze met mine over Lenny's shoulder.

"Len…" I warned, shaking my head.

Lenny pulled away and turned back to me with a shrug and mischievous smile. "What will you kids have?"

Grayson let me order, and watched Lenny make his way back to the kitchen. "Does he really have Mafia connections?" he whispered, once Lenny was out of earshot.

"I dunno." I shrugged nonchalantly, holding back my laughter. "Probably."

He paled a little and nodded slowly. "You guys seem close."

"Um, yeah. He's been like a substitute father since I arrived here." I smiled affectionately towards the kitchen, listening to the clatter of pot and pans. "He lived in the same street in New Jersey where my dad grew up. They were like brothers."

"So, your mom was Australian?"

"Yeah, Dad left everything to be with her."

Grayson offered me a warm smile. "Where in Australia did you live?"

The bittersweet memories of my childhood home flashed through my mind. "Melbourne."

Grayson nodded. "I can see why you like New York then. It's like Melbourne on steroids."

I burst out laughing. "You're so right. That's probably why it feels like home. Have you been to Australia?"

"Yeah, when I was little, but I don't remember too much, except for being *petrified* of your wildlife."

I chortled. "You've gotta watch out for those drop bears."

Grayson's eyes grew large. "Don't even start. I had nightmares for months."

We both cackled with laughter.

"What made you move to the States?" he asked when our laughter died down.

Breathe…

I shifted my gaze to the window and swallowed down what felt like a rusty nail. "After my parents died, everything and everyone reminded me of them. I guess I just needed a fresh start." Turning towards the kitchen, I willed the pizza to come out to stop the conversation.

Grayson appeared to take the hint and remained quiet for a long moment. "So, how's your job going? You seem stressed about it."

I exhaled, thankful for the change of subject, even if it was an unsettling one. "Yeah, a little. I'm finally finding my feet here, but I feel like the carpet is about to get ripped out from under me."

Grayson rubbed his short stubble. "What do you think is going to happen?"

"I have no idea. They've had a ton of meetings lately. Rumour has it, they're going to sell, or worse…fold."

"I doubt they will fold. It just needs a few changes here and there to bring it into the 21st century."

I tilted my head, and tapered my gaze. "How do you know all this?"

He ran his hand through his hair. "Well…it's the same story with most companies. Adapt or die."

My eyes widened.

Grayson's hand slid over mine. "Your company will be fine. You said there's been a lot of meetings, which means there must be a lot of interest. You shouldn't have anything to worry about."

I smiled tightly. "I hope so. Either way, change is on the way and change is unsettling."

"It can also be new and exciting." Grayson waggled his eyebrows and I laughed.

"I never really thought of it like that."

Lenny brought out our pizzas and we ate quietly, stealing glances at each other as we devoured nearly every slice. Wanting to retain some dignity and appear 'lady-like', I purposely didn't finish the entire pizza. But there was no way I was going home without the rest, so I asked Lenny to box it up for me.

Grayson's gaze left mine for the first time that evening as he turned to stare out the window. "It's getting late."

I lowered my eyes to hide my disappointment. "Yeah, I should get home."

Lenny came back with my leftovers and another stick of garlic bread, and we stood to leave. Grayson shook Lenny's hand and I gave him a peck on the cheek, before attempting to pay the bill. Lenny refused my money, so I shoved it in the tip jar.

As I stepped out onto the sidewalk, I shivered. The temperature had dropped somewhat and I stupidly forgot to bring a jacket. I had no intention of being out so late.

"I'd offer you my coat, if I had one," Grayson said, rubbing his own arms.

"It's okay, I live close by."

Grayson shoved his hands in his pockets, and peered up at me. "May I walk you home?"

I smiled up at him. "I'd like that."

As we walked, Grayson obviously saw me shiver again because he slid his arm around my shoulders, and pulled me in to share the warmth of his body. My heart sped up and tingles spread through me as his fingers wrapped around my arm. I peeked up at him and smiled, but we didn't speak.

Not wanting the night to end, I slowed my pace as we approached my apartment.

"This is me," I said, at the bottom of the steps leading up to the entrance.

He dropped his arm and ran his gaze up the four-storey building. "Nice," he said, approvingly. "Which one is yours?"

"Are you going to throw stones at my window?"

He chuckled. "Maybe."

I looked up and pointed to the third floor. "That one there. With Garfield stuck to the window."

His left eyebrow rose. "You're a fan of Garfield?"

"He's sarcastic, lazy, hates Mondays and loves Italian food. Dude's my spirit animal." *Did I just fucking say that?*

When Grayson didn't laugh, I lifted my eyes to find him staring at me. His Adam's apple bobbed up and down as his gaze penetrated mine, making my heart race. I licked my lips, and the movement drew his eyes. Without another word, he slid his hand around the nape of my neck and slammed his mouth down onto mine.

I drew back in surprise at the unexpected softness of his lips, then kissed him again, desperately needing more. He pulled my waist towards his as I circled my arms around his neck. His hands glided up and down my back and through my hair as we devoured each other.

Finally and reluctantly pulling apart, I realised we were on the verge of indecent exposure.

"When do you leave?" I panted, feeling like I'd just run a marathon.

He ran his hand down my cheek. "Tomorrow."

"Oh." Disappointment sat heavily on my shoulders.

"I need to report back to my father, but hopefully I'll be back in a week or two. Can I see you then?"

I wanted to scream yes, but I knew better. "Gray…"

"I don't want this to end before it's even begun," he said, with a sense of urgency.

This is a bad idea. "But you live on the other side of the country."

"They're just details."

I shook my head. "They're *facts*."

He placed his hands on his hips and pursed his lips.

I looked away uncomfortably. "I can't start something knowing there's an expiry. I…I don't take heartbreak well."

He reached for my hand. "I don't intend to break your heart."

Before his fingertips found mine, I abruptly turned and walked up the stairs. "Goodbye, Grayson."

"Josie…"

I lingered on the top step before turning back.

A mixture of frustration and sadness swirled behind his eyes. "Our story doesn't end here." Before I could respond, he dropped his gaze and continued up the road. His fading footsteps felt like a countdown, and I was running out of time.

"Gray!" I yelled, temporarily losing my mind.

Pausing mid-step, he slowly turned around.

I dropped the pizza box and practically flew down the stairs, launching myself into his arms as my lips crashed into his. "Don't go yet," I murmured, between breaths.

Without saying a word, Grayson hitched me up around his waist and carried me up the stairs. After two failed attempts at entering my code into the keypad, he placed me back on my feet so I could concentrate. At the sound of the buzzer, we both exhaled, and Grayson opened the door.

"Wait!" I cried, coming to a halt. "My pizza!" I ran back and retrieved the leftovers that thankfully hadn't fallen from the box.

Grayson chuckled and shook his head as he chased me up the stairs to my apartment. Trying to ignore his hot breath on my shoulder, I unlocked the door and threw the pizza on the kitchen bench as Grayson dropped his backpack by the door.

"Great plac—" Was all he could mutter before my lips were on his again, and we were stumbling towards the bedroom.

Buttons scattered over the floor as I tore off Grayson's shirt and threw his hat across the room, leaving him half-naked in his expensive jeans and looking…magnificent. My gaze travelled down his well-built arms and hard chest, and all I wanted to do was lick every god given part of him.

Stalking me to the edge of the bed, I fell down with a giggle. He parted my legs with his knees and stepped between my thighs, looming over me with hunger. Grayson pulled my hair free, pushing each rainbow coloured stand over my shoulders to expose my neck to his mouth. He lay a gentle kiss under my ear and ran his finger across my collarbone, slipping it under the strap of my dress. He asked permission with his eyes and I gave him a small nod.

Pushing one strap off my shoulder, followed by the other, he slid the dress down to my waist, exposing my lacy cornflower blue bra that I thanked the lord I decided to wear. He ran the back of his hand down my cheek, drinking me in. His fingers travelled further south, drawing a line from my neck, between my breasts and over my stomach, building an ache I was growing desperate to soothe.

As he climbed over me, engulfing me in his muscular frame, he slid his hand under my lower back. And with one swift movement, he threw me further onto the bed.

Soft kisses travelled over my stomach as he unlatched my bra leaving it loose over my chest. When he finally dragged it away, his mouth found my breasts. His five o'clock shadow tickled my delicate skin and drove me wild. As he moved closer to my throbbing core, I was sure I would combust.

My dress hung low on my hips, barely covering anything. He ran both hands down my sides, before sliding them under my body and cupping my arse cheeks. Grabbing my dress and panties, he pulled them down over my legs and dropped them to the floor.

I should have felt vulnerable lying there completely naked in front of him, but I felt powerful. The desire in his eyes was undeniable and reflected how I felt. I needed him inside me.

He kicked off his shoes, and undid his belt to slide out of his pants. When his erection sprang out, I gasped and my heart kicked up a notch. *Holy crap!*

Kneeling back onto the bed, he eased my legs to each side of him.

"There's a condom in the nightstand," I said, breathlessly.

He shook his head. "We're so not there yet."

"Oh," I said as he lowered his grin between my legs. His hot breath grazed my swollen lips. "*Oh...*"

His chuckle muffled as his tongue met my seam and almost sent me flying off the bed. "Fu...ck me," I cried out in pleasure.

"*Not...yet.*"

My fingers threaded through his scruffy brown hair as his tongue worked expertly deep within my thighs. I could have sworn he had a manual down there.

"Gray, I...I'm coming..." I stammered as my body began to jerk.

This only made him press harder and I lost my mind.

Smiling, he slowly trailed kisses back up my body to my breasts. A deep growl rumbled through his chest as he took my nipples into his mouth one by one. His hardness rubbed against my core and my body begged for more of him.

Grayson reached into my nightstand drawer and pulled out a condom. Snatching it from his hands, I grinned and slowly removed it from its wrapper to roll it on. I peered up into his heated gaze as he watched me stroke his erection.

"That was so fucking hot," he uttered and slammed his mouth down on mine, stealing my breath away.

Our kisses were rough and urgent, and we couldn't wait any longer. Pausing at my entrance, he devoured my mouth again and slowly pushed his length all the way inside, making me cry out in ecstasy. *Hooooly craaaap!*

Once I adjusted to his size, our natural rhythm began and it was to the beat of the best fucking song ever. Each thrust was neither gentle nor rough, but the perfect mixture of both that had me coming multiple times throughout the night, until we both collapsed in each other's arms and drifted off to sleep.

Chapter 9

"Joooosssie," a low voice called, waking me up from my morning slumber. I reluctantly pushed up onto my elbows, trying to locate the noise. A deep growl sounded from the living room and I jolted upright. *Luci?*

"Luci, no!" I yelled, flying out of my bed and wrapping my silk robe around my naked body.

I skidded out of the bedroom to find a paling Grayson standing extremely still, wearing yesterday's jeans, no shirt, and carrying two coffee mugs. I followed his terrified gaze down to Luci who stood between us, blocking his return to the bedroom. Reed must've dropped him back this morning while we slept.

Luci growled again.

"Luci. No!" I repeated sternly and stomped my foot. He was almost deaf, so I had to send vibrations to get his attention.

He let out a whimper and trotted over for a pat. "Luci, this is my friend Grayson. Grayson, this is my dog, Luci."

His eyes remained wide. "Dog?"

I chuckled. "He's a gentle giant, I promise," I said, taking Luci out onto the terrace.

"He's bigger than you!"

I nodded. "Yes, *that* was unexpected."

Grayson's brow furrowed, clearly confused.

"He was a stray. I thought he was a fully-grown dog when I took him in, but turned out he was just a puppy and well...he kept on growing."

Grayson peered through the window, fascinated by the mass of fur. "Did you also think *he* was a *she*?"

I chuckled. "Oh, Luci's just a nickname."

"For what?"

I winced. "Luci-fer."

Grayson blinked a few times, then burst out laughing. "You named your dog after the devil?"

I threw my hands in the air with a laugh. "He was such a crazy puppy, tearing shit up and wreaking havoc wherever he went. It seemed to fit at the time."

"And now?"

"Now he's old, partially deaf and blind, and, as you just found out, super protective. I couldn't ask for a better friend." I smiled at Luci through the floor to ceiling windows that overlooked the terrace.

Grayson's eyes sparkled as he passed over a coffee.

"Thank you." I said, wrapping my hands around the warm mug.

"Sorry, I helped myself. I can't function without coffee in the morning."

I cringed. I didn't have a fancy coffee machine. "I bet you don't have instant often?"

"I'll take what I can get. I'm feeling especially tired this morning." He winked and my cheeks warmed.

"You hungry?" I asked, as my stomach rumbled. I spotted the empty pizza box on the floor and groaned. "Luuuci." That *was* my breakfast.

"Should we get dressed? I can take you somewhere."

"No way! It's Sunday. Pyjamas don't come off until *at least* midday."

Grayson slipped his finger through the gap in my robe, attempting to take a peek. "You're not wearing pyjamas," he said, smugly.

I brushed his hand away and laughed. "You know what I mean." I smirked. "I'll make us something."

Grayson's eyes widened and a twinkle appeared. "You can cook?"

"We can't all afford to eat out every night." I poked his chest as I moved past him towards the kitchen.

I rustled up some bacon and eggs from the fridge, and turned on the stove.

As I cooked, Grayson sat on the kitchen stool watching me. "I haven't had a home cooked meal in months."

I scrunched up my face. "You're kidding, right?"

"I wish I was."

"What about when you go home to your folks?"

He rubbed his stubble, which was now longer than it was the night before. "I guess that's the closest I get. They have a chef."

My eyes widened. "Wow. We are from *very* different worlds."

Grayson glanced around my apartment. "Are you sure? This apartment would've cost a fortune."

I followed his gaze. "It did." I muttered, feeling a little sick about the $1.5 million I spent on it.

"How can you even afford this on your wage?"

I narrowed my eyes. "How do you know how much I earn?"

"Sorry, that was rude of me. I...er...don't exactly, I'm just guessing this would be a stretch for an unknown photographer."

I wasn't offended, because he was right. "Well, you're spot on. My inheritance paid for this. I didn't want to live off my parent's money for the rest of my life, so I invested it all in this apartment. But the fun stuff, like bills and food...that's up to me. I guess in some way I'm still trying to prove to them I can make it on my own."

"You seem switched on. I think you'll do just fine." He wandered around the large living area, staring at the photos on the walls and the lone couch on the floor. "Did you just move in, or do you spend all your money on artwork instead of furniture."

I laughed. The small amount of furniture I did own, didn't do the place any justice. I had a massive open plan living room with polished floorboards and trendy exposed brick walls, yet all I had to compliment it with was a tiny old couch, a small television sitting precariously on a dining chair, my record collection and a torn-up dog bed. At least my walls weren't empty. They were covered in photographs.

"I've actually been living here for almost six years...and the artwork is all mine."

His mouth dropped, but I couldn't tell if he was shocked or impressed.

"Looks more like a gallery than a home, doesn't it?" I continued. "At least I don't have to worry about Luci destroying anything."

"Is that why you have no furniture? The dog?"

I should have said yes, but it wasn't the truth. "The only furniture I have was either given to me or taken off the street."

Not daring to look up into Grayson's sympathetic eyes, I concentrated on dishing up our breakfast onto three plates. The third was for Luci, who was drooling profusely at the window, watching my every move.

As we sat side by side at the island bench, hoeing into our meal, Grayson's eyes glistened as he chewed on the simplest meal known to man.

"Is any of your work for sale?" he asked, scanning my walls for the second time.

"No." I shrugged and picked up a piece of bacon. "But maybe someday."

"Why not today?"

I laughed and took a bite. "Why? You want to buy one?"

"I'd buy them all if you'd let me."

My chewing slowed. I couldn't tell if he was joking. "It doesn't feel right selling them. They're other people's moments, not mine."

"But it's your take on them that makes them so beautiful."

I shrugged. Maybe he was right. Maybe he was just being nice.

"Those photos at Lenny's last night, they were yours, weren't they?"

"Yeah." I nodded. "He thinks he can sell them."

"I know he could."

I let out a nervous laugh. "So, when do you fly out?" I asked, pushing the subject back onto him.

He blinked as if he'd forgotten he had somewhere else to be, then sighed. "This afternoon."

"Back to the mothership?"

He chuckled. "It definitely feels like that."

"Well, hopefully your father has cooled off by the time you get back."

"Ha, I doubt that. The man knows how to hold a grudge."

"Do you ever think about leaving the family business?"

He ran his hand through his hair. "All the fucking time."

"Why don't you?"

He pondered me for a moment and smiled. "One day I will."

Grayson was practically licking the plate when I pulled it out of his hands.

"Let me," he said, picking up the rest of the dishes. "Since you cooked, I'll clean." He dumped them into the sink and turned on the tap. Except when he reached over for the dish detergent, he pumped the hand soap under the running water instead.

I giggled and nudged him out of the way. "You've never washed a dish in your life, have you?"

Grayson stood closely behind, peering over my shoulder. "Is it that obvious?"

I reached over and tapped the soap. "Hands." And then the detergent. "Dishes."

"I should take notes," he said, laying a soft kiss on my shoulder.

I drew in a deep breath as he moved closer, eliminating any space between us. His growing bulge protruded from his jeans as he pushed me up against the counter.

The thin layer of silk did nothing but enhance every movement he made. He scooped my hair away from my shoulder and kissed my neck. As he nibbled my ear, his hands encircled my waist. One slipped inside my silk robe and over my breast, while the other moved lower causing me to drop the plate into the sink with a loud clatter.

"Fuck the dishes," Grayson said in a husky voice. "I'll buy you new ones."

With another giggle, I closed my eyes. "God, that feels good," I murmured, loving the feel of his hands exploring my body.

"I can make it feel better than good," he whispered as he pulled the smooth material over my behind.

The zipper of his jeans sounded, and a condom materialised

from his back pocket. A moment later, he slid into my crease with one swift thrust, almost splitting me in two. My back arched as he drove into me, again and again until I was grasping the counter and crying out his name.

After we desecrated the kitchen bench, we took ourselves back to the bedroom for yet another round. We had enough protein at breakfast to sustain us for the rest of the day.

As I fell back onto the bed with a giggle, Grayson nudged me with his elbow. "What?"

"I'm just…giddy." *Pete never made me feel this way.*

He shifted onto his side to face me. "I'm glad I'm not the only one."

I matched his move, and lifted my gaze to his.

His smile faded as his now hazel eyes drew me in. "Can I see you again?"

I smirked. "You really are persistent, aren't you?"

"It's one of my better traits."

I lifted the bed sheet, peeking underneath. "Definitely not your *best* trait."

With a chuckle, he grabbed my waist and pulled me on top of him. "Come on, Josie." He raised his brow, waiting for a response.

"Alright," I muttered, pretending like it was an effort to give in to his charm.

His mouth curved into a smile. "Good, because I have a plane to catch and if I don't leave now, I'm going to miss it." He flipped me over and gently kissed my lips. With a long groan, he moved off the bed, searching for his clothes that were scattered all over the apartment.

I shifted to the edge of the bed and watched him pull up his jeans. As he scanned the room for his shirt, the welcomed memory of tearing it off the night before flashed through my mind, until I remembered where I threw it. *Oh no…*

"Hang on." I slipped on my gown and scooted out of the room, predicting its fate before I found the evidence. Sure enough, his shirt was there…in tiny pieces all over Luci's bed.

"Fuck," Grayson muttered from behind. "He really is the devil, isn't he?"

"I'm pretty sure I ripped it first, if that helps. I'll buy you a new one."

"Don't be silly. I'll call my driver and get him to pick one up on the way here."

I blinked. *Driver? Of course he has a driver.* "Wait, I might have something."

I bounded back into the bedroom and rummaged through the closest until I found the bag of clothing Pete had left behind and clearly not missed. Pulling out one of his old work shirts, I turned and handed it to Grayson. "It needs an iron, but it should just fit."

Grayson's eyes narrowed. "This is your ex-boyfriend's shirt, isn't it?"

I shrugged. "It could be. I've had many lovers." His eyes grew large and I punched his shoulder. "I'm joking. Yes, it's his."

He slid it on and buttoned it up. It was too tight around his arms, but it made him look so damn sexy, I wanted to tear it off immediately.

"Don't look at me that way." He chuckled as he straightened the collar.

I grinned mischievously and sat back on the bed, letting my gown slip off my shoulder. "What way?"

A little blush touched his cheeks. "The way that will make me miss my flight," he said, leaning down to kiss me goodbye. Taking one step towards the door, he paused and returned a second later to claim my lips again. As he pulled away with an enduring groan, his eyes morphed from hazel to green, and before I knew it, he was unbuttoning his shirt and climbing back over me.

"But your flight…" I mumbled as Grayson's tongue dipped in and out of my mouth.

He parted from my lips, breathing heavily as he stared down into my eyes. "Fuck it, I'll catch the next one."

When Grayson left an hour later, still in a rush, I dressed in my pyjamas for the first time that day and ambled through my apartment, picking up after our trail of destruction. Torn clothes, dirty dishes, and empty condom wrappers littered the floor…plus one cell phone.

In his haste to catch his flight, Grayson must've dropped his phone. I picked it up and pushed the home button, waiting for the screen to light up. It was locked, but the screen was full of notifications.

Adam: **6 missed calls**

Dad: **3 missed calls**

Mel: **10 missed calls.**

His phone lit up with a text message.

Adam: **Why the fuck aren't you answering my calls? Dad read your report. He's actually impressed. He wants you to stay and make the deal.**

And again a few minutes later.

Adam: **Where are you? Quit fucking around. Dad's getting pissed.**

Adam: **Great. Now he's sending me over to babysit you.**

I pressed my lips together and slowly placed the cell phone on my nightstand. I had no business reading his messages.

For once, I didn't mind that it was Monday. After a thoroughly satisfying weekend, I went to work feeling a lot lighter—I guess multiple orgasms would do that to you. I wasn't going to get down about the uncertainty of my job, because Grayson was right. Change could be a good thing, and it was probably just what our magazine needed.

"You look...different," Amy said, smirking in my doorway.

I shrugged and smiled before peeking up at her.

Her eyes twinkled as she performed a victory dance across the room. "You got laaaaid!"

"Shhh. I don't want the whole office knowing. Especially Pete."

She bounced on her feet. "The hydrangeas did it, didn't they?"

I glanced across at my potted mass of blue snowballs and chuckled. "I don't know how he knew, but—" I paused and narrowed my eyes at her. "How *did* he know, Ames?"

Her eyes popped and she hurried back into her office.

"Amy!" I charged after her.

She glanced up at me, typing aimlessly on her keyboard. "I'm right in the middle of something, can we chat later?"

"How did he know?" I asked, ignoring her.

"Well, he was trying so hard and you were giving him nothing…so, I maaay have sent a text to the number on the card." She sheepishly peered up at me.

"Ames." I groaned.

Shrugging indifferently, she leant back in her chair. "I'm not sorry though. Just look at you, you're glowing."

My cheeks warmed and I pursed my lips, trying to think of a clever response. "Righto…well, I need to get back to work," I muttered before heading for the door.

"It suits you," she sang out, and I quickened my steps towards my office.

That evening, I arrived back to my apartment after a breezy day in the office. Marlene had been at an off-site meeting all day and I was ahead with my work, so I didn't have much else to do but fight off X-rated flashbacks of my night with Grayson.

"Hey, Josie!" Reed called out from the bottom of the stairwell.

I paused mid-step and looked down. "Oh, hey, Reed."

He lugged up a large cardboard box. "You got a delivery this morning," he said, meeting me as I unlocked my door.

Reed was a dream neighbour. His profession meant he barely left his apartment, so he was always there to watch the place and take deliveries. He also helped me with Luci, who was now slobbering all over him.

I narrowed my eyes at the box as he carried it inside. "I haven't ordered anything. Are you sure?"

"There's only four people living in this building, and I'm pretty certain you're the only Josie Spencer, so yes, I'm sure," he replied, placing the box on my kitchen bench.

"Okay." I chuckled. "Well, thanks for bringing it up. You're a legend."

Blush crept up into his cheeks and he smiled bashfully. "No problem, Jos."

"Got any new gaming videos out?"

He grinned. "Just uploaded one today. Already has 1.2 million views."

"Niiice." I held up my hand and we high-fived, before he disappeared out the front door.

Throwing my handbag and keys onto the kitchen bench, I meandered over to my delivery. I grabbed some scissors out of the drawer and began cutting away the tape that held it all together. Unfolding the cardboard, I peered inside to discover a brand-new porcelain dinner set. I burst out laughing as I picked up the accompanying note.

It appears I left my phone at your place. Please keep it safe until I return (soon!). Feel free to take as many naked selfies on it as you like.
~ G.

I was half tempted until I reminded myself I barely knew the guy, so I took a photo of Luci's gorgeous face instead.

Chapter 10

After taking Luci for an early morning run at the park, I dressed for work in my usual jeans, faded Stones t-shirt and Chuck Taylors. I was entirely grateful for *Maude's* super relaxed dress code. The thought of wearing corporate attire on a daily basis made me shudder.

As I picked up my handbag, Grayson's cell phone vibrated along the nightstand. I was surprised it hadn't fallen off the table, given the amount of calls that came through overnight. Grayson was obviously a busy man.

It stilled as I approached, and I hesitated before picking it up to see who wanted to talk to him so badly. Suddenly, his phone lit up with a text message.

Unknown: **Josie, this is Gray. Please pick up. I need to talk to you.**

The phone rang again and I swiped to answer, but the screen went black. *Crap.* Rummaging around my bedside, I found a phone charger and plugged it in. I tapped my finger impatiently on the screen, but it didn't light up. Glancing at the time on my own phone, I grimaced; I was already running late. With a sigh, I left his phone on charge and raced out the door.

When I finally walked into the office, uncharacteristically late, everyone was on edge.

Some were attacking their keyboards, some were wiping away tears and some were gathered in small circles whispering amongst themselves. I was left wondering what the hell I had missed in the last ten minutes.

I poked my head into Amy's office. "What's going on?"

She sat at her desk, face down in her hands, before peering up at me with eyes full of anguish. "I can't handle all this. The energy around here is…too much."

I glanced down at the small rose-coloured crystal sitting firmly in her palm, and tried again. "What's going on, Ames?"

"Management just called a meeting…with everyone. It's the one we've all been waiting for."

I looked towards Marlene's office at the end of the hall. "Oh, fuck."

Her face fell back into her hands. "I know."

"When's the meeting?"

"In twenty-two minutes," she muttered through her fingers.

I entered my office and sunk into my chair. Twenty-two minutes. *Shit*. Everything was changing in twenty-fucking-two minutes. *No, scratch that. Twenty-fucking-one.*

Needing to keep my cool, I decided to keep working. There was no need to freak out just yet, but my thoughts kept travelling to the worst-case scenario. I didn't have enough money saved for my trip so I'd have to work at Lenny's until I found a new job. Or perhaps I could sell my apartment…no, I had Luci to think about and that place was perfect for him.

As I switched on my laptop to load my latest article, a notification pinged on my computer screen from Marlene's assistant, Linda.

L. Evans: **All staff are to report to the conference room immediately.**

I glanced through my glass wall into Amy's office and met her worry-stricken face. I wondered if she already knew what was going to happen.

We met in the hallway between our offices and walked to our impending doom together. A handsome man in an expensive suit, exited Marlene's office and strolled towards us. As I moved aside to let him through, his eyes met mine and I felt the slightest twinge of recognition. He smirked and tipped his head. "Ladies."

I offered him a small smile and kept walking, wondering where I'd seen him before.

Amy glanced back at him. "He was checking you out."

I rolled my eyes. "You think everyone is checking me out." My thoughts drifted to Grayson and shrugged. "Guys like that really aren't my type." *Grayson for that matter...*

She scoffed. "That guy is *everyone's* type."

I shook my head and grabbed Amy's hand tightly as we entered the conference room. Pete was already seated, and I decided to join him at the back of the room, proving to everyone that we were, despite all the rumours, still friends.

I smiled tightly. "So, it's really happening."

He scratched the back of his neck. "Seems that way."

Marlene flew through the door with her assistant trailing closely behind. A deathly silence fell over the room as we anxiously awaited her speech. Linda looked terrified.

"After ten amazing years, our little indie magazine has grown into something bigger than I ever imagined. It has the potential to be so much more and I'm both saddened and excited to announce that *Maude* has been bought by a much larger company that will help it grow into what it deserves."

I threw Amy a sideways glance as Marlene continued.

"Representatives from the company will be here tomorrow to meet you all and discuss your future. Now, I've been assured that most of you will retain your jobs, however it is inevitable that some changes will need to be made and a few of you will be let go, but not without a glowing recommendation from me, of course."

Gee, thanks, Marlene. You're a real sport.

Amy leaned towards my ear. "I think I'm going to vomit."

I rubbed her back, but I felt the same. "At least we still have jobs."

"For now," Pete muttered.

The meeting ended with Marlene hugging each and every one of us. It was fine for her. She would be retiring after they appointed a new editor. The rest of us had mortgages, rent, kids and bills to think about, and there weren't many other jobs like this around.

I dragged myself back to my office and slumped into my chair, ignoring my office phone as it persistently rang. Instead of checking my messages, I picked up my cell to ask Lenny to leave a job open for me, but Pete interrupted from the doorway.

"We're all heading to The Edge after work tonight. Want to join us for some commiseration drinks?"

I would normally decline any invitation from Pete, but this was different. He looked as drained as I felt. "Sounds perfect."

His frown turned upward. "Perhaps we could grab a bite to eat afterward…"

I mentally face palmed. "Pete…"

"Okay, okay." He chuckled before retreating down the hall.

Later that night, I stumbled into my apartment after consuming copious shots of whiskey to dull my anxiety for what the next day would bring.

"Hey Luuuuuci," I slurred, cuddling my gentle giant until we were rolling around on the floor. *Perhaps I'm a little drunker than I thought.*

I searched the fridge for a snack and washed down some pain killers with three glasses of water, trying to avoid the inevitable hangover coming my way.

As I crawled onto my bed and under my blankets, I spied Grayson's phone sitting on my nightstand. I picked it up and squinted my eyes as I attempted to turn it on, but nothing happened.

Twisting myself in the sheets, I hung my head over the side of the bed, my rainbow hair swishing over the floor. My blurry gaze met the power point on the wall and I groaned. It was switched off. I half-heartedly attempted to reach over and flick on the switch, but I clearly passed out instead.

―――

The raspy vocals of *Born to Run* blared in my ear, and I knocked over my lamp trying to find the phone with my eyes glued shut.

"What?" I cried, when I finally focused enough to perform basic functions.

Amy's voice was unusually low. "Josie, where the fuck are you?"

"Huh?" I glanced at my clock and my heart stopped. 9:15am. *Please be Saturday? Please be Saturday?* "Fuuuuuck! I slept through my alarm!"

"They haven't arrived yet, but get here as soon as you can. I won't be able to cover your ass this time."

Launching out of bed, I came crashing down onto the floor, still tightly tangled in my bed sheets. *Fuck!* Quickly unravelling myself, I lunged into the closet and threw on my favourite jeans and my last clean shirt, along with my darkest sunglasses.

I grabbed my gear and raced out the door, down two flights of stairs and ran, all while my head screamed at me to slow the fuck down. I darted across roads and weaved around pedestrians, while cursing at myself for being so stupid. *Of all the fucking days to be late!*

Arriving to work in record time, I glanced at my phone and cringed. 9:40am. Avoiding the irritatingly slow elevator, I sprinted up the stairs, praying I would arrive before my new boss.

I reached my floor and pushed open the emergency door, panting heavily. Confusion set in. The place was empty. Perhaps it really was a Saturday and this was all some elaborate prank.

A deep voice sounded from up the hall, towards the conference room, and my heart sank. To my horror, the meeting had already started. I crept up to the open door and sucked in my breath, ducking my head as I turned into the room, trying to make it to the back without being noticed.

"And that brings me to our next rule. Tardiness."

I froze and lifted my gaze to find everyone's eyes on me. Feeling a burning stare on the back of my head, I slowly turned around, preparing myself to apologise. But when I met those familiar eyes, swirling between hazel and green, my mouth fell open and no words came out.

"Sunny, is it?" Grayson asked, and the man beside him smirked.

I slipped off my sunglasses, revealing my bloodshot eyes. "Um…no."

Grayson's jaw twitched before breaking eye contact. "Take a seat."

I sank into the first empty chair I could find, wanting to disappear. Blood surged through my body making my temperature rise as I tried to figure out what the fuck was going on. This wasn't the Grayson I knew. The two suits at the front of the room were cold-hearted business men. Not at all like the man who spent the weekend in my bed. *In me.*

As they listed all the new company policies, I tried to join the dots, but more and more questions flooded my mind and I racked my brain for answers.

Why would his family want *Maude? My Maude?* What business were they in anyway? Did he even tell me that? *Fuck.* Did he tell me anything about himself? *FUCK!* Why didn't I look him up? He practically told me to. *Stupid, stupid, stupid!* Was this some sort of game to him? Like a cat playing with its prey before he eats it. *Am I the mouse?!* Argh, my head was pounding.

"The next rule is one we take very seriously," the other man said. I assumed he was Grayson's brother, Adam, by his similar appearance. No wonder he looked so familiar in the hallway yesterday.

Grayson's face lowered and his shoulders tensed as his brother continued.

"There will be no relationships in the office, except for professional ones. It never ends well and it's disruptive to the team."

I accidently laughed out loud, and the entire room shifted their gaze to me. Including Grayson.

Adam raised his brow. "Is that going to be a problem, Miss…?"

I flickered my eyes over Grayson and then back to Adam. "Spencer. Josie Spencer. And no. That one definitely *won't* be a problem. It's actually the best policy yet."

While Adam narrowed his gaze at my weirdness, Pete shot me a dirty look and Grayson cleared his throat, eager to move to the next item.

The meeting wrapped up an hour later and I was dying to get out of there. My stomach was churning, the lights were entirely too bright and I shivered from the cold sweat coating my body. All the signs were there…I was going to vomit.

As soon as Adam finished his spiel, he headed straight for Marlene's office, while Grayson remained at the front of the room, packing away their notes. Quickly wiping the perspiration from my forehead, I bolted for the exit, praying I'd get to the toilet in time.

"Miss Spencer, can you wait a moment?"

Amy turned to me with worried eyes as she retreated, leaving me alone with a very different man to the one I thought I knew. I couldn't believe I'd been fooled again. Once everyone had disappeared back to their offices, Grayson closed the door.

"Josie..."

I held up my hand to stop him from talking.

Clearly seeing my paling face, he took a step forward. "Are you okay?"

I still couldn't speak. A lump was forming in my throat as I battled the nausea.

He took another step. "Jos—"

Quickly scooping up the small wastepaper bin sitting by the door, I heaved.

"Fuck," Grayson uttered, watching me uncomfortably as I brought up a mixture of whisky and last night's tacos. *Thank god I skipped breakfast.*

After taking a deep breath, I straightened my back. "Would you mind if we postpone this surprising reunion until I find some dignity?"

Grayson nodded quietly and opened the door. I didn't dare meet his eyes as I strode out of the room, head down, embracing the bin.

Amy raced out of her office as I passed, catching up with me as I entered the ladies' room. "That's him, isn't it? Are you okay?"

I whirled around to face her. "Did you know?"

"I didn't see this coming, I promise. When I saw him here a couple of weeks ago, I assumed he was looking for you, not buying the business."

My mouth fell open. "He was the one in the hallway, wasn't he?" *I'm such an idiot.*

Amy winced as she nodded. "Did he yell at you for being late?"

"He didn't get a chance," I said, handing her the evidence before bending over the sink. The cool water felt glorious as I splashed it over my face, and I thanked the lord I decided to wear waterproof mascara...*last night.*

She glanced down and gagged. "Oh my god, you didn't?"

"He's lucky I didn't vomit on his Armani shoes." I gazed up at my dishevelled reflection and moaned. "What have I done?"

Scurrying back into my office a short time later, I switched on my laptop. While waiting for it to load, I noticed Linda carrying boxes into the room beside Amy. The room that had laid vacant since the last job cuts. My gaze shifted to Amy, and she motioned to her computer as mine chimed.

A. Mitchell: **Do we have a new neighbor?**

Linda unloaded bundles of files onto the desk in the middle of the room, and shuffled the furniture around until she looked content.

J. Spencer: **Linda is preparing it for someone. Marlene perhaps?**

A. Mitchell: **It can't be for Marlene. She's already downsized into the office next to the conference room.**

J. Spencer: **Hopefully they're just using it for storage.**

A. Mitchell: **Boring!**

My chuckle dissolved when I spotted Grayson enter the office and converse with Linda. He settled into the chair behind the large desk and opened his laptop. *For fucks sake.*

His eyes flickered across to mine and I quickly dropped my gaze back to the computer screen.

A. Mitchell: **Who is it?**

J. Spencer: ***angry face* You know who.**

A. Mitchell: **I'll happily swap offices if I get to stare at that all day.**

J. Spencer: ***face palm***

I opened my email, and watched my inbox fill. The last three to come through were from William Harlow. The first, a group email, welcoming us all to Harlow Corp. The second, another group email, with an attachment of the new agreement we all had to print, sign and return. And the third, to me.

Josie, we need to talk.

Ha! Not a chance.

I closed the window and opened up the story I'd been working on, keen to get well and truly distracted. Hours passed as I sat, staring at my computer screen, trying to ease my temper. My neck hurt from being frozen in the same position, fearing

I'd make eye contact with Grayson if I moved. Why couldn't he share Marlene's old office with his brother? Was the room not big enough for both of their egos?

My message window popped up.

W. Harlow: **Got a minute?**

My breath caught. I knew Grayson was watching because he had full view of my desk from his, even with all the shrubbery.

J. Spencer: **Who dis?**

W. Harlow: **Please?**

I had nothing nice to say, and now that he was my boss, it was all the more reason not to say anything.

Grabbing my coffee mug, I stood up and noticed Grayson's back straighten in my peripheral vision. He was anticipating my visit, but instead of walking straight into his office, I turned and marched down the hallway to the lunchroom.

I was making sure to savour every last drop of my coffee, when Pete walked in.

"Oh, hey, Josie."

"Hey, Pete. How's your day going?"

He shrugged. "Feels like the calm before the storm, doesn't it?"

I pressed my lips together and nodded. "How much do you know about Harlow Corp.?"

"Only that they're the biggest publishing company on the east coast."

What the actual fuck? I disguised my shock with a long sip.

"They're renowned for buying little magazines like ours to either build them up, shut them down or merge them into their other publications. But not before getting rid of all the dead wood."

I clenched my teeth. *How could Grayson not tell me this?*

Pete reached up and ran his thumb down my cheek. "You look tired," he said, his eyes full of warmth. His longing gaze panned past my face and widened. Quickly dropping his arm, he stepped around me and held out his hand to the new arrival. "Mr. Harlow, I'm so glad to finally meet you. I'm Peter Wallis, head of accounting."

I turned to find Grayson's eyes burning into mine. After a few long seconds he diverted his cold stare to Pete and shook his hand. "Yes, I recognise the name."

Pete motioned to me. "And this is Jo—"

"We met in the meeting," he interrupted.

I tapered my gaze. There was no need to be rude.

Pete's round eyes met mine as Grayson scanned the room's facilities.

"I don't mind you all having the occasional coffee, but don't make a habit out of socialising outside of your lunchbreak," Grayson said, not making eye contact.

My eyelids fluttered. "Riiight, well I better get going then," I uttered, shaking my head as I marched back to my office. *What an absolute jerk.*

The day almost ended without any further interaction with Grayson. He'd been in a meeting with his brother and Marlene all afternoon, and when I overheard Linda ordering their dinner, I breathed a sigh of relief.

It wasn't until I was shutting down my computer, when Linda appeared in my doorway. She was an older lady, mid-sixties and completely old school. She still used a paper-diary and email was a foreign concept. It was both refreshing and annoying at the same time.

"Josie, Mr. Harlow would like to see you in his office."

I looked past her and frowned. "But he's not in there."

"Yes, he's currently in a meeting, but he would like you to wait until he returns."

With a growl, I pushed up from my desk. "Fine." I may as well get it over with.

I crossed the hallway into his empty office. His desk was covered in paperwork and files. Files with our names on them. My heart rate picked up as I scanned his desk for my name. Perhaps he didn't want to talk to me at all, perhaps he was going to fire me.

"You won't find your file."

I jumped. Grayson strode into the room like he owned the place. *Oh, wait…*

He motioned for me to sit, and I cautiously slid into the chair in front of him. Instead of returning to his, he leant back on his desk and crossed his legs.

"You asked to see me?"

His expression softened. "I need to explain."

"Why you lied to me?"

"I didn't lie. I *don't* lie."

I crossed my arms and lifted my brow. "Sorry. I meant deliberately withhold information."

"Listen, I never thought my father would go ahead with it, so there was no point in telling you."

Pursing my lips, I looked away and remained silent.

Grayson rubbed the back of his neck. "After Hank and Sabrina's wedding, I was desperate to talk to you, so I found out what magazine you work for. I did a little research on the company, with the sole intention of finding your contact details, when I discovered it was for sale. I did my due-diligence and it was an amazing deal, exactly the sort of business I've been looking for. My father isn't keen on these types of magazines, so I didn't think anything would come of it."

"You could have at least given me a heads up," I said, still fuming.

"Trust me, I tried. When I got back to LA to find out Adam had already left to finalise the sale, I wanted to call you, but your number was in my cell. I tried calling your office yesterday, but you never answered."

I shook my head and stood to leave.

"Josie, I had no prior intention of pursuing this business. Only you."

My breath hitched and I turned back to him.

His eyes bled honesty. "But this is a big deal for me. It's the first time my father has *ever* supported one of my ventures."

The door swung open and Adam marched into the room.

Grayson stood up and his expression instantly changed. "Consider this a formal warning. Be late again and you're done here," he said sternly.

I blinked a few times like I'd been slapped. Adam's eyebrows rose and he flicked his head to the door. With a scowl, I stormed out of the room, hearing Adam chuckle as I slammed the door behind me.

Luci enjoyed an extra-long walk that night. I strolled around the park numerous times until the sun had set and only darkness remained. I never had to worry too much with Luci by my side. Even in the daylight, no one ever seemed to bother me.

As I turned the last corner to my apartment, Luci let out a low growl. Shadowing his foggy senses, I discovered Grayson sitting at the top of the stairs that led to the entrance of my building. He lifted his eyes at the sound and met my narrowing gaze.

Luci continued his menacing rumble and I let him.

Grayson rose and slid his hands into his pockets, warily walking down to meet me. His blazer was gone and his tie hung loose from his buttoned-down shirt. As his foot left the last step, Luci's growl grew louder and he froze.

"Take your hands out of your pockets," I ordered.

His eyebrows pulled together. "What?"

"Just do it."

He pulled out his hands and Luci moved closer. He sniffed the air and whimpered before sitting and lifting his paw to shake hands. *Traitor.*

Grayson laughed and shook his giant paw. "Hey, Luci."

"What are you doing here, Grayson? Or do I have to call you William now? Or is it Mr. Harlow?"

He lowered his gaze. "Grayson is fine."

"And at work?" I asked, looking away.

He sighed. "The latter is preferable."

I chuckled and pushed past him to climb the stairs.

"I'm sorry, Josie. I—"

"Let's just forget last weekend ever happened, okay?" I blurted, cutting him off. "It will be easier on everyone."

"Josie..." He reached out and encircled my wrist. "I don't want to forget."

I drew in a shaky breath and spun around. "Well, I have to." My eyes pleaded with his. "I need this job."

His other hand reached for my shoulder as his eyes softened. "Your job is safe."

"These people are my family. Are *their* jobs safe?"

His mouth parted and he paused before speaking. "We can't keep everyone."

My eyes welled as my anger surfaced and I brushed him off. "Just the ones sleeping with the boss, right?"

Grayson shook his head. "It's not like that. That's not why you're keeping your job. *Maude* would be nothing without *Capturing Love*. You're the reason for its success."

"How many?" I asked, ignoring him. "How many people are losing their jobs?"

He looked away. "Ten by the end of the week. We're introducing a digital team and we need the space."

Pain radiated through my chest and I blinked back tears. "I need to go."

"Josie…"

I threw up my hands as I continued up the stairs. "What?!"

"Can I grab my cell?"

The question threw me. "Oh. Yeah sure. Wait here."

Mumbling obscenities as I trudged up the stairs with Luci by my side, I unlocked my apartment and went straight to the bedroom to yank Grayson's phone off charge.

Consumed with anger, I made my way to the window and slid it open. Spying Grayson waiting patiently below, I poked out my head and held out the cell. "Head's up!"

Grayson's eyes grew large as he lifted his hands in desperation, anticipating my next move. "Josie, no!"

But instead of dropping it down to him, I threw it as far as I could, across the street. It exploded into a thousand pieces as it collided with the road underneath. I guess I was just taking the 'lose my number' speech to another level.

His shoulders slumped as he gazed out onto the street. "What the fuck, Josie?!"

"Whoops," I said with a small shrug, before slamming the window shut.

Chapter 11

The next morning, Linda was pacing the hallway on the verge of tears.

"Are you ok?" I asked, catching her elbow as I returned from the lunchroom with a coffee.

Her lower lip trembled as she shook her head, and I pulled her into my office.

"What's going on?"

"I'm going to get fired," she whimpered, lowering her gaze.

My eyes widened. "Have they announced—"

"Oh no, not yet," she said, meeting my fretted eyes. "I'm going to get fired if I can't fix this." She held out her hand to reveal a tiny chip sitting loosely in her palm. "I don't even know what it is," she cried.

My heart stopped. It was a sim card from a cell phone. I didn't need to guess whose.

"He said if I can't figure out how to get all the numbers off it, then I'm not much of an assistant."

"He *what*?" My hands clenched at my sides as I glared through Grayson's office window. He was leaning back in his chair, feet up on the desk, with the phone pressed against his head. Probably barking orders no doubt.

Linda was nearing retirement age. She wouldn't have a clue about these things. She had been with *Maude* since they launched and knew everything about everything…except all the necessary components of a cell phone.

She let out a defeated sigh. "It's okay. I'll figure it out. My grandson may know about these things. I'll call him."

She turned to leave, but I held on to her hand. "You won't need to do that. I'll sort this out."

Linda peered up at me in awe. "Really?" she gushed, her eyes welling. "Oh, Josie, you're such a gem."

She dropped the little chip into my hand and I wrapped my fingers around it, forming a tight fist. Linda left my office, and once out of sight, I marched into Grayson's, slamming the sim card onto his desk.

His jaw tightened as his eyes travelled from my hand up to my pursed lips. "I'll call you back," he uttered, hanging up the phone.

"What is this?" I demanded.

He dropped his feet to the floor and eyed the sim card. "*That* is the remains of my entire professional network," he said, with a growing smirk. "Great arm, by the way."

"Why did you threaten Linda with her job? She can't do this type of thing."

"Isn't that what assistants are for?"

I growled and picked it back up. "I'll do it. I don't need others to clean up the messes I make." I turned and marched towards the door.

"Josie," he called, and I slowed my pace. "Don't barge into my office again. No matter what our history is, you need to remain professional around here."

I scoffed and spun around. "Professi—are you kidding me?" Heat surged to my cheeks. "No one has ever questioned my professionalism."

He regarded the mountain of paperwork on his desk and peered up at me, baring no emotion. "Looks like no one has questioned anything around here for a while."

My mouth fell open, and I drew in a long breath, before storming out of there.

Harlow Corp. gave us one week to prove ourselves, before they started their 'restructuring' phase. And after my outburst at Grayson, I could only assume I was on top of their 'to go' list. Nonetheless, I did my work and knew I did it well. If Grayson decided to sack me, it would have to be for personal reasons and *then* we would see who lacked professionalism. I even got his stupid sim card fixed, minus my number, thanks to Reed.

Our entire office had turned into a funeral home. There was barely a smile behind anyone's eyes anymore. Even Amy, who always added a little spark to the workplace, had gone quiet, only fuelling my fury towards Grayson.

Grayson seemed to make a point of creating enemies. He was nothing short of rude, arrogant and heartless, and made me question my ability to read people. How could I have gotten it so wrong with him? How could the man I met over a burger in Las Vegas turn into this cold-blooded creature?

Adam was away, tending to another business, leaving Grayson in complete power for the remainder of the week. Between ordering people around and threatening jobs, I wondered who he was trying to impress. From the snippets of information he shared with me, I got the impression his father expected a lot from him. But it was no excuse, and I totally understood why the majority of the office despised him.

The day Adam returned, we knew our time had come. Various staff were called into the conference room, one by one. It was when they walked out with an empty cardboard box that broke me. I couldn't bear to look their way. Maria from Payroll, Gemma from Marketing, and about five others all returned to their desks to pack up their belongings.

Maude wasn't large enough for this to go unnoticed. We had a unique business structure that enabled us to produce a quality publication with minimal staff. We all put in more than our job roles entailed, because we loved where we worked... until now.

When the day from hell was finally over, I was packing up my things, eager to leave, when Linda sent out a group message:

L. Evans: **All staff to the conference room in 5 minutes.**

Five minutes?! I could be half way home in five minutes! *Not really, but that isn't the point.* I was twiddling my thumbs, waiting for the clock to wind down, when I glanced over at my wilting hydrangea. It hadn't been watered all week. I wasn't intentionally trying to kill it, I just didn't want Grayson thinking I cared for his gift. Plus, I didn't need the reminder of how stupid I was to believe he was a good person.

Picking up the potted beauty, I slipped into Grayson's empty office, and left the plant on his desk. Even in its limp state, it brightened the room instantly. Brushing my hands, I snuck back out and slipped into the line of employees entering the conference room.

Grayson and Adam were already standing at the front, deep in conversation. Their voices hushed as I edged past and felt both sets of eyes trail after me. *God, I hope he hasn't told his brother.*

As staff numbers were declining, it became easier to find a spare chair to sit on. I plonked myself between Amy and Janice, to avoid the empty seat beside Pete.

Amy leant to my ear and murmured. "Don't cause a scene this time. I can't survive this place without you."

I smirked and lifted my gaze to the front of the room and met Adam's intense blue eyes. Grayson followed his brother's gaze and his jaw twitched.

After the last staff member hurried in, Adam patted his brother on the back and moved to close the door. Grayson lifted his gaze to meet my deathly stare, but remained expressionless.

"Well, congratulations on surviving round one," Adam announced.

Wow. Really?

"Over the next few months, we will continue to review and assess what, *and who,* is needed in the continuing success of this business. This is not the time to become complacent in your jobs. You will need to prove to us you belong here every single day."

Gasps echoed through the room.

"If you're wondering who will be picking up the extra workload, well, this will be you. All of you will be taking on more responsibility. If you have a problem with this, please speak to William. He'll endeavour to work on a more *suitable* arrangement for you." He smirked at his brother, and Grayson nodded.

"We will be meeting with each of you individually over the next week to discuss your roles and expectations at *Maude*. I look forward to getting to know you all better." His eyes found mine as he finished his last sentence and I cringed. *Well, that was sleazy.*

I kept my eyes lowered and rushed out of the room to avoid any more unwanted eye contact. As the conference door closed, a muffled argument arose from behind. Adam and Grayson were clearly disagreeing over something, but it was impossible to make out the words as I made my way to my office. I glanced across at Amy and she shrugged, clearly hearing it too.

Grayson stormed back into his office, but paused in front of the new leafy addition on his desk. He tapped his finger beside the pot, obviously contemplating what to do with it. With a sigh, he continued around to his chair and began hammering away on his keyboard.

"They're ready to see you now," Linda said from my doorway, smiling tightly.

Trying to slow my erratic heart, I followed her to the room at the end of the hallway. Marlene's old office, Adam's new torture chamber. Not many people had come out unscathed.

She knocked twice and opened the door. Adam sat behind a large mahogany desk, while Grayson paced the room behind him. I sent Linda a 'don't leave me' glance and she offered me a sympathetic nod as she closed the door, leaving me alone with the Harlow brothers.

"Please sit," Adam said, motioning to the chair in front.

Hesitantly, I perched on the edge of the visitor's chair and took another deep breath.

"You can relax," he said finally. "We won't bite...muc—"

"Josie, we're happy with your output so far, but we think you can take on a bit more." Grayson cut him off and Adam's grin faded.

I blinked a few times. *Is he joking? I'm already doing two jobs.*

"We want you to cover the New York music scene. Concerts, reviews and the like. Marlene said you were more than capable."

My eyes went round. "But isn't that Susan's—"

"She's moved on," Grayson answered abruptly. "Do you have a problem with the extra workload?"

I swallowed and shook my head, but didn't meet his eyes. "No."

Susan had worked off site. She attended gigs most nights and slept through the day, meaning she worked different hours to the rest of us. I wasn't sure how I was going to make it work, but I would have to.

"I'll have Linda handover all of Susan's files by the end of the day. You'll need to be up to scratch by Monday."

There goes my plans for the weekend. *If I had any.*

"Will there be anything else?" I asked.

Adam's grin returned. "Well, now that you mention—"

"There will be nothing else," Grayson uttered. "You're free to go."

With a quick nod, I left the room, closing the door softly behind me.

"You're kidding me?" Amy almost spat out her wine after I told her about my additional workload. "You're already doing so much."

"Tell me about it." I glanced at the time on my phone. "I have one weekend to get familiar with the entire New York music scene."

"At least you like music," she said, trying to cheer me up.

"Old music, Ames, not the new stuff. Most of the artists I listen to are dead." I dropped my head into my hands at the bar.

Amy rubbed my back. "You'll be fine. You'll just take it in your stride like you al—" Her hand stilled on my back. "What the…"

I lifted my head and followed her glare. Adam and Grayson sauntered into The Edge, ambling towards the bar. As Adam ordered their drinks, Grayson's eyes panned down the counter, widening when his gaze collided with mine. His back straightened as he scanned the bar, meeting unhappy faces of employees who just wanted to relax.

His lips pursed as he nudged his brother. Adam chortled as he regarded all the familiar faces, but didn't seem surprised at all. A few words were spoken between them, leaving Grayson's jaw clenched.

"They have some nerve," I murmured under my breath.

"Josie..." Amy warned as I placed my empty wine glass on the bar.

Amy let out a squeak as I approached them, and quickly hid from the scene she thought I was about to cause.

Grayson stepped forward before Adam noticed I was there. "Josie, I didn't know you were all going to be here. Adam didn't tell me—"

"Tell you what?" Adam appeared next to Grayson and handed him a neat whiskey. His blue eyes brightened when they met mine. "Josie, what a surprise."

I narrowed my gaze. "So you had no idea this is where we all come for drinks on Fridays?"

The corner of Adam's mouth twitched. "I had no idea...until Linda let it slip this afternoon."

Grayson groaned and ran his hand through his hair, watching me with tired eyes.

Adam shrugged. "I wanted to see what all the fuss was about," he said, pretending to be interested in the décor as he sipped his drink.

"We'll have one drink, then leave. Enjoy your night, Josie," Grayson said, attempting to turn his brother away.

"No, stay. Maybe if you see us as human beings, you'll show a little more compassion."

Grayson gave a short nod, before pushing his amused brother to an empty table in the quickly filling bar.

I spun around and headed back to my workmates, all wary of the new arrivals.

Instead of going home early as planned, I ordered another round of drinks, then another, and another. After I gave Pete the low-down on my job, he told me he also absorbed someone else's role and understood the pressure I was feeling. We spent the next hour venting about our week, until Pete's fingers grazed my leg.

"Pete," I whispered, straining my eyes at him.

He quickly lifted his hand and winced. "Sorry, sorry! It's a hard habit to break."

"You need to be more careful. I don't want you getting in trouble."

"What? For the no romantic relationship rule?" He chuckled. "Can they even do that?"

"They seem to do whatever they want," I murmured, glancing over to the two gorgeous women who had joined their table.

Adam was lavishing the women with attention, but Grayson kept his distance, sipping his beer every time one of the girls moved closer. It made my skin crawl.

"I need another wine," I professed, as the blonde ran her hand over Grayson's bicep.

"I'll get you one," Pete said brightly, sliding out of the booth before I could protest.

Once he was gone, Amy launched into the empty space beside me, but I barely noticed. She nudged my side to get my attention. "Somebody's jealous." She giggled and broke my trance.

My mouth dropped open. "I'm not jealous, I'm just…just… argh, fuck." I threw my head back and stared at the rafters above.

"It's okay, Jos," she said, sliding her arm around my shoulders. My head rested beside hers. "He's been watching Pete with the exact same expression."

I grimaced. "Did he see his hand…"

Amy laughed. "Who didn't?"

"It's not funny, Ames. We'll lose our jobs if they suspect anything."

"I'd be more worried about Pete getting a broken nose, than losing your jobs."

I groaned. I was getting way too tipsy to process anything and desperately needed food in my stomach. "I need to go home before I do something stupid." I grabbed my bag and shuffled out. "Can you say goodbye to everyone for me?"

She rolled her eyes and laughed. I was known for my disappearing acts, but the truth was, I hated goodbyes. Without a peep in Grayson's direction, I snuck out of the bar, pulled on my cardigan and began my journey home.

"Need a ride?" a familiar voice called from a slowing car as I walked briskly down the sidewalk. Lenny's Pizzeria was closing in twenty minutes.

"No, I'm fine," I replied, briefly glancing at Grayson in the back window of his chauffeur driven car.

"Your place is about ten blocks away. It's safer to ride with me."

I snorted. "Doubt that."

"Come on, Josie." He sighed. "Get in the car."

I stopped and turned to him, raising my brow. "Is that an order?"

"Josie…"

"I'm fine, Gray." I continued to walk as his car followed. "I just want to get some food, go home and forget, okay? Just leave me alone."

"Very well," he said and his window slid shut. The car rolled away and sped off down the street and around the corner. *Well, that was easier than I thought.*

Just shy of twenty minutes later, I spotted Lenny's pizzeria and to my delight, the lights were still on. I jogged across the road and walked into the restaurant that always smelt heavenly.

"Josie girl!" Lenny hollered, strolling out of the kitchen with a pizza box in hand.

"Hey, Len," I replied with a smile, glancing around the restaurant to see who the order was for. "Sorry I'm a bit later than usual. Is the kitchen closed yet?"

Lenny frowned. "Did you want something else?"

I shook my head. "No, just my usual."

"Oh." He chuckled. "Well, here you go." He handed over the large pizza and garlic bread.

I scrunched my nose. "How did you know I was coming?"

Lenny's smile grew larger. "Your friend. The handsome man with the fancy watch told me you were on your way."

"Oh." It was all I could say as my cheeks heated.

Lenny held my face in his weathered hands. "You should give him a chance."

I shook my head. "Not gonna happen."

Pressing his lips together, Lenny's eyes saddened. "You deserve a little happiness, Josie."

"What makes you think I'm not happy?"

"Your eyes." He kissed my forehead and pulled me into a hug. I swallowed back tears because I knew he was right. I was so busy reading and capturing other people's emotions, I was ignoring my own.

As I stepped back out onto the street, cradling dinner in my arms, I almost crashed into Grayson, who was waiting outside. Minus his car.

"Hey." He chuckled, stabilising the pizza box before I dropped it.

I cleared my throat and peered up at him. "Hey," I replied, suddenly nervous. "Thanks for the pizza."

He shoved his hands in his pockets. "Now will you let me walk you home?"

I shrugged. "I guess so. But I'm not sharing." I meant it too. That pizza was also my breakfast and possible lunch for the next day. Luckily I was blessed with a ridiculously high metabolism.

Grayson laughed and my heart almost exploded, for I hadn't heard that beautiful sound since our weekend together. I shook my head in disbelief.

"What is it?" he asked, narrowing his eyes.

"You actually sound like...like the person I thought you were."

He ran his hand over his face and let out a long sigh. "Look, I know I've been..."

"A jerk?"

He pursed his lips.

"An arsehole?"

He shook his head.

"A fu—"

"Difficult!" he blurted, with a laugh.

"Difficult?!" I snorted. "Gray, you've been the devil incarnate."

He threw his hands in the air. "Alright, alright, well, that's the way I've been taught to run a business."

I scrunched my face. "By making everyone hate you?"

"Well…yeah. It works for my father and brother."

"There *are* other ways."

Grayson quietly contemplated my words as we crossed another road. "I really am sorry, Josie. For everything. This version of me…it's not one I'm proud of."

I stopped walking and turned to him, humour leaving my face. "Then be one you *are* proud of."

He opened his mouth to speak but nothing came out. I smiled sadly and we continued to walk on in silence, stealing sideway glances until we reached the steps to my apartment building.

With his hands still firmly wedged in his pockets, he found it hard to meet my eyes. "So…Peter's the ex-boyfriend slash almost fiancé?"

He did see. "Um, yeah. He's struggling with the idea that it's over."

Grayson's jaw twitched. "I noticed."

"I'm surprised you saw anything with that leggy blonde all over you." I squeezed my eyes shut. *I did not just say that. I did not just say that.*

He smirked. "Did you also see them *both* leave with my brother?"

I screwed up my nose. "Eww."

Grayson smiled, seemingly pleased with my reaction.

An awkward silence followed as I wrestled with the temptation of inviting him in. "Well, thank you for walking me home," I blurted, edging towards the stairs.

He pressed his lips together and gave a gentlemanly nod.

"And I'm sorry about your cell phone," I continued. The guilt had been weighing on me.

Grayson chuckled. "I'm pretty sure I deserved it."

"Yeah, you did," I said, trying not to smile. "But I still shouldn't have done it."

"Well, nevertheless, thank you for retrieving all my numbers. I did find one problem though."

"What's that?" I asked, worried Reed had missed something.

"I appear to be missing a very important number."

"Oh...who's that?"

Grayson smirked. "A particular staff member. She's exceptional at her job, but a total pain in my ass."

I turned my head to hide my fleeting grin. "Linda has a list of all the work numbers. I'm sure she'll give it to you."

"I know, but I'm not sure if this specific employee would like me calling her."

"Depends which version of you is calling, I guess." The side of my mouth lifted as I bounded up the stairs and punched in the security code. The door buzzed and I pushed it open, turning back before I entered. "Goodnight, Gray."

His warm smile made my heart race. "Goodnight, Josie."

Chapter 12

Tension was at an all-time high Monday morning as everyone adapted to their new roles and responsibilities. I spent the entire weekend listening to every New York based band and musician in Susan's files, and added their upcoming tour dates to my calendar. I wasn't sure when I was going to get any sleep, but that's what coffee was for…*right?*

I glanced over at Grayson's empty office and found my hydrangea where I left it, barely clinging to life. *He didn't water it!* Pulling off a fluro-pink sticky note, I scrawled 'Water me *sad face*', before sneaking into his office and slapping it to the front of the pot. There was no way he could miss it. Feeling better, I returned to my office and set to work, waiting for Grayson to return from his morning meeting with Adam and Marlene.

An hour later, the click of his door grabbed my attention and I watched him settle at his desk. He picked up the note and smirked, before scrunching it in his hand and throwing it in the bin. My mouth fell open. Wondering if he was toying with me, I waited and waited. But he clearly had no intention of resurrecting the plant.

With a scowl, I stood and marched over to his closed door.

"Come in, Josie," he called, a moment before my knuckles collided with the glass.

I stepped in and found him leaning back in his chair with an irritating grin. He intertwined his fingers as I approached.

"It will die if you don't water it," I said, crossing my arms and glaring at him.

He chuckled, and ran his fingers through his hair. "I'll just add it to Linda's long list of jobs to do."

My shoulders slumped. "No, don't do th...You seriously can't water one measly plant?"

"I'm a busy person," he said, with a shrug.

"Too busy to give something *you bought* the basic necessities to live?"

"Well if we're getting into specifics. It was a gift. Therefore, shouldn't its survival be bestowed onto the receiver?"

With a frustrated growl, I picked up his glass of water—that Linda filled for him—and tipped it into the pot. "It needs to be watered daily," I stated, before retreating towards the exit.

"I look forward to your daily visit then." I didn't need to turn around to know he was smiling.

―――

Morale in the office was in a serious decline and I couldn't stand it. I tried to stay out of the office for as long as I could, careful not to get caught up in the bitterness.

Searching the streets and parks for my stories in the morning, I wrote them up at my desk in the afternoon and attended gigs at night. I was incredibly busy, but if I kept my head down I would get through it, although I remained unsure of what was on the other side. The Harlow brothers obviously wanted to see how well we worked under pressure and I was determined to show them I was a motherfucking diamond.

With the few hours I spent in the office, I wrote steadily and met my targets. Others however, were struggling. The ones with families mostly, but I didn't have that problem.

The only interaction I had with Grayson each day was due to his inability to care for anything but himself.

"Hi," I said quietly, slipping into his office with my watering can.

Instead of his usual playful smirk, he was massaging his temples and frowning.

"All okay?"

He took off his glasses and rubbed his eyes before peering up at me. "Can you close the door?"

Panic flooded me. I slowly pushed the door closed, making the room virtually soundproof, and prepared myself for the worst. "Should I sit?"

Grayson sighed as he regarded my expression. "You're not getting fired, Josie. I just want to ask your opinion on something."

"Oh, okay." My eyelids fluttered.

He chuckled at my surprise and motioned to the chair. "Please sit."

Panning my gaze around the room, I searched for signs I'd fallen into an alternate universe. I placed the watering can on the desk between us and gradually lowered myself into the chair.

"My father wants me to cull more employees," he stated, remaining expressionless.

I gasped, but remained quiet. When I didn't meet his eyes, he continued.

"I don't *want* to, but some people aren't pulling their weight. Their work is good, but they're not producing like they have in the past. Good is not going to cut it anymore. I need great."

I chuckled. *Is he really this clueless?*

"What?"

My eyes grew large. "Honestly?"

His mouth twitched upwards and he nodded. "Go."

"Well, what did you expect would happen?" I blurted, almost rolling my eyes. "You come in here pressuring us, threatening our jobs, treating us like...like dirt, and then you expect great results?" I shook my head and frowned. "Unhappy people will never give you their best."

"Are you unhappy here?"

Heat crept up my neck. "Yes."

"But your work is excellent."

I shrugged. "I don't count. I don't have anywhere else to be." My jaw clenched as I tried to remain composed. "These people...they have families. They're expected to be home at dinnertime, to spend time with their kids, to come home with a smile on their face. These new conditions have caused so much stress and anxiety, and you haven't shown one ounce of empathy."

His eyes and shoulders lowered simultaneously. After a noticeable period of self-reflection, Grayson looked up with a sigh. "What should I do?"

I smiled sadly. "You need to connect with them. We're a family here. We care about each other. Prove to us that you're on our side. Be that version of yourself I know you can be."

He leant back and exhaled, rubbing the back of his neck.

I grimaced. "Shit. I said too much. I'm sorry," I said, wiping my damp palms over my jeans.

"Don't apologise."

Unsure of what to do, I stood up. "Okay, well…I'll just get going."

Grayson nodded but was clearly in a daze. I edged out of the room, totally forgetting my reason for visiting in the first place.

The very next day, everything began to change.

"Oh my gosh, Josie, have you seen it?" Amy guiltily glanced back into Grayson's office as she snuck into my mine, clearly trying to go unnoticed.

"See what?" I whispered, following her gaze to find Grayson on a call with his back turned.

"The new coffee machine!" She squealed quietly. "It does evvvvverything!"

I leant back into my chair with a growing smile. "Reeeally?"

"It's amazing. You just push a couple of buttons, and whammo!" She held out her mug proudly. "Almond Chai."

I chuckled. It was impressive compared to the instant coffee we were used to.

"Perhaps they don't hate us after all." She smiled and brought the mug to her lips, breathing in the delicious scent.

"Perhaps not."

Amy left my office with a renewed bounce in her step which made me smile. As she passed Grayson's office, our eyes met through the glass. I offered him a discreet nod, which he swiftly returned.

With Adam away again, Grayson made every effort to improve morale in the office. He interacted with employees, learnt their names, asked about their families and genuinely listened to their answers. He even let everyone call him William. The workload remained, but smiles were returning and the tension in the air was dissipating.

On my way back from the lunchroom with my fourth cup of coffee of the day, the loud hammering of buttons in the photocopy room caught my attention. I peeped in to discover Grayson standing by the machine, brow furrowed, looking like a fish out of water.

"Are you lost?" I asked, trying to muffle my giggle.

Grayson glanced my way before turning his attention back to the machine as his cheeks grew pink. "Ha-ha, Josie. No, I'm not lost. I…I just can't stop this thing from beeping."

I ambled up next to him with an amused smirk. "First time?"

As he cleared his throat, his jaw twitched. "Yep." The beeping persisted and he continued to tap a button that was making everything worse.

I pulled his arm out of the way. "That's not going to help."

"Do I need to buy a new one?"

I laughed and placed my coffee onto the small table beside us. "No." I pointed to the flashing light on the screen. "This means the printer is out of paper."

"Oh."

I opened the supplies cupboard and pulled out a ream of paper. "So, where's Linda?" I asked, curious to find out why he was attempting such a task.

He grumbled. "At her granddaughter's recital."

My fingers paused as I unwrapped the packaging and I peered up at him with a smirk. "You better be careful, Gray."

His forehead creased. "What? Why?"

"People might actually start to like you."

His cheeks turned a slightly deeper shade of pink, and he looked away with a smile. "Come on, quit giving me grief and help me out here."

I pulled out the empty tray and reloaded it. "Now just push—"

"Here?" His fingers slid over mine on the print button and we froze.

Sparks surged through my body, staggering my breath as I slowly peered up into his alluring green eyes. There was something swirling behind them that both frightened and excited me.

He ran his thumb back and forth over my hand, sending tingles from my head to my toes and settling somewhere in-between. As his eyes burned into mine, he opened his mouth to say something.

Pete strode into the room, sorting through a sack of documents in his arms, while I quickly pulled my hand away and picked up my deserted coffee.

He saw me first and smiled. "Josie."

"Hey, Pete," I uttered, smiling tightly.

His attention shifted to Grayson who removed his printout from the tray. "William?" He was clearly just as surprised to see him there as I was.

"Good afternoon, Peter. How's that report coming along?"

Pete nodded. "Great actually. Just printing it off now."

"Excellent. I'll wait here then."

"Oh, I don't mind bringing it to your office," Pete said, looking nervous.

Grayson waved him off. "It's fine. You can fill me in on your last racquetball match while we wait." *Whaaaat?*

Pete's eyes lit up. "Sure," he said, with a huge smile. "Hey, great shirt, by the way," he added, pointing to Grayson. "I have one just like it."

My eyes went round. He was wearing Pete's shirt. "Well, I better get back to my office," I uttered as Grayson smirked knowingly.

Pete beamed over at me. "Are you coming to The Edge tonight?"

I smiled. "I should be able to sneak one drink in."

"Great. I'll see you there."

As I left the room, my gaze flickered to Grayson, but he was too busy sending silent daggers into the back of Pete's head. *Oh dear.*

Friday night drinks were, once again, a joyous occasion. No longer did we need to vent about the evil that were the Harlow brothers, and it was a welcomed relief. With Adam away, Grayson turned the office around, and it hadn't gone unnoticed.

"So, it's his brother who's the douche?" Amy clarified as we made our way to The Edge to meet the others.

I shrugged. "It seems to be panning out that way. Gra...I mean *William* still has a lot of work to do to win everyone over, but at least he's trying."

Amy narrowed her eyes. "Are you guys still..."

"No!" I replied too quickly. "I'm not going there."

She grinned. "But you want to?"

"Can you stop fishing?" I cried, trying not to laugh. "Come on, let's get a drink."

As we walked in, I spotted our team towards the back and froze. Grayson sat in the booth, surrounded by our colleagues, deep in conversation.

Amy drew in a breath. "This is new."

In a panic, I redirected her to the bar.

"Curiouser and Curiouser," Amy mimicked Alice in Wonderland with a giggle. "He's taking this team bonding thing to a new level, isn't he?"

I ignored her and ordered two gin and tonics from the barman.

With drinks in hand, we approached the table and greeted everyone. My eyes slowed over Grayson and his smile grew large. I sucked in my breath and began chatting to Anton from marketing to distract myself from Grayson's lingering gaze.

After a few drinks, I relaxed a bit more and started to enjoy myself. I moved around Grayson, determined to keep him at a safe distance, because after the incident in the photocopy room, I knew any further contact could send us into dangerous territory.

People left to go home to their families, and a space opened up in the booth. Before I could offer it to anyone else, Amy grabbed my arm and pushed me in.

"Come on, Jos, my feet are killing me," she said, nudging me along until I was pressed up against Grayson. I shot her a nasty look and she shrugged, pretending to be oblivious to my discomfort.

Grayson turned his body towards me the moment our arms touched. The same tingling sensation arose and I wondered if he felt it too. Offering me a small smile, he returned his focus back to Pete who was rambling on about something on his alternate side.

As I participated in the conversation on my side of the table, Grayson politely listened and nodded in his. I propped my elbow up on the table and rested my chin in my hand, swivelling my straw as I pretended to laugh along with the others. The week had caught up with me.

My breath caught when the edge of Grayson's hand brushed against the side of my exposed thigh under the table. At first I thought it was an accident, but it happened again. Wide awake, I lifted my head as my temperature rose, sipping my drink in a feeble attempt to cool down. His gentle touch crept towards the hem of my skirt and I sucked on the straw too quickly, causing me to cough and splutter and unintentionally make a scene. Grayson faced me with concern and rubbed my back with a knowing twinkle in his eye. Amy rushed off to get me a glass of water.

When I finally recovered, Grayson leant towards me. "You okay?"

I nodded. "Yep, excuse me." I slid out of the booth and ran into Amy who was returning with my water.

"I'm just going to go freshen up," I said, pointing to the restroom.

Amy narrowed her eyes. "Okay, sure. You'll be back…right?"

I nodded quickly and left, turning back to see Amy whisper something into Grayson's ear that he seemed to find quite fascinating.

Instead of heading back to the table, I snuck through the crowd and out the front door, calling an end to my night. I paused momentarily to breathe in fresh air to soothe my lungs, when a voice surprised me from behind.

"Amy said you might pull a stunt like this." Grayson was leaning against the wall, smirking.

I groaned and continued walking up the street, but he caught up with me easily.

"You know it's rude to leave without saying goodbye," he said, matching my strides.

"Giving *me* etiquette tips now, are you?"

He chuckled. "No. I just wanted to talk to you before I fly out."

I stopped walking and turned to face him. "Where are you going?"

"Back to LA for a couple of weeks."

"Oh, okay," I said, trying my hardest not to sound disappointed. "What did you want to talk to me about?"

He shoved his hands into his pockets and lowered his gaze. "I was hoping you could keep an eye on things for me. Adam is back, and well...he operates very differently to me."

My forehead creased. "Can't you talk to him? Isn't this supposed to be *your* project?"

His jaw twitched. "Under his supervision, yes."

I shook my head. "Jesus, Gray." I wanted to tell him to grow some balls, but the frown on his face made me reconsider.

"I'm trying my best here, Josie."

I scoffed. "Really?"

"Under the current circumstances, yes."

"Alright." I sighed. "I'll keep an eye out, but you need to do something for me."

He stepped closer as the side of mouth quirked upwards, while his heated gaze traced the curves of my body. "What's that?"

"You need to cool it with all *this*." I motioned between the two of us. "I'm not going to risk my job for a roll in the hay with a Harlow."

He frowned. "Do you really think that's all *this* is?"

"Yes...I don't know, isn't it?...Argh!" This man was giving me a headache.

He shook his head as he turned to walk in the opposite direction. "Enjoy your pizza, Josie."

I scrunched up my nose as he sauntered away, leaving me even more confused. "Pizza?"

Sure enough, my favourite pizza was waiting for me at Lenny's when I arrived, courtesy of Grayson.

Chapter 13

Grayson: **How bad is it?**
Josie: **He fired Anton.**
Grayson: **Fuck. What happened?**
Josie: **He had a differing opinion.**
Grayson: **That would do it. How are you doing?**
Josie: **Fine.**
Grayson: **Fine?**
Josie: **Fine.**

I didn't want to elaborate. I was a big girl and could sort out my own problems. Since Adam's return and Grayson's departure, we were all suffering from whiplash. The office had regressed to what it was before; a miserable place to be.

"Josie, Mr. Harlow would like to speak with you in his office," Linda whispered, from my open door.

I exhaled. "Okay." He'd been watching me lately, so I expected to get pulled up for something eventually.

As I entered his office, he looked up from his desk with a blank face. "Josie, I understand you're required to spend time out of the office, but coming in after lunch every day isn't acceptable. I want you here by 9am like everyone else."

My mouth fell open. With my new role covering music, I wasn't getting home until at least 2am. That would only leave me approximately five hours to sleep before I'd have to get up for work. *Fuck.*

Normally I'd sleep until 10am, head to the park to take photographs and interview people for *Capturing Love*, before heading into the office just after lunch. I had it all sorted, and I was managing fine...until now. I should have pleaded my case, but Anton's defeated face flashed through my mind and I thought better of it. I would just have to work out a new routine.

"Yes, Mr. Harlow." I offered him a quick nod and turned on my heel.

"And Josie...please call me Adam."

The next few days were a nightmare. Although nightmares required you to be asleep, and I hadn't had any decent sleep in days.

I set three alarms each morning, and dragged myself out of bed every day to get to work on time. Thank god Adam hadn't taken away the new coffee machine, because I wouldn't have been able to face anyone without it, and would probably be in jail for murder by now.

My computer chimed with a new message, startling me awake.

A. Mitchell: **Wake up!**

My heart was racing as I adjusted to my surroundings, which weren't my bedroom.

J. Spencer: **Thank you.**

A. Mitchell: **I'm guessing you're not coming out for drinks tonight.**

J. Spencer: **Not a chance. Bed is calling and I still need to go to the park to 'capture some love' *rolling eyes***

A. Mitchell: **We'll miss you xox**

I glanced at the time, but was too exhausted to be excited by the fact that it was 4:45pm on a Friday. All I could think about was my head hitting the pillow and not leaving it until Monday morning.

"Hey, Josie." The voice in my doorway drew my tired gaze. Grayson stepped into my office rolling a small suitcase behind him. "Are you okay?"

"I'm just a little tired, that's all," I murmured, drawing in a shaky breath.

"A little tired? You look exhausted."

I swallowed and began shutting down my computer.

His eyes narrowed. "What haven't you told me?"

"Ask your brother," I snapped, uncharacteristically.

Grayson pursed his lips before nodding and marched back out the door and down the hallway. *Oh shit.*

I winced as a muffled argument erupted behind Adam's door. *Shit, shit, shit.* Grabbing my bag, I bolted for the elevator before either of them resurfaced.

———

I stirred awake the next morning after a twelve-hour sleep and smiled. It was Saturday...finally. As I wiped my eyes, I reached for my phone and gasped at the missed calls and messages.

Amy: **Drinks aren't the same without you. I'm bored. *sad face***

Grayson: **2 missed calls**

Grayson: **Please pick up.**

Amy: **Boss man is looking for you. So is Pete *rolling eyes***

Lenny: **You didn't pick up your pizza. All okay?**

Grayson: **I'm coming over.**

My eyes grew large and I shot up in bed in a panic.

Grayson: **On second thought, I'm guessing you're asleep. Sweet dreams, Josie. I'll talk to you on Monday.**

I relaxed back into my pillows. *Thank god.*

The rest of the weekend consisted of napping and binge-watching Netflix, which would've been heaven if I hadn't spent the entire time fretting about the week ahead. I deliberately left my laptop in the office, because I knew I'd end up catching up on work instead of a week's worth of sleep.

As I lay in bed Sunday night, mentally going through the week ahead, my phone lit up.

Unknown: **Josie, this is Adam. I've just been given word from Ben Archer's manager that there's a secret gig happening tonight at Hell Fire, East Village @ 11pm. You'll need to cover this. The ticket is waiting for you at the venue. I want your review on Marlene's desk by 9am tomorrow to make the next edition.**

My jaw clenched tight as I glared down my phone. *Is he fucking kidding me?!*

I wrote a nasty message back, but hesitated over the send button. Instead, I grudgingly typed the singer's familiar name into the search engine to see who he was. It seemed my week of sleep deprivation would be starting a little earlier than expected.

To my surprise, he was originally from Australia and already had a huge following in the United States. He could easily fill a stadium, so this show must've been super exclusive. My heart picked up when I read a description of his music. Hard rock with bluesy undertones. It was much easier to write about music I actually found enjoyment in, so I flicked back to the text message that would surely get me fired, and pressed delete.

Gazing down at the pyjamas that hadn't left my body in two days, I groaned. I rolled out of bed and into the shower, before rummaging through my closet to find an outfit that would help me blend into the crowd. Thankfully, I still had my mum's old leather pants. They remained in mint condition and I loved them, but there was rarely an event that warranted such an item.

With a cheesy grin, I pulled them out and rolled them up my legs. The black leather was tight and super flattering, making my legs appear much longer than they really were. Digging out my Black Sabbath t-shirt and some ankle boots, I was genuinely impressed when I reviewed myself in the mirror. After applying more makeup than usual, I released my hair from its twisted bun and the multi-coloured strands fell over my shoulders, peeking out from under the auburn waves. The hint of colour was the only accessory I needed.

Scooping up my handbag and camera, I blew Luci a kiss and flew out the door to get to the gig on time.

On a high, after an amazing show, I was desperate to write my article. With no laptop at home and a deadline of 9am, my only option was a few blocks away.

The streets were eerily quiet, and every noise made me skittish. Picking up my pace, I quickly reached the entrance to *Maude* and hurriedly swiped my pass. I punched in the security code, and to my relief, the door unlocked. Not all employees had 24hr access to the building, but I'd worked so many all-nighters for Marlene, she found it easier to give it to me, than constantly let me in and out at all hours.

The *Maude* offices ran along the top of five existing street level shops, in an old corner building that radiated character with its unique patterned brickwork. The two floors above housed the bare necessities our little publication needed to survive, and for me, it was a second home. I took the stairwell to my level, not wanting to risk the elevator at night, and flicked the switch that lit up the entire floor. My first stop was the lunchroom, where I made myself an extra-large cup of coffee before heading to my office.

Half an hour later, I was in the zone, completely entranced, when movement startled me from my office doorway. I knocked over my coffee cup as I lunged at my purse for the mace.

"Josie!" Grayson cried. "What are you doing here?!"

My eyes almost burst out of their sockets. "What are *you* doing here?! You frightened the absolute shit out of me!" I yelled back as my heart returned to a healthier pace.

"You set off the silent alarm."

I lifted my eyebrows. "Oh. I didn't know there was one."

"I just had it installed, but we've had some false alarms and it's costing a shitload to keep sending security out. Luckily for you, I decided to check this one out myself."

I winced. "I'm sorry, I just needed to finish this…" My voice trailed off as I glanced down at my laptop, which was now covered in coffee. "Shit," I murmured, grabbing the box of tissues from my desk and piling them over the keyboard.

Grayson exhaled and placed his hands on his hips. "Seriously, what couldn't wait?"

"Your brother apparently," I spat, sitting back down and tapping the keyboard, hoping like hell it still worked.

He let out a low growl. "I told him you needed a break, and this is what he does."

I was too focused on my computer to comprehend what he was saying. "Nooo…no, no, no!" I cried as I tapped the keys even harder.

Grayson ambled around my desk and grimaced. "Did you save it?"

"No, I didn't save it!" I tried to hold in my emotion, but it was no use. I burst into tears and dropped my face into my hands to muffle the uncontrollable sobs.

"Whoa, Josie." Grayson's voice softened. His warm hand slipped over my shoulder, but I shrugged it away.

"This is your fault!" I snarled.

"Just calm down."

"Calm down? This article is due in six hours. At some point, I was hoping to get some sleep tonight! And I really need some fucking sleep."

"Don't worry, I'll speak to Adam."

Grayson's relaxed demeanour aggravated me even more. "I don't need you to bail me out."

"He's out of line," he said, running his fingers through his bed hair. "I told him to stop pushing you so hard."

"I can fight my own battles."

"I can see that."

I wiped my eyes and turned back to my laptop, switching it off and on again.

"Use my computer."

"I can't even remember what I wrote now," I whined.

He motioned for me to follow him into his office. "Come on, it will come back to you."

Turning on his computer, he ushered me into his luxurious office chair and left the room. I logged into my profile, but as suspected, my story was gone. I drew in a deep breath, kicked off my heels and composed myself.

Grayson re-entered with two fresh cups of coffee.

"You're staying?" I asked as he handed one over.

"You shouldn't be here on your own. Any bets you walked here too."

I ignored his tapered gaze and shrugged. "I don't mind, I'm used to it."

"I mind."

My eyes shot up to his, but he turned away, making himself comfortable on his visitor's lounge.

"I'll just wait here until you're finished, then I'll drive you home."

With a little nod, I proceeded to open a new document.

An hour later it was done and I let Grayson do the final read through while I paced the room waiting for his verdict. I watched him curiously as his eyes darted across the screen. Sitting there in his old hoodie and sweatpants, he looked like a normal human, not the billionaire business man everyone else knew. My heart fluttered when his eyes lifted to mine.

He leant back in his chair and exhaled. "If this is the quality of your work at 3:30am, I'd love to see you at full capacity."

Leaning over him to press the print button, I accidently grazed my breast across his shoulder. "You already have," I murmured, unintentionally breathing him in.

Grayson tilted his head and smirked up at me. "I'd like to see it again someday."

I chuckled and crossed my arms, leaning my hip against his desk. "You don't give up do you?"

"Not on a good thing, no." His hazel eyes swirled into emeralds. Grayson's fingertips found mine and he tugged me onto his lap.

My leather coated legs straddled his sweatpants. "Grayson, we shouldn't. What about the rules?"

"They're Adam's rules. I play by my own." He pulled my lips down to his, while his hands entwined through my hair, drawing me closer. Our tongues interwove greedily as I ran my hands over his body, while Grayson's fingers glided over my legs and settled on my arse. "Fuck, Josie. These pants should be illegal." I laughed into his mouth as he lifted me up and placed me onto his desk, pressing his growing bulge against my core. "In fact, I think they should come off. They're way too dangerous."

I grinned and leant back on my elbows to give him access. He unfastened my pants and slowly peeled them over my arse, exposing my hot pink G-string. It was the sluttiest thing I owned, but rarely saw the light of day. He growled deeply as he shimmied the leather pants down my legs, dropping them to the floor with a thud.

He ran his hands back up my legs, and toyed with the straps of my underwear. I shuddered in anticipation, but he redirected his attention to my top half.

Grayson pulled off my t-shirt and threw it across the room. I unzipped his hoodie to reveal his naked chest and released him from his sweatpants, adding to the growing pile of clothing on the floor.

Pens and pencils scattered everywhere as he pushed me flat onto the desk and trailed his tongue across my collarbone. His mouth found mine and I moaned as he pushed his erection even harder against the flimsy material between my legs.

Sliding both hands under my arse, he lifted me off the desk and dropped me onto his soft leather visitor's lounge. He climbed over me and pulled down my bra, licking and kissing each nipple while his other hand hooked onto the strap of my G-string and slid it down my legs. *Finally!*

Grayson reached for his pants and pulled a condom from his wallet. I eased back and watched as he rolled it on, his penetrating gaze barely leaving mine. Growing impatient, I wrapped my legs around his muscular body and pulled him in until I was gasping at the fullness I craved. Grayson's eyes glistened as he began to rock back and forth, watching me come undone with every thrust of his hips.

"Josie, we need to get dressed," whispered Grayson, grazing my face with his thumb.

I snuggled deeper into his neck, wanting to stay there forever.

He kissed my ear before he spoke into it. "People will be here soon."

Opening my eyes, I wearily took in my surroundings and tensed immediately. "Holy shit, what time is it?"

Grayson wiped his sleepy eyes. "I'm not sure. I drifted off too."

I scooped up my t-shirt from the floor and pulled it over my head while Grayson stepped into his sweatpants.

The faint ding of the elevator sounded and my eyes struck Grayson's in a panic. I dove for my pants but there was no time to navigate the tight leather as footsteps were already coming down the hallway. Just as Adam greeted Grayson, who endeavoured to block his view, I scurried under his desk and held my breath.

"Do I need to ask why you're half naked?"

Grayson cleared his throat. "I came straight from the gym. I always have a spare suit in the office."

I rolled my eyes. *Of course he does.*

"Well make sure you're dressed before Josie arrives. Wouldn't want her getting any ideas."

I got more than an idea.

Grayson cleared his throat. "Right…"

"Oh, did you check up on that security issue last night?"

"Yeah, yeah. Just another false alarm," Grayson replied, nonchalantly.

"Good to see you're finally taking this seriously. Dad will be pleased to hear it."

It was silent again, but I didn't come out until I'd successfully pulled on my pants and shoes. *If only I knew where my panties were.*

"You can come out now," Grayson whispered, already fully dressed in a fresh suit and tie, looking incredibly handsome.

Stumbling a little as I stood up, blush filled my cheeks. The heels I had on were ridiculously high, and definitely not day wear. As I tried to formulate an explanation for my colleagues, I grabbed the article from Grayson's printer and rushed out of the room.

I hadn't even made it into my office when Adam's door flew open. "Josie, you're here early. How'd you go last night?"

Freezing at my door, I back stepped into the hallway to face him. "Great actually, I'm just about to do a final read through."

Adam's gaze slowly travelled down my body to the paper in my hand. "Can I take a look?"

I cleared my throat. "Um, sure."

As he skimmed over the draft, I looked through Grayson's window and spotted a sliver of pink material peeking out from under a cushion on the couch. Grayson followed my alarmed gaze and smirked. Sitting down beside my G-string to tie up his shoes, he slid it deeper into the chair to hide the evidence and I smiled in relief.

Adam lifted his gaze. "Glad to see someone around here values their job."

My smile faded.

Grayson materialised next to Adam. "Josie, feel free to leave early today. You must have had a late night."

Adam glared at his brother, and Grayson held his gaze without expression.

"Seems…fair," Adam said, turning back to me. "Good job, Josie."

"Thanks, Adam."

Grayson's eyes shot to mine and narrowed. His jaw clenched as he panned back to his brother. Adam grinned and patted Grayson on the back, before chuckling all the way back to his office.

"Did I just miss something?" I whispered.

Grayson rubbed his stubble and shook his head, but his shoulders remained tense. "Listen, I'll get a new laptop sent to your apartment. Feel free to work from home as much as you need. Go home and get some sleep."

"Oh, okay, thanks…" My forehead furrowed as I returned to my office. "I guess?"

I woke up late in the afternoon to the ping of my phone. My heart quickened when his name appeared on the screen, but I frowned when I read the message.

Grayson: **Since when do you call my brother by his first name?**

Although I wanted to, I didn't respond. His text rubbed me up the wrong way.

To blow off some steam, I threw on jeans and a t-shirt and took Luci to the dog park. I let him off his leash and he went nuts; running laps, rolling in mud and sniffing as many dog butts as he could. I just sat on a park bench watching in awe. Dogs had it good.

"You didn't respond to my message."

I looked up to find Grayson, still suited up, gazing down at me. "How did you know I was here?"

"You weren't home. I guessed. Now, why didn't you respond?"

"I didn't like the question," I muttered, returning my gaze to Luci. "But if you must know, he *asked* me to call him Adam."

"That's even worse," he said, running his fingers through his hair.

"What? How exactly?"

Grayson shook his head, bewildered. "Are you that blind?"

"You're talking in riddles, Gray."

"He has a thing for you. *Fuck*. Every male in the office does, it's driving me crazy."

I burst out laughing. "What!?" I glanced around, expecting to find a hidden camera. "Are you fucking with me?"

Grayson sat down beside me and loosened his tie. "You're so damn clueless."

"Gee, thanks," I said, rolling my eyes.

"I didn't just send you home today because you needed sleep, I sent you home because of those damn pants you had on. Jesus, Josie, you were every boys' wet dream."

My cheeks grew red. "I never *intended* to wear them to work."

Grayson moistened his lips. "But I'm so fucking glad you did."

"You're a very confusing man, Grayson Harlow."

"I just can't think straight around you."

My heart fluttered as I glanced across at his smile. We sat in a comfortable silence, until Luci started getting verbally abused by a chihuahua.

"Dammit," I cried, running over to pull Luci away from the incessant yapping.

Grayson waited by the fence, smirking. "What's his problem?"

Luci's ears pricked up at the familiar voice.

"Small dog syndrome," I muttered, watching the owner cradle his dog like a baby.

Luci leapt out of my hands and bounded towards Grayson.

"Luci, no!" I yelled, but it was too late. He lifted his paws up onto Grayson's shoulders and licked his face. I winced, knowing exactly where that tongue had been a few minutes ago.

Their height was evenly matched, but Grayson started to crumble under his weight. I jogged over and dragged Luci off, before returning my attention to Grayson. I struggled not to laugh, but his shirt was now completely soiled with mud.

"I'm sorry." I grimaced, attempting to brush it off, but all I was doing was rubbing it in.

His eyes met mine, but they weren't angry. His shoulders weren't even tense. Grayson smiled and raised an eyebrow. "Has Pete got any more shirts?"

As soon as we walked into my apartment, I took Luci out onto the terrace to wash him down and left him there to dry.

"I'll just, um...get you that shirt," I stammered, when I returned to find Grayson shirtless in the living room.

The side of his mouth twitched. "I don't think we need it just yet, do you?"

A familiar ache began to stir below. "Gray...I don't think we should keep doing this."

He stepped closer. "Why?"

I maintained the distance. "Because you're my boss."

Grayson continued to move forward until I backed myself into the living room wall. "And?"

"And...we're not allowed to have romantic relationships in the office."

He shrugged. "We're not in the office...and it doesn't have to be romantic..."

"Gray..." I whined, glancing out the window as his face drew closer.

His hot breath grazed my cheek. "Josie..."

My heart hammered and my core pulsed as his lips touched my neck.

"No one can know," I whispered.

His mouth curved into a smile before giving me a little nip. "Know what?"

I let out a squeak as his pressed me up against the wall, and I playfully pushed back his chest. "You always get what you want, don't you?"

He grinned, mischievously. "Mostly."

Bending down, he wrapped his arms around my legs, and threw me over his shoulder. I burst out laughing as my rainbow hair bounced over his arse while he cave-man carried me to the bedroom. *God help me…and my heart.*

Chapter 14

Due to my ridiculous schedule, I barely had enough time to breathe, let alone start a fling with my boss. I only appeared in the office for a few hours each day before rushing off to a gig most nights. Thankfully Grayson kept to himself, leaving me to concentrate on my work and recover from our last...session.

With nothing organised for the weekend ahead, I wondered if Grayson had anything planned. Probably attending some charity gala no doubt. *Isn't that what rich people do?*

Sitting in the lunch room with Amy and Pete, I devoured my leftover lasagne while listening to Amy reel off something about Mercury Retrograde and her computer not working. As usual, Pete stared at her blankly, patiently waiting to change the subject.

Pete was super conservative. He worked in accounting, wore a suit to work every day even though the dress code was relaxed, and never swore. Like ever. What he saw in me was a fucking mystery.

I paused mid-chew when Grayson sauntered into the lunchroom with his empty mug. His eyes skimmed over mine and met the others. "Good afternoon, team," he greeted with a nod, and continued on to the coffee machine.

Pete's back straightened and Amy grinned up at him after a quick glance in my direction. I hadn't updated her on what happened, so she must've seen something in my aura. Psychic friends were annoying like that.

"Good afternoon, William," Amy chirped as he fiddled with the machine settings. "Would you like to join us?"

I scrunched up my face at her and whispered. "He doesn't have time for a lunch br—"

"Actually, I will," he interrupted, moving to our table. "I haven't had a break all day."

"Great!" Pete said, overenthusiastically.

I smiled tightly and lowered my gaze to my food. *Stay cool, Josie. Stay cool.*

"Josie was just about to tell us her plans for the weekend." Amy's eyes twinkled with mischief. "Weren't you, Jos?"

"I was?" I mumbled with a mouth full of food.

Amy raised her brow and nodded, while Pete went quiet.

Grayson smirked. "So, what are your plans, Josie?"

I shifted uncomfortably in my seat. "Um, nothing really. Sleep, I guess." I peeked up at Grayson who was watching my every move as he sipped his coffee.

"Well, at least you'll be able to make drinks tomorrow night. We missed you last week," Pete remarked happily.

I nodded and forced a small smile his way.

"What about you, William? What's on for the weekend?" Amy switched her attention to Grayson with the sweetest of smiles. *What is she up to?*

He took a sip of his coffee as he considered the question. "Well, I've been invited to a few charity galas, but…"

I threw my hand over my mouth to smother a giggle. *I knew it!*

Grayson tapered his gaze at me before returning his attention to Amy. "*But* I haven't decided which one to go to."

The conversation continued for a gruelling twenty minutes, before I excused myself. I couldn't stand being so close to Grayson and not being able to touch him.

Ten minutes later my phone vibrated on my desk.

Grayson: **Spend the weekend with me.**

I glanced into his office, but his back was turned.

Me: **I thought you had plans.**

Grayson: **Not anymore.**

I thought about it for a moment.

Grayson: **Please?**

I smiled.

Me: Only because you remembered your manners.

Grayson: I'll pick you up from The Edge. Pack a toothbrush. Clothing optional.

Thankfully, I didn't have a gig that night so I was able to get a full eight-hour sleep in preparation for the weekend ahead. Reed happily took Luci, leaving me guilt free and bubbling with excitement.

Grayson was in a meeting with Adam and Marlene when I arrived at work the next morning, which meant I'd be able to concentrate on the finishing touches of the story I'd been working on. I glanced down at my usual tote, with a spare set of clothes and some toiletries hidden inside and grinned. Nothing looked out of the ordinary.

"Hey, Josie."

I jumped. "Oh hey, Pete."

He seemed oblivious to my edginess. "You mentioned yesterday that you didn't have any plans this weekend, so I was wondering if…"

Grayson materialised beside him and Pete's words caught in his throat. "You're not about to ask Josie out, are you?" he probed, remarkably expressionless.

"Well…argh…no, I was just seeing if she…"

Grayson crossed his arms as he waited for a response.

"It doesn't matter." Pete hung his head and sulked back down the hallway.

Grayson turned to me with a grin.

"Really?" I asked, raising my eyebrows at his childish behaviour.

He shrugged. "Rules are rules."

My mouth fell open and I shook my head. "You're unbelievable."

He winked. "You should know."

Grayson walked back into his office, chuckling. He was so arrogant, yet so charming and irresistible, making me want him in every possible way.

The day dragged on. I finished my article by lunchtime, and was planning the week ahead. Grayson appeared to be struggling too, taking every opportunity to glance my way. His gaze burning hotter as each hour passed.

By 4pm, my body was on fire and I needed a break before I imploded. I escaped to the lunchroom to fill my glass with cool water and took a long sip, closing my eyes as the water slid down my throat.

When I opened them, Grayson was standing in front of me.

"Shit, Grayson," I cried. "You frightened me."

He smirked. "Glad to see you're hydrating," he said, refilling his glass. His eyes locked onto mine as he brought it to his mouth.

Mesmerised by his glistening lips, I mirrored the action of his tongue picking up the excess water, but it did nothing but fuel the fire.

"Meet me in the photocopy room in thirty seconds," he whispered, placing his glass down on the bench beside me.

I drew in a shaky breath, and watched him leave, waiting thirty long seconds before following the trail of his familiar cologne.

As soon as I pushed open the door to the photocopy room, Grayson pulled me inside and pressed me up against it, engulfing my lips with his. I circled my arms around his neck and pulled him closer, but nothing was close enough. His tongue danced with mine as his hands rummaged over my silky top, grasping my breasts.

"Do you have to go to drinks?" he panted, before returning his mouth to my neck.

"Yes," I replied, breathing heavily. "I promised I would."

He took my face in both hands and pressed our foreheads together. "I want to bury myself inside you, Josie. Don't make me wait. I have no patience."

I chuckled and pushed him away so I could catch my breath. "I can see that."

"I'll have a car waiting at 6pm," he stated firmly, before leaving me to frantically fix my dishevelled appearance as he rushed out of the room. *Jesus Christ. That was hot.*

Grayson's driver opened the door to a dark sedan that lay waiting for me at exactly 6:01pm. Quickly glancing around to see if I knew anyone outside The Edge, I thanked the driver and stepped towards the passenger door. Instead of sliding in like a lady, which was my intention, a hand reached out and grabbed mine, pulling me inside.

I squealed as I fell amongst the leather interior and into Grayson's arms. His lips slammed against mine. "You're a minute late." I tried to defend myself, but he hushed me with his finger. "Shhh. We're behind schedule."

With a giggle, I let Grayson maul me in the backseat of his private car, while his driver discreetly wound up the privacy window and drove. The city traffic made it increasingly difficult to keep our clothes on, and we both exhaled in relief as the car rolled to a stop outside an exquisite apartment building on the Upper East Side.

The car door opened and I climbed out, bashfully thanking the driver. Grayson pulled me close, hiding the bulge in his pants as we walked into the building.

"Mr. Harlow," the doorman greeted, and tipped his hat at me. "Miss."

Grayson nodded and pushed me forward before I had a chance to acknowledge him. He pressed the button of the elevator and it opened immediately.

We stood on either side of the rising cube, watching each other. Grayson's eyes narrowed like he was sizing up his prey and my body heated at the thought of being devoured by him. The ding of the elevator sliced through the tension and I followed Grayson towards the grand entrance of his apartment. He swiped his card and opened the door, motioning me inside.

I gasped. I knew he was wealthy, but knowing and seeing it were very different things. I'd seen money before, but this was something else.

"I'd hate to see what your permanent place of residence looks like," I joked, feeling a little sick inside.

"I don't have one. I'm on the move too much. This is one of many Harlow properties. Adam's staying in another one in Midtown."

My eyelashes fluttered. "So where do you call home?"

He shrugged. "Probably where I grew up."

"In LA?"

His cheeks grew pink as he lowered his eyes. "Bel Air, to be precise."

I shook my head and chuckled. *Of course he did.*

Ambling around the open plan living space that was at least three times the size of mine, I noticed it lacked a personal touch. There was expensive artwork on the stark white walls, but not a photo in sight.

"Are you sure you live here?" I asked. The place was immaculate. There wasn't a cushion out of place or fingerprint on the glass dining table. *How is that even possible?!*

The whole place was professionally decorated with ultra-modern furniture and a mono-chrome colour scheme. It reminded me of William Harlow. A façade.

"It's not exactly my taste, but this makes up for it." He wandered over to the drawn curtains, and flicked a switch on the wall. The drapes drew apart like the beginning of a stage show, revealing something just as exhilarating. My mouth dropped open as the most picturesque view of Central Park materialised before my eyes.

"Oh my," I gushed. "I've never seen anything so beautiful."

"I used to think that too."

I turned to find him watching me and my heart somersaulted. "Really?" I asked, raising my brow at his corny line. *That totally worked, mind you.*

The doorbell rang and Grayson chuckled. "Saved by the bell," he said, opening the door to the same doorman as before. But this time, he was holding a pizza box.

"Delivery, sir."

"Thanks, Nigel." He slipped him a note and closed the door.

My mouth fell open. "Is that what I think it is?"

His eyes sparkled as he grinned, opening the box to reveal my favourite pizza from Lenny's.

Instead of launching for the pizza, I threw myself at Grayson. Tearing open his shirt as he precariously balanced the precious cargo in one arm.

"Whoa, Josie. Don't you want to eat first?" He laughed, happily accepting my sudden affection.

"It's even better reheated."

Grayson's mouth curved into a smile. "You know best," he uttered, lobbing it onto the kitchen bench. "I guess a little snack before dinner couldn't hurt."

He hitched my body up around his and carried me to his bedroom to start his first course.

Grayson was right. Clothing was *not* required over the next two nights. Every time we dressed was pointless; it wasn't long before we tore each other's clothes off again.

"What are we doing, Gray?" I sighed, staring up at the ceiling from his enormous bed.

He ran his finger down my arm, leaving goose bumps in his wake. "I thought it was obvious," he said, with an endearing smirk.

"You know what I mean." I rolled onto my side and poked him in the chest. "You're my boss. We shouldn't be doing this."

He took my offending hand and entwined his fingers with mine, bringing them to his lips. "Is this about Adam's stupid rules again?"

My forehead wrinkled. "No, this is about my rules. I vowed never to get involved with someone I work with again, not after Pete."

"Another reason to hate him."

"Be nice. He's still my friend…well, I hope he is anyway."

Grayson sighed. "I get it. I feel the same about Mel. We were best friends before we made the colossal mistake of getting involved. As much as she drives me crazy, I'll always care about her."

"How is she doing?" I asked, wary of crossing the line.

Sadness flickered through his eyes. "Okay. I'm trying to distance myself from her. She needs to know she's capable on her own."

"And your parents? Have they eased up on you?"

He rolled onto his back and took my hand with him, resting it on his chest. "I'm avoiding their calls."

"Oh, but what if…"

He laughed. "Don't worry, if it was important, they'd send their messenger pigeon."

"Adam?"

"Yep."

"Are you sure you aren't adopted? You're nothing like your brother."

"He's not as bad as everyone thinks he is. He puts up a good front, but he's just as fucked up as the rest of us."

My eyes widened as a distressing thought crossed my mind. "You're not going to tell him, are you? I don't want him, or anyone else at work, thinking less of me because of what we're doing."

"No one will think less of you," he said, squeezing my hand. "Plus, if they do, I'll fire them."

"Gray!"

"I'm joking." Grayson chuckled as he rolled back onto his side. "As much as I want to," he said, tucking a stray hair behind my ear. "I think it's safer to keep this between us…for now."

My lips curled upward. "So, we can stay in this uncomplicated bubble?"

Grayson grinned and pulled the bed sheet over our heads as he leaned over to kiss my neck. "Yes, we can stay."

Sunday morning came around too quickly and I reluctantly edged my way out of bed.

"Pyjamas till noon," Grayson groaned, grabbing my waist and dragging me back under the sheets. "Your rule, not mine."

Laughing as he pulled me on top of him with a sleepy smile, I leant down to kiss his soft lips, feeling a subtle twitch below. I smiled at the instant effect I had on his body.

"Gray, you home?!" yelled a familiar voice from the living room.

My breath caught and my eyes burst open. "Is that your brother?" I jumped off Grayson and stumbled around, looking for my clothes.

"Get in the shower," he whispered, clearly as alarmed as I was.

With my clothes bundled in my arms, I bolted for the ensuite, just before Adam walked through the bedroom door.

"What the fuck, Adam?" I heard Grayson hiss at his brother. "Ever heard of knocking?"

I turned on the shower and scooted back to the door to listen to their conversation.

There was a moment of silence before Adam erupted into laughter. "You have company? I'm proud of you, little brother. About time you tried someone new."

Grayson blew out an impatient breath. "What are you doing here?"

"So, how was it? Is she hot?"

"Adam…"

"Speaking of, did you see Josie in those leather pants the other day? *Fuck me.*"

I gasped. *Those pants really do have magical powers.*

"Stay away from Josie, will you? We need her."

"Yeah, I guess you're right, but I need her to—"

"Why are you here?" Grayson snapped.

"Well, you haven't been answering your cell. Mom's pissed. She wants to know if you're coming home for Thanksgiving."

"Christ. Isn't Thanksgiving a couple of months away?"

"You know Mom."

Grayson groaned. "She needs to take on more charity work."

Their voices faded away, leaving me straining my ear against the door.

Once the front door closed and I knew Adam was gone, I took advantage of the divine shower that occupied half the room. It wasn't long before Grayson joined in and decided to take advantage of me.

Chapter 15

The line blurred from that point onwards. As much as we tried to keep our distance, we found it impossible to keep our hands to ourselves. We completely ignored each other at work, but the minute we were alone all bets were off.

On the nights I worked, Grayson would organise a private car to take me back to his apartment, and on the nights I had off, he stayed at mine. We always made sure we started work at different times so we wouldn't draw any suspicion.

Grayson appreciated me staying out of the office as much as possible, that way he wouldn't have to worry about his brother's advances. Every time I came in, Adam would find an excuse to visit my office, leaving me extremely uncomfortable and Grayson furious.

Amy knew something was going on, but she never pried. She looked entirely fascinated every time we were together, watching our auras, I assumed. I never asked her not to tell anyone, I just trusted she wouldn't.

Two months had passed since the first night at his apartment. We used no labels, had no expectations, and it suited us just fine until a few days before Thanksgiving.

"So, what are you working on today?" Grayson asked, leaning over my shoulder. His hand rested on my chair and his thumb moved in discreet circular motions over my back as he reviewed my latest piece of photography. "That's an amazing shot."

I rolled my eyes and chuckled. "You're not wearing your glasses. Plus, there's no need for flattery, you know you're getting lucky tonight."

His smile grew large. "I can see just fine," he said, poking me with his finger. His gaze panned across my desk and settled on my Pantone book. He fanned out the colours and ran his fingers over the different shades. "This reminds me of your hair," he said, leaning closer to my ear. "...spread over my pillow while I'm fuc—"

His voice halted when Adam walked into the room. Grayson stood up straight and moved away from my desk. "Great work as usual." He shifted his gaze to his brother. "Were you looking for me?"

"No, actually. I was hoping to have a word with Josie."

Grayson's eyes narrowed as he nodded, and reluctantly left my office. I leant back in my chair and looked up at Adam curiously.

"How's that article coming along?" he asked, with his hands sitting casually in his pockets.

"Great actually. I should have the first draft to Marlene by tomorrow."

He nodded, but he didn't appear to hear what I said. "Listen, I've been given an extra ticket to see Magnus Brayshaw tonight, so I thought, considering you're already going, that we could go together."

"I don't know." I glanced nervously into Grayson's office. "I wouldn't be much company. All I do is take photos and write notes."

"That's totally fine. I'll pick you up at 8pm. We'll grab a bite to eat beforehand."

He left the office before I had a chance to respond.

A few seconds later my computer chimed breaking me from my daze.

W. Harlow: What did he say to you? You look like you're in shock?

J. Spencer: I am.

W. Harlow: ???

J. Spencer: I think your brother just asked me out.

W. Harlow: And what did you say?

J. Spencer: He didn't give me a chance to say anything. Apparently he's picking me up at 8pm.

I flinched as something clattered to the floor in Grayson's office.

W. Harlow: **Don't go.**

J. Spencer: **I have to. It's my job. You have nothing to worry about.**

Dinner with Adam wasn't as bad as I thought it would be. I prepared myself for his infamous womanising ways and kept our discussion strictly business related. He seemed content to talk about work, so I continued to throw questions at him to avoid any coming back my way.

At the realisation he wasn't getting anywhere with me, he called for the bill early and we arrived at the gig sooner than planned.

"What would you like to drink?" he asked as we walked into the venue.

"Um, water is fine. I don't drink when I'm working," I replied, pulling out my camera.

"You can relax a little, you know. I won't tell the boss." He winked at me and I laughed at his blatant attempt to flirt. Adam smiled at the perceived encouragement.

I grimaced. "No really, water is fine."

As I walked around the venue, trying to find the best position, Adam ordered my water and a whiskey for himself and brought it over. He passed the glass and I took a long sip. Anything to avoid talking.

"So, how long have you been a fan of Magnus?" I asked.

"Who?" he replied, a line forming between his eyes.

I chuckled. "The singer...?" I pointed to the stage.

"Oh! Since...forever." He took a giant gulp of his whiskey as his cheeks turned pink.

An arm appeared around Adam's shoulders. "Oh yeah, Adam here is a huge fan."

My heart leapt at the sound of Grayson's voice.

"What are you doing here?" Adam asked, pushing his brother off him.

"I could ask you the same question," he said as his gaze travelled to mine and softened. "Josie," he greeted with a nod.

I smiled tightly, but his presence infuriated me. I told him I could handle it. Dropping my gaze to my camera, I pretended to fiddle with the settings as they spoke.

"How did you even get a ticket? I thought it was sold out," Adam asked, turning back to the bar to order another drink.

Grayson shrugged. "It is. But I managed to convince someone outside to sell me theirs."

I peeked up to find Adam rolling his eyes, before turning to me. "Josie, you want another one?"

I was about to reply when Grayson intercepted. "Since when do you drink on the job?"

My mouth dropped open and I narrowed my gaze at the insinuation.

"Whoa, Gray, give her a break, she's been drinking water all night."

"Oh," he muttered, lowering his eyes, clearly realising his mistake.

Blood crept up my face and I took a deep breath to calm myself. "I'm fine, Adam, but thank you for asking." I swallowed the lump in my throat. "Excuse me. I have work to do."

With a forced smile, I moved away to get a better position before the show started. I threw Grayson a sideways glance, before lifting the camera to my face to hide the tears that welled behind. Unfortunately, little did they realise, I could still hear their conversation.

"You're really not going to let me near her, are you?"

"Nope. She's too important." Grayson paused. "...to the business."

"There *are* other photographers."

"Not like her."

Adam went quiet, but I could feel the weight of his stare. "I bet she's great in bed."

Grayson growled. "Just stay the fuck away from her, will you?"

"Oooh, I see..." His brother chuckled.

"What?"

"You *like* her."

Silence.

"I wonder what Melanie would think about that."

"Melanie doesn't need to know shit," Grayson snarled.

"Well this just got a whole lot more interesting. So, do you reckon she'd be up for it?"

"Up for what?"

"You know…you…me…her in the middle…"

"Shut the fuck up, Adam!"

"Jesus, Gray, I was only joking. You've really got it bad, don't you?"

I couldn't bring myself to look back at them. I was mortified. Thankfully, the venue was filling quickly and it was getting too loud to carry on any sort of conversation. The singer appeared on stage, and I proceeded to take as many photos as I could in the first five minutes, because the next five minutes consisted of me disappearing into the crowd and exiting through the back.

Not long after I arrived home, my doorbell rang. With a grunt, I pressed the buzzer to let him in. I knew who it was.

"Why did you leave without saying anything?" Grayson asked as soon as I opened the front door.

I crossed my arms and leant against the doorframe. "I didn't think I needed to."

"You could've at least returned my messages. I was worried."

I glanced over at my cell phone, sitting face-down on the kitchen bench and turned back. "I'm perfectly capable of looking after myself, Grayson."

He sighed. "I know, but—"

"Then why did you come tonight?"

His jaw clenched. "Because I know what he's like."

My blood boiled. "What did you think would've happened if you didn't show? Did you think I would've fucked him?"

He frowned. "No."

"Am I *that* easy to get into bed?" My eyes burned.

He shook his head. "No."

"Then why where you there?"

"I was jealous!" he blurted. "I hated the thought of him taking you out, when I never have."

"Oh." My gaze softened.

His shoulders slumped as he ran his hand through his hair. "I'm sorry, it was a dick move."

A small smile played on my lips. "That really hurt, didn't it?"

"What did?" His brow furrowed.

"Apologising."

He smirked and shoved his hands into his pockets. "We Harlows aren't designed for such things."

I shook my head with a chuckle and pulled him inside by his collar. "Come to bed, we have work tomorrow."

The next day, everyone was frantically finishing up jobs in order to get home to their families for Thanksgiving. Most of the staff originated from outside Manhattan and were leaving early to beat the traffic. Amy's dad lived upstate, Pete's parents lived in Philly, and Grayson…well, he and Adam were returning to the West Coast.

"What are your plans for Thanksgiving?" Grayson asked casually as I watered the plant he deliberately refused to care for to ensure my visit.

"Um…I'm just…staying here, I guess."

His gaze shot up from his computer. "You have no other family in the US?"

"I don't have family anywhere." I chuckled to keep my face from falling.

His jaw dropped. "I assumed you…"

"Oh, I've got plans." *Lie.* "Lenny always invites me to spend Thanksgiving with his family in Jersey." *Not a lie. I just never go.*

Grayson exhaled. "Oh, okay then. Jesus, I thought you were going to be alone for the holiday for a second there."

I smiled tightly. "So, you're heading home I see." Glancing down at the suitcase sitting beside his desk, I nodded towards it.

"Ah yeah. Mom makes a big deal every year. She obviously has way too much time on her hands."

"No, it's nice." I could only imagine. "Does she put on a big turkey with all the trimmings?"

Grayson laughed. "With the help of her chef, yes."

"That sounds amazing." My eyes glazed over, but I quickly blinked the tears away.

Adam rolled his suitcase down the hallway and stopped at Grayson's door. "Ready?"

"Yeah, I'll meet you downstairs," he said, his eyes not budging from mine.

"That's fine. I can wait." He leant against the doorframe and pretended to check the time.

Grayson's jaw tightened and he eyed me apologetically as he stood. "Have a good weekend, Josie."

"You too," I replied, turning for the door.

Adam nodded as I walked past, and I returned the gesture with a small smile.

I placed the watering can back on my desk and sank into my chair, just in time to see Grayson follow Adam down the hallway with their suitcases trailing behind them.

Five minutes later my phone chimed.

Grayson: I'll miss you.

His text made my heart ache.

A few minutes later it chimed again.

Grayson: Lenny doesn't have any sons, does he?

I laughed.

Me: Only three *wink face*

Grayson: I'm turning the cab around.

Me: All happily married.

Grayson: Phew.

Grayson: Perhaps when I get back...I could take you out some place?

I smiled.

Me: Like a real date?

Grayson: Yes. A real date.

I giggled.

Me: I'd like that.

Grayson: Me too.

As much as I was envious of everyone's plans, I was relieved. I hated Thanksgiving. I didn't dread the holiday itself, just what came with it. While everyone was catching up with loved ones and 'being thankful', it was a time of year I wasn't thankful for anything.

I locked myself in my apartment, turned off my phone, ate and drank myself into a stupor, listened to music at full blast—because no one was there to complain—and wallowed in the misery that was the anniversary of my parents' untimely death.

Seven years prior, my parents and I planned to have a traditional American Thanksgiving with Lenny's family in New Jersey, except we never even made it to the airport. A driver lost control of their car and veered onto the wrong side of the road, ploughing through ours. I somehow managed to survive with minor injuries, but my mum died on impact, and I watched my dad slip away days later in hospital.

The faint ringing was driving me mad. I'd passed out on the floor, again, and was rummaging through my scattered records, searching for my phone. Remembering I had switched it off and hidden it in my nightstand, I curiously looked around the room trying to figure out what the time was…or day for that matter.

The ringing sounded again, but it wasn't my phone, it was the doorbell.

"Who the fuck…" I stumbled over to the receiver, clearly still drunk. "Wrong number, buddy!" I yelled into the mouthpiece. There was no one left in my little building except me and my best mate, Luci.

"Josie, let me in."

I froze. "Grayson? What are you doing here?"

"Just let me in, Josie."

"You really need to work on your manners," I mumbled as I pressed the buzzer.

I tried to flatten my hair and straighten up my clothes, but it was useless. I wasn't expecting to see anyone, so all I had on were my sweatpants, Dad's old Creedence t-shirt, and my sheepskin slippers.

I almost pulled the door off its hinges when I opened it, welcoming Grayson after he jogged up the stairs. "Happy Thanksgivvving!" I cheered and giggled to myself.

Grayson's scrutinising gaze tapered. "You lied to me," he said, nudging me aside as he entered my apartment.

"Come on in!"

His eyes burned into mine. "You're drunk."

"It's Thanksgiving! You're supposed to get drunk."

"You're supposed to be with family and friends, not…" He panned his gaze around the room at the empty takeaway containers, bottles, records and Luci who was fast asleep in the middle of it all. "Jesus, Josie."

"Luci's my family," I muttered, crossing my arms.

His jaw twitched. "You said you were going to Lenny's."

I lifted one finger and shook my head. "No, no I did not. I said I was *invited* to Lenny's."

He pursed his lips and ran his hands through his hair. "Well, I called Lenny…"

"What?!" My eyes widened. "Why? Why did you do that?!"

"You weren't answering your phone!"

I growled. "I just want to be left alone, Gray! I just want everyone to leave me the fuck alone for a few days."

"He told me what happened."

Fear surged through my body. "I want you to leave."

"I'm not leaving," he said, shaking his head as he stepped closer.

My eyes welled. "Please leave."

"No."

I burst into tears. Drunken, messy tears. Grayson pulled me into his embrace and held me tighter than any hug I'd had before. And for the first time since my parent's death, I finally let someone in.

"Please don't leave," I whispered into his chest, between sobs.

And he didn't.

Regardless of the puffy eyes, I woke the next morning feeling lighter. The ache in my heart had eased and I felt a distinct shift in my mood. The smell of something cooking drew me out of bed, and I crept out to see what Grayson was up to.

The apartment was clean, with two full rubbish bags sitting by the front door. Grayson stood with his back to me, hovering over the stove. It was a divine sight.

I slid my arms around his naked waist and peered over his shoulder to see what he was cooking.

Grayson smiled as I lay a kiss under his earlobe.

"Pancakes?" Perhaps he wasn't as clueless in the kitchen as I originally thought.

He shrugged and pecked me on the lips. "It's the only thing I can cook."

"I love pancakes. I haven't had them since…in a long time."

"Well, grab a plate, because this one is almost done."

I did as I was told, and Grayson flipped the first pancake onto my plate. Digging the maple syrup out of the pantry, I poured it on top and grinned. The smell brought back memories of my dad, dancing in the kitchen on a Sunday morning, stacking up pancakes as high as possible. A memory I'd normally shake off.

"You look a little better today," Grayson said as he dropped another onto my plate.

My eyes met his and my face warmed. "I'm sorry you had to see me that way."

"You have nothing to be sorry about, except the fact you didn't tell me you were alone for Thanksgiving."

"I didn't think you would…"

Grayson narrowed his eyes. "What? Care?"

I swallowed and lowered my eyes. "I didn't want to cross the line…"

He leant back against the counter. "I think we crossed the line months ago, don't you?"

"But I thought we were keeping this thing…uncomplicated."

"As long as I'm waking up with you every morning…you can call it whatever you like," he said and turned back to the stove.

My eyelashes fluttered along with my heart, and I smiled down at my pancakes. I quietly ate as Grayson continued to fill my plate and then his.

"Thank you," I said as I polished off the last pancake.

He offered me a small smile. "You're not used to someone looking after you, are you?"

"No, not really."

"Pete never…"

I shook my head. "I didn't let him."

"Not even after two years?"

"I'm not exactly an easy person to get close to," I said, avoiding his gaze.

Grayson nodded slowly, but didn't say anything.

I took my plate to the sink and rinsed it. "You know, if you need to get back to your family, I totally understand. You really shouldn't have come home early and ruined your trip."

"Oh no, my parents did that already."

I glanced up at him. "What happened?"

"What didn't?" He chortled. "They're just so…fucking interfering."

"Isn't that what parents are supposed to do? Interfere? It's just their way of showing you they care."

Grayson's expression softened as he regarded me from across the counter. "You know what, you don't need to worry about my family drama. Let's just enjoy the rest of the holiday together."

"Okay." I smiled. "Pyjamas till noon?"

He grinned. "Pyjamas till noon."

Chapter 16

THE HARLOW-WARREN EMPIRE STRIKES BACK

It wasn't the headline on the back of Pete's newspaper that caught my attention. It was the photograph. I stared at the striking features of the man who shared my bed most nights, sharing an intimate kiss with his ex. The caption confirmed what I was seeing.

William Harlow and Melanie Warren reunite over Thanksgiving, much to the delight of their families.

My stomach dropped and bile crept up my throat as I strained my eyes to read the article from across the table. I tried to inconspicuously tilt my head, but Pete was so absorbed with the finance section, he wouldn't have noticed if I was sitting there naked.

Grayson strolled in a minute later and I shot upright, pretending to nibble on my sandwich.

"How is everyone today?" he asked, taking his lunch out of the fridge. The lunch I made for him that morning.

"I'm well, William. How was your Thanksgiving?" Pete asked, folding up his paper and placing it in the middle of the table.

I smiled tightly, but didn't meet Grayson's eyes.

"Bumpy start, but ended well," Grayson replied, sitting at the end of the table, between the two of us. I sensed him looking my way, but I kept my eyes lowered. "I trust you both had a good holiday?"

I gave a quick nod, but Pete continued. "Always nice to head home for a few days. Josie, you went to Jersey again, right?"

"Like always," I muttered.

Pete's brow furrowed. "Are you feeling okay? You look pale."

Grayson's eyes darted to mine and narrowed.

"I'm fine. Just tired, I guess." I packed up my half-eaten sandwich, and pushed up from the table. "I better get back to work." With a light tap on the newspaper, I smiled over at Grayson. "Great photo by the way. Perhaps I'll do a feature on you and Melanie in the next edition of *Maude*."

Grayson's gaze dropped to the article, and quickly bounced back to me as I strode out of the lunch room, feeling like a fool.

Don't be that girl, Josie. Don't be that girl! I sank into my desk chair and rubbed my temples. I'm sure there was a totally reasonable explanation for the photograph...and the kiss.

Footsteps stormed down the hallway and my body seized. Grayson flew past my office with the newspaper folded under his arm, and into his. He slammed the door closed and picked up his phone, pacing the room until someone answered.

My computer chimed.

A. Mitchell: Can you hear that?

J. Spencer: Yep.

A. Mitchell: I'd hate to be on the other end of that phone call.

When the muffled yelling through the walls finally subsided, I peeked up from my desk into Grayson's office. My heart skipped a beat when I discovered him standing at his window studying me, before signalling me to come to him with his finger.

I sighed and hesitantly rose from my chair. He held open his door as I ambled over, and closed it behind me.

"I need to explain that photo," Grayson said as he edged around his desk and sat down, motioning for me to do the same.

Sliding into the visitor's chair, I crossed my arms, refusing to meet his eyes. "Go."

Grayson exhaled heavily. "My parents invited the Warrens for Thanksgiving. If I had any idea, I wouldn't have gone at all. Mel got a little carried away when she arrived and pulled me in for a kiss. I promise you, it didn't last long, nor did I enjoy it."

"You could have told me she was there, I wouldn't have been mad."

"I'm sorry, Josie, I'm not used to *sane* women in my life."

"I'm barely sane."

He ran his fingers through his hair. "Compared to Mel, you're the definition of the word."

"So..." I twiddled my thumbs in my lap. "How did the photo end up in the paper?"

His shoulders dropped. "My mother leaked it to the press."

"Why would she do that?"

"My parents want us back together. This was her gentle nudge."

I tapered my gaze. "And Melanie?"

Grayson pursed his lips. "She's still getting used to the idea that it's over."

Pinching the bridge of my nose, I tried to take it all in. "So, who were you talking to just now?"

"Mum. I told her to stop meddling and..." He paused, and caught my gaze.

My heart quickened. "And what?"

"I told her I've met someone."

"Wh...What?" *Oh Shit.*

"It just came out," he blurted. "I didn't know how else to get through to her."

"So much for uncomplicated," I muttered, as my thoughts and heart began to race.

He sank back into his leather chair. "With you, it *is* uncomplicated."

I cleared my throat and rubbed the perspiration from my neck. "And how did she take it?"

Grayson went quiet for a moment, before his mouth grew into a tight smile.

"Gray?" *It must be bad.*

"She wants to meet you."

My eyes bulged. "What?!"

Grayson chuckled. "Don't worry, Christmas isn't for another month, so we'll have some time to prepare."

"Christmas!" I struggled to breathe. "Christmas with your family? Noooo, there is no way I'm going to LA to spend

Christmas with a bunch of people I already know aren't going to approve of me."

Grayson shrugged. "That's fine, because they're coming here. We spend Christmas with my Grandfather in the Hamptons."

Shit.

"But I have Luci. I can't leave him alone."

"We'll bring him. The property is huge. He'll love it."

"Gray…"

His eyes softened. "Josie, it'll be okay."

I tried not to hyperventilate.

Grayson winced, clearly remembering something. "We have one problem though."

I laughed nervously. "Just one?"

"Adam will be there."

My eyes rolled back and my head fell onto the chair. "I guess that means you'll have to tell him."

A smile crept over his lips. "So, you'll come?"

I groaned. "Do I have a choice?"

"Not really, no," he said with a glint in his eye.

"Just don't tell them any more about me."

"Why not? They're going to find out anyway."

"I know, but I want them to know as much about me as I do about them. It's only fair. Plus, I don't fancy being followed by a private investigator for the next month."

Grayson chuckled. "They're not the FBI, Jos." Then his laughter faded. "Actually, you're right. It is something they would do."

Due to Adam's disregard for privacy, we rarely stayed at Grayson's apartment. But when Adam was out of town, we lapped up the luxury. As much as it was nice to be in an apartment with furniture, the whole place weirded me out. It was too perfect. Just to feel more comfortable, I deliberately threw cushions on the floor and rearranged the colour coded bookshelf. Anything to make the place look lived in.

A couple of weeks before Christmas, Grayson and I spent the day on his couch, both catching up on work while playing footsies in the middle.

"Have you told Adam yet?" I asked when Grayson slammed his cell phone back on the coffee table for the seventh time in the last hour.

"I was hoping to tell him this week, but he extended his trip. I'm not complaining though. My couch is slightly more comfortable than yours."

I poked out my tongue, and he grinned before refocusing on his laptop. Not a minute passed before Grayson's phone buzzed again and he scowled down at it.

"Who are you avoiding?" I asked, becoming even more curious.

He groaned. "Mel."

My heart dipped at the mention of her name. "Oh…you can't block her?"

"She's a friend, Jos." He ran his hand through his hair. "I can't shut her out."

I pressed my lips together and nodded.

When his phone buzzed a third time, I glanced down to see a selfie of Melanie Warren entirely top-less. Grayson snatched up his phone as quick as my eyebrows rose.

"Gray! Is that what she's been sending you?! I *bet* you don't want to shut that out."

Grayson deleted the photo, and looked up at me, exasperated. "She's just trying to get my attention."

I snorted. "Well she certainly has mine."

"If I respond in any way, she'll take it as encouragement."

I held in my laughter. "Riiight. Well then…" I picked up my phone and angled its lens down my top.

Grayson stilled. "What are you doing?"

"Well, if you have naked photos of your ex, I figure it's only fair mine does too."

I pretended to take a photo and scrolled down my contact list. "Now, where is Pete's number?"

Grayson's eyes grew huge. "Don't you dare."

He climbed over his laptop and straddled my legs, trying to snatch my phone away as I giggled uncontrollably. He wrestled it out of my fingers and dropped it out of reach.

Laid over me, he watched my face as my laughter melted into a chuckle. "You drive me crazy, you know that?"

My mouth curved into a smile as I stared into his swirling green eyes, just inches above mine. "Show me," I whispered, pressing my pelvis into his. A low growl rumbled deep within his chest, and he wiped the knowing smirk off my face with his soft lips.

Adam arrived back the day of the office Christmas party, leaving Grayson only one week to tell him about our relationship. We finished the work day early and celebrated with champagne and nibbles in the conference room, which Linda had elaborately decorated for the evening.

Moving in different circles to avoid any romantic slipups, Grayson charmed his way through the staff, looking happier than ever. Christmas was apparently his favourite time of year and it showed. Occasionally his eyes would graze over mine and twinkle, causing my heart to flutter every time.

My cheeks warmed as I sipped my champagne, quietly observing everyone mingle. We finally felt like a family again.

"It's great to see you smiling Josie," Adam said, appearing at my side. He had been eyeing me curiously throughout the night, making me wonder if his brother had finally spoken to him but neglected to fill me in.

"Well, 'tis the season." I lifted my champagne glass, still grinning.

He chuckled. "My brother is a sucker for Christmas too."

"I've noticed," I said, watching Grayson hand out gifts to all the employees from a giant Santa sack.

"See, we're not all bad."

I lifted the glass to my mouth and took a sip. "No, apparently not." As much as I was enjoying myself, I couldn't wait for the party to end; Grayson was taking me out on our first official date afterwards and I was beyond excited.

Grayson called over to Adam. "Can you go to my office and grab the rest of the gifts?"

Adam nodded and turned to me on his way out. "Would you mind giving me a hand?"

"Sure," I replied, placing my glass down on the table amongst the array of festive food platters.

I trailed after him into Grayson's office, but as soon as we walked through the door, Adam's pace slowed. Assuming he was scanning the room for the gifts, I pointed to the floor next to the desk and manoeuvred around his stationary frame to pick them up.

As I began piling them into my arms, I glanced up to find Adam staring at me.

"I was actually wondering if I could speak to you privately for a moment," he said, rubbing the back of his neck.

I smiled in relief. Grayson must've spoken to him. "Yes, I was hoping we'd have a chance to talk."

His eyes lit up as he stepped closer. "Or we could just skip the talking part."

Before I knew it, his mouth was pressing against mine.

"Don't forget to grab th—" Was all I heard before Adam's lips were torn away, and I was stumbling backwards and dropping presents all over the floor.

Grayson grabbed Adam's shirt and threw him against the wall, eyeballing his older brother with a clenched jaw. "I told you not to fucking touch her."

"Fuck, Gray, what's *wrong* with you?" he yelled, shoving him off. "It's a Christmas party, loosen the fuck up."

My mouth dropped open. "You didn't tell him?!"

Adam narrowed his eyes as they darted between us. "Tell me what?"

Grayson rubbed his hand down his face and hung his head. "Josie and I...we're together."

"What?" he spat, stepping backwards.

Grayson peered up at Adam and swallowed. "We're...a couple."

"Since when?!" His forehead creased. "When Mum questioned me about the woman you were seeing, I assumed it was...wait." His face dropped. "That girl in your apartment, in your shower...that was *her*?" He moved his eyes to me. "That was you?"

I nodded reluctantly, my face burning.

Adam pursed his lips and pulled his fiery gaze back to his brother. "Why didn't you tell me, Gray? Or were you enjoying watching me make a fool out of myself?"

I stepped forward, feeling horrible. "Adam, we had no inten—"

"That's Mr. Harlow to you!" he barked, making me flinch.

"Adam..." Grayson warned, moving between us. "I'm sorry you had to find out this way, but I won't let you speak to her like that."

"What? Am I supposed to treat her differently to the rest of the staff, just because you're fucking her?"

"No, I expect you to treat her with the respect she deserves."

He shook his head with a laugh. "I can't wait to see you explain this one to Mom and Dad, not to mention Mel."

Grayson pinched the bridge of his nose and groaned.

With an amused snort, Adam turned my way. "You know he's supposed to marry Melanie Warren, don't you? This *thing* between the two of you, it won't last."

Grayson exhaled. "What the fuck are you doing, Adam?"

"Saving her the grief," he muttered before storming out of the room, leaving behind an unsettling silence.

I lowered my stinging eyes. "Well, that went well," I mumbled, picking up the presents I dropped.

"I'm sorry, he's just—"

"Can we just get back to the party?" I interrupted, hiding my face behind the pile of gifts sitting precariously in my arms.

"Yeah, sure, let me help with that." He slid the boxes from the top of the pile into his arms, revealing my glistening eyes. "Jos, are you okay?"

"Yeah, yeah. I'm fine," I said, shaking off my anxiety.

"Don't worry about Adam. He'll get over it."

"Will the rest of your family?"

His gaze bored into mine. "They don't have a choice."

I swallowed the lump in my throat. "Gray, about Christmas… maybe I shouldn't come."

"I can't possibly survive my parents without you there." His tired eyes begged me. "Please don't back out on me now."

My shoulders dropped. "Melanie won't be making a surprise appearance, will she?"

"My parents assured me the Warrens will be staying on the West Coast these holidays. You have nothing to worry about."

"Alright." I sighed, but something in my gut made me think there was.

While the others went to The Edge to continue drinking, I hurried home to get ready for my date with Grayson. He was picking me up at 7pm, leaving me half an hour to look my best. Without a clue as to what was planned, I decided on my leather pants, ankle boots and a flowy silk blouse with a soft blazer on top. Not only would my choice in pants drive Grayson crazy, but they would also keep me warm. *Win, win!*

The doorbell rang and I buzzed him in, leaving the front door ajar so I could feed Luci.

"Jesus," Grayson moaned from behind as I bent over to fill Luci's water bowl.

I grinned knowingly and turned to find Grayson in the middle of the lounge room rubbing his hand over his mouth, staring at my legs. "You can't wear those."

My brow arched as I placed one hand on my hip. "Why not? You didn't tell me what we were doing."

"You're not going to be doing anything, other than me, if you wear those."

I laughed and placed the empty glass on the kitchen counter. "Down, boy. We'll see how this date goes first."

He shook his head as I approached him with a small smile playing on my lips.

"Josie..." he rumbled.

Rolling my eyes, I ran my hands over his tense shoulders. "I'll wear a long coat."

Grayson exhaled. "Good."

As I kissed his lips, something rustled at his side. I peered down at the brown paper bag tucked under his arm. "What's this?"

"Well its customary to bring flowers on a first date, but knowing you're not into that, I brought you these instead."

Eyeing him curiously, I opened the bag and peered inside. My eyes widened as my mouth began to salivate. "Rosie's donuts?"

"I figure they're made of flour, so...it's a decent substitute, right?"

I pulled his lips down to mine to show just how much I appreciated them. "How about we skip this whole date thing and go eat these in bed naked?"

He nipped my neck with a low growl. "Nope, we're going out."

"Fine." As much as I was looking forward to our long-awaited date, I was nervous. Until today, no one knew about us and I'd been happy in our bubble. Although the likelihood of running into anyone from work was low, I still worried how everyone would take the news once it finally came out.

A private car took us to Lumière. Possibly the fanciest restaurant I'd ever seen. I was instantly intimidated, but Grayson took it all in his stride like he ate there every night.

"Relax, Josie," Grayson whispered, walking closely behind as we were escorted to our table.

"I know, I'm sorry. This is just a little different from Lenny's Pizzeria."

"Say the word and we'll leave."

I caught his eye as we were seated and his expression was dead serious. "No, no. This is fine. More than fine. It's amazing." I gazed around the room at the elaborate chandeliers, expensive silverware and crystal glasses, wondering how the hell I got there.

A few people glanced my way, eyeing my hair. I'd worn it up so my rainbow streaks were prominent amongst the auburn curls, but now I regretted it. Feeling self-conscious, I took out a few pins and let my hair spill over my shoulders.

Grayson reached out and slid his hand over mine. "You look stunning, Josie. Don't change for them."

Heat crept up my neck and I shrugged, keeping my eyes lowered.

A waiter appeared at our table and handed us menus. As I perused over the mains, I scrunched up my nose—it was all written in French. I peeped over the menu at Grayson, who was watching me with an amused smirk.

"Need some help?"

I chuckled and shook my head. "How's about you just order for me?"

The waiter came over and Grayson reeled off an array of French dishes, rolling each 'r' with perfection.

"You speak French," I said. *Of course he does.*

He shrugged. "A little. Enough to understand what I'm eating." He winked and flashed me his dazzling smile.

"I'm guessing you've been to France, too?"

His face turned pink and he cleared his throat. "Yeah. I've spent a few summers there."

"Just a few summers, hey?" I almost laughed. "I hope to get there one day."

"You will."

His confidence surprised me. "You seem pretty sure about that."

"I am," he said, with a casual shrug. "Where else do you want to go?"

I leant back in my chair, mulling on the question I asked myself weekly. "Europe, initially. Then Asia, maybe Africa—oh! And South America...*argh*, all of it really. My list keeps getting bigger unfortunately. I need to stop watching those bloody travel shows."

Grayson laughed before narrowing his gaze. "And when do you plan on doing all this travel?"

"As soon as I can afford it," I stated with a smile, before rolling my eyes. "So never."

"I can't say I'm not relieved. *Maude* needs you to stick around for a while." He opened his mouth to say something else, but our attention was stolen by the arrival of our meals.

Without the faintest idea what I was eating, I devoured everything. The portions were concerningly tiny, but the incredible flavours made up for it, and after six courses, I was ready to curl up and sleep.

"We better get going if we're going to make the show," Grayson said, signalling the waiter for the cheque.

My heart leapt. "We're going to a show?"

"Broadway."

"Really?" I clapped my hands like a seal, before remembering where we were. "I've always wanted to go to the theatre."

"You live in New York and you've never seen a Broadway show?"

I gave his foot a tap under the table and widened my eyes. "Struggling artist, remember?"

"You're only struggling because you haven't attempted to sell your work yet."

I grinned. "I think you're a little biased."

"I appreciated your art well before I found out you were great in bed."

A loud laugh erupted from my mouth and the couple on the next table looked my way, making me wince. "You need to get me out of here."

Grayson smirked and rose from the table, holding out his elbow. I latched on like he was a life preserver, and he guided me towards the entrance.

As he helped me slip on my long winter coat, a female voice sounded from behind us.

"Grayson? Is that you?"

I turned to find a petite brunette with large brown eyes, standing before us, grinning ear to ear.

"Staci, hi," Grayson said reluctantly, leaning over to greet her with a hug.

Her eyes met mine over his shoulder and her smile faltered. I had seen her face somewhere before, but couldn't place where.

Staci's hand remained on Grayson's arm, making my skin crawl. "I haven't seen you since…well, you know…" She waved it off. "How have you been?"

"Good. Busy. What brings you to the East Coast?"

"One of Mum's fundraisers. You know how it is."

With a quick nod, Grayson smiled tightly before Staci tilted her head in my direction.

As I stepped forward to introduce myself, Grayson's hand slid around my elbow, steering me away. "Well, it was great seeing you, but we better get going."

"Oh, okay," she uttered with a shrug, "I'll tell Melanie you said hi."

Ah-ha! Melanie's Hens' night! I remembered her, but I doubt she remembered me. She was off her face on God knows what.

We walked in silence for an entire block.

"Well, that was—"

"Awkward, I know," he blurted, running his hand down his face. "I should've introduced you, I'm sorry. I just…"

"Freaked out?" I chuckled, but it was forced. *Is he ashamed of me?*

"I wasn't expecting to see anyone from home."

My pace slowed and I peered up at him. "Would you have taken me out if you had?"

Grayson lowered his eyes, but remained silent.

"Maybe you should take me home."

"No," he retorted, before taking my hands in his. "I think it's time everyone starts getting used to the idea."

"Are you sure? You were pretty uncomfortable back there."

"I'd rather Mel heard about you from me, rather than Staci, that's all."

I chewed on my lower lip. "Maybe you should talk to her."

"I'm going to," he said, with a sad smile. "I'm just waiting for the right time."

He gave my hand a squeeze, before we continued our brisk walk down West 45th Street so we wouldn't miss the start of the show.

Grayson's hand lay entwined with mine throughout the entire production, but his mind was clearly elsewhere. Even after the show, when we strolled back up 5th Avenue to admire the Christmas lights, he remained deep in thought. It wasn't until we were standing in front of the spectacular Rockefeller Christmas tree, he returned to the present.

"I still can't believe I live here," I said, gazing up at the twinkling lights.

Grayson slipped his arms around my waist, resting his chin on my shoulder as he followed my gaze. "New York City definitely has a lot going for it."

My heart raced as I built up the courage to ask the next question. "Do you think you could live here…*permanently,* I mean?"

Grayson spun me around and slid his arms into my jacket, cradling my arse with his hands. The warmth sent tingles straight to my core. "I know I could."

I tried to hide my smile, but it was no use.

Grayson pressed his lips to my forehead. "Should we go and eat those donuts now?"

"Oh, I assumed we were staying at your place."

"We are," he stated with a glint in his eye. "I bought extra."

I poked him in the chest. "You're going to make me fat."

"Unlikely, but we can always work it off afterwards," he said, giving my bum a little squeeze.

I shrugged. "Or during."

Grayson's pupils dilated as he gazed down at me. "I like the way you think."

Chapter 17

On Christmas Eve, Grayson carried my suitcase down the stairs while I struggled with Luci. His long legs found it difficult to navigate the steps and it was always a challenge getting him down safely, even though we did it on a daily basis.

"Are you sure it's okay if we bring him?" I winced, thinking of all the damage he was likely to cause.

Grayson smiled. "It's fine. Once he runs around the property a few times, he'll be too tired to destroy anything."

I stepped outside to find a large SUV parked out front and raised my brow. "This is your car?"

He smirked. "One of them."

"Oh, the places we could go, Luci." I scuffed his head and peered up at Grayson. "Just warning you, Luci's never been in a car before."

He opened the back door and Luci bounded inside, settling beside our suitcases. "Ever?"

"Nope."

Grayson shrugged. "What's the worst that could happen?"

A half hour into the trip, we were forced to drive with all the windows down, letting the freezing wind aerate the car. Luci was anxious, and apparently when dogs get nervous, they release gas. A lot of gas. And the smell was horrendous. By the time we reached the Hamptons, our faces were almost frozen solid. I feared the smell had infiltrated my pores and would never wash out.

"Oh my god, I stink like dog farts," I cried, jumping out of the truck as soon as we parked.

Grayson wrapped his arm around me and stuck his nose into the crook of my neck. "You smell just fine." I giggled as he kissed me. "But I might keep the windows down for a while."

I pulled my eyes away from Grayson and lifted them up to his grandfather's mansion. My mouth fell open. "Wow."

"It's beautiful, isn't it?" Grayson followed my gaze as he pulled me into his side.

"It's…magnificent." I gasped, mesmerised by the intricate brickwork and the barn style pitched roof. It was like something from a storybook, and I felt like a princess standing in front of it. *I am way out of my league here.*

Grayson let Luci out of the car and popped on his lead. "There's about four acres of land so this guy can go nuts."

Luci let out an excited whimper as if he understood. I smiled down at my dog, wishing I felt the same.

"You'll be fine, Josie. I'll be with you the whole time."

I took the lead from his hands and gazed back up at the house. "Promise?"

"Promise."

He looped his arm through mine as we approached the grand columned entrance. Grayson pressed the doorbell, his hazel eyes twinkling back at mine while we waited.

My heartrate accelerated when approaching footsteps sounded inside. A moment later, a man in his early sixties opened the door and I straightened my back.

"Mr. Harlow." He greeted Grayson with a nod and I relaxed when I realised he couldn't be his father.

"Hi, Max. This is Josie. Josie, this is Max. He's been my grandfather's butler for fifteen years."

My eyes widened. *Oh my god. A butler?* "Pleased to meet you, Max."

He offered me a warm smile. "The pleasure is all mine. And who do we have here?" He peered down at my dog with a glint in his eye.

"This is Luci," I said.

He lifted the back of his hand to Luci's nose. "An Irish wolfhound, no doubt."

Luci gave him a lick and Max chuckled.

I smiled. "You know your dog breeds."

"I'm quite fond of these gentle giants," Max said, ruffling the hair on Luci's head.

Grayson took Luci's lead from my hand and stepped towards him. "How would you feel about taking Luci for a quick walk around the grounds? Get him used to the property?"

"I would be honoured," he gushed.

Grayson passed over the lead and Luci jumped around impatiently.

"I'll take your bags up to your room when I return. Your grandfather and parents are in the parlour."

I grinned as I watched Max walk away with Luci trotting happily beside him. "He is going to love it here."

"So will you, come on," Grayson said, taking my hand and pulling me inside.

The interior was just as divine. It was warm and inviting, nothing like I thought a Harlow residence would be. I assumed they'd all be similar to Grayson's apartment. Cold and impersonal, but this was the exact opposite.

Grayson nudged my side as I drank it all in. "Are you ready?"

"No," I replied, and he chuckled.

His fingertips grazed my lower back as he ushered me down a wide hallway. I nervously glanced around, like I was walking through a house of horrors, waiting for something to jump out at any moment. His hand found mine and squeezed it, before rolling open the French doors.

Three sets of eyes turned to us.

"William, my dear." His mother smiled tightly as she glided over to Grayson. She kissed his cheek, observing me over his shoulder with cool blue eyes, like Adam's.

"Good afternoon, William." A man in his late sixties slowly rose out of his chair, presumably his father, but didn't approach.

"Grayson, glad to see you, son. And who is this lovely young lady?" asked an elderly man, hobbling over with his cane. He patted Grayson on the shoulder, but approached me instead.

"Grandpa, this is Josie. The one I've been telling you about."

My eyebrows rose. *He's been talking about me?*

The old man grinned. Reaching out, he enveloped my hand in his.

"Lovely to meet you…" I looked at Grayson for help because I had no idea what to call him.

"You can call me Grandpa too." He winked, and I noticed he had Grayson's eyes. "It's getting a little confusing around here with all these Williams in the family."

Grayson cleared his throat as his parents moved closer. "Mum, Dad, this is Josie."

"Josie…" They peered up at Grayson, waiting on a last name.

"Josie Spencer," I answered for him, reaching out to take his mother's hand.

Her fingers felt limp in mine. "Hmm…Spencer. I'm not familiar with that name."

"Oh, I keep a low profile."

Grayson's mouth curved into a smile, but his mother remained expressionless—or perhaps it was the Botox disguising how she really felt.

"Josie, this is my mother, Caroline, and my father, William."

"Pleased to meet you both." I shook his father's hand, but he didn't meet my eyes.

Instead, he narrowed them at Grayson and glanced at his wife. "Australian."

I'm not sure if it was a statement or a question, but I nodded regardless.

Fear laced Caroline's expression and Grayson groaned impatiently. "She's a dual-citizen, Mum."

My eyes darted between their worried looks. "My father was American," I offered, hoping to ease their minds.

Caroline tried to raise an eyebrow. "Was?"

"Mum…" Grayson uttered, in a low voice.

"It's okay, Gray." I touched his arm. "Both of my parents passed away a while ago."

Grayson's grandfather gasped. "Oh, Josie. I'm so sorry to hear that."

I swallowed, but managed to keep myself composed. "Thank you."

"What on earth is *that*?" Caroline clutched her chest as she stared out the window.

We all followed her gaze to find Luci bounding around the front lawn with Max frantically chasing after him.

"*That*…is Luci," Grayson declared proudly, without any further explanation. "Come on, Josie." He reached for my hand and grinned. "Let me show you around."

The rest of the day flew by. Grayson gave me the grand tour of Harlow Manor along with the brief history of his family. His great grandfather and grandfather were responsible for most of the Harlow fortune, but his father built it into an empire he planned to pass on to his sons when he retired. So far, according to his dad, Adam proved ready, but Grayson was lacking.

We explored the enormous grounds, with Luci alternating between trailing behind and running ahead at every flicker of movement. The stoned pathways were lined with boxed hedges that had a small sprinkling of snow sitting on the top. It was a winter wonderland.

"It's really picturesque out here," I said, breathing in the crisp air.

"Just wait until they turn on the Christmas lights and the snow falls. I used to pretend I was in the north pole."

I gazed around in awe.

"Every season here is amazing," he continued. "My grandmother was a painter, and she filled the garden with an assortment of plants so each season would bring something new and beautiful to inspire her."

"Sounds like my sort of lady." I grinned.

Grayson's cheeks grew pink. "You sometimes remind me of her."

"Did she swear a lot?"

He let out a laugh and shook his head. "Like a sailor."

As we sat down for dinner, the doorbell rang.

A moment later, Adam walked into the dining room, shrugged off his winter jacket and handed it to Max. "Good evening, all."

We hadn't seen him since he walked out of the office Christmas party and had been ignoring Grayson's messages all week.

Caroline jumped out of her chair and wrapped her arms affectionately around her eldest son. "Adam, you finally made it. We feared you'd get snowed in, leaving so late."

William stood up and shook his hand firmly. "Well done on the Ferguson deal."

Adam smiled tightly as his eyes panned across to the two of us.

"Adam," Grayson greeted shortly.

His brother nodded. "Gray." And then to me. "Josie."

"Hi," I responded, hoarsely.

Caroline's lips pursed. "Oh, so you've already met your brother's new...*friend*?"

Grayson's hand slid under the table and over my knee, giving it a squeeze.

Adam grinned at his mother's response. "It seems we met a while ago." His eyes sparkled as they met his brother's tense gaze.

Everyone settled down into their seats and started their meals.

"So, just how long has this...been going on?" Caroline asked as she cut up her steak.

Adam smirked. "I've been wondering that myself."

Grayson cleared his throat, and I shifted uncomfortably in my chair. "We've been seeing each other for a while now," he replied as honestly as he could.

Grayson's grandfather seemed to notice the tension and attempted to change the subject, but it only got worse.

"What do you do for a living, Josie?" William asked, speaking over his father.

I finished chewing my food and placed my cutlery on my plate. "I'm a photographer."

"Oh, an artist. Like my dear Betty." Grandpa's eyes sparkled as he smiled.

Grayson nodded and caught my eye. "Josie is really talented. I keep telling her she should have her own exhibition."

I laughed nervously. "No, the magazine keeps me busy enough."

A silence lulled over the table, and I realised I'd fucked up. *Big time*.

William stopped chewing. "What magazine do you work for?"

My eyes darted from Grayson to Adam, who was now leaning back in his chair with a sly grin.

I felt sick.

"She works at *Maude*, Dad," Grayson answered instead.

"God dammit, William!" His father stood up abruptly and threw his napkin on his plate. "You're fucking the help now?"

"Whoa, Dad, calm down," Adam said, looking worriedly across at Grayson, whose eyes burned into his father.

"I brought you up to be better than that," his father continued.

"Do you even know anything about her?" Caroline joined in as if I wasn't there. "It seems convenient that she has no family. For all we know, she's just after a green card and half your bank account."

"Jesus, Mum." Adam wiped his hand over his face, clearly embarrassed by their reaction.

With a racing heart and nauseous stomach, I placed my hands on the table and rose. "Excuse me," I said, needing to escape.

Grayson reached out and seized my wrist, standing up next to me. "No, Josie." His face grew red as he glared at his parents. "Don't you ever speak about her like that."

"We had a plan, Grayson!" William retorted with a growl. "Have you ever stopped to consider how this affects your family? Is it really worth throwing it all away for some…some *office fling*?"

Grayson's hands balled into fists at his sides. "She's not some fling! I fucking *love* her."

My heart stopped as the room fell deathly silent. All eyes travelled to where I stood, cheeks ablaze and trembling. I slowly lowered my burning eyes and ran from the room.

I bounded up the stairs, taking three at a time, trying to put as much distance between myself and his family as possible. I'd never been so humiliated, and Grayson's surprising declaration was like the cherry on top of a pile of dog shit. *Could his timing be any worse?*

Finally finding our bedroom, somewhere in the east wing—*yes, the fucking east wing*—I slammed the door and resisted the urge to scream. But instead, I burst into tears.

Swinging my suitcase onto the bed, I started repacking what I unpacked earlier that day. I was stupid to think they would accept someone like me into their lives. The door clicked closed behind me, and I jumped. I hadn't even heard it open.

Grayson stood in front of me with slumped shoulders and tired eyes. "I'm so sorry, Josie."

I shook my head. "I shouldn't have come."

"You have every right to be here. My parents were out of line. Grandpa is giving them all a stern talking to as we speak."

My face scrunched at the thought. *Grandpa?*

"He may look docile, but trust me, you never want to cross him."

I drew in a deep breath and exhaled, trying to compose myself. "I just want everyone to be happy. It's Christmas, for Christ's sake." *What the fuck did I just say?*

Grayson chuckled and stepped closer. "I'm happy."

"Yeah, right."

"A few minutes alone with you and I will be," he said, grazing my cheek with his thumb.

The corner of my mouth lifted. "Just a few minutes?"

"You know what I mean," he said, nudging my arm.

Blush crept up Grayson's neck as my smile grew.

He lowered his gaze. "I didn't mean to say what I did downstairs."

My heart dropped. "Oh."

His eyes shot back up. "I mean, I wanted to tell you in private, preferably a few months from now so it wouldn't freak you out."

"Oh." I chuckled. *Phew.*

"I'll yell it from the rooftops, if you prefer?" With sparkling eyes, he slid his arms around my lower back and pulled me towards him, pressing his forehead to mine. "I love you, Josie. Please don't go. I want to wake up to you on Christmas morning."

I twisted my head towards the window, watching the falling snow. "I think I'm snowed in anyways."

His mouth curved into a smile and he hung his head heavenward. "Thank you, Father Christmas."

Peering up into his now green eyes, I experienced something I'd never felt before. Something that frightened me as much as it excited me, but the words caught in my throat. As my walls crumbled, his lips crashed down onto mine.

Not another word was uttered as we tore off each layer of clothing and edged closer to the four-poster bed. Our lips only parted for Grayson to pull a condom from his wallet on the nightstand, and within seconds, they were back on mine, breathing me in as though I was his source of oxygen.

His tongue explored every inch of my body, visiting all my favourite places along the way. Moaning as my need for him grew more and more intense, he locked onto my hungry gaze and filled me with his length. I pressed my lips together, muffling my screams as he pushed deeper and harder than ever before. Perspiration slid down my face as I let out a cry of pleasure, before Grayson collapsed beside me.

After we caught our breath, I threw on my Creedence t-shirt and curled up in Grayson's arms, falling straight to sleep.

A gentle nudge stirred me awake and I discovered a tiny gift box resting on the pillow beside my head. Rubbing my eyes, I peered across at Grayson who lay completely still, watching me.

"Merry Christmas, beautiful," he said with a lazy smile. He rolled over and switched on the bedside lamp.

I glanced at the time and chuckled. 12:01am. *He really does love Christmas.* Climbing over my gift and onto him, I kissed him softly and smiled. "Merry Christmas. But your gift is under the tree, so you'll have to wait until morning."

"That's okay, I wanted you to open this in private."

Still straddling Grayson's lap, I peeked at him as I picked up the box. He sat up to meet my eye level and slid his hands over my butt. I untied the ribbon and lifted off the lid to reveal a delicate chain with an exquisite rainbow speckled opal glittering at the bottom. I gasped at its beauty.

"It reminded me of you," he said, sweeping forward a few strands of my coloured hair and giving them a gentle tug. "It's an Australian Opal."

I blinked away tears and smiled down at the precious stone. "Thank you. It's so beautiful."

Grayson took out the necklace and placed it around my neck, kissing me as he finished clasping it.

Warmth spread through my body as I touched the pendant. "I love it. I love you." I gasped as the words flew out unexpectedly.

The corner of Grayson's mouth twitched and his chest swelled, but he didn't call me out on it.

"Although…" he said, grazing his lips over mine. "I think it would look much better without this." He tugged on my t-shirt and proceeded to pull it over my head.

I giggled. "Better?"

"Much." He threw me onto the bed and grinned down at me mischievously. "Now for your next present."

Early Christmas morning, I crept downstairs to check on Luci, hoping to hide any evidence of his destructive behaviour before anyone else woke.

I froze in the hallway when the parlour doors opened and Grandpa poked his head out. "Josie," he whispered, motioning me over with his hand.

"Grandpa? Why are you up so early?" I asked, following him into the room.

He smiled and ushered me over to the window. "I'll show you."

I gazed outside, but all I could see was white. Blinking a few times to refocus, I soon realised it wasn't going to help. Snow blanketed every surface of the garden, glowing as the sun rose. All I wanted to do was capture its beauty, but I knew by the time I raced upstairs to get my camera, the moment would've passed.

"Betty used to paint in here, right by this window."

"I can see why; the view is beautiful."

A loud yawn sounded behind us and I spun around to find Luci curled up by the fireplace. My mouth fell open.

"Well, I couldn't have this fine beast sleeping in the mud room." He chuckled and returned to his chair beside Luci and the roaring fire.

"Thank you," I gushed, settling into the lounge opposite. "He's not going to want to go home."

"Fine with me." Grandpa chortled, pouring a creamy liquid into two mugs.

Eyeing him curiously as he passed one over, I brought it to my nose and raised my eyebrows. "It's a little early for eggnog, isn't it? Shouldn't we at least have breakfast first?"

"Well, it has eggs in it. Seems like a good breakfast to me."

I smirked and shrugged. "You have me there."

"But if you prefer to eat with *that* lot, you're most welcome."

My eyes widened. "No, no, this is fine."

Grandpa leant further back into his chair. "So, how long have you lived in New York?"

"Almost six years now," I replied, blowing on the hot liquid.

He tilted his head. "And Australia before that?"

"Yeah, most of my life." A twinge of homesickness crept up on me.

"Wow, must be quite the change. Are you thinking of returning some day?"

I fleetingly wondered if he was trying to pry information out of me for Grayson's parents, but he appeared genuinely interested in my life.

"For a holiday perhaps. I loved it there, but all my memories are laced with sadness now."

Grandpa nodded slowly. "Grayson mentioned you lost your parents in an accident. I lost mine early in life also."

My heart ached for him. "It's still hard to talk about," I said, swallowing the familiar lump in my throat.

"The pain never really goes away, but you'll find a way to move forward. It's hard to let people in after something like that, knowing what real loss feels like. But don't be afraid to. I'm lucky Betty was so persistent with me. If it wasn't for her, well, I never would have opened myself up to real love." He smiled sadly at the memory of his late wife.

I discreetly wiped away a lone tear as it rolled down my cheek, and drank another mouthful.

Tucking my feet under my body, I melted into the lounge while Grayson's grandfather spoke about his parents, his childhood, and told hilarious stories of sibling rivalry between Grayson and Adam as kids.

He didn't have much to say about his own son except, "I didn't tell him 'no' enough as a child." He blamed himself for not teaching his son to value people over money. "At some point, he lost sight of happiness and pursued what he thought I wanted from him; wealth and status."

The parlour doors flung open and Grayson barged into the room, exhaling when he saw me. "There you are. I couldn't find you or Luci, and thought you'd left." He spied Luci curled up in front of the fire and his shoulders relaxed.

"You're not leaving yet, are you?" Grandpa asked, with a frown. "Don't you worry about those bullies. You will not be insulted under my roof ever again."

"Thank you, Grandpa," Grayson said, before turning to me.

I met Grayson's pleading gaze. "I guess I could stay a little longer."

Grandpa clapped his hands. "Wonderful! Well, let's go open some presents then."

Even though the only gift to me under the tree was an exquisite silk scarf from Grayson's grandfather, my fingers played with the opal pendant hidden under my top. Grayson eyed me and smiled as he knelt down to pick up the remaining gifts under the tree.

"Last ones," he announced, handing one of the gifts to his parents. "To Mr. & Mrs. Harlow, love, Josie."

Caroline shifted uncomfortably in the Chesterfield lounge and William's back straightened.

"There was no need to get us anything," muttered Grayson's mum as she quickly unwrapped the present. She pulled out a small frame and stared at the image inside.

I watched on nervously. "Grayson and Adam had just finished working on the monthly projections for *Maude*. They were so proud of their achievement they didn't even notice I took the photo."

Caroline swallowed and William's body stiffened.

"Let me see that." Grayson's grandfather reached for it, but Caroline clutched it to her chest.

"There's one for you too." I smiled and Grayson handed over his matching gift. Grandpa quickly unwrapped it. "Oh, Josie. Now I see why Grayson wants you to have an exhibition. This is a beautiful photograph. You've captured their personalities perfectly."

My cheeks warmed and I lowered my gaze.

"To Mr. A. Harlow, love, Josie," Grayson said, tossing the present over to his brother.

We all watched as he tore away the wrapping to reveal a signed copy of Magnus Brayshaw's latest album. He burst out laughing, and when Grayson saw the gift, he joined in.

My forehead creased. "You said you were a fan."

Grayson shook his head as tears formed in the corners of his eyes. "It wasn't the band he was a fan of."

Adam winked at me and my mouth fell open. "Oh." My face fell into the palm of my hand and I groaned.

"Thank you, Josie. That's actually very thoughtful," Adam said.

Still chuckling, Grayson found the last gift sitting under the tree. "Ah, to me, love, Josie." He smiled warmly as I recovered from my embarrassment, and his grin only grew as he unwrapped his gift, carefully pulling out a cookie jar shaped like a Las Vegas slot machine.

"Charming." Caroline snorted, rising from her chair to leave the room.

Ignoring his mother, I focused on Grayson's smile. "Look inside."

He lifted the lid and peered into a jar before erupting into another fit of laughter. Hugging the jar close to his body, he leaned towards me with sparkling eyes. "Best. Present. Ever."

He slid his hand through my hair and pulled me in for a kiss, warming my cheeks.

Adam peeked into the jar full of penis shaped candy and scrunched up his face. "You guys are fucking weird."

Christmas dinner was a lot less eventful than the night before. Grayson's grandfather dominated the conversation while Caroline and William spoke endlessly about the Warren family, bringing up Melanie at every opportunity. Adam remained quiet.

Each time Grayson showed affection towards me, his parents shot each other worried glances, making me more and more uncomfortable. So, I did what most people would do: I ate. Christmas dinner was an elaborate spread of roast meats, vegetables, sauces, and desserts, and left me barely functioning as I slipped into a food coma. Grayson took me to bed not long after, and we both fell asleep, wrapped up in each other's arms.

Chapter 18

The following afternoon, I took Luci for a stroll while I photographed the picturesque gardens. There wasn't as much snow as the day before, giving me the perfect opportunity to explore more of the vast grounds. I left Grayson to spend time with his grandfather. I could tell they were close and he didn't see him often, so I decided to make myself scarce for a while.

As the sun was setting, Adam ambled over with an extra coat. "If you're going to stay out here any longer, you'll need this."

I warily slipped it over my shoulders. "Thank you."

"Still avoiding our parents?"

I chuckled. "Is it that obvious?"

"You really should come inside; your lips are turning blue."

"It's a better fate," I uttered, looking back towards the house.

Adam fell in step as I continued walking. "Listen, I'm sorry," he said, shoving his hands into his pockets to keep them warm. "If I'd known how deeply Grayson felt about you, I never would have pursued you, or treated you the way I did."

I lowered my eyes. "We shouldn't have kept it from you for so long."

"I understand why you did. I can be a pretty shitty brother at times, and an even shittier boss."

"You definitely keep everyone on their toes."

Adam held back a smile. "I'm lucky to have Grayson by my side. Without him, I wouldn't have half the success I've had."

"Or any employees." I peered up at him with a smirk.

Adam chuckled. "True."

We continued to wander around the property talking about work, while I took photos of Luci bounding through the oak trees, over patches of snow and splashing through puddles. Adam seemed much more passionate about the family business than Grayson, and I wondered if his father could see it too. His eyes lit up every time he talked about acquiring businesses and stripping them apart, whereas Grayson preferred to build them up and watch them grow. I guess that's what made them a good team.

I turned down a new path which led behind the six-car garage, and my eyes bulged. "Holy crap, is that a helicopter?"

Adam laughed. "Grandpa is an avid golfer, but he doesn't care for the drive."

"He can fly it?" I asked, with a gasp.

"God, no. He has a pilot on call."

I screwed up my nose. "How many staff does it take to look after one person?"

"Apart from Max, Grandpa has a driver, a pilot, a chef, a nurse, multiple housekeepers and a few gardeners."

My brow lifted. "Wow."

"That's nothing compared to my parents."

I shook my head in disbelief. The more I learnt about Grayson's parents, the more I disliked them, and clearly the feeling was mutual.

After a moment of reflection, I let out a long sigh. "They're never going to accept me, are they?"

Adam winced. "Our parents have never been comfortable with outsiders. When you have the sort of money we do, you need to be wary of anyone new who comes into your life."

"So, Melanie is perfect for Grayson," I said, lowering my eyes.

"Mel is a nutcase, but yes, she comes from good stock."

"You make her sound like a prized cow."

Adam chortled. "I have heard her described that way."

"If she's such 'good stock', why don't *you* marry her?"

His eyes went round. "*Me? Marry Mel?* Hell no, I'm never getting married. In my opinion, it's an archaic ritual. Why settle with one woman, when I can have many? Plus, I'm married to my job. I don't need, or want, the distraction."

I glanced up at him. "And your parents are happy about that?"

"As long as their bank balance is going up, they're ecstatic. I made it clear to them early on I have no intention of giving them grandchildren, so that's on Gray."

"Perhaps you just haven't met the right girl yet," I said with a shrug.

"I don't believe in 'the one' bullshit. That's just for lazy fuckers who don't get laid as much as I do. I'm perfectly content with my life the way it is."

I laughed at his frankness. *He won't even see her coming.*

When we walked into the mud room an hour later, urgent voices erupted from deep within the house. My worried gaze shot to Adam, who left to find the source, and I hurried after him until he came to a standstill at the open doors of the parlour. I sidled up beside him to watch the scene unfold.

"What do you mean she's in the hospital?" Grayson snapped, staring at his mother who was pacing the room.

Caroline drew in a shaky breath. "All we know is she was found unconscious at a friend's place, with a bottle of pills beside her. They're pumping her stomach as we speak."

Grayson ran his hands through his hair, the pain on his face was palpable. "Fuck. Was it deliberate?"

"We won't know for certain until she wakes. But we can only assume, given the rough time she's been having since you called off the wedding."

"Caroline!" Grandpa barked, tapering his gaze at his daughter-in-law.

"She sounded fine last time we spoke," Grayson said, pinching the bridge of his nose.

Caroline shook her head. "Well, finding out your fiancé is seeing another woman would certainly change that, don't you think?"

"She not my fiancé, and how the fuck did she even find out?"

"Well you haven't exactly been discreet," she bit. "Not according to the rumour mill."

"Fucking Staci," Grayson muttered, lowering his head. "I should've known she wouldn't keep her mouth shut."

"There is only one person to blame here, and it's not Staci Warner."

Grayson let out an exasperated sigh. "I need to go."

Grandpa rested his hand on his shoulder. "I'll get the helicopter and jet ready. Don't worry, son, you'll be there in no time."

"Thanks, Grandpa," he said softly.

"We're coming with you," his mother stated. "That girl is like a daughter to us."

"You need to fix this, Grayson," His father spoke in a low voice. The threat was evident.

Grayson pursed his lips before turning to leave. When his eyes collided with mine, he froze.

"Remember, this is a private matter," his father continued. "Make sure *she's* aware of that."

Grayson closed the distance between us in a few strides. He took my elbow in his hand and guided me away without looking back.

"What's going on, Gray?"

He ignored my question and took me upstairs to our bedroom, leaving me standing in the doorway while he retrieved his suitcase.

"Is Melanie okay?"

He lifted his glistening eyes. "I don't know."

"Gray..." I stepped towards him, but he flinched.

"All I know is that she needs me and I have to go. I'm sorry, Josie, but it's complicated and messy, and I don't have time to get into this with you right now. I have to get home."

"Of course," I whispered, lowering my gaze so he wouldn't see the quiver of my lower lip.

"I'll arrange for Adam to take you and Luci home in the morning."

He shoved his clothes into the suitcase and zipped it up, before turning back my way. "We'll talk soon." As he wheeled his suitcase out the door, he paused beside me. "I'm sorry to leave you like this." Grayson placed his palm over my cheek and kissed me softly, staring into my eyes like he was taking in every little detail. It made me wonder how long he planned to be gone, but before I had a chance to ask, he disappeared out the door.

While Adam filled the car with gas, I gave Luci a toilet break before heading inside to grab some coffees for the road. I was in desperate need of caffeine after waiting up all night for a call or text from Grayson that never came. Walking back to the car, I noticed Adam on his cell phone. He saw me approaching and his lips formed my name to the person on the other end. *Grayson.* I quickened my step, desperate to talk to him.

As I climbed back in, Adam muttered his goodbye and slipped the phone back into his pocket, without explanation. *Perhaps it wasn't Grayson.*

I placed his coffee into the drink holder between us, but held mine tightly in my hands as Adam started up the car and pulled back out onto the road.

"Was that Grayson?" I asked hesitantly.

He cleared his throat. "Yeah, he's with Mel now. Apparently she's stable, but still asleep."

"Oh…That's good news." I was genuinely relieved, but a sharp pain radiated through my chest. I glanced down at my phone, willing it to light up.

Adam threw me a sideways glance, before gazing back at the road ahead. "He probably just expected me to relay the news. I'm sure he'll contact you soon."

"He really cares about her, doesn't he?" I asked, keeping my eyes on the passing scenery.

"He always has. They've been through a lot together."

I nodded, pretending to know, but I really had no idea. Grayson never spoke about her and I never asked. I took a sip of coffee and let it burn my throat. It was a welcome distraction.

"That's why this whirlwind romance of yours has taken everyone by surprise," he continued. "We all just expected they'd get back together. Clearly Melanie did too."

My heart sank. "Do you think that's why she…is that why she's in hospital? She found out about us and…hurt herself?"

"It seems that way." Adam sighed. "Just like the last time they broke up."

"They've broken up before?"

"Yeah, back in college. Grayson ended it and Melanie went off the rails. Started drinking and partying too much, anything to get his attention."

"Why can't she just let him go?"

"Because she's dependent on him. Always has been. And Grayson thinks he's responsible for her."

"Why on earth would he be responsible for a fully-grown woman?"

Adam went momentarily quiet as his shoulders tensed. "He hasn't told you, has he?"

My head snapped back to his. "Told me *what*?"

"Fuck Grayson," he muttered, gripping his steering wheel tighter. He glanced my way. "Why do you think they got engaged so young?"

I winced. "I assumed they were in love."

"*In love?*" he snickered. "That maybe came later, but not in the beginning. If Grayson wasn't so shit scared of her father, I doubt he would've proposed at all."

"I...I don't understand."

Adam took his eyes off the road to meet mine. "He got her pregnant."

"What?!" My eyes bulged and my heart lurched.

Adam rambled on like my brain didn't just explode all over the interior of the car. "I guess he was trying to do what was right. A baby out of wedlock would be the ultimate embarrassment for our families, not to mention social suicide for Melanie."

Bile crept up my throat. "Gr...Grayson...has a child?" *How did I not know this? How could he not tell me?!* Coffee spat out of my cup as my hands shook, burning my fingers, but I didn't feel a thing.

Adam glanced my way, clearly seeing my distress. "No, Josie. *Shit.*" With a quick glance in the rear-view mirror he pulled over to the side of the road and stopped the car. He reached over and took the coffee from my hands, placing it in the spare cup holder. "There was no baby. Melanie lost it about a month later."

Oh god. Relief and despair churned my stomach. "Jesus..."

Adam sank back into his chair. "It got pretty messy after that, but Grayson didn't leave her side. She came to rely on him, and with the added pressure from our parents, I think he found it easier to stay engaged."

I screwed up my nose. "If she's such a hot mess, why are your parents so hell bent on him marrying her?"

Adam chuckled. "Do you know how much Melanie Warren's family is worth? If Grayson marries her and our companies merge, we'll be one of the most powerful families in the country."

"So, this is all about money?"

"Money, power, status…it all goes hand in hand," Adam responded with a casual shrug.

"It's all bullshit. It all means nothing if you're unhappy."

A small smile touched Adam's lips. "I can see why Grayson likes you, he used to think the same way."

I crossed my arms and stared out the window. "Maybe he still does."

Adam pulled the car back onto the road. "Regardless, Grayson has always done what's best for the family. Ours *and* hers."

My gaze tapered in on his profile as he drove. "What's that supposed to mean?"

"Just that he has responsibilities."

I shifted uncomfortably in my seat, knowing where the conversation was heading.

"Look, I'm not saying he has to give you up. He'll just have to learn to be more discreet when he's with you."

"Right." I chuckled in disbelief. "Because that's all I can be to someone like him…a seedy love affair."

"Josie, I just want you to know what you're getting yourself into."

I pursed my lips. "Well, there's no chance of that."

Leaning forward, I upped the volume of the radio until it eliminated any chance of continuing the conversation. As the Def Leppard song *Love Bites* filled the car, I curled up in my seat and closed my eyes. It wasn't long before I succumbed to sleep, freeing myself from my noisy mind and heavy heart.

As the car rolled to a stop, I grudgingly opened my eyes and stared up at my apartment building. It seemed minuscule compared to Harlow Manor, but it was home. I didn't need a butler, or a cleaner, or anyone to wipe my arse, because unlike Grayson's family, I was comfortable on my own.

Adam jumped out of the car to help me with my bags, but I beat him to it.

"I've got it," I said quickly, picking up my suitcase and Luci's lead. "Thanks for the ride, it was…enlightening."

"No problem," he uttered, leaning back against the car with his arms crossed.

An awkward silence fell between us, and I gave Luci's lead a gentle tug towards the stairs. "I guess I'll see you at work."

Adam nodded. "I'll be running things while Grayson's gone."

"Great," I murmured through my tight smile.

"I'll behave. I promise." He chuckled, before climbing back into the car and winding down his window.

I rolled my eyes, and turned to find his expression had morphed into something more serious. "Look after yourself, Josie."

With a sad smile, I shrugged. "It's what I do best."

I needed to hear his voice. It had officially been twenty-four hours since I'd last spoken to Grayson and I was not okay. He hadn't returned any of my calls or texts, and I was beginning to worry. Before heading to bed, I decided to make one last attempt.

Me: **Is everything ok? I'm worried.**

Three little dots appeared and my heart leapt. I waited for the message to appear on my cell, but it never came. "Where did you go?" I murmured, staring down at my phone. A few minutes later, they reappeared.

Grayson: **All ok.**

That's it? *That's fucking it?!* My blood boiled. I'd been waiting all day for an update, and all he could manage were two fucking words. I drew in a shaky breath as my eyes welled, but I blinked away the tears.

After everything Adam told me on the way home, I realised there was a lot we needed to talk about, but not over the phone. With the Melanie situation looming over him, he didn't need the extra pressure. So as much as it hurt, I placed my phone back on the nightstand and closed my eyes, letting a stray tear roll down my cheek.

It wasn't until the next night, that my ringtone infiltrated my dreams.

"Grayson?" I answered in a husky voice, rubbing my eyes. I glanced at the clock. It was 1am.

"Hey, Jos, sorry for calling so late," he whispered.

I sat up in my bed. "Why are you whispering?"

There was silence on the other end and I heard the click of a door closing.

Grayson cleared his throat. "No reason," he said, returning to a normal level. "How was the drive back with Adam?"

"Fine," I replied, shortly.

He sighed. "I'm sorry it's taken me a while to call you. My phone's been off most of the time. Hospital policy."

"You called Adam." I couldn't hold back the bitterness in my voice. *Hospital policy my arse.*

"I'm sorry, Jos, this stuff with Mel, it's really messed up and I'm trying to keep you out of it."

My jaw clenched as I held back my tears. "Clearly."

"That's not what I meant, I—"

"So, where are you now?" I interrupted. I hated the way I sounded, but I couldn't control my mouth.

Grayson was quiet for a moment. "What do you mean?"

"Well your phone is on now, so obviously you're not at the hospital."

A guilty silence followed. "I'm at Melanie's parents' house. They hired a nurse so she could come home."

"And you're staying there? With her?"

"Just until she's feeling better," he said quickly. "She's in a bad way and needs my support."

"Shouldn't she be going to rehab or something?"

"We're dealing with it privately. If this gets out, it will ruin her."

What the fuck? "Isn't her health more important than what people think?"

"You don't understand," he said, tiredly. "We look after our own."

Pain seared through my chest. "Of course, how stupid of me."

"Jos, it's complicated."

My nostrils burned. "It seems like the only complication right now is me."

"You're not a compli—" He paused when a female voice sounded in the background.

"Who are you speaking to?" she asked.

"Go back to bed, Mel. You need to rest," Grayson replied.

"Is that her?" she asked.

Grayson sighed. "I need to go, I'll speak to you soon."

Before I could respond, he hung up the phone, leaving me breathless.

As I sunk into my bed that still smelt like him, I burst into tears. How could everything change so quickly? A couple of nights ago, he told me he loved me and I returned that love, but now he was on the other side of the country with the woman he was supposed to marry. I wanted to be okay with it. I tried to be okay with it. But I wasn't. Not in the slightest.

Chapter 19

I lay in bed the next morning, tracing my fingers around the delicate opal pendant that rested at the base of my neck, staring at the message on my cell phone.

Grayson: **Melanie's parents want me to stay for a few more days. Please understand, I'm the only one who can get through to her.**

My heart trusted him, but my head kept screaming 'Bullshit'! His connection to Melanie was much deeper than I imagined, and it made me wonder if Adam was right.

Me: **When do you think you'll be back?**

Grayson: **I don't know. Dad has called a family meeting, so I'll have to stay until Adam can get back here.**

Was he stalling? Was he having second thoughts about us? Had Melanie convinced him to stay with her? An avalanche of self-doubt tumbled through my mind, causing me to do something I'd never done before.

Opening the web browser on my phone, I typed 'Melanie Warren' into the search bar. Moments later, my screen filled with photographs, articles and posts relating to the Californian beauty. Just like I remembered, she was textbook gorgeous. Blonde and blue-eyed with scarlet red lips. There wasn't an image in sight that depicted anything other than perfection.

I scrolled down to what looked like an official social media account and clicked through.

381K Followers. *Wow.*

Her grid was full of glitz and glamour, holiday snaps, and selfies. So many selfies. Every time I attempted a selfie, my chin multiplied and my eyes crossed, or I'd drop the phone on my face, almost breaking my nose. Melanie knew exactly how to arrange herself, the precise way to tilt her head and pout her lips, all while steadily holding a cell phone in her hands. It was impressive.

I scrolled through the images until I caught sight of the same photo Grayson's mother sent to the newspaper after Thanksgiving. I read the caption.

Surprising my man at Thanksgiving #togetheragain

I took a deep breath. Grayson explained that one and I believed him. *Move on, Josie.*

As I delved further back, Grayson featured in almost every second post. All the photos, captions, hashtags and comments made my head spin. It was too much. I knew Grayson had a life before he met me, but I never imagined myself having front row tickets to the re-play. As much as I didn't want to look, I couldn't help but be drawn into their perfect high society world.

My heart sank. No wonder Grayson's family were shocked about me. I was nothing like this girl, and never would be. She was born into their lifestyle and I was clearly an unwelcome visitor.

Not one to dwell on the past, I scrolled back to Melanie's more recent posts. There were countless images of her sun-baking, cocktail-drinking and calorie counting until there was nothing. After Christmas day, total radio silence. My stomach churned, knowing I was part of the reason. Had she not found out about Grayson and I, she never would have hurt herself. The guilt weighed heavily upon my shoulders, and Grayson's reluctance to share her progress only made me feel worse.

Although the uncertainty of where I stood with Grayson was gnawing away at my heart, I was determined to give him the time he needed. I couldn't compete with a girl like Melanie, and I wouldn't. The last thing he needed in his life was more pressure, and as much as I wanted to fight for him, I needed to prepare myself. There was obviously much about his life I didn't know, and the fact he hadn't told me everything about Melanie made me think there was some validity to what Adam had told me about their relationship.

Dropping my phone into the empty space beside me, I rolled onto my back. My vision glazed over as I stared at the ceiling, repeatedly telling myself how fucking stupid I was to get involved with a man I barely knew.

As the new year approached, I kept myself busy watching bad horror movies, eating ice cream and drinking wine...all my usual avoidance behaviour. But I managed to balance it out with long walks in the park with Luci and my camera, getting lost in other people's worlds and emotions. Anything to avoid my own.

While Luci bolted around the dog park, I took my phone from my pocket and stared down at the empty screen. It was New Year's Eve and still no word from Grayson. My thumb hovered over the phone and I reluctantly tapped on Melanie's social media account which I'd accidently-on-purpose, saved to my favourites list.

Four new posts had been added since my last visit and my heart beat rapidly as the images loaded onto the screen, each one cutting deeper than the last.

The first one, uploaded December 28th, was a picture I knew well, for it was the view I'd been waking up to for the last few months. It was Grayson, sprawled out in bed, fast asleep and presumably naked. The caption read:

Sorry for being MIA the last few days. I've been preoccupied #sleepinglikeababy

In the second photo, uploaded December 29th, Melanie held Grayson's hand as they strolled along the beach. She smiled at the screen, while he looked out towards the ocean.

Just like the old days #reminiscing

The third photo, uploaded yesterday, showed Grayson dressed in a tux and Melanie dolled up in a glamourous gown at some event.

A charity that means so much to us #doingitforthekids

But the fourth, uploaded just seconds ago, split my heart in two.

It wasn't Melanie's flawless smile that caught my breath, or her hand intimately grazing Grayson's cheek. It was the sharp daggers of light piecing the camera lens, each one originating from the source of my turmoil. The diamond on her finger.

New year, new beginnings #itsbackon

The pain in my heart multiplied with each 'like' and supportive comment that accumulated underneath. I wanted to vomit.

"Excuse me!" a flustered woman in her early sixties called out from across the field. She frantically waved her hand as she marched over with a miniature poodle trotting by her side. "Excuse me!"

I broke out of my trance when I realised she was approaching me.

"Is that your dog?" she asked, pointing towards Luci and her new-found friends. "The big ugly one."

Keep your cool, Josie. "If by ugly, you mean beautiful, then yes. He is mine."

The lady scoffed at my response and continued. "Well, I doubt you noticed with your head stuck in that cell phone, but he has deposited a rather large…" She cleared her throat. "Poop on the lawn over there. So, if you could be a responsible dog owner and clean it up, that would be great."

My head snapped to hers. "Excuse me?"

"You need to clean up your dog's…"

"Oh, I heard that part, and I intend to, but there is absolutely no need to be a bitch about it."

The lady grasped her chest. "How dare you!"

Anger rushed through me. "No, how dare you!" I bit. "What makes you think I wouldn't pick up after my own dog? Is it the way I'm dressed? The colour of my hair? Or perhaps my botox-free face gave it away?"

Her eyes grew larger as I continued my rant.

"Seriously, what is it? What makes you think you're better than I am?"

Another two ladies appeared by her side. "Is this lady bothering you, Patricia?" One spoke, narrowing her eyes at me.

My mouth fell open. "Bothering her?! She approached me! All you upper-class snobs just stick together, don't you?" With clenched teeth, I pivoted in the direction of Luci and stormed away, pressing my trembling lips together.

"Stupid cows," I muttered as I pulled a poop bag from the dispenser on Luci's lead.

Leaning over to scoop up Luci's enormous turd, my cell burst into song and Grayson's name flashed onto my screen. My heart lurched and I fumbled my phone, dropping it from my hands into the pile of shit below.

"Fuck." I gasped, hovering above it.

It continued to ring, but the steaming faeces surrounding it screamed 'do not answer', and I took it as an omen. The universe couldn't have made it any clearer.

Part of me considered abandoning the phone altogether, but I couldn't afford a new one. Thankfully, I had a spare bag and managed to pluck it out without making any skin to poop contact. I would figure out how to wash it later, once I got the hell out of there.

As the group of snotty nosed women watched on, I attached Luci's leash to his collar and dragged him away from his favourite place, lifting my middle finger as I retreated.

Slamming the door as I got home, I threw the vibrating poop bag in the kitchen sink and marched over to my dad's record player. Squeezing my eyes to hinder the inevitable tears, I ran my hand over his vast collection of music, praying for guidance.

Laughing at the blind selection of *The Stranger* by Billy Joel, I opted for something a little louder. The bold guitar intro of AC/DC's *Back in Black* filled my apartment as I gloved up and precariously removed the cell phone from the foul-smelling bag.

My teeth gnashed as I gazed at the screen.

Grayson: **4 missed calls**

Grayson: **Please pick up. I need to talk to you about something. It's important.**

"A little late, Grayson," I grumbled, trying to push him from my mind.

With more force than necessary, I switched off my phone and turned on the tap.

As I incisively scrubbed away the grime, I thought about my parents. The despair I felt after losing them was as real in that moment as the day it happened, except *they* didn't choose to leave.

The water flowing from the faucet mirrored the tears spilling down my face as all the emotion I held onto so tightly crept to the surface. A sob rattled my body, causing my cell to slip from my soapy hands into the shallow water below. "No," I cried, desperately fishing it out and shaking off the water.

I grabbed a plastic bag from the cupboard and filled it with rice, before throwing my phone inside and sealing it shut. I knew the protocol. After losing my last phone to the toilet bowl a year ago, Reed showed me what to do if it happened again. *It did.* Hopefully my phone's brief swim wouldn't cause any permanent damage, but only time would tell.

Just before midday, I crawled back into bed with puffy, bloodshot eyes and stewed over Adam's revelations. He may have been harsh, but at least he was honest. He had a whole twenty-nine years of intel on Grayson to know his next move, and I'd stupidly ignored him. All I had with Grayson was seven months of…what? A relationship? *Barely.* We were a secret. A secret that almost cost the life of the woman he clearly loved.

Loud banging jerked me out of my sleep. It was dark out, but I had no idea what time it was, or what year, for that matter. I dragged my feet to the front door, rubbing my swollen eyes and looked through the peephole. A huge blue eyeball filled my vision and I stumbled backwards. *What the fuck?*

"Come on, Josie, open up! I know you're in there," Amy called out.

Luci whimpered at my feet as I opened the door a fraction. "How did you get up here?"

Amy grinned. "I snuck in behind your neighbour." She pushed past my lax stance and I followed her to the living room. "Why is your phone off? I've been trying to call you all afternoon," she said, leaning over to pat Luci's head.

"I've…um…been in bed."

Amy turned my way as I lowered my eyes. "Oh no, are you sick?"

"No." I exhaled and lifted my despondent gaze to meet hers. Her face fell. "Josie, what happened?"

I gave her the short version, minus the emotion I was trying to compartmentalise.

Amy's eyebrows rose as she assessed the images from Melanie's social media account on her own cell phone. "I guess even I get things wrong sometimes," she uttered with a long sigh.

"It's fine." I shrugged, refusing to let myself shed another tear. "I guess he was just sowing his wild oats before settling down with someone more…suited."

She reached for my hand. "I don't think it was like tha—"

"Ames, I don't want to talk about it anymore," I said, clenching my jaw. "I just want to forget."

Amy fell momentarily silent. "Well I can definitely help with that."

I peered up at her, half expecting her to pull out some magic crystal, but she smiled instead.

"Go get dressed," she said, pushing me towards my bedroom. "We have a new year to celebrate."

As I pulled my soft leather jacket over my vintage Bowie t-shirt, I reviewed my look in the mirror. My fitted ripped jeans and heels topped off my rocker chick vibe, making me feel sexy, and purposely intimidating. I planned on getting drunk, not hit on.

"Are you ready?" Amy called out from the living room. "I told Pete we'd be at The Edge in twenty."

I stared at my reflection through a haze. "Almost." With sharp ache in my chest, I unclasped my delicate opal necklace and let it slide from my hand onto the bathroom bench below. "Let's go!"

Midnight was approaching, and I was well on my way to drunkville. Most of the *Maude* team were there, because we barely had time to maintain friendships outside of work. Amy was making moves on some hot British backpacker, and Pete was entertaining two women, both vying for his attention before the clock struck twelve. I just sat alone in the booth, sipping my whiskey, watching and wondering.

Perhaps I was wrong to give up on Pete. Perhaps my feelings would have grown for him, had I just let him past the walls I'd built. *The walls Grayson tore down.*

Pete was warm, friendly, smart, handsome, and way closer to my league than Grayson would ever be. I peered up at him through a wine fuelled glaze and caught his kind eyes.

"Josie?" Lines appeared on his forehead as he examined my face. "Are you okay?"

I let out an awkward laugh. "Just peachy," I said, but my lower lip trembled.

Ignoring his company, he slipped into the booth. "What's wrong?" he asked, bringing his arm around me.

"It doesn't matter. Not anymore," I murmured, but the falling tears outed me as a liar. As he rubbed my back, I hid my face in the crook of his neck attempting to settle my sobs with long, deep breaths.

"Wanna talk about it?" he asked, his voice full of concern. "I know we're not going out anymore, but we're still friends, right?"

I nodded and smiled sadly. "You're a good guy, Pete. I'm sorry I was such a bitch to you when we were going out."

"You weren't a bitch," he said with a soft chuckle. "You wouldn't even know how to be. You're perfect, Jos, you just don't give yourself enough credit. Why do you think I keep trying my luck with you?"

I stared into his eyes—so different to Grayson's—and wondered if I could be happy with him. As the countdown rolled onto midnight, his gaze lowered to my lips. My heart beat accelerated when he leant forward, pressing his lips to mine as cheers erupted around us. I wanted to feel something, *anything,* but there was nothing.

Jerking away, I glanced up at Pete. "I'm sorry, I can't do this."

"Josie, I don't care about the rules anymore, I'm..."

His voice faded into the background when my gaze collided with familiar green eyes across the room. Grayson looked away, turned and exited the bar before anyone noticed his arrival.

"I have to go," I uttered, pushing past Pete and rushing out the door into the freezing night air. Spotting his receding trench coat, I marched up behind him. "What are you doing here, Grayson?"

He stopped dead and turned around slowly. His face wore no emotion. "I was hoping to ring in the New Year with my—"

"Your what? Your side piece?!" My voice rose with my anger.

His shook his head. "What?"

"Your mistress? Or is there some other word your kind uses to describe someone like me?"

Grayson's mouth opened, but only fog escaped. "Josie, I'm not sure what you've heard, but—"

"Heard?!" I gasped. "I've heard nothing from you! But Melanie's photos sure helped fill in the gaps."

His eyes tapered. "What photos?" As if answering his own question, his face fell. Grayson quickly pulled his cell from his pocket and searched his phone. Scrolling through the images that would haunt me forever, he ran his hand down his stubbled face and growled. "She wasn't supposed to post this until after I'd spoken to you."

My eyes burned. "How could you?"

His shoulders slumped. "Fuck, Jos, this isn't what it looks like," he said, taking a step towards me.

"It isn't?" My eyebrows shot up. "Because it looks like she's wearing an engagement ring."

Grayson ran his hands through his hair. "Just let me explain," he pleaded, moving closer.

"You should've been honest with me from the beginning. If I'd known how much she still meant to you, how much you'd been through together, I never would've got myself into this mess." I wiped a tear from my cheek before it froze to my face, and turned to leave.

"Josie, wait!" He grabbed my arm and pulled me back.

I shook my head, trying to hold myself together. "I'm not going to be the other woman when you marry her, Gray."

His voice softened as his other hand reached for my face. "I'm not marrying her."

"Your ring is on her finger!" I growled, shoving him away.

He stumbled back in surprise, but quickly recovered. "That doesn't mean anything!"

"It means everything!" I yelled, glaring at him through blurring vision.

He stood there silently, not moving except for the twitch in his jaw.

The lump in my throat grew and I swallowed it down. "I don't fit into your world, Grayson."

"So, Peter is a better match for you, is he?" he asked, pursing his lips as he gazed back towards the bar.

I looked away. "Like Melanie is for you."

The heat in his gaze burned. "You can't believe that."

"You clearly do though." I took a step backwards.

Grayson eliminated the distance between us in less than a second, before slamming his mouth down on mine. I let myself taste him one last time before pushing him away.

"No!" Tears grazed my cheeks as a small sob escaped my mouth. "I can't do this." Not meeting his eyes, I spun on my heel and left before my words or lips betrayed me.

Chapter 20

Shittiest. Year. Ever. That was my prediction. I spent the entire first day of the year in bed, curled up with Luci, crying my heart out into his shaggy fur. The doorbell buzzed incessantly, but I refused to answer it. Peeking out my bedroom window, I watched Grayson pace the sidewalk below, waiting for me to let him in. *Ha! No fucking chance.*

Later that night, while rummaging for some food, I discovered my phone still sweating away on the kitchen bench. Ignoring the forty-eight-hour rule, I opened the bag, brushed off the excess rice, and turned it on. The screen lit up and my heart raced as I prepared myself for a tirade of messages from Grayson. Surprisingly, there were none.

Pete: **That was a spectacular disappearing act you performed last night. Do you think we should talk about what happened?**

Fuck.

Me: **Sorry, Pete. Too many tequilas. What happened last night?**

Pete: **Nothing to be embarrassed about. I'll see you tomorrow.**

I groaned. Tomorrow couldn't come slow enough.

My chest pounded as I walked up the hallway to my office. Grayson's door was closed, but with a quick glance through the glass, I noticed he had company. My heart dropped. It was Pete, and by the look on his face, he wasn't talking about racquetball.

A few minutes later, Grayson's door closed and Pete strode down the hall with an empty cardboard box in his arms. My temper sparked, but instead following Pete, I marched into Grayson's office.

"That got your attention," he uttered, without looking up from his computer.

My gaze tapered as my blood boiled. "What did you do?"

He leant back into his chair, finally meeting my eyes. "I didn't *do* anything."

"You just fired Pete because we kissed, didn't you?!" He opened his mouth to speak, but I didn't let him. "Then you should fire me too!" *What am I doing?!*

"I probably should," he said, nonchalantly. "But *Maude* needs you."

I crossed my arms. "*Maude* needs me?"

"I haven't been keeping you around because we're sleeping together, Josie. You're great at your job."

"What about Pete? He's a great accountant."

"He's replaceable," he said with a shrug.

"*Everyone* is replaceable."

His hard gaze didn't budge from mine. "Not everyone. Not you."

I looked away as my breathing shallowed. "This is ridiculous. I should go," I muttered, preparing my escape. He wasn't going to make this easy.

Avoidance was my only defence against Grayson. If I didn't see him, I didn't have to look into his warm hazel eyes, or notice how the right side of his smile hitched a little higher than the left, or have my heart skip every time I heard his voice. I could just pretend like nothing happened between us and move on. *Who am I kidding?*

"I came by your apartment yesterday. *Twice* actually."

"You shouldn't have," I grumbled.

"You have to let me explain what's going on," Grayson said, taking off his glasses and rubbing his eyes. "But it has to be in person. I can't do it over the phone."

"If it's to clear your conscience, I'm not interested."

Grayson rose from his chair. "Josie, about the engagement, it's all—"

Adam stepped into the room, clearing his throat to announce his arrival. "Dad's on his way up, Gray. You need to wrap this up." His eyes darted to mine and then back to his brother.

Grayson's eyes bulged. "What is *he* doing here?"

A shiver rolled over my body. William Harlow was the coldest man I'd ever met and he gave me the innate urge to run and hide.

"He says he wants to check on a few things," Adam replied.

"Since when is he interested in…" Grayson's gaze panned to mine. "Fuck."

A line formed between my eyes. "What?"

"Josie, you need to go back to your office." Grayson's voice was gruff and full of warning.

I let go of a little chuckle. "Oh, but I wanted to say hi." My voice dripped with sarcasm as I left his office, shaking my head at my abrupt dismissal.

"Does she know what's at stake here?" I overheard Adam ask before closing Grayson's door behind me.

My brow furrowed as I returned to my desk. *At stake? What the hell is he talking about?*

Before I had a chance to analyse his words, William Harlow III strode down the hallway with Linda fussing at his side. Adam stepped out of Grayson's office to greet his father and guided him towards his office, while Grayson held my gaze through the glass. Lowering his tired eyes, he trailed after them.

For the next hour, Amy and I threw each other worried glances as their muffled argument travelled down the hallway. I couldn't understand what was being said, but whatever it was, it left an unsettled feeling in my gut.

My computer chimed and broke the tension. It was group message to all staff.

P. Wallis: **I know it's short notice, but I'm having goodbye drinks tonight @ The Edge. I hope to see you there.**

Why would he want *me* there? I'm the reason he was fired.

The computer chimed again, but this time it was from Amy.

A. Mitchell: **You going?**

I wasn't ready to face him. The guilt was too much.

J. Spencer: **I'm not feeling up to it. Tell Pete I'll call him in a few days.**

A. Mitchell: **Totally understand *sad face* Hope you're ok.**

My ears pricked at the sound of the conference door opening. The footsteps down the hall were unlike Grayson's, or Adam's. They were heavier, full of purpose and…slowing at my door.

I lifted my gaze to find their father glaring down at me. I drew in my breath and stood. "Mr. Harlow."

He wore no emotion. "I'm glad to hear your relationship with my son has dissolved. It will be in your best interest to keep it that way."

And with that, he continued down the corridor, leaving me to process his words and the underlying threat.

For the rest of the week, Grayson yelled abuse at everyone. Thankfully his father hadn't made another appearance, but his presence prevailed in Grayson's demeanour. Poor Linda copped the brunt of it, while the rest of the staff hid behind their computers trying not to draw attention to themselves. Surprisingly, Adam became good cop to Grayson's bad.

"Grayson wanted me to give you this," Adam said, handing me a copy of the latest edition of *Maude* to add to my collection.

I tilted my head around his intimidating stance and found Grayson in his office. "He couldn't do it himself?"

"Under the current circumstances, I think it'll be wise to limit your interaction with him for a while."

I peered up at Adam, making sure I made direct eye contact. "I have no intention of pursuing an engaged man, if that's what you're implying."

Adam's brow creased. "That's not…" His voice trailed off with a sigh.

"What?"

"Nothing," he muttered, shaking his head. "Grayson's a big boy. He can clean up his own mess." Swivelling on his heel, he strode towards the door.

"Adam, wait!"

He slowed his pace and turned back to me, while I reached into my bag. Slipping out the necklace I couldn't bring myself to wear anymore, I held it out to him.

His body tensed as he stared at the pendant in my hand. "What are you doing?"

"Can you give this back to him?" I held it out, but he didn't move. "Please?"

After a moment of hesitation, he snatched it from my hand. "Fine, but I'm done being a messenger pigeon," he growled, before marching out of my office and straight into Grayson's. He dropped the necklace on the desk in front of him and Grayson's shoulders fell. His eyes slowly travelled to mine, and I quickly dropped my gaze, swallowing the lump in my throat.

———

"Is Pete okay?" I asked Amy as we settled down for lunch. "He hasn't answered any of my calls or texts"

"Jos, he's in Mexico. I doubt he's even looking at his phone. Haven't you seen his posts?"

My mouth fell open. "Mexico? Since when?"

"Since our boss waived his two weeks' notice."

"Two weeks' notice?" My eyebrows drew together. "But I thought he was fired."

"Fired?! Pete?" Amy laughed. "Why on earth would you think that?"

"Because...well..." My thoughts travelled back to the day I stormed into Grayson's office, firing accusations he neither confirmed or denied. "Shit."

"He accepted a job at a big accounting firm in Midtown. Some swanky corporate company that's way more his style. Apparently William was so pissed off when Pete handed in his notice, he told him to pack up his things and leave immediately. I believe it too. He's been a total dick since...well...you know."

"I know." I tore the crust from my sandwich. "Everyone around here seems to be paying for my epic mistake."

"This isn't your fault, Jos."

I nodded unconsciously, but the guilt churned my soul.

"Is *you know who* still coming by your apartment?" Amy asked, in a low voice.

"Every night," I said, with a sigh. "I don't know why he bothers, I'm not going to let him in."

"Maybe you should."

My irritation flared. "Why? There's nothing he can say to make this hurt any less."

"Okay, okay," Amy said, raising both hands. "It's just tha…"

Our conversation halted when a couple of guys from the new digital team entered the lunchroom, and I quickly wiped away the tears that stung my eyes.

"You'd think a man engaged to Melanie Warren would be a little happier," Simon muttered as he dumped his tuna salad on the table.

Amy discreetly glanced my way as I pretended to nibble on my sandwich. My jaw was too tight to take a bite. I needed to get out of there.

Brian chuckled. "I know, right. If I had a woman like that, I'd…"

As if on cue, Grayson sauntered into the lunchroom carrying an empty coffee cup and my chest tightened.

Simon cleared his throat to cover Brian's words. "William, I hear congratulations are in order."

Grayson's hard gaze darted to mine, then back to Simon. "Thank you, Simon."

"Have you set a date yet?" Brian asked.

Scooping up my leftovers, I manoeuvred my way around Grayson and out of the lunchroom before I could hear the rest of the conversation.

Amy shadowed me down the hall and pulled me into the photocopy room, shutting the door as I sank to the floor, struggling to breathe. Crouching beside me, she took my hand and massaged a pressure point to help me relax. "I don't know what's going on with you two, but your energy is all over the place. You really need to talk to him."

"There's no point. He made his choice. I was stupid to believe we could be anything more."

"You weren't stupid, you were brave," she said, running her hand down my hair. "You finally let someone in. That takes guts."

A little snort erupted from my mouth. "And look how it turned out."

Amy smiled sadly and squeezed my hand. "You'll get through this, I promise."

"Not if I keep working here. I need to find a new job."

"No, you can't leave," she pleaded. "No one else understands me."

"I don't think I have a choice."

Struggling to concentrate that afternoon, I opened a new window on my computer and started my job search. It wasn't surprising when nothing came up with the same wage and skill set. I considered myself lucky to have this job; not only was I paid to take photos, I got to see them published in a popular magazine every month. It also put a healthy sum into my savings account each week, pushing me closer to my dream trip.

"What are you doing?"

I jumped so high I nearly fell off my chair, frantically hitting the keyboard and mouse trying to close the incriminating screen.

My shoulders slumped when I realised it was too late. I swivelled my chair around to face Grayson, who stood motionless behind my desk with his arms crossed. His jaw twitched as he stared at my monitor.

"I...I'm...looking for a friend," I stammered, knowing my cheeks were turning pink.

He leant forward, reading the screen over my shoulder. The scent of him made my heart ache. "This *friend* of yours seems to have a very similar skill set to you. Would they be interested in working here?" The corner of Grayson's mouth twitched.

"They're not suited to a place like this," I muttered.

He rubbed his stubble. "If they gave it a chance, perhaps they'd be surprised."

"Grayson..."

He pressed his lips together and looked away. "You can't leave, Josie."

"I have to," I whispered.

"The company won't survive without you."

I scrunched my face in disbelief.

"You run our most popular segment," he continued. "If you go, our readers will follow."

My temper sparked. "Is this how you plan on keeping me around? Emotional blackmail?"

He shook his head. "Regardless of our situation, I care about this magazine and that's the truth."

The blood drained from my face as Grayson's eyes confirmed his words. "Can I work from home then?"

"What? Why?"

"Because I can't sit here and see you every day and pretend everything is okay. So, unless *you* plan to leave, we'll need to find another solution."

Grayson's expression softened as he reached for the tear on my cheek. "Josie, it doesn't have to be like this."

I flinched away from his touch. "I've already told you. I'll never be *that* girl."

With a frustrated growl, Grayson spun around and just when I thought he was about to leave, he closed the door and returned to the visitor's chair.

"What are you doing?" I asked, narrowing my eyes as he made himself comfortable.

He leant forward and rested his elbows on his knees. "You need to listen to what I have to say."

"We're at work, someone may hear you," I whispered, glancing out into the empty corridor.

"I don't fucking care at this point. I've tried to keep this out of the office, but you've left me no choice."

I sunk into the chair, crossing my arms. "Fine."

"My father is threatening to ruin your career."

"What?" I gasped, sitting back up.

"If I don't marry Melanie, he made it very clear you'll never work for *any* publication again."

My eyes grew wide with panic. "He can do that?"

"He's a powerful man with *a lot* of connections. I have no doubt he'll follow through with his threat if he suspects anything is going on between us. That's why I haven't called or texted you, he'll be looking at our phone records."

"He would stoop that low?"

"There's a reason Harlow Corp. have broken all the biggest stories. He has eyes and ears everywhere."

Swallowing down my fear, I slowly gazed around my office wondering if it was bugged.

Grayson lowered his gaze. "I'm sorry, Josie."

"How could he make such a cruel request?" My stomach churned.

"That's the way he operates."

"Even with family?"

"Our families have been planning to merge Warren Media and Harlow Corp. for years, but Melanie's parents want us to marry before it happens. That's why my father has been so furious with me." Grayson sighed. "I just thought if they met you and saw how happy we were together they'd let it go, but all I did was expose my weakness."

"What's that?" I asked, my voice hoarse.

He exhaled. "You."

My mouth parted, but I remained silent.

"He's used to getting want he wants, and will destroy *anyone* who gets in his way."

"And I'm at the top of his hit list." I couldn't believe this was happening.

He pursed his lips and nodded. "Unless I can prove to him how serious I am about the family business."

"So you're marrying Melanie to save my career?" *This is ridiculous*.

He shook his head. "No, that's what I've been trying to tell you. The engagement is a smoke screen."

My eyes grew wide as I lifted them. "Does Melanie know that?!"

The corner of his mouth quirked up. "Of course she does. I wouldn't have considered it if it didn't benefit her as much as me."

"So, you told her about us?"

"She knows I'm seeing someone—someone I'm serious about—but I'm sparing her the details."

My heart dropped. "Because she loves you."

"No more than a friend," he responded, shaking his head.

"Then why did she react so badly when she found out about us?"

Grayson winced, clearly effected by the memory. "Because she isn't stable, and when Staci told her she'd seen me with someone new, she spiralled. I'm the only person she trusts and she felt like she was losing me. I should've prepared her."

I lowered my gaze. "She really is dependent on you, isn't she?" The conversation I had with Adam on the drive home from the Hamptons flashed through my mind.

"I thought if I put some distance between us, she would learn to cope on her own, but she's only getting worse. Her parents are more toxic than mine, so they're no help. The only time they've ever eased up on her was when we were together."

"Can't she just tell them to back off?"

"She's not strong enough, not yet anyway. If her parents believe we've reunited, they'll leave her alone. Melanie can finally get some help, and it'll buy me some time to figure out what to do about my dad."

"So your solution is to lie to everyone?" It didn't sit well with me. Lies tend to snowball.

"Not to the people who matter," he answered softly.

"Does your brother know what's going on?" Surely he wouldn't support this.

"Yes. Adam may be ruthless like Dad, but even he doesn't agree with this."

I rubbed my temples. "Is that why your father was here last week? To check up on you? On *us*?"

Grayson scowled. "He's pretending to care about the company, wanting to know the ins and outs of the business, but yeah, he's making sure I'm falling in line."

I slowly blew all the air from my lungs. "I guess that explains his little visit to my office."

His eyes snapped to mine. "He spoke to you?"

"Oh, he just wanted to tell me how happy he was that we'd 'dissolved our relationship'," I said, mimicking his dad's deep voice.

Grayson ran a hand down his stubbled face. "And what did you say?"

"Nothing," I said, with a shrug. "He didn't say anything that isn't true."

Grayson's expression grew dark. "Josie, this isn't the end of us."

I dropped my eyes to avoid his burning stare.

A rumble rolled through his chest and his voice lowered. "Josie…"

After a long moment, I lifted my gaze. "Well…maybe it should be."

Rising from the chair, he leant over my desk until his green eyes were level with mine. "How I feel about you hasn't changed, and I'm pretty sure you feel the same—fuck, I *know* you do. So, don't give me this bullshit."

My heart pounded. "But this isn't just about you and me. If you don't marry Melanie, I'll not only lose my job, but *Maude* will fold and everyone here will suffer the consequences. I won't be responsible for that."

Grayson's glistening eyes bored into mine. "Just give me some time. I'll find a way out of this. I even got us some burner phones so we can talk without my fath—"

"Burner phones? Are you serious?" I shook my head vigorously. "No, I'm not doing it."

"Josie, please. I miss you. I'll figure this out…"

I looked away as my lower lip trembled. "Then call me when you do, because until then, I don't want any part of this."

He ran both hands through his thick hair as his jaw tightened. "I'll make this right, Jos. I promise."

I wanted to believe him, but self-preservation was something I'd mastered over the years since my parents died, and I could already feel myself rebuilding my walls.

Grayson's phone buzzed and he slid his hand into his pocket to silence it. "Adam is waiting for me downstairs," he said, gazing towards door. "We've been summoned back to LA for a family dinner."

My mouth went dry. "Will Melanie be there?"

Grayson's shoulders sagged. He didn't need to answer.

"Well don't let me hold you up," I muttered, moments from crumbling.

He remained frozen in place. "Jos…"

"Just go," I bit.

With a pained expression and small nod, Grayson left my office and my mind with too much to humanly process.

At the end of the day, I quickly gathered my things and raced out of the building, desperate for fresh air. At least now I had a valid excuse to skip Friday night drinks. My head was pounding. The walk home eased the pain somewhat, so I dropped in to see Lenny. I needed a healthier distraction than the bottle of wine awaiting my homecoming.

"Hey, Lenny!" I yelled as I walked through the door.

"Josie! You're early today. I'll be out in a second."

"No rush," I said as I moseyed around the empty restaurant, gazing at the old photos. "I've got nowhere to be." My eyes were drawn to an empty space on the wall. "Len, did you move my prints?"

Lenny came out from the kitchen drying his hands with a tea towel, before taking an envelope out of the cash drawer. "I told you if you put a price on them they'd get snapped up." He threw the envelope over with a huge grin.

My eyes grew wide at the weight of it. "Are you kidding me?"

"There's enough there for a ticket to Italy," he said with a twinkle in his eye.

I smirked, but didn't comment. Unfortunately, I needed much more than that for the trip I had planned.

"Come on, you need a holiday. Look how pale you are. A little Italian sun and my sister's cooking will fix you right up."

Amusement tugged at the corners of my lips. "Your sister's cooking?"

"Yes, you'll stay with her of course," he stated firmly.

I laughed. "That's sweet, but my life is too complicated right now."

Lenny's eyes narrowed as he folded his arms across his chest. "Work life or love life?"

"Both actually," I said with a sigh.

His forehead wrinkled. "Are you doin' okay?"

"Yeah, I'll be fine." I hated when Lenny worried about me.

"Well, it sounds like something needs to change, and change is as good as a holiday."

"I think you're right, Len." I grinned, picking up the menu. "Maybe I'll start by ordering something different tonight."

"Whatever makes you happy," he said, with the warmest of smiles. I could always rely on Lenny to lift my mood.

As I sat at home, munching on my new favourite pizza topping, I thought about Lenny's words while I stared at the fat envelope on the kitchen bench. Perhaps my dream of travelling was closer than I thought. I'd only need to sell a couple more pieces before I'd have enough to visit a portion of the world, and if I couldn't quit my job, perhaps a long holiday would give my heart the break it needed.

I'd been resistant before, but now I desperately needed something to distract myself, so I gave up on my job search, in lieu of a new plan. I was going to have an exhibition.

Chapter 21

The weekend was spent sorting through old photography files, picking out my favourite images from the ones I'd taken over the years. I created a contact sheet, and wrote an email to a few smaller gallery owners in the area, asking if they would be interested in hosting an exhibition for an unknown artist.

My jaw dropped when I received an email back within minutes.

Hi Josie,

Thank you so much for contacting us in regards to hosting your photography exhibition. We are already familiar with your amazing work with Maude, and are blown away by the images you have sent. We would be honoured. Adrian, our curator, will call you on Monday to work out the details.

We look forward to working with you.

Faye Westwood

Manager

AG Galleries

I squealed in delight. Finally, something to keep my mind off the train wreck that was my life.

Returning to work on Monday didn't seem so bad now I was working towards something bigger than my next article for *Maude*. Thankfully, Grayson and Adam hadn't returned from LA as yet, so I was available to take Adrian's call to nut out the finer details of my first show.

"Loved your latest *Capturing Love* piece," Marlene said, poking her head through my doorway.

I smiled. "Thanks, any changes?"

"Nope, it's perfect as usual. I just need to run it past the big bosses, but I'm sure they'll be fine with it."

"Speaking of, where are they?" I asked, trying to sound casual.

Marlene ambled into my office, nursing her morning coffee. "Linda received a message from Adam early this morning telling her they had to reschedule their flight. Something to do with an unexpected meeting. Personally, I think they're still recovering from the engagement party."

My eyelashes fluttered. "The what?"

"It's all over social media, I don't know how you missed it."

Fuck you, online world. "Oh, I've been a little busy," I said, lowering my eyes.

Marlene slipped her cell from her tailored suit pants, pressed the screen and passed it to me.

"Too much coffee or not enough?" she asked, eyeing my shaky hand as I reluctantly reached for her phone.

"Clearly not enough." I smiled tightly as I gazed down at the photo of Grayson and Melanie holding up their champagne glasses in a toast.

The caption from Harlow Corp. read...

Celebrating with @MelanieWarren and @WGHarlow #surpriseengagementparty

"Wow." *So much for their family dinner.*

"I'm amazed they didn't ask you to photograph it," Marlene said as I handed back the phone. "This photographer did nothing to capture how they feel for each other."

"I doubt I could've either." I couldn't even look at them without wanting to puke.

Marlene frowned. "You really shouldn't put yourself down, Josie. You have a very unique talent and your work is amazing."

Her comment took me by surprise, because compliments from Marlene were rare. Perhaps her looming retirement was softening her up.

"You're right. Thanks, Marlene."

Her warm smile returned. "I hope I've been a good mentor to you over the years."

"Yes, you definitely have," I said, thinking back to my first day at *Maude*. "It's going to be weird when you're gone." Marlene took a chance on me five years ago, and I was determined to never let her regret it.

She took a long sip of her coffee and exhaled. "Well, I hope these two trust fund kids can keep *Maude* alive. I'd hate to see my company fold after all the hard work we've done here."

My chest tightened, knowing I played a major role in the future of the magazine. "I'll do whatever it takes to make sure it doesn't."

"You're a sweetheart," she said, receding from the room. "I hope they give you a good bonus this year."

"Thanks, but I'm hoping I won't need it."

Adam and Grayson arrived just before home time, wheeling their small suitcases up the hallway. Neither said hello, nor spoke a word to each other before their collective doors slammed closed. Something was stirring.

Moments later, all of our computers chimed.

Linda: **Compulsory meeting for all staff in the conference room in 5 minutes.**

I closed down my computer and packed my bag, hitching it over my shoulder before making my way up the hall. As I passed Grayson's door, my tote was yanked sideways into his office.

"What are you doing?" I growled, shrugging him off.

His intense gaze pierced mine. "I need to tell you something."

"I already know about your little engagement party."

Grayson's chest rose and fell, his eyes full of remorse. "No, it's something else."

"Then tell me after the meeting," I said, glancing over my shoulder as my colleagues passed by. "I'm going to be late."

"Just promise you'll hear me out afterwards. It's about Mel."

I narrowed my gaze, studying him. "Whatever. Can I go now?"

With his nod, I hurried out of his office and into the conference room.

As I moved to the back, Adam strolled in and his brother closed the door behind him. Grayson scanned the room until his gaze settled on me, but I kept my focus on Adam.

"Good afternoon, all," Adam welcomed, with a forced smile. "Before you read about it in the papers, we thought we should inform you first, that Harlow Corp. has sold half its share of *Maude* to Warren Media."

Fuck.

Adam continued. "Now, there is no need for alarm, for the business will run as usual. But as of tomorrow, Melanie Warren will be joining our team of directors to build on the furthering success of this company."

Fuck. Fuck. Fuck.

Burning fury flowed through my veins as my gaze panned over to Grayson, who had been watching my reaction closely. Adam finished his spiel and sent everyone on their way, until just the three of us remained. I was paralysed with anger.

Clearly aware of my presence, Adam placed his hand on Grayson's shoulder, urging him to leave. "Gray, we need to go."

Grayson didn't move, nor did his eyes leave mine. "Just give me a minute."

"It's not a good idea. Remember what Dad said…"

He shrugged him off angrily. "Just give me a fucking minute."

Adam grumbled something incoherent as he left the room, shaking his head.

Rising from the chair, I moved towards Grayson, watching his jaw pulse as I edged closer. I opened my mouth to speak, but I couldn't even form a word. Instead, I dropped my gaze, stepped around him and left.

I rushed out of the office as quick as humanly possible and ran home, mumbling obscenities with every step. Hoping to calm my inner turmoil, I grabbed Luci and went straight to the park for a long run.

Hours later, I trudged up the stairs with Luci, feeling no better than when I left. And once I reached my apartment, I felt even worse. Because there, on the floor, leaning back against my door was Grayson, fast asleep.

His hair was scruffy, his shirt loosened and his jacket lay piled at his side. He looked more homeless than a billionaire, and I almost felt sorry for him. Before I had a chance to nudge him awake with my foot, Luci lunged forward and slobbered his face with wet kisses. Grayson's eyes shot open before scrambling to his feet.

"How did you get up here?" I asked, as my anger resurfaced.

"Um…the guy downstairs let me in."

I groaned. *Bloody Reed.*

"He thought I was the pizza guy."

Luci licked his chops as I peered down at the empty pizza box at Grayson's feet. "At least I don't have to feed him dinner now."

"Shit," Grayson muttered, picking up the remains.

"Why are you here?" I asked, unlocking the door to let Luci in.

"You promised to hear me out."

I glared at him. "That was before you unleashed my own personal hell." I moved inside, but blocked the doorway.

Grayson raised his eyebrows. "Can I come in?"

"No." I crossed my arms and leant against the door frame.

"Please?"

"No."

His eyes met mine, and the hint of a smirk hid behind his lips. "What are you afraid of Josie?"

I pursed my lips, but remained silent. *You.*

"I just want to talk."

Grudgingly, I stepped aside to let him pass, then proceeded to the kitchen to pour myself some wine. "You have until the end of this glass," I said, before gulping down two mouthfuls.

His jaw tensed and I raised my eyebrows impatiently.

"Our parents made the deal behind our backs. We had no idea it was happening until it was too late." He lowered his eyes to the hardwood floor. "It was a surprise engagement present."

I took another sip, but struggled to swallow it down. "You said her parents wouldn't merge until you were married."

"And they won't, not entirely. They're just trying to push things along because Melanie hasn't been coping. They think she'll benefit from being closer to me, and with *Maude* to keep her busy, she'll stay out of trouble."

"And what do you think?"

Grayson placed his hands on his hips and sighed. "I think they may be right. I can get her the help she needs out here."

"So, she'll be *living* with you? Here in New York?"

"Yes. They trust her with me."

"Can *I* trust her with you?"

He grimaced. "She's difficult, but I can handle it," he said, stepping forward. "You have nothing to worry about."

I drained the rest of the wine down my throat. "Do you realise how fucked up this all is?"

"I know," he said, running his hand down his face. "But hopefully it won't be for too much longer. We just need to keep up the façade until—"

"Until *what*, Gray?" I snapped. "Until you're married?!"

Grayson's forehead creased. "No! Adam and I are working on a plan, but I need to make sure Melanie is in a good frame of mind before we proceed."

"I don't get it, *why* is she your responsibility?"

Grayson looked away as his whole body stiffened. "Because I'm the reason she's like this. I really fucked up when we were kids, and I've been paying for it since."

My shoulders wilted. "Is this about the baby?" I placed my glass down and stepped out from behind the island bench.

Grayson mouth parted. "How did you know about—"

"Adam told me."

His expression softened as he moved closer. "I should've been the one to tell you."

I nodded, my eyes filling with tears.

Grayson's hand ran down my arm and settled on my wrist. "It's not that I didn't want you to know, I'm just used to keeping it to myself. No one knows the truth, except our families. The rest of the world assumed our engagement was the result of young love."

I frowned. "Surely you felt something for her. You were together for eleven years."

His casual shrug didn't match his tortured eyes. "I think it somehow eased my guilt. By staying with her, I thought she'd eventually return to who she was before she lost the baby, but she's only getting worse. She's drinking more than I realised and the drugs—*fuck!* I didn't even know she was into that shit."

"This isn't your fault, Gray."

He shook his head and started to pace. "You know what the worst part is? I don't even remember the night it happened. Mel and I have been best friends since we were kids, but never anything more. She threw this big party after her boyfriend dumped her, and I clearly drank too much because the next morning, I woke up in her bed. We found out she was pregnant a few weeks later."

I sucked in a breath, imaging how scared they must have felt.

"Our parents forced us to get engaged to avoid embarrassing both families." He let out a despondent chuckle. "It was what they'd always planned for us, we just sped up the timeline."

"Jesus, you were just a kid," I said, disgusted with their parents' intentions.

Grayson stopped pacing and turned to me. "It doesn't matter. I screwed up her life, Jos, and I owe it to her to make it right."

"And if you can't?" I grimaced, knowing he had little control over her self-destructive behaviour.

"I...I don't know." His eyes glistened. "I've made such a mess of everything. Of her...of us..." He moved towards me and lifted his hand, running it slowly down my cheek. "I've missed you so much."

I trembled. "I meant what I said, Gray. I can't be with you like this."

With a silent nod, he dropped his hand and stepped back, but his longing gaze penetrated my soul more intimately than his touch. Grayson's cell phone blasted from his pocket, like a wrecking ball smashing through the tension between us.

As soon as he answered, Adam's voice bellowed through his phone. "You fucking better not be where I think you are!"

"I know, I know. Just buy me some time until I get there, okay?" he replied, quickly glancing in my direction and moving away.

I couldn't hear Adam's response, but Grayson winced. "Well, she can wait!" He hung up the phone and lifted his gaze to mine. "I'm sorry."

He left without a second glance.

Chapter 22

"I know you."

I froze before reluctantly turning to Melanie Warren as she stood between Grayson and Adam at the front of the conference room. Dodging my colleagues as they exited the room after Melanie's introduction, I approached them, wishing I'd been faster in my escape.

Swallowing the lump in my throat, my gaze glided over Grayson and Adam's paling faces.

"You're Josie Spencer." Melanie's signature red lips curved upwards. "You took the photos at my bachelorette party in Las Vegas last year."

I stared into icy-blue eyes that weren't as cold as I'd expected, and my heart slowed. "Um, yes…I did."

"That was one wild night." She chuckled. "Sorry you had to leave early."

I smiled tightly and pretended to laugh along, before shooting Grayson a nervous glance.

"We'll have to get you back to cover our wedding, won't we Grayson?"

My eyes widened.

Adam cleared his throat, and placed his arm around Melanie's shoulders. "Let's go find you an office, shall we?" He quickly ushered her out of the room.

I lifted my eyes to Grayson. "She doesn't know, does she?"

He shook his head. "It's better if she doesn't."

"For who?"

"For everyone. Trust me."

———

The next morning, I took my time wandering around the park searching for couples to feature in my next article, but nothing inspired me. Arriving at work later than usual, I was startled to find Melanie sitting at Amy's desk.

I slowed at the doorway. "Hi," I said, panning my gaze around the room.

Melanie's head shot up and a dazzling smile splashed across her face. "Josie, hi! I was wondering when I was going to see you today."

"Um...where's Amy?"

"Who?" She scrunched up her nose. "Oh! You mean the girl who was in this office?" She lifted her shoulders in an easy shrug. "Gone, I suppose."

My eyes bulged. "Pardon?"

"I don't know. Grayson just said he'd sort it out."

A fresh swell of rage roared through me. With a forced smile, I continued down the hallway and through Grayson's open door.

He lifted his hand to calm me before I unleashed hell. "Relax, Josie, Amy hasn't been fired. She's just been moved to the next floor."

My mouth dropped. "The next floor?!"

He sighed. "Melanie wanted the office next to mine."

"She couldn't take mine?"

"I wouldn't let her," he stated in a low voice. "I like my view."

My hands found my hips. "So now I have to stare at the both of you all day?"

"You're barely in the office anyway," he argued. "I'll buy you another tree."

"Make it a big one," I snarled, and stormed across the hallway.

With one last angry glance back at Grayson, I switched on my computer.

J. Spencer: **Where for art thou?**

A. Mitchell: ***sad face* Between Accounts and IT.**

J. Spencer: **Wanna swap?**

A. Mitchell: **Hell no.**

J. Spencer: **How's Janice?**

A. Mitchell: **Very funny. You better be coming to drinks Friday.**

J. Spencer: ***thumbs up***

The next few weeks dragged by. I kept out of the office as much as possible, only returning to upload my work and take on new assignments. When I wasn't reviewing gigs at night, I was working tirelessly on my exhibition, which was getting closer by the day.

"What's this?" Melanie asked, after hovering around my desk for the past ten minutes.

I glanced up at the newest director of *Maude*, who never seemed to have work to do, and sighed. "Oh, it's just a little project I've been working on in my lunch breaks."

She picked up the contact sheet of photography pieces I was collating for my exhibition, and her eyes lit up. "Oh my god, are you having a show?"

"Um, yeah. I am actually." I couldn't help but smile.

Melanie clapped her hands. "Oh, please let me help. I know so many people who would love your work."

My eyelids fluttered. She looked genuinely excited and I knew how well connected she was. "Well...I *have* been worried about no one showing up."

"Are you kidding me? Your work is sensational. Leave it with me."

I frowned, unsure of her motive, or if she had one at all. "Thank you, Melanie."

She waved me off and grinned. "Oh, this is what I do best. I have one condition though..."

"What's that?" I asked curiously.

"I want to be in it."

"Huh?"

"I want a photo of *me* in the exhibition." A sparkle appeared in her eye. "We could do a photoshoot."

As much as I didn't want to spend any more time with this woman, I couldn't help but be infected by her buzz. She definitely had a way about her that drew you in, and it wasn't just her beauty. Perhaps I'd been too quick to judge.

"Okay," I said warily. "Let's do it."

Just days later, Melanie called me into her office as I made my way to the lunchroom to meet Amy.

"I want to show you something," she said, waving me over. "My designer friend in LA put this together for me. What do you think?" She handed over an elegant invitation to an upmarket art exhibition and grinned.

My eyes grew large when I read my name in the heading. "Oh my god, is this for my show?"

Melanie giggled. "Yes, silly. I told you I know all the right people. I've also made a spreadsheet of everyone who is anyone in New York, and we're inviting them all."

Panic surged through my body. "Oh, I can't afford that," I said, grimacing. "Maybe we could just print...like...twenty or something?"

"Don't worry about the money, I have it sorted."

"I can't let you do that."

Melanie scrunched up her nose. "Of course you can."

I was about to disagree when Amy popped her head in the door. "You coming to lunch?"

"Um...yeah. I'll be there in a sec." I glanced back at Melanie's falling face, but she disguised her disappointment with a tight smile. "Would you like to join us? I'd like to hear what else you have planned."

Her face brightened. "I would love that."

"Awesome," Amy said, smiling. "But you'll need to move fast before Simon pollutes the lunch room with his cat food salad."

From that day on, Melanie joined us at our lunch table. She quietly listened to the banter between our work mates, but rarely joined in. Some may have taken this as snobbery, but the more I observed her, the more I realised she was uncomfortable around them. And when it all got too much, she escaped into her phone.

Once our lunch break ended and the room cleared, Melanie exhaled and turned to us. "So, your invites were delivered this morning."

"Really?" I squeaked. *I never squeak.* "Can I see them?"

"Sure, but they're at the apartment. I was actually wondering if you guys would like to come over tomorrow night and help me stuff envelopes?" Her cell phone pinged and she looked down to read the message.

I glanced at Amy and her eyes widened.

"We can make a night out of it," Melanie added while she rapidly typed. "Order some take out, watch a movie…" She lifted her gaze. "I have plenty of wine."

"I…I dunno…" My voice caught in my throat.

Melanie's smile faltered. "It's Saturday night, of course you've already got plans," she muttered while her cheeks grew pink.

"No, it's not that…I—"

"If you're worried about seeing your boss, don't be. He'll be out."

My breath caught.

"It sounds like a great idea," Amy said, jumping up from her seat. "Just text us the details and we'll be there." Her eyes found mine and bulged, urging me to agree.

"Okay, sure. What should we bring?" I asked, mimicking Amy's enthusiasm.

"Nothing at all, just wear something comfortable," she said, straightening out her dress as she stood. "I have to go to some tedious meeting now, so I'll see you tomorrow." Her phone rang and she let out an exasperated sigh before answering. "I'm coming! Stop being so pushy."

Amy giggled and shot me little wave as I threw my half-eaten sandwich in the bin. As Melanie continued her heated conversation down the hall, I trailed behind until Grayson's unmistakable presence blocked our path. With a groan, Melanie ended her call and Grayson dropped his phone from his ear.

"Where have you been?" he asked, with a quick glance my way.

"At lunch."

He scoffed. "In the lunchroom?"

"It's where people eat," she replied, rolling her eyes.

Grayson chuckled. "Not you."

"It's not like *you* invite me anywhere," she said, pushing past him.

As we both watched Melanie disappear into the conference room, my heartrate accelerated. I attempted to edge past Grayson and into my office, but he whirled back, almost bumping me over. His hand spread over small of my back while his other hand ran down my arm to steady me. I drew a shaky breath as his touch ignited every molecule in my body.

"Sorry," he said, but his smirk wasn't apologetic at all. "I should be more careful."

"You should," I rasped, lowering my gaze. "Excuse me."

With a quick nod, he waited for me to enter my office before continuing up the hall to his meeting.

Out of breath, I sank into my desk chair and woke up my computer.

A message awaited on my screen.

A. Mitchell: Don't stress, he won't even be there.

J. Spencer: I shouldn't be there.

A. Mitchell: She's obviously lonely. Maybe she doesn't have many friends in NYC?

J. Spencer: He's going to freak when he finds out.

A. Mitchell: After the crap he's put you through lately, he deserves it.

J. Spencer: True dat.

A. Mitchell: Don't hate me, but I kind of like her.

J. Spencer: *face palm* me too.

The next night, I hid behind Amy as she rang the doorbell, praying Grayson had already left. When the door swung open, I exhaled in relief to find Melanie standing in front of us in baggy sweatpants, a Laker's t-shirt, and ridiculous narwhale slippers. She almost looked...*normal*.

"Come in, your timing is perfect. The food just arrived," she said, ushering us over to the couch I'd had sex on *at least* a dozen times. "I didn't know what you guys liked, so I got a bit of everything."

My eyes bulged at the array of food piled up on the coffee table. "No, no...this is more than enough."

"For like a month," Amy muttered, before the amazing view of Central Park distracted her.

As I examined the living room, my eyes were drawn to the subtle differences that could only come from a feminine touch. Fresh flowers donned the mantlepiece, fashion magazines polluted table tops, and the additional artwork softened the room.

"Is that a Louise Birmingham?" I gushed, moving closer to the painting on the wall.

"Sure is," Melanie said. "I found it at a gallery last week and had another sent back home."

"You must have an amazing collection."

Melanie chuckled. "Just not enough walls."

"Who took these?" Amy asked, edging over to a set of familiar photographs on the wall.

My stomach flip-flopped as Melanie followed her.

"I'm actually not sure, but they're gorgeous, aren't they? Grayson found them in a little restaurant in Greenwich."

Why didn't Lenny tell me?

The corners of Amy's mouth rose as she glimpsed my way. "He's got a good eye."

Melanie let out a little snort. "All those years of dragging him along to galleries and art shows has finally paid off."

The bedroom door opened and we all whirled around. "Adam's on his way up. We better not miss the start of the game…" Grayson stopped dead in his tracks. "What are you doing here?" he blurted, staring directly at me.

My mouth fell open, but nothing came out.

Amy stepped in front of me with an overenthusiastic smile. "We're having a girl's night!"

His eyes tapered in on Melanie. "You didn't tell me you were having people over."

She scowled. "I didn't think I had to."

Before he could say another word to make us feel even less welcome, Adam sauntered through the front door.

"Finally," Melanie cried, throwing her hands in the air. "You were supposed to pick him up an hour ago."

Ignoring her, Adam spotted Grayson's paling face and followed his gaze. "This looks like fun," he said, his eyes sparkling with amusement as he panned over the three of us.

Melanie groaned. "Trust you to bring the sleaze."

A snigger erupted from my mouth and Grayson's eyes darted to mine from under his faded Lakers cap.

"What? No pillow fights?" Adam asked with a chuckle, before turning to his brother. "Come on, Gray. The car's waiting."

"Hang on a sec!" Melanie hollered, before grabbing a purple Lakers cap from the hallway table and placing it on her head to conceal her dishevelled hair.

Adam hung back his head and groaned. "Come on, Mel, not again."

"It won't take long," she uttered as she applied her usual shade of lipstick. Grabbing her phone, she pulled Grayson beside her and leant into him to take a selfie. "Say *Go Lakers!*"

"Go Lakers," Grayson mumbled with absolutely no enthusiasm.

After Melanie reviewed the photo, she took off the cap and threw it back on the table. "Thanks, you can go now."

Adam placed his arm around his brother and guided him out of the apartment. "Bye, ladies!"

"If you want to go to the game, we can reschedule," I said to Melanie as she furiously wiped the red from her lips.

Melanie laughed while she typed something into her phone. "God no, I hate basketball."

Amy shot me a look and I shrugged.

"Grab some food and make yourselves at home," she said, walking towards the kitchen. "I'll get the wine."

Settling on the couch with an unusual combination of noodles, tacos and a side of fries, Melanie handed me an empty glass and filled it until the red wine ran dry. "Sorry, I started a bit early," she said, placing the empty bottle on the coffee table. "I have plenty more though."

Amy held up her hands and smiled. "No judgement here."

"I finished stuffing all the envelopes this afternoon, so I figured we could just relax and have some fun tonight," Melanie said, dishing up smallest serve of spaghetti I'd ever seen.

I winced. "Oh, Mel, you shouldn't have done it all yourself."

"It's okay." She shrugged. "Grayson helped, so it didn't take long."

My mouth fell open.

"Don't look so surprised. He's not so bad outside of work."

Amy cleared her throat to smother her laughter. "Mmm… this Pad Thai is amazing."

I filled my mouth with noodles and scowled across at her. If I didn't feel guilty before, I felt guilty now.

Steering the conversation away from Grayson, Amy and I relayed stories about how *Maude* used to be before Harlow Corp. took over. Melanie laughed along to our comfortable banter, until tears stung our eyes and it hurt to breathe.

"Shall I open another bottle of red or are you ready for something a little stronger?" Melanie asked after pouring the remains of the wine down her throat.

"Maybe we should slow down a bit," I said, remembering what Grayson told me about her excessive drinking. "Some coffee perhaps?"

She grinned and stood up. "Espresso Martinis it is!"

Hiding my grimace, I helped Amy clear away the empty take-away containers while Melanie returned to the kitchen.

"Can someone check the basketball score?" she yelled over the rattling cocktail shaker.

"Sure thing," Amy said, looking at me quizzically. She turned on the television and scrolled through the channels. "The Lakers are beating the Knicks by 10 points at half time!"

"Thanks for that," Melanie said, returning to the lounge room carrying a tray of cocktail glasses. "You can turn it off now."

"Why are you interested in the score if you hate basketball?" I asked curiously, as she placed the tray on the coffee table.

"Because everyone thinks I'm at the game," she said, picking up her cell phone and passing it over. "See?"

Amy peered over my shoulder as I looked down the photograph of Grayson and Melanie in their Lakers caps. The post read:

Off to the basketball #golakers

Melanie laughed at our scrunched-up faces. "My followers have certain expectations on my social life. Eating take-out and watching rom-coms in my sweats is *not* one of them."

"Do you do this often?" I asked, wondering how many of her old posts were staged.

Her eyes twinkled. "All the time."

Clearly as curious as I was, Amy moved towards Melanie and took her hand, facing it palm up. "May I?"

"Okay..." she said warily, while Amy examined the lines.

I handed back her phone with a frown. "Don't you get tired of keeping up the façade?"

"Sometimes." She shrugged nonchalantly. "But I've been playing this game for a while now. I'm used to pretending."

Amy hummed. "You definitely have a lot of secrets."

With a tight smile, Melanie slipped her hand from Amy's grasp and turned to me. "Oh, I forgot to mention I have some leftover invitations. Did you want some for your friends and family?"

"Sure," I replied, narrowing my eyes at Amy. *What did she see?*

Melanie guided me over to the dining table, covered with overflowing boxes of addressed envelopes, and handed me a pile of spare invitations.

My smile grew as I ran my hand over the slightly embossed letters that spelt out my name. "This is amazing."

"Once these are sent and I promote you online, there won't be an art collector in New York City who doesn't know your name."

My heart fluttered. "How did you get so good at this?" I asked, picking up her elaborate to-do list.

"My mother is the queen of event planning. Parties, fundraisers, anything to keep herself in the spotlight. I guess I picked up a few things over the years."

"Do you get your exceptional taste in art from her too?"

"Oh, no. I majored in Art History in college." Melanie cheeks turned pink. "My parents said I'd never need a career, so I chose something I liked. I'm not creative like you, but I appreciate the beauty in art."

I smiled at her. "You should open your own gallery."

"I...I would actually love that," she replied, but the light in her eyes dulled. "But my parents wouldn't approve."

"But with your collection and ability to—"

"Shall we watch that movie now?" Melanie interrupted, moving back to the lounge.

My eyebrows rose. "Sure." It was clearly a sensitive topic, so I let it go.

We deliberately chose a predictable romantic comedy, so we could talk throughout and not miss any major plot turns. The endless drinks, together with our hilarious narrative, made the movie way more entertaining than expected, and I was genuinely enjoying myself.

Our laughter was so loud, we barely heard the key in the door as the credits rolled. Nursing the remains of my cocktail, I poked Amy to see if she had passed out (she had) and watched Melanie pour herself another glass of red wine. *This girl can drink.*

My amusement faded when Grayson's gaze struck mine as he walked through the front door. He looked so damn sexy in that faded Lakers cap, I shoved a cushion in my face to stop myself from gawking.

"Hey, babe! How was the game?" Melanie asked, turning towards him.

"Shit," he mumbled, throwing his keys on the entry table.

Melanie chuckled. "But didn't you win?"

I peeked over the pillow as he trudged into the kitchen, grumbling. "We should go," I said, tugging Amy's arm to stir her awake.

"But I'm soooo comfy," she slurred, snuggling deeper. "You never told me how cosy this couch was."

Anxiety filled my body, hoping Melanie wouldn't read anything into Amy's words. "I'm calling a cab."

"You shouldn't be catching a cab at this time of night," Grayson said, walking into the room with a bottle of water. "I'll drive you both home."

"No, no, it's fine." I slipped on my oversized hoodie in preparation to leave.

"No, it's not. You're clearly drunk, and it's in my best interest to get you home safe."

"I'm not *that* drunk," I muttered.

Grayson impatient gaze fell to my outfit and Melanie laughed.

I dropped my chin to see what was so funny. *Fuck*. My hoodie was on backwards.

"Just let him," Melanie said, rolling her eyes. "He just loooves coming to the rescue."

I let out a defeated sigh as I rearranged my clothing. "Alright, thanks."

"Grab your things. I'll carry Amy to the car." Grayson handed me the bottle of water before scooping Amy off the couch with little effort.

"I'm going to bed," Melanie mumbled as she stumbled across the lounge room and into the bedroom opposite Grayson's. "Goodnight."

A knot untied in my stomach at the confirmation they weren't sharing a bed. "Goodnight, Mel."

"You coming?" Grayson asked, with an irritated edge to his voice after observing my relief.

With a small nod, I picked up my bag and followed him out of the apartment.

As I entered Amy's East Village address into the GPS, Grayson strapped her into the backseat while she mumbled something incoherent about secrets. Less than a minute later, her endearing snores filled the car as we pulled away from the curb.

"You'll feel like shit tomorrow if you don't drink that water," Grayson said, staring out of the windshield.

I stopped picking at the label and placed the bottle into the drink holder between us. "I know how to handle a hangov—"

"Are you deliberately trying to make this harder?" he snapped, gripping the steering wheel tighter.

I screwed up my face. "Fine! I'll drink the damn water!"

"That's not what I meant," he growled. "Why were you at my place?"

I exhaled loudly. "Melanie asked me over, what was I supposed to say?"

"Say no! You're not her friend."

"Why can't I be?" I asked, crossing my arms. "We could be best friends."

Grayson scoffed, irritating me even more.

"What's the problem? Afraid she'll start liking me more than you?" I tilted my head as I watched him closely, before putting on a baby voice. "Is somewon a liddle bwit jealwous?"

He stopped at a red light with more force than necessary, and turned my way. "I'm jealous because you were in my apartment spending time with my ex, rather than in my bed screaming my name. So yeah, I am pretty fucking jealous."

"*Daaaamn*," Amy drawled, poking her head out from between the seats.

"Ames!" I cried. We'd clearly forgotten she was in the car.

"That was...*hot*," she moaned, before sinking back into the seat.

Blush rose up Grayson's neck as he continued to drive, while I stared out the window trying to cool the heat in my cheeks.

"Does anyone else feel like a burrito?" she asked, oblivious to our embarrassment.

I pressed my lips together, holding back a smile, but Grayson's sideways glance set me off. I burst out laughing and Grayson followed. The tension between us evaporated as his deep chested laughter, and my drunken giggles, filled the car.

As we pulled up beside Amy's East Village apartment building, I jumped out of the car to help Grayson convince Amy to leave the comfy confines of his leather interior.

"Thanks for the ride, boss man," Amy slurred as she crawled out of the car and wrapped her arms around Grayson.

He momentarily froze before giving her a light pat on the back. "No problem, Amy." His eyes met mine over her head and a smile played on his lips. *His soft, beautiful lips.*

Ignoring my pounding heart, I pulled her away. "Come on, Ames. Let's get you upstairs."

Thankfully she climbed the staircase with little support, while we hovered behind, waiting to catch her. Once she was safe inside her tiny studio apartment, we tucked her into bed and returned to the car, driving on in silence.

"I like that hat on you," I said, staring a little longer than I usually let myself. "It's cute."

The corner of his mouth twitched, but he remained focused on the road. "Cute?"

"Mmmhmm." Unfortunately, I wanted to rip it off and run my fingers through his hair. *Down girl.*

"How much have you had to drink tonight?" he asked, rubbing the back of his neck.

I turned my gaze out the window. "Too much. Waaay too much."

As he parked the car outside my apartment building, he leapt out and opened the door for me.

I chuckled. "You're such a fucking gentleman," I said, refusing to take his hand as I jumped from the car onto the sidewalk.

Grayson shadowed me to the entrance. "You say that like it's a bad thing."

"It *is* a bad thing," I muttered, entering the security code into the keypad. It made me want to take him upstairs. "I'm not having sex with you." *Did I just say that out loud?*

The door unlocked, but Grayson's hand slid over mine preventing me from turning the handle. Every hair on my body stood to attention as he lowered his mouth to my ear. "I never mentioned sex."

I whirled around and peered up into eyes that were entirely too close to mine. My core ached and it pissed me off. "You don't have to. I just have to look at you and…*sex.*"

The corner of his mouth rose. "You're drunk," he said, running his thumb down my cheek. "I wouldn't take advantage of you like that."

I refused to meet his gaze. "What if I wanted you to?"

"Josie, I want you in every non-gentlemanly way, but not like this."

"Whatever," I grumbled. "It's not like I'll remember tomorrow anyway."

Grabbing both sides of my hoodie, he drew me closer. "Then I guess this won't hurt." He pressed his lips to mine and my mouth parted instantly, wanting more, *needing* more, but he didn't comply. "Goodnight, Josie," he whispered, before dropping his hands. "I'll see you Monday."

As he strode back to his car, I blinked away tears before stumbling through the entrance door. Savouring his taste on my lips, I climbed the stairs, wondering if he would wait for my apartment to light up before driving away.

Hesitating over the light switch, I walked into my bedroom and peeked out the window. My heart warmed at the sight of him sitting in his idling car. As his gaze travelled up to my window, I leant down and turned on my bedside lamp. *I'm so fucked.*

Chapter 23

Once the invitations were sent out, Melanie managed to get word of my exhibition to every newspaper, A-list celebrity, and blogger in New York. We worked through lunch breaks and after hours on every aspect of the event, until every job on Melanie's extensive list was checked off.

"How's it going?" Grayson asked, pulling me out of my creative zone.

I'd stayed back to finish some editing, before I headed out for drinks. My show was only a week away. "After this, I'll only have one piece left to work on."

"Thanks for including Mel in your exhibition. I haven't seen her this excited about anything in a long time."

My eyes darted across the hall into Melanie's office.

He followed my gaze. "She left early."

"She's been an amazing help," I said, rotating my chair towards him. "She's definitely not as bad as I thought she was going to be."

Grayson's smile was tight. "We all have our demons."

"How's she going…with everything?"

He leant his backside against my desk and crossed his arms. His shirt tightened around his biceps causing the heat in my body to rise.

"Good. No dramas yet, which is refreshing. She's finally seeing a therapist."

I raised my eyebrows. "That's good."

"This project of yours has been the perfect distraction for her," Grayson said as he threw my world globe stress ball from one hand to the other.

"And for me," I muttered, lowering my gaze.

He placed the globe back on my desk and slid his fingers over mine. "Adam and I are heading to the Hamptons this weekend to speak to Grandpa about our situation. We may have found a solution."

I pulled my hand away to slow the fluttering in my belly. "Are you sure Melanie is okay with all this? She keeps posting about the wedding like it's going ahead." I cleared my throat. "So I hear."

"I wouldn't worry about her social media. That's how she wants everyone to see her. I guess it gives her some semblance of control, since it's only thing in her life her parents have no say in. Her reality is a lot darker."

I narrowed my gaze. "So, not only is she striving for her parents' approval, she's also searching for validation from strangers? Sounds healthy."

"I know." He rubbed the back of his neck. "It's not great, but she's hoping to build something out of it. I think you may be helping her figure out what that is."

"Well, she's definitely a natural with all this. I couldn't have done it without her."

Grayson shook his head. "Maybe not as quick, but your artwork certainly speaks for itself."

My cheeks warmed. "Will you be coming to my exhibition?"

"Of course." He frowned. "I wouldn't miss it."

"As Melanie's date, no doubt?"

"I'm coming for you, not her."

I pressed my lips together and looked away.

"Do you have plans for the weekend?" Grayson asked softly, attempting to change the subject.

The corner of my mouth lifted. "You mean apart from all the hot dates I've been invited on?"

"Very funny," he uttered, narrowing his gaze.

I shook my head with a chuckle. "I'll just be working on this, I guess."

With a gentle nod, Grayson stood up, preparing to leave.

My heart dropped. I wasn't ready for him to go yet. "Grayson…"

He drew in a deep breath and turned back, the longing I felt mirrored in his eyes.

The words stuck in my throat. "Say hi to Grandpa for me."

His mouth curved into a sad smile as he back stepped out of my office. "I will."

Melanie arrived a half hour late to our meeting place in Central Park, covered in a long fur coat and dark sunglasses. All she needed was 101 spotted puppies chasing after her to complete the picture.

"I'm sorry I'm late," she groaned, dropping onto the park bench beside me. "I…um…slept in."

I glanced at the time on my cell and my eyes grew large. "That's one hell of a sleep in."

Melanie giggled. "It was one hell of a night."

My eyelids fluttered, but I kept my attention on the camera. "Should we get started?" It was best I didn't know any more.

"Of course," she said, slipping out of the hopefully faux fur to expose an exquisite black gown that hugged every inch of her body impeccably.

"Wow." I gasped. "That is some dress."

Melanie smoothed her hands down the intricate lace as she stood. "There's no other like it."

"You aren't too cold?" I panned my gaze over the snow-covered ground and frowned.

"There is no beauty without pain," she said, flashing a tight, but charming smile.

Her profound statement stunned me, but they didn't sound like her words. "I'd rather you didn't die of hyperthermia."

Melanie shrugged nonchalantly and slipped a hip flask out of her coat. "Don't worry, this will keep me warm."

I winced. "I'll be quick, and we'll take breaks," I said, concerned by how little Melanie cared about her health.

We moved to a more secluded position, where the snow was thicker, creating a striking backdrop against her dress. The crisp air brought out the pink in her cheeks, complimenting her crimson lips. It was like photographing an actress from a classic 1950s film.

Melanie was the definition of beautiful, but I needed more from her. If her photograph was going to feature in my show, I'd have to find out who she truly was. Not just who she wanted the world to see.

While I snapped token shots to warm her up, I asked questions about her life, hoping to work towards something deeper. Surprisingly, she was quite open and candid, like we'd been friends for years. It made me wonder if she actually craved a real connection, or if the contents of the hip flask let down her guard.

"So, how are you finding New York?" I asked, genuinely interested in her answer.

"Oh, I'm loving it. The night life here is amazing...I just need to convince Grayson to loosen the leash a little."

I lifted my gaze to meet hers, but didn't say anything.

"He thinks I party too much," she continued, rolling her eyes. "He's always acted more like a big brother than a fiancé. Always trying to fix me." *Snap.*

"It must be nice, having someone care for you that much."

"Grayson has always been there for me, even at my lowest points." She sighed. "I wish I could say the same about my parents." *Snap.*

I watched her closely through my lens. "High expectations?"

"The highest, and I'm not meeting a single one." She laughed, but it quickly faded. "At least I have room to breathe out here."

I chose to stay quiet, fearing I would say something to reveal how much I already knew about her situation.

"Grayson can be just as bad sometimes, always on my case about this and that. I had to tell him I had an appointment with my therapist, just to get out of going to the Hamptons with him this weekend."

My mouth gaped behind my camera.

"It's not like I *need* therapy. He's just overreacting." Her face dropped a little before she quickly gathered herself. "Little does he know my therapy session was of the beauty variety." A chuckle escaped her lips as she inspected her latest manicure.

I cleared my throat, suddenly really uncomfortable.

She let out a long sigh. "I just wish everyone would get off my fucking case."

"If you don't mind me asking…why are you with him?" I needed to know if she'd trust me with the truth about her pretend engagement, or keep up the façade. At least then I could gage how genuine she was about our growing friendship.

Melanie straightened her posture. "Apart from being a dream match for our families, he can give me the life I want."

My heart dipped. I'd have to play along with the lies. "What sort of life is that?"

"You know," she said, tilting her head with an underlying smirk. "Money, status…expensive jewellery."

"What about love?"

She shrugged. "That's the sacrifice, I guess. You can't have it all, especially when he's in love with someone else."

What? My heartbeat accelerated and I fumbled my camera. "How…how do you know that?"

"He told me," she stated, matter-of-factly. "He's using our engagement to distract his parents from whatever plan he's devised to make it work with her."

Her unexpected honesty rendered me speechless.

"It's okay though, it won't work out." She twirled the giant diamond ring around her finger. "I'm just biding my time until he realises it."

All the blood rushed from my face. "What makes you think it won't work?"

"From what I can tell, she isn't Harlow material. He wouldn't be so secretive if she was," she said, rubbing her arms. "I've known him my entire life, and he's never gone against his parents wishes. He tried once, but we all knew he wouldn't follow through. So as much as he thinks this girl is *the one*, he's engaged to me. It maybe for the wrong reason right now, but it won't be long before he realises it's just easier this way."

I nodded like I understood, but I was in shock. Melanie's

intentions were entirely different to what she'd led Grayson to believe.

"It's not like he's the only one who's had to give up love for the greater good of the family," she muttered, before tipping the flask into her mouth.

Say what? I brought the camera back to my face. "So, you had someone?"

"Oh, it doesn't matter, not anymore. We were just stupid kids." *Snap.* Her eyelids fluttered at the sound of my camera, but she kept on talking. "My parents didn't approve of him, so it never would have worked out." A single tear ran down her cheek, but she quickly wiped it away. *Snap.*

I wondered if he was like me. *A nobody.* "Why didn't they approve?"

"He wasn't Grayson," she said, with a laugh to mask her obvious pain. "Our parents have been planning our wedding since we were kids. They weren't going to let anyone get in the way of that."

"What did they do?"

"They didn't have to *do* anything. Some shit went down with Scott's dad, and he spilt. No explanation. Not even a goodbye." Her lower lip trembled. *Snap.* "The best part was finding out I was pregnant weeks later."

My eyes bulged.

"Oh, don't worry," she uttered, watching my reaction. "I miscarried."

"How old were you?" Surely I had the timeline wrong.

"Seventeen. I know, how stupid right? It all worked out for the best though. Grayson was there to pick up the pieces…" She smiled tightly. "And the rest is history."

Breathe, Josie, breathe. My chest tightened over my hammering heart. "Did you…" I cleared my throat. "Did you ever find out what happened to him?"

She stared at the ground. "A few years ago, I heard rumours he'd moved here and become some hotshot lawyer. Apparently has his own firm in Midtown called Blackwood & Associates."

"Have you seen him since?"

"God no. I won't even venture to that side of town just in case." Her jaw twitched. "There's no point anyway. I almost have everything I want."

Lines creased my forehead as I tried to fathom her logic. "Almost?"

Melanie gathered up her coat and wrapped it around her body before settling back on the park bench. "How important is love in the scheme of things anyway? My parents seem to do okay without it."

I thought about my parents. Their love for each other, their love for me. "I think it's *the* most important," I replied, barely above a whisper. I sat down beside her.

Melanie chuckled. "Spoken like a person in love. Who's the lucky guy?"

"Oh, no." I flustered, packing away my camera. "It's just... well, it's my job to believe that."

She narrowed her eyes and the corner of her mouth lifted. "There's definitely someone."

I smiled tightly as I held my breath, keeping the tears at bay. "It's...it's complicated."

Melanie smirked and handed me her flask. "*Life* is complicated."

Even though I tried to talk Melanie into going home, I was certain she kicked on after we parted ways.

"I'm not wasting this outfit," she said, reapplying her lipstick. "I only have one night left of freedom before Grayson gets home and I'm going to make the most of it."

She wanted me to join her, but with the exhibition only a week away, I still had a ton of work to do. Plus, I needed time to process everything. I never dealt with secrets well, especially hurtful ones, and now I was sandwiched between the lies of two people I cared about.

When Melanie spoke about Grayson, the guilt was unbearable. I felt like the other woman, and the very notion made me sick to my stomach. Over the past month I'd become someone she confided in, and clearly needed. She deserved to know the truth about my relationship with Grayson, but I wouldn't be able to live with myself if it pushed her over the edge.

Grayson must have felt the same, but his motivations were derived from a lie. Melanie had somehow made Grayson believe the baby was his, and he'd lived with a sense of responsibly for her since. It was unforgivable.

Unfortunately, I had to spend the rest of the weekend staring at Melanie's flawless face on my computer screen, which annoyingly didn't require much retouching at all. With a few slight adjustments, I was left with one of my favourite pieces for the show.

It wasn't even Melanie's overall appearance that pulled me in, it was her expressive eyes. There was so much anguish behind them, it made me curious about her lost love and what happened between them so many years ago. There was so much pain there, a pain that could only come from losing someone you love, and as much as I wanted to hate her, I couldn't. I knew that pain well. My heart ached for her.

Opening my web browser, I hesitantly typed 'Blackwood & Associates' into the search bar and came up with one hit in Midtown. *Bingo!* I perused their super slick website until I found the 'about us' tab, and clicked through.

I immediately recognised the first face to appear and frowned, trying to figure out where I'd seen him before. *Scott Blackwood.* I repeated his name several times in my head, until a memory jolted me. *Hank and Sabrina's wedding!*

No wonder Grayson acted strangely towards him. Scott Blackwood was the ex-boyfriend of his ex-fiancé. *Awkward.* He shared the singles' table with us, but I barely remembered the conversation we had before Grayson monopolised my attention.

I skimmed over his profile, which included the details of his fancy college and law school, until I found something that made him sound remotely more human.

In his free time, Scott enjoys long drives, vintage cars, and collecting fine art.

An art collector? *Interesting.*

I opened the spreadsheet of invited guests Melanie created for my event, and scanned down the list. I rolled my eyes. Of course his name was missing. Why on earth would she invite the man who left her pregnant and broken-hearted at seventeen?

Flicking back to the picture of Scott and his genuine smile, I found myself wanting to know his story. According to Melanie, he wouldn't have known about the pregnancy, and his reason for leaving her eleven years ago remained a mystery. Perhaps he had a valid excuse. Perhaps he never had the chance to explain himself. Perhaps he could now…

Maybe if they reconnected, Melanie would find the closure she needed. Or maybe she'd remember how it felt to love someone, and would finally let herself—and Grayson—move on.

Without dwelling on all the reasons why I should and shouldn't interfere, I opened a new email and sent Scott an invitation to my exhibition. I knew it was selfish, but in the moment, I refused to care. There was a good chance he wouldn't come, or even open the email, so the risk was minimal. I was simply giving the universe a little nudge.

Chapter 24

My exhibition was a success. There was barely an inch of standing room as I squeezed through all the guests admiring my work. *My work!*

It was impossible to miss Melanie as she waltzed into the gallery, wearing a spectacular scarlet red designer gown, but it was the accessory on her arm that drew my attention. *Grayson.*

He looked so devilishly handsome in his suit, combed hair and glasses, I couldn't help but gawk. He'd been in and out of meetings all week so I'd barely seen him, and apparently my body needed a fix.

"You're drooling," Amy whispered, giving me a little bump.

"Oh god, am I that obvious?" I mumbled, lowering my eyes as I turned to her.

"Not as obvious as him." I peeked back and found Grayson's eyes glued to my body as he stalked up to me, holding two champagne glasses. My heart quickened as he approached and Amy discreetly moved away.

"Congratulations, Josie, you're truly remarkable." He kissed my cheek and handed me a glass as Melanie edged up beside him.

"I couldn't have done it without Melanie's help." I smiled at her. "Thank you."

She leant in and offered me an air kiss. "It was a pleasure."

I nervously sipped my drink, avoiding Grayson's constant stare while Melanie's eyes searched the walls.

"So…where is it?" she asked excitedly.

I smirked at her enthusiasm. "Over there." I pointed to the large photograph on the back wall, surrounded by admirers.

Melanie manoeuvred through the gathering to get a better viewpoint, and Grayson and I followed closely behind. Deep within the crowd, his fingertips grazed my lower back and my breath hitched. He still had such an effect on my body, and he knew it.

She paused in front of the image, taking it all in. I nervously glanced up at Grayson—whose eyes were fixed on me instead of the photo—then back to Melanie and her portrait.

Melanie looked fierce amongst the snow, posing like a professional in her black couture gown. There wasn't a strand of blonde hair out of place, or a blemish on her fair skin, creating an image of perfection. If it wasn't for her vibrant red lips, you would almost believe the entire image was black and white.

But what made the photograph unlike any other of Melanie Warren, was the subtle sheen over her icy blue eyes and the residue of a tear that slid down her cheek, taking the tiniest amount of mascara with it. This unassuming flaw was the pivotal part of the piece, because it was a rare glimpse at the deep emotion that simmered deep beneath her compelling façade. I titled it *There is no beauty without pain*.

Whirling back with tears gleaming in her eyes, Melanie threw her arms around me.

I let out a relieved chuckle. "So you like it?"

"Like it? I *love* it," she gushed. "Name your price."

Faye, the gallery manager, stepped forward. "Unfortunately, this piece has already been sold."

Melanie growled. "What? To who?"

I winced. "Don't worry, I can have another printed for you."

Faye skimmed over her clipboard. "This piece was sold to a… Mr. Blackwood."

My heart stopped and I slowly turned to Melanie's paling face. There were so many people, I didn't even know he was there.

Grayson's expression grew dark as he scanned the crowd. "Are you referring to Scott Blackwood?"

Faye smiled. "Yes, he was very interested in the piece."

"More like the subject matter," Grayson muttered as Faye moved away to make another sale.

Melanie's hand trembled as she brought her drink to her lips.

We all spotted him at the same time, but he wasn't alone. An attractive young brunette hung off his arm, devouring his every word. *Shit*.

Grayson's hand slid around Melanie's elbow, turning her away. "Melanie, why the fuck would you invite Scott?"

"I...I didn't." Her eyes glistened as she peered up at him. "I haven't seen him since...since he left."

He shook his head and sighed. "Maybe we should go."

"What? No! This is Josie's big night."

A sharp pain radiated through my chest. "Maybe you should speak to him," I said softly, trying to ease the situation.

Grayson's hard gaze snapped to mine. "I need another drink," he grumbled as he stormed towards one of the roving waiters.

"I need some air," Melanie mumbled and headed for the door.

Before I had a chance to follow either of them, a familiar voice called my name.

"Pete!" I cried, throwing my arms around him. "Thank you so much for coming."

"I couldn't miss this, Jos," he said, keeping my hand in his as we parted. "I'm sorry I haven't returned your calls. It all happened so quickly and I wanted to wait until everything settled down before seeing you again."

Squeezing his hand, a sense of relief washed over me. "I totally get it. You've been busy with your new job. Congratulations by the way, we've missed you at work."

He nodded. "You know *Maude* was never my long-term plan."

I felt a light tap on my shoulder and turned to find Grayson standing closely behind. "Can I speak with you in private for a moment?"

Pete rolled his eyes while Grayson refused to acknowledge his presence. "It's fine, Josie. I have to leave anyway, but perhaps we could catch up for dinner sometime?"

"Sure," I replied.

"Next Saturday? I'll make reservations at Bellini's for 7pm. I know how much you love Italian food." Pete glanced up at Grayson with defiant eyes. "It's not like we work together anymore."

I swallowed. "Yeah, okay. I'll...um...meet you there."

Grayson glared at Pete as he walked away and I nudged his side to draw his attention.

He cleared his throat and leant down to my ear. "Did Mel say anything to you about leaving?"

"No, she just said she needed some air."

"I've already checked outside," he muttered impatiently.

I exhaled. "I'll see if I can find her."

After a few laps of the gallery, I decided to check outside again, so I made my way into the cloak room to grab my jacket.

"Jesus," I cried, finding Melanie hiding amongst the leather and fur. Her dilated pupils shot up in horror and back down to her hand where the compact mirror lay covered in white powder.

"Lanie?" a voice rasped from behind me.

I spun around to find Scott's paling face as he froze at the sight of the girl he used to know.

Melanie's cheeks reddened as she quickly wiped her nose and lowered her eyes.

"What the fuck?!" Grayson snapped as he entered the small room a moment later.

Before I could even grasp what was happening, Grayson grabbed Scott around his collar and shoved him out of the gallery and onto the sidewalk.

"Grayson, stop!" Melanie cried, chasing after them.

Grayson's face grew red as he tried to contain his rage. "Is he your new dealer?"

"What? No! I told you, I haven't seen him in years."

"Apple doesn't fall far from the tree, does it?" He sneered at Scott, and turned back to Melanie. "What did he give you?"

Scott shoved Grayson hard, making him stumble backwards. "I didn't give her anything. I'm nothing like my father."

Grayson secured his footing and glared up at Scott. "Excuse me if I don't believe you."

"I don't give a shit what you believe." He moved in Melanie's direction, but Grayson stepped between them.

"Stay the fuck away from her, she doesn't need someone like you in her life."

"I'm not in her life," he bit.

I stepped forward, hoping to diffuse the situation. "Grayson, maybe you should just let them talk. It's been a long ti—"

"Maybe you should stay out of this," he snapped, glaring back at me. "This has *nothing* to do with you."

I sucked in an icy breath at his harsh tone. "Actually, it does," I said, as a shiver rolled through my body. "I invited him."

Three bewildered faces turned my way and I swallowed the lump in my throat, realising how much I'd fucked up.

"Why would you do that?" Grayson's fiery gaze singed my skin.

Melanie grimaced. "I didn't tell you about him so you could play matchmaker!"

Scott turned back to Melanie in surprise, but didn't utter a word.

I peered up at Grayson, but he refused to meet my eyes. "I'm sorry."

"We need to go," he said quickly, texting his driver.

"There you are!" A high-pitched voice floated from the entrance. "I knew you'd forget our coats, so I grabbed them on the way out."

Scott turned to his date as she stepped outside. "Thanks, Cindy."

"It's Mindy," she corrected, smiling tightly.

"Right, sorry." His eyes softened as he gazed over Melanie one last time, before taking his date's hand. "Let's go."

We all stood completely still, and deathly quiet, until they were out of sight.

"I truly am sorry," I said, turning back to face the music. "I just thought…"

"I'll get our coats," Grayson muttered, striding back into the gallery.

Melanie didn't seem to hear either of us. Her faraway gaze crumbled into her hands as tears ran down her cheeks.

"I'm sorry, Melanie," I whispered, placing my hand on her shoulder as she sobbed.

Flinching at my touch, she straightened her posture like nothing happened. "It's fine. I'm fine," she said, unusually bright.

Grayson reappeared with their coats under his arm and ushered Mel into the private car that rolled up beside us. Before climbing in after her, he met my gaze, baring no expression. "We'll talk later."

As the car sped off, I returned to my exhibition to find the curator speaking animatedly to the gallery director. His eyes lit up when he saw me and almost bowled me over.

"Josie! There you are! You won't believe it," he gushed.

That I'm a horrible person? I got the memo.

My brow lifted, too drained to match his excitement. "Believe what?"

"You've sold everything!"

I should've been celebrating, but I was pissed off, upset and riddled with guilt. After wrapping up my long night at the gallery, I walked out onto the street, praying for a cab to take me home to bed.

Instead, I found Grayson leaning back against his car with his arms crossed.

"What are you doing here?" I asked, instantly annoyed.

"It's late. I'm driving you home." He opened the passenger door.

"I'm fine. I have a cab coming." *I just haven't booked it yet.*

"Cancel it. We need to talk."

I crossed my arms. "I've already apologised."

"I'm not after an apology, I want to know why you invited him."

My nostrils burned as I lowered my glistening eyes. "I thought I could make Melanie remember, that's all."

His brow furrowed. "Remember what? How much he hurt her?"

"No!" I cried, "I wanted her to remember how it felt to love someone."

"He destroyed her, Jos. She couldn't possibly still have feelings for him."

"That's where you're wrong," I said, shaking my head.

Grayson scoffed. "I think I know her a little better than you."

I raised my eyebrows.

"What?"

"Forget it." I attempted to continue up the sidewalk, but he reached for my hand.

"No, wait...tell me."

I jerked out of his grasp. "She's lying to you, and confiding in me! She considers me a friend and has told me things. Things I shouldn't know."

"Like what?"

"It's her truth to tell, not mine."

"Josie..."

"No, I'm not going to betray her trust anymore."

"So your friendship with her is more important than our relationship?"

"I could say the same thing to you!"

He pursed his lips. "I'm just trying to do the right thing here."

"So am I!" I cried. "But I'm drowning in all the lies, the half-truths and the missing puzzle pieces. My heart can't take it anymore."

His jaw tightened. "What are you saying?"

"It shouldn't be this hard," I whispered as tears threatened to escape.

His heated gaze burned into mine as he stepped closer. "I've put everything on the line for you...*for us*."

"Well, now you don't have to." I growled, stepping backwards while trying to hail a passing cab. "Now you can slip back into your high society life, with your trophy wife and stop slumming it with the rest of us." I couldn't control the words coming out of my mouth.

His face fell. "You know that's not what I want."

"But it's not about what either of us *want*. It's about what your parents *want*, what Melanie *wants*, what her parents *want*...and I don't *want* them controlling my life anymore." I exhaled in relief when the cab pulled into the curb

His shoulders slumped. "Josie…"

Without looking back, I escaped into the car, telling the driver where to go before the tears started streaming down my cheeks.

———

The following week was torture. Grayson was in a foul mood, and everything I did was subjected to criticism, which was more surprising to my colleagues than it was to me. I'd barely set a foot wrong since my first day at *Maude*.

"What did *you* do to piss off the boss?" Marlene asked as we left the conference room after our weekly staff briefing.

With a quick shrug, I scooted back into my office to gather up my photography gear. After Grayson's last outburst, I planned to spend the rest of the afternoon as far away from him as possible.

"Excuse me, Josie. Adam would like to see you in his office," Linda said, poking her head through my door.

"Sure," I muttered, dropping my bag onto the desk and making my way up the hall. I knocked twice on Adam's door before entering.

Adam glanced up and sighed, before closing his laptop. "Josie, take a seat."

I did as directed.

"I want you to take the rest of the week off."

My eyebrows drew together. "What? Why?"

"Because it's becoming increasingly obvious something is going on between you and my brother, and we need to tread very carefully at the moment."

"There's nothing going on between us."

He scoffed. "If that were true, he would've told me."

"I'm perfectly capable of being professional around Grayson. *He's* the one who's embarrassing himself."

"Regardless, I want you to make yourself scarce for a few days. Work from home, take a mini break, I don't care. I have to fly to LA to sort out an urgent contract, so I need Grayson thinking straight while I'm gone…which he doesn't seem to do when you're around."

My mouth fell open.

"And keep clear of Melanie. She's a loose cannon right now… no thanks to you."

I hadn't seen Melanie since the exhibition, but according to her latest posts, her social life had been pretty wild. Adam clearly thought I was to blame, and it pissed me off.

He rubbed his eyes. "You couldn't have picked a worse time to bring Scott Blackwood back into the picture."

I gnashed my teeth. "Don't you get it? He was always in the picture! She never got over him."

"I think you're mistaken," Adam said, leaning back into his leather chair while tapping his pen on the desk. "Melanie moved on remarkably quick after he left. Hell, she jumped into bed with Grayson just days later."

I raised my eyebrows. "Don't you think it's a little coincidental she got pregnant just *days* after Scott left, to someone who conveniently doesn't remember anything that happened that night?"

The tapping slowed. "What are you saying?"

"I'm saying…that unlike Grayson, I won't take responsibility for something that has nothing to do with me."

Adam's face fell. "Jesus," he muttered, closing his eyes. "How do you…"

"She told me," I said quickly, before I lost my nerve.

"Does Grayson know?"

My eyes glistened as I shook my head. "I can't tell him. He'll be crushed."

"Leave it with me," Adam said, rubbing his forehead. "Just go home and I'll see you next week."

The door opened and I jumped, glancing back to find Grayson pause in the doorway.

"Oh, I didn't know you had company," he said, darting his gaze between us. "I'll come back."

"No, it's fine. I'm going," I uttered quickly, edging past him with my eyes lowered.

Grayson blocked my path and placed his finger under my chin, lifting my face, before turning to his brother with fire in his eyes. "What did you say to her?"

My heart raced. "I'm fine," I bit, reluctantly pulling away from his touch.

"Let her go, Grayson. We need to talk."

Chapter 25

Pete: **See you at Bellini's @ 7pm.**

"Fuck!" I launched off the couch, skidded into my bedroom and began rummaging through my closet. *Crap, crap, crap!* I had had such an emotionally charged week, I totally spaced on my dinner plans with Pete.

I settled on the short black dress I wore to Hank and Sabrina's wedding and quickly straightened my hair to disguise the colourful underlights. Bellini's was super conservative, and well…I wasn't.

Scrambling out of the cab, I adjusted my dress as I walked into the restaurant only five minutes late. *I deserve a fucking round of applause!*

The waiter guided me through to our table and Pete stood as I approached. Feeling a strong pull in the opposite direction, my gaze travelled across the room to discover Grayson eating dinner with a couple I didn't recognise.

I hadn't seen or heard from him since I left Adam's office a few days prior, and I preferred it that way. His mere presence brought up too many emotions, and I was done with all of it. Whether Adam told him about the baby or not, it had nothing to do with me.

I narrowed my eyes and the corner of Grayson's mouth twitched.

Pete sighed. "Yeah, I know. Of all the restaurants in New York City, William Harlow has to be having dinner here. We can go somewhere else if it makes you uncomfortable."

I swallowed. "No, no, this is fine."

He held out my chair, and I sat down, immediately picking up the menu to hide behind it. The quicker we ordered, the quicker we could get out of there.

Pete returned to his chair, and I cringed. Grayson was in my line of sight, already making it difficult to focus on whatever Pete was saying.

"Pardon?" I mumbled, shaking my head. "Sorry, I'm a bit out of it today."

"Totally understand. I know how busy you are. I just asked how the rest of your exhibition went."

My face brightened. "Great. I still can't believe I sold everything."

"Wow! That's amazing, Josie."

I blushed. "Thanks, Pete."

"It's a shame you can't make a decent living out of that sort of thing."

Irritation rippled through me, but I kept smiling. "What makes you think I couldn't?"

Pete chuckled. "The term 'starving artist' comes to mind. I highly doubt you could make as much money as you do at *Maude*."

"Why is everyone around here so focused on money?"

Pete grinned. "It's my job to be."

I changed the subject before I got too worked up. "Speaking of which, tell me more about this job of yours."

Pete delved into a load of financial talk and as much as I tried, I had no interest in what he was saying. Instead, my focus kept drifting to Grayson. Every time he glanced in my direction, I looked away, getting more and more worked up. Relief washed over me when our main course was served, because it meant I could focus on my food, instead of constantly battling the attention of two men.

As I finished chewing my last bite of salmon, Grayson's laughter drew my gaze to his table. He caught my eye and threw me a wink. My temperature rose, and I reached for my water to cool myself down. But instead of pouring it down my throat, I fumbled and spilt it all over the front of my dress.

"Shit..." My cheeks flamed red.

"Wow, Josie." Pete chortled. "Are you okay there?"

I picked up my napkin and patted down my dress, trying to absorb the excess water. "God, I'm such a klutz."

"There should be a dryer in the restroom. Go dry off and I'll order us some dessert."

I hesitantly pushed up, too embarrassed to glance over at Grayson, who I could only guess witnessed the whole thing. As I walked along a tiny hallway and past the noisy kitchen, I sighed in relief when I finally located the restroom sign.

Pete was right, there was a dryer, but it was only for hands. I tried to manipulate the nozzle, but it wasn't going to work. As I attempted to precariously angle myself under it, the door opened and I jumped away, pretending to act casual.

"Everything okay in here?"

My eyes bulged when Grayson entered. "You can't be in here!"

"It's a unisex restroom, Josie. Get with the times." His eyes travelled down my body before his panty-dropping smirk appeared. "Need a little help with that?"

I grumbled. "Not unless you have a hair dryer in your pocket."

He looked down at his pants and chuckled.

Realising what I said, I blushed. "*Not* what I meant."

"Come on, take off your dress."

"What?! No!"

Grayson rested his hands on his hips. "You can hide in the cubicle while I dry it for you."

"You'd do that for me?" I asked, narrowing my gaze.

He ran his hand through his hair and pointed towards the toilets. "Just take it off."

I darted into the cubical and shuffled out of my dress, flinging it over the door to Grayson. My dress disappeared, and a moment later the restroom door opened and closed, followed by silence.

My heart sank and fear surged through me. *Did he just do a runner with my dress?!* "Grayson?"

A fit of laughter broke out, right before the dryer started up.

I collapsed against the wall in relief. "Fuck you, Grayson."

"Sorry, I couldn't help myself."

"You're such a jerk."

We remained quiet while the dryer did its thing.

"That should do it," he said as the noise died down.

I reached my hand over the stall door and waved my fingers. With a moment of hesitation, Grayson handed over my dress. Slipping the warm material back over my body, I opened the door to meet Grayson's hard stare. I attempted to walk out, but he boxed me in.

My heart raced. He was angry at me, and I knew why. "Adam told you, didn't he?"

A flicker of sadness passed over him. "I don't want to talk about that...I want to talk about why you're here...with Peter?"

"He...he invited me."

His jaw flinched. "I know, I was there when he asked. You should've said no."

I rolled my eyes, frustrated by his jealousy. "It's not a date or anything. We're just friends catching up."

"Does he know that?" His eyes never left mine as he waited for my answer.

"Yes! No...I dunno! It's none of your business anyway. Who I go out with, outside of work, has nothing to do with you."

He stepped closer, pushing me further into the stall until the door swung closed behind him. His swirling green eyes penetrated deeper. "It has *everything* to do with me."

"It's over between us, Gray. I thought I made myself clear."

Grayson pursed his lips. "Shouldn't I get a say in that?"

"Why? Because you're my boss?" I growled, attempting to shove past him.

With a firm grasp of my sides, Grayson pushed me up against the wall. His hot breath grazed my ear. "No...because you're mine."

I gasped for air as his tongue trailed down my collarbone, and moaned when he ran his hands down my body, pausing at the hem of my dress. He slipped one underneath, and trailed his finger along my seam. I drew in a shaky breath, already on the verge of release.

"You're still wet," he murmured with a smirk, his eyes locked on mine. "Perhaps we should take these off to dry?"

With an unsteady nod, the tiny piece of fabric dropped to my ankles and Grayson's lips crashed down on mine. His consuming kiss muffled my scream as his fingers entered me, driving in again and again, until I could take no more. Shuddering over his hand, Grayson supported my weight with his other, and lay a gentle kiss on my forehead.

The door to the restroom opened and I pushed Grayson away, glaring at him as I lifted my panties and adjusted my dress. After patting down my dishevelled hair, I exited the cubicle and nodded politely to the wide-eyed lady reapplying her lipstick, before rushing out of the restroom.

I returned to the table just as dessert was being served, still trying to catch my breath.

Pete smiled up at me as I took a seat. "Great timing. Are you all dry now?"

I smiled tightly as Grayson made his way back to his table. "Yes, all good."

We ate our dessert in silence until an unwelcome voice drew our attention.

"Josie, Peter, fancy running into you two here," Grayson said, standing by our table. He rested his hand on the back of my chair and I almost choked on my soufflé when his thumb grazed my shoulder.

My cheeks grew red and I forced myself to smile. Pete mimicked my greeting.

"How's that new job working out for you?"

"It's great," Pete said, puffing out his chest as he gazed across at me. "Looks like a few things are working out for me since leaving *Maude*." He reached for Grayson's hand. "No hard feelings?"

My eyes widened. *God, I hope Grayson washed his hands.*

Grayson grinned. "No, not at all." As they shook hands, Grayson peeked down at me and winked. He looked so smug, I wanted to punch him. "I'll see you later, Josie."

I gave him a quick nod, but looked away when he smiled.

Pete leant back into his chair as he watched him leave. "You know, he's not so bad."

I scoffed. "You think?"

The restaurant wasn't too far from my apartment, so Pete walked me home. He was doing and saying all the perfect things, but I couldn't stop thinking about the fleeting look of despair in Grayson's eyes before he distracted me with his hands.

As I approached my apartment stairs, Pete tugged me back. "This isn't going to work out between us, is it?"

I lifted my hand to his face as my eyes welled. He was so handsome and lovely, and I hated myself for not making it work. "I'm sorry. It's just…"

"There's someone else, isn't there?"

I nodded.

"I hope he knows how special you are, Jos," he said, with a defeated sigh.

My lips rose into a sad smile and I pecked him on the lips. "Stay in touch, okay?"

"Bye, Josie," he uttered, and we parted ways.

As I typed in my security code, a shadow cast over me.

"Pete, I told you…" I turned around and my voice faded. It wasn't Pete, it was Grayson.

His chest rose up and down as he moved closer. His glistening eyes bored down into mine. "I still don't want to talk about it."

My heart ached for him. "Just be gone before I wake up, okay."

He lowered his eyes with a nod, and I let him follow me up to my bedroom.

I walked into work on Monday morning on high alert. It was only a matter of time before Melanie's secret imploded, and it wouldn't take her long to work out who was responsible.

"I wouldn't go down there," Amy whispered, grabbing my arm and pulling me aside as I entered the foyer.

A few of our colleagues hovered nearby and we all simultaneously flinched when a loud crash sounded down the hallway.

I gasped. "What's going on?"

"Tell me who she is!" screamed Melanie.

Oh, shit.

Leaving Amy behind, I slowly edged my way down the hall, eyeing Grayson's trashed office as I crept to my desk. Grayson's back was turned, while Melanie waved a familiar pink G-string in front of his face.

Oh, fuck.

My wall of plants concealed the scene, but did nothing to muffle their argument.

"Just calm down, Melanie," Grayson said, remaining composed. "Maybe when you're sober we can have this chat, but you're not remotely capable of having a civil conversation right now."

"Don't tell me to calm down, just tell me who you're fucking!"

Grayson sighed. "Why the fuck do you even care? This relationship isn't real."

"But our parents don't know that."

Panic surged through me.

Grayson's voice grew low and menacing. "Go home and sleep it off before I say something I'll regret."

"Are you really doing all this for some slut from the office?"

"Don't *ever* call her that! She's none of your fucking business."

"I'm your fiancé, I think she is."

Grayson growled. "Not anymore you're not, real *or* fake."

"No. No, no! You can't just dump me. You need me!" Panic laced her words.

"Actually, I don't *need* you for anything anymore."

I sucked in a breath at the finality of his words.

"What are you going to do, send me back home to my parents?"

"Well you clearly have no intention of getting better out here."

"Why should I?" she cried. "So you can move on with someone else? After everything we've been through together."

"That shit's not going to work on me anymore. I refuse to be manipulated by you, or our parents, any longer."

"I'm nothing like them," she snapped.

"Take a look in the mirror! You're the walking picture of your mother, with just as much venom."

A slap ricocheted off the walls and I winced.

"How dare you!" she yelled.

The tension heightened as the silence grew.

"The Melanie I grew up with would've despised someone like you. She never would've lied and manipulated to get what she wanted, or hurt the people who cared about her. I have no idea who you are anymore."

Her tone softened. "I'm your best friend."

"No, my best friend died the day she made me believe she was having my baby."

My thumping heart filled the silence that followed.

"Who told..."

"You should've told me!" he yelled. "I've lived with that guilt for eleven years! You made me believe I was responsible for you for eleven...fucking...years."

The pain in his voice made my heart ache.

"But I didn't have anyone else," she pleaded. "You were the only one who ever cared about me."

"Stop, just stop! I can't listen to this any longer. I can't even look at you," he muttered angrily. "And as soon as Adam gets back from LA, I won't have to."

"What's that supposed to mean?" Melanie cried, but Grayson's footsteps were already fading down the corridor.

A prickly sensation rolled over my body, and I warily peered up into Grayson's office to find Melanie's mascara streaked face staring back at me.

She knows.

I lowered my eyes as she took slow purposeful steps towards my desk, and drew in my breath when she dropped my long-lost G-string in front of me.

"Aren't I the fool?" she muttered, emotionless.

Squeezing my eyes shut, I prepared myself for a tirade of abuse, but there was only silence. "Mel, I'm sorry. I never meant to..." I lifted my gaze, but she was already storming down the hallway.

"Is anyone else fucking my fiancé?" she hollered as she reached the foyer. "Or is it just Josie?"

I winced. *Perhaps no one heard...*

Chapter 26

A. Mitchell: **Let's go out for lunch today.**

J. Spencer: **Is that your way of telling me to avoid the lunchroom?**

A. Mitchell: **Not unless you like everyone staring at you.**

I grimaced.

J. Spencer: **What are they saying about me?**

A. Mitchell: **It's all Chinese whispers, don't worry.**

Bile crept up my throat.

J. Spencer: **I've lost my appetite.**

Instead of eating, I stared blankly at my computer screen. Knowing Grayson was hurt and upset, and Melanie was a complete mess, made me worry about both of them. On top of that, my body was consumed with anxiety about my job, my career, and the future of *Maude*…and it all lay in the hands of two extremely volatile people.

"What the fuck happened here today?" Adam asked, pausing in my doorway with his suitcase and a mountain of paperwork tucked under his arm. His eyes remained glued on Grayson's office, clearly assessing the damage.

"Melanie happened," I grumbled. "She found something of mine in his office and was evidently pissed."

A line formed between his eyes as he turned to me. "What?"

I dangled the G-string from my hand with a tight smile.

Adam ran his hand down his face. "Fuck, Josie. A little cliché, don't you think?"

"It was from months ago. Before we ended things."

He ignored me. "Where's Grayson now?"

"He left."

"Shit," he muttered, glancing down at the paperwork. "I need to find him, preferably before this incident gets back to our parents."

"Fuck your parents." I quickly covered my mouth, but the words had already slipped out.

Adam's eyes grew wide. "Did you just say, 'fuck your parents'?"

I winced. *If I hadn't already lost my job, I was about to.*

Instead of firing me, he burst out laughing.

"Why are you laughing?" I asked, with wide eyes.

His laughter settled into a chuckle. "Because you're a breath of fresh air."

My eyebrows drew together, unsure of his meaning.

"Look, I need to go find Grayson and sort this shit out. Can you tell Linda to cancel my afternoon meeting?"

"Um…sure…"

"Oh, and don't forget to review that gig tonight. Your name's at the door."

He left my office and continued to cackle all the way down the hall.

Mid-way through the show, a familiar mop of blonde hair caught my attention, bobbing up and down to the music amongst the crowd. The venue was dark, but even with the strobe lighting, I could have sworn it was Melanie.

I lifted the camera to my face, squinting as I zoomed in. Sure enough, it was her. Wearing next to nothing and rubbing herself against a seedy guy with wandering hands. I inwardly cringed as she stumbled over her heels, spilling her drink on some poor guy's shirt before attempting to lick it off.

Sliding my phone from the back pocket of my jeans, I brought up Grayson's number.

Me: **Melanie's at Hell Fire. I think you need to come get her.**
Grayson: **She not my responsibility anymore.**
Me: **She's wasted.**

Grayson: **What's new?**

I let out a frustrated growl.

Me: **Forget it. I'll text Adam.**

"Trouble in paradise?" Melanie appeared in front of me, and I quickly shoved my phone away. "Oh, relax." She laughed and pushed herself through to the bar. "Grayson can fuck whoever he pleases. I know I do."

"You're not angry?"

She shrugged. "Nothing a few drinks couldn't fix."

I looked into her light blue eyes, wide and dilatated, and knew it had taken more than a few drinks. "Maybe you should slow down a bit," I said, hovering close behind as she ordered two martinis.

"Jesus, Josie, lighten the fuck up." She groaned. "You sound just like him."

As the barman passed over the drinks, my phone buzzed. I glanced down and discreetly read the message.

Adam: **No need to text me. I'm with Grayson and we're on our way.**

I lifted my gaze to meet Melanie's growing smile as she handed me a martini.

"No, thanks." I pointed down to the camera hanging around my neck. "I'm working."

She rolled her eyes and took a sip instead. "I'll just have to drink both of them then."

"Fine," I muttered, snatching the drink from her other hand and pouring it down my throat. She really didn't need another and I could use ten more.

Melanie stared wide eyed at the empty glass in my hand before erupting into giggles. I clearly missed the joke.

"You know, for someone who's fucking the boss, you sure seem to work a lot," she said, leaning back on the bar before taking a mouthful of her drink. "Doesn't Grayson give you any special treatment?"

I clenched my jaw. "I work just as hard as everyone else."

"Maybe your new boss will give you more perks," she said, with a chuckle.

"What are you talking about?"

Melanie's mouth fell open in mock shock. "You didn't know? The magazine's been sold."

"*What?*"

"Apparently our parents were offered a deal too good to refuse and it was all signed off this afternoon."

"And Adam and Grayson were okay with that?"

"According to my father, it was their idea to sell. Something to do with cutting losses."

My stomach dropped. Grayson clearly wasn't as invested in *Maude* as I thought he was. *Or me.*

Melanie smirked. "They're probably out celebrating right now."

"No doubt," I muttered through clenched teeth.

"It's a shame. I really like *Maude*...but working there was such a fucking drag." A flicker of regret passed over her expression, although it was gone in an instant. "I'm gonna go dance," she announced, already bouncing to the beat. "You should probably drink some water."

As she slipped into the crowd, I was left to fester in her revelations. My temperature rose with my anger as I thought about how much my life had been turned upside by these people.

All I wanted to do was go home, but my racing heart and weighted legs prevented me from leaving. Too lightheaded to keep standing, I staggered over to an empty bench seat. *What is wrong with me? Is this what a panic attack feels like?*

I rubbed my temples as I glanced down at my phone, trying to figure out how much time had passed since Adam texted me.

Three songs later, I was struggling to hold myself up.

"Where is she?" The words hit me like a truck and my eyelids fluttered, trying to focus on the figure in front of me. Adam's lips fell in and out of focus as he spoke. "Where's Melanie?"

I gazed off into the sea of bodies, all bobbing in slow motion. "I...I don't know."

Adam growled and stormed off into the crowd.

Grayson appeared in front of me, staring intensely into my eyes. "What's wrong with you? Have you been drinking?"

"I...I only had one," I mumbled.

The room began to sway until Grayson's hands found mine, drawing my focus. "Josie...I'm going to get you some water."

I clenched his hands in desperation. "No, please don't leave me."

"It won't take long." He pried my fingers off, leaving me petrified and alone, pulling me into a distant memory of the moment my father's life support was turned off.

Returning with a bottle of water, he brought it to my trembling lips. "Have you eaten today?"

As I shook my head, Adam reappeared with Melanie trailing behind.

"Did you give her something?" Grayson snapped at Melanie as she stumbled up beside him.

"Not on purpose!" she said, with a chuckle. "That drink was meant for me."

Grayson's fiery gaze tapered in on her, making her squirm. "What was in it?"

"Just a little Molly. I don't see what the big deal is."

"It's a fucking big deal!" Kneeling in front of me, placing his hands on my forehead and cheek. "Adam, she's on fire. We need to get her to the hospital."

"I'll get the car ready," he replied instantly, already dragging Melanie away.

While drowning in perspiration and tears, my hands climbed up to Grayson's unshaven face and pulled him close. "I don't know what's wrong with me, Gray. I'm scared."

"It's going to be okay, you just need to stay with me." Grayson gave me a little shake to keep me alert, but it was no use.

My eyes rolled back into my head and I felt my body rise into the air.

Lenny, my next of kin, sat quietly at my bedside, staring out the window. My eyes fluttered open moments before his worried gaze travelled back to where I lay.

"Oh, Josie girl, thank god." He leant forward and took my hand, touching his head and chest in a cross formation.

"Where am I?" I moaned as the beeping machines infiltrated the fog that consumed my head. "What happened?"

"You're in the hospital, sweetie. You were drugged at some club you were at last night and your body couldn't cope. The police are outside waiting to take your statement."

My forehead wrinkled as I tried to recall the events of the night before. As the hazy memories floated in, I grimaced. "Who called the police?"

"Grayson. He's in the waiting room with another man and a blonde woman. They won't let any of them through without your permission."

My heartbeat picked up on the machine beside my bed. "Good."

Lenny furrowed his brow. "Are you sure? Grayson is desperate to see you."

"You said there was a blonde girl out there?" I asked, ignoring Lenny's concern.

"Ah, yes. Melissa...I think..."

"Melanie?"

"Yes, that's it. She's in a bit of a state."

I drew in a deep breath. "Len, I want to see her."

His forehead wrinkled. "Not Grayson?"

"Not Grayson."

He studied me with sadness in his eyes before nodding. "Very well." He squeezed my hand. "I'll let her know."

Before Lenny left, I gave him the keys to my apartment. Last night's outfit now lay in the corner of the hospital room, tied up in a plastic bag and marinating in vomit, so I desperately needed a change of clothes. Plus, Luci would have torn the place apart by now, searching for his breakfast.

Half an hour later, there was a soft knock on my door.

"Come in," I croaked, gazing up as Melanie entered the room.

Her head was lowered as she took small delicate steps towards my bed. As soon as our eyes met, she burst into tears. "I'm so sorry, Josie," she sobbed. "I never meant for you to get hurt."

I stared at her numbly and didn't respond straight away. "I believe you."

"You do?" Her blue eyes grew large on her grief-stricken face.

"And I'm not pressing charges," I continued, without expression.

She exhaled and almost smiled. "Oh god, thank you...you don't kno—"

"There are stipulations though," I interrupted firmly.

Her eyes darted to mine and her chest stopped moving. "Anything. Just tell me how much money you want and I'll arrange it."

My gaze tapered. "I don't want your money...I want you to get professional help."

She opened her mouth to speak, but I hushed her.

"Under all your bullshit, I actually think you're a good person, but you need to start taking responsibly for your own actions. Stop using your shitty upbringing as an excuse. Tell your parents to fuck off if you need to. This is *your* life, and you may not believe it right now, but you're more than just a billionaire's daughter with a pretty face."

"How can you be so nice?" she sobbed. "After everything I've done?"

My voice softened. "Because you deserve a chance to make things right."

"I will, I promise you. Grayson and I are heading back to LA tonight to confront our parents about our fake engagement and I've already booked myself into a facility in Malibu to get treatment. I'm serious about getting better this time. I won't let you or Grayson down."

"Do it for yourself, not for us," I said, relieved Grayson was going with her. He needed closure as much as Melanie did.

With a small nod, Melanie pressed her lips together and turned to leave, before pausing at the door. "He really loves you, you know?"

I rolled over and squeezed my eyes shut. It didn't matter anymore. Grayson and I needed to move on from the ridiculous notion it would ever work. Selling *Maude* was obviously his first step and now I had to take mine.

"I saw the way he looked at you last night," she said, quietly. "He's never looked at me that way…not the way Scott used to."

I turned back, surprised by the emotion in her voice, but she was gone.

Late that afternoon, I was allowed to leave the hospital. Lenny took me out the back exit as Grayson was still stalking the hallways, waiting to see me.

We arrived back at my apartment to a very lonely and bored Luci.

"I'm sorry Lucifer," I said, throwing my arms around his neck. "I'll get Reed to come and take you for a walk. I'm not feeling up to it today."

At the mere mention of my neighbour's name, Luci bounded all over the living room in anticipation. I gave Reed a quick call, and within minutes he appeared at my door. When he offered to take him for the night, I jumped at the chance. I highly doubted Luci wanted to watch as many Buffy reruns as I did.

Once I assured Lenny I'd be fine on my own, I made my way to the fridge desperate to put something back in my stomach. Praying for the bare necessities—ice-cream, chocolate or leftover pizza—my mouth dropped when I discovered it full of home-cooked meals. *Aww, Lenny.*

Settling on his famous lasagne, I popped it in the microwave and went to plug in my cell phone, which had gone flat overnight. I flinched as each message came through.

Grayson: Please call me. They're refusing to let me see you.

Grayson: Why won't you let me in?

Adam: In light of recent events, I want you to take a week off. PS. Please call my brother. He's acting like a lunatic.

Grayson: Why aren't you pressing charges? She could have killed you.

Grayson: ???!

Amy: Is everything okay? I just got a cryptic text from boss man wanting to know if I've heard from you.

Amy: I just did a reading. I'm coming over.

Grayson: **So, I just got myself arrested for breaking into your room, only to find you've already gone home.**

Grayson: **Don't worry, Adam bailed me out.**

Grayson: **I'm coming over.**

The doorbell rang and I froze. My feet felt like lead as I shuffled over to the bedroom window to peek below. I caught a glimpse of snow coloured hair, and breathed a sigh of relief.

I waited for Amy at the top of the staircase, but she took longer than expected. A thud sounded with each step, and I curiously waited until she appeared, dragging a large suitcase behind her.

"I'm here to look after you for a few days," she said, between puffs.

"A few days? It looks like you're moving in."

Amy blushed and waved me off as she made her way into my apartment.

As we both settled into my little couch, eating ice-cream and watching the vampire slayer kick demon arse, I picked up my phone. Ignoring all the missed calls from Grayson, I logged into my bank account to check the state of my savings.

"Holy crap!" Ice-cream dripped onto my top and I didn't even care.

Amy looked up. "What is it?" she mumbled with her mouth full.

"There must be some mistake." I scrolled through my recent payments and found a large sum from AG Galleries. "The money from my art sales…it's all there."

Amy grinned. "See, Josie? I told you your photography would pay off one day."

"I can't believe it. I actually have enough money now." My heart raced.

"For what?"

As if she doesn't know.

"My trip to Europe!" I squealed, feeling joyful for the first time in weeks. "I don't have to wait anymore, and the timing couldn't be more perfect."

"So…you're just going to leave?" Amy frowned. "What about your job?"

I sighed. "They've sold *Maude*, Ames."

There was no element of surprise in her eyes. "And?"

"I don't know what that means for everyone else, but as soon as Grayson's parents find out he isn't marrying Melanie, his father will destroy my career. I need to get away before it all goes pear-shaped."

"So, what are you going to do?"

I smiled. "I'll photograph my way through Europe and blog about everything I see. It'll be like *Capturing Love*...but on the road."

"That actually sounds amazing, but what about your apartment? And Luci..."

I looked over at her over-stuffed suitcase and back at Amy's not-so-innocent face. "Ames, how would you feel about living here until I get back? My neighbour will help you with Luci...he can be a bit of a handful."

"Luci or your neighbour?" she asked, with a cheeky smirk.

I laughed wholeheartedly. "I'll leave that for you to find out."

As our laughter died, Amy grew serious. She reached out and took my hand. "But what about Grayson, Jos?"

"Grayson's not a factor," I responded, nonchalantly, but Amy clearly sensed something else.

The doorbell rang and my stomach dropped.

"Speaking of..." Amy pressed her lips together and waited for me to move.

Crossing my arms, I sunk further into the couch, refusing to budge.

"You need to talk to him. He's worried about you."

I winced as the doorbell sounded again.

"Josie..." Amy's shoulders dropped. "Don't do this."

I threw up my hands. "Do what?"

"Push him away. Just like you push *everyone* away."

"I let you in, didn't I?"

She snorted. "I didn't give you a choice."

"It's easier this way," I retorted, fiddling with my hair to avoid eye contact.

"Easier on who?"

"On both of us."

Amy voice softened. "He loves you, Jos. I can see it all over him. Why are you doing this?"

My lower lip trembled. "Because what if one day, he's gone? What if he leaves me, or worse..." I burst into tears as the memory of my parent's death, and the loneliness that came after, slammed into me. "I won't let myself go through that again."

"Oh, Jos." She wrapped her arms around my shoulders and squeezed. "I'm sorry, I didn't mean to open old wounds."

I wiped my eyes. "It's okay, I'm just too tired to talk about him right now. I need to go to bed."

Amy pulled me off the couch. "Come on then, I'll tuck you in." She guided my exhausted body to the bedroom and I climbed under the sheets. As soon as my head hit the pillow, I could barely keep my eyes open. Amy sat quietly at my side until a light tap sounded from my bedroom window. Followed by another, then another. My heart quickened. *Is Grayson actually throwing stones?*

I pretended to be asleep as Amy moved over to the window and peered outside onto the street below. With a little gasp, she unlocked the window and slid it open.

"Amy, can you please let me up? I need to see her." His voice was faint as it travelled up three stories.

"She's asleep."

There was a pause and some possible curse words. "Is she okay? She won't return any of my calls."

"Just give her some time."

"Can you let her know I'm heading to LA for a few days? I'm going to sort everything out."

"I will," Amy said before sliding the window shut. I quickly closed my eyes before she turned my way. "Catch all that?" she asked, jumping into the spare space next to me. *Busted*.

I offered her a sleepy smile. "Thanks, Ames."

"Goodnight Jos," she whispered. "Everything will work out."

"Goodnight."

"I thought I told you to take some time off?" Adam asked, when I walked into his office a few days later.

I slowly approached his desk. "I am, except it's going to be a little longer than a week."

He pursed his lips and nodded. "Very well, how much time were you thinking?"

With a tight smile, I placed my laptop and security pass on his desk.

His eyebrows pulled together. "Josie…"

"I can't work here anymore."

"If you're worried about Mel…she's gone. Grayson's taken her back to LA."

"This isn't about Mel. It's about me."

"And Gray? Where does he fit in?"

"He doesn't," I said, ignoring the ache in my chest.

Adam winced and ran his hands through his hair. "Well, what are you going to do instead?"

I smiled. "Something I've wanted to do for a long time. Travel."

He thought about it for a moment. "Where to?"

"Italy…to start with."

Adam picked up his phone and started dialling. "Okay, well, I'll give you a four-hour head start."

I scrunched up my nose. "Huh?"

"That's how long it will take from the moment this call connects, to the moment Grayson is back in New York chasing down your ass."

My mouth dropped. "You wouldn't…"

He lifted the phone to his ear with a smirk. "Grayson, hi."

"Fuck," I said, and sprinted out the door.

Hurrying back home, I picked up the bags I'd spent the last few days packing and dropped them at my door, ready to escape as soon as my cab arrived.

"Whoa, what's the rush? Your plane isn't leaving for another six hours," Amy said as she finished carrying in the rest of her things.

"Oh, you know me. Just eager to start my next adventure." I smiled a little too forcefully.

Amy narrowed her eyes. "Oookay...well, you still haven't introduced me to this neighbour of yours."

"Oh crap, let's do that now." I grabbed her hand, pulled her down the stairs and knocked on his door.

"Hang on," Reed called out as loud gunfire erupted within his apartment.

Amy's eyes grew wide. "What is he doing in there?"

"He's a professional gamer," I said, tapping my foot.

She scrunched up her nose. "That's a thing?"

The door flew open. "Yeah, it's a thing," Reed said, dropping his headpiece around his neck.

Amy's eyes fluttered as she looked over Reed, who stood before us, shirtless and dishevelled. Her cheeks grew pink.

I muffled a giggle. "Reed, this is Amy. She'll be staying in my apartment while I'm overseas. Amy, this is Reed. He can help you out with Luci when he gets too much."

They both uttered hellos and stood there, silently admiring each other.

I clapped my hands together to draw their attention. "Well, now that's done, Amy can you help me bring my bags down?"

"Oh, I don't mind helping," Reed intercepted, closing the door behind him.

"But what about your game?" I asked, guiltily.

He threw a sideways glance at Amy. "There'll be others."

"You've been holding out on me," Amy whispered as we tailed him up the stairs.

I giggled. Reed was exactly Amy's type. A little nerdy, and a whole lot of sexy. I didn't need to be psychic to know they were going to have fun together.

Saying goodbye to Luci was the hardest thing. He jumped around excitedly, without a clue I'd be disappearing from his life for an undetermined period of time. He licked away my tears as I assured him he was in good hands, and then bounded away. Peering up at Amy and Reed, I found them making googly eyes at each other and groaned. I'd become the third wheel in my own apartment.

I gave Reed a hug goodbye, before Amy walked me out to my waiting cab.

"Please don't break my bed," I said, with a knowing smirk.

Amy laughed and shrugged. "We'll try not to."

My laughter faded as the cab driver closed the trunk, signalling he was ready to go.

"Look after yourself, Josie," she said, turning serious.

"I will."

She pulled me in for a hug. "One day, you'll let someone else do it for you."

"Well until then, I've got all I need." I held up my passport and camera bag, with a cheesy grin, and slid into the cab.

Chapter 27

As I sat in the airport terminal with only two hours left before take-off, my leg bounced up and down incessantly. For the fiftieth time, I rose from my chair to check the schedule of incoming flights from LA. The next one wasn't for a few hours, so I breathed a sigh of relief.

"Funny thing about private jets, they can take off and land anytime, anyplace."

I jumped out of my skin and whirled around to the voice that made my heart swell. "Grayson…what are you doing here?"

He raised an eyebrow. "I was going to ask you the same thing."

"I…I'm heading to Europe." My jaw twitched. "Like I always planned."

Grayson pursed his lips. "And when did you *plan* on telling me?"

"Look, it'll be better for the both of us to just let this…this *thing*…go."

"This *thing*?" Irritation flickered through his expression.

"That's all it is…a passing infatuation that was never meant to last." Pain speared through my chest.

His hard stare penetrated mine. "Why do you keep lying to yourself?"

Struggling to breathe, I lowered my gaze. "Our worlds are too different, Gray. I need to leave before…" My voice trailed off as I faced my underlying fears.

"Before what?" he uttered, impatiently. "Before we've even had a chance?"

My eyes filled with tears as I lifted them to meet his. "Before you leave *me*."

"Jos..." He stepped forward. "I don't plan on leaving you... ever."

"Well, things don't always go to plan," I muttered, folding my arms.

"No, they don't," he said, shaking his head. "I never planned on meeting you, and you're the best goddamn thing to ever happen to me."

I scowled. "Don't say things like that."

"Like what?"

I huffed. "Don't make this harder than it needs to be."

He chuckled. "So I shouldn't say things like...I miss you so much it hurts?"

"Exactly that," I cried, turning away from him.

"Then I definitely shouldn't say I think you're the most beautiful woman I've ever seen, and I think I'm dreaming every morning I wake up next to you."

My breath hitched. "Please stop."

"What about...I love you and plan to marry you, just as soon as you'll let me?"

I gasped and spun back to him, wide-eyed and mouth agape.

Grayson closed the distance between us. "We may be from different worlds, but I want to create a new one...with you."

I drew in a deep breath as my resilience began to crumble. "Grayson, please..." My eyes burned. "I've been saving for this trip since I moved here. This is something I need to do."

Grayson shrugged. "Fine." He pulled out his phone and typed a long message, lifting his sparkling gaze to mine as he pressed send.

"What are you doing?" I asked, tapering my eyes.

His sly grin grew. "Well, if you're not going to stay, then I'll have to come with you. I'm due for some time off."

"But...you can't..."

He folded his arms. "Why not?"

"Your parents, for one..."

"They have no hold over me anymore. As of yesterday, I'm no longer with Harlow Corp."

I gasped. "You left the family business?"

"Kind of," he said with an easy shrug. "I left one, and started another."

"What about Adam?"

"He'll be running Harlow Corp. as soon as Dad retires, and I'll be heading something new. Grandpa was blown away by my ideas, and wanted to back me. Can you believe it?"

I stopped breathing as the realisation struck me. "You bought *Maude*?"

Grayson cupped my face in his palm. "It was the only way. My father can't ruin your career if he has no control over it."

My eyes lit up. "So everyone keeps their jobs?"

"Yes," he chuckled. "Except for maybe Janice. She's a bitch."

I burst out laughing, right before the tears started. "She is, isn't she?"

Grayson pulled me to his chest and I exhaled into his arms. "I've missed you," he said, kissing the top of my head.

I peered up into his hazel eyes and melted into him. "I've missed you too, so fucking much," I said, pushing up onto my tiptoes to kiss his soft lips.

His hands travelled up my back and rested in the nape of my neck as he devoured my mouth, pressing his body into mine.

"You're really coming with me?" I murmured, when our mouths parted.

"Well…no…" he said, clearing his throat. "You're actually coming with me."

I scrunched my nose. "Huh?"

"We're taking the private jet."

My eyes grew wide. "Are you sure you're allowed—"

"It's Grandpa's jet, and he loves you almost as much as I do."

Heat rose up my neck. "Oh…"

His face fell. "This new world of ours can have a private jet, can't it? Please don't make me fly…" he shuddered. "Commercial."

I laughed. "Only if we can keep my apartment." The words left my mouth before I could even register what they meant, and my face heated.

A huge smile covered Grayson's face. "Sounds fair...but as soon as we get back, we're buying a new couch."

"We might need a new bed too." I chuckled as we began to manoeuvre through the crowded airport.

Grayson slowed his pace. "Care to explain?"

"Let's just say, my house sitter has taken a liking to my neighbour and I'm pretty sure they'll hit it off." I screwed up my face. "They're probably *hitting it off* right now."

He laughed and discreetly ran his hand over my arse as we walked. "Well, if we didn't manage to break the bed, I doubt they could."

I threw him a sideways glance and a familiar ache grew below. "So, just how private is this *private* jet of yours?"

He shot me a wink. "You're about to find out."

Grayson's anxious hand glided up and down my leg as the plane took off. He kept his focus on me, instead of the descending landscape to ease his irrational fear. Barely looking at the air stewardess, he requested a blanket, then when she returned, surprised her with the rest of the flight off.

Lying the soft material over our legs, his hand returned to its original position...only a little higher. As his fingers ran over the denim between my thighs, my core throbbed and a quiet moan escaped my lips.

As soon as the air stewardess returned to the front cabin, it was on. I hurriedly unbuckled my seatbelt and threw myself onto Grayson, straddled him in his chair. "Still afraid of heights?" I asked, dragging my tongue along his bottom lip.

"Not with a distraction like this, I'm not," he mumbled, between our urgent kisses.

I tore off his shirt while he slipped his hand up my back and unclasped my bra. He cupped my breasts while his thumbs entertained my nipples, making me clench my thighs over his. With one swift motion, my top and bra disappeared and his mouth consumed mine.

Wrapping his arm around my lower back, he pulled my hips closer until I felt his hardness through both layers of denim. Leaning forward, he ran his tongue between my breasts at an agonising pace. *I need him now.*

As if reading my thoughts, Grayson lifted my body, flipped me onto my seat, and tugged down my pants. His tip pressed against my entrance and paused. "Shit, Jos. I don't have anything."

I could barely breathe in anticipation. "Please don't stop. I'm clean and on the pill." I looked up at him, praying for the same response.

"I haven't been with anyone but you, since my last test, which was 100% clean."

As he carefully reclined the chair, I cried out in ecstasy when he finally entered me, giving me everything I desired.

"I love you, Jos," he whispered huskily into my ear as he began to thrust.

"I…love…you…too," I murmured, trying to delay my inevitable release. "Please don't stop."

His eyes pierced mine. "I'm never…going…to stop."

Slightly disorientated after a few hours' sleep, we woke when the pilot made an announcement over the PA that we were about to start our descent.

I looked over at Grayson in alarm. "We can't possibly be there yet."

He winced and his cheeks grew pink. "I may have made a slight adjustment to our itinerary."

My eyes grew wide. "What?"

"It's just a stopover," he said, keeping his voice level, but the corner of his mouth rose. "We have a little unfinished business to attend to."

I narrowed my gaze. "What are you talking about?"

He pulled a torn piece of napkin from his back pocket and straightened it out in his hands.

"My list," I gasped. "You kept it? All this time?"

Grayson's smile melted my insides. "Are you ready to see number one?"

Happiness swelled within and I threw myself against the window of the plane. The glowing casinos and twinkling lights below confirmed what Grayson was trying to tell me. We were back where it all started. *Las Vegas*.

EPILOGUE

Grayson

I stood behind Josie, watching her kaleidoscopic hair blowing back in the breeze as she gazed over something almost as beautiful as her. *The Grand Canyon.*

A smile played on her lips as she reached back and took my hand, tugging me beside her. "It's incredible," she gasped and peered up at me. "I never thought I'd get here." Her striking bronze eyes glistened. "Thank you, so much."

I wrapped my arm around her shoulders and pulled her close as the sun set over the rocky horizon. The sky glowed deep shades of orange and pink, leaving Josie so awestruck, she was forgetting to take her own photos. Giving her a nudge, I motioned down to her camera with a raised brow.

"Shit," she muttered. Quickly lifting it to her face, she began clicking relentlessly.

I let out a little chuckle and watched her in wonderment.

It may have taken a while for me to convince her, but she was it for me. Her walls were built so high, I feared I'd never get through to her. But brick by brick, she let me in and I felt like the luckiest man alive.

I'd never met a girl like her in the circles I ran in. So strong willed, independent, hardworking and loyal. Traits my parents weren't comfortable with in a female, let alone one who didn't come from old money like ours. Josie had no ulterior motive, wanted nothing to do with our fortune, and refused to play into any part of that world.

If it wasn't for her, I never would have stood up to my parents, and Mel and I would've been in the same position we'd been in for years. Unhappy. Our parents were so consumed with their desire for power, they lost sight of what it cost to attain it. I wanted to marry for love, not for money or status. For simple, old fashioned, heart pounding, butterfly inducing love. The love I felt for Josie Spencer.

Finally letting go of the guilt I felt over Melanie's health and my parent's expectations, I was free to make my own decisions. Josie was my first. *Maude* was my second.

My brother and I could both see the potential of our little publication, and with my Grandfather's help—and my healthy trust fund—I made an attractive offer to Harlow Corp. and Warren Enterprises, knowing they'd take it. They didn't know who they were dealing with until the contract was signed.

Adam still worked for my father, and was content to live that way, but I wasn't anymore. I wanted to build something and watch it prosper, not just buy, build and sell, which my family were notorious for. I wanted to make a difference and do something worth putting my name on.

I dropped my arm from Josie's shoulders, and fished out her list again.

"So, I may not be 'devilishly handsome', but I was hoping to cross the last item off your list."

She frowned. "But we did them all…I don't kno—" Her voice caught and her eyes widened as I unfolded the napkin and slid my glasses over my nose.

I cleared my throat. "I believe there was a bonus item…"

Josie gasped and snatched the list from my hand, letting out a nervous laugh. She turned away to hide her reddening face as she reread the miniscule scrawl at the bottom of the napkin.

While her back was turned, I knelt down and pulled a tiny box from my pocket. "Josie…"

She shook off her embarrassment, and turned back to me, dropping her eyes to where I rested on one knee. Her mouth fell open.

My heart raced, but I tried to keep my voice steady. "Josie Spencer, will you marry me?"

She clutched her chest when I lifted the lid to reveal a shimmering opal ring surrounded by diamonds. She took deep breaths but said nothing.

"Josie?" I called, hoping to break her trance.

Her eyes gleamed. "Grayson, you're wrong…"

My heart dipped, but her face didn't match her words of rejection.

She stepped towards me with a glint in her eye. "You're the very definition of 'devilishly handsome'."

My smile grew as my heart resumed. "Is that a yes?"

Tears rolled down her cheeks as she launched into my arms. "That's a *hell yes*." She laughed, and tilted her face towards me with a smile I'll never forget. She kissed me hard, and I matched her ferocity. Her hands held my stubbled cheeks as I wrapped my arms tightly around her waist, easily taking her weight.

"Hang on…" I said, easing her down onto her toes. I took her hand and squeezed it. "We forgot something."

As I slipped the ring onto Josie's finger, her breath caught.

"Is this the same opal?" she asked, wide eyed.

I nodded and stared straight into her deep brown eyes. "I had no intention of ever letting you go."

Full of emotion, she slid her arms around my neck and I lifted her up until her lips were level with mine.

"So, when do you wanna do this?" she murmured, her mouth hovering over mine.

I chuckled at her enthusiasm. "How does tomorrow sound?"

Josie's eyes grew as I continued.

"I know this great little chapel in Vegas, and they just happen to have the best Elvis in town."

Her sparkling eyes warmed my heart. "It sounds perfect," she said, grinning ear to ear.

Josie lowered her gaze and smiled down at the little list that brought us together. "I guess I won't be needing this anymore."

I took it from her hand and slid it back into my pocket. "You'll have to make a new one," I said, tucking a strand of hair behind her ear.

She lifted her eyes. "I can't think of anything else I want to do right now, except you."

My pants tightened under her heated gaze. "Well, there's your first item."

She laughed and lay gentle kisses on my smiling lips. "And second…and third…and fourth…"

"Come on." I chuckled, holding her at armlengths to avoid an embarrassing situation. "There must be a million things you want to do."

"Well, this isn't just about me anymore. What would you put on there?"

"Easy." I shrugged nonchalantly. "Number one. Same as you." I winked and she smirked. "Number two. Travel the world with you. Number three. Move in with you." Her smile grew. "Number four. Work with you. Number five. Have babies with you." I ignored her wide eyes. "Number six. Grow old with you. But I'll happily interchange number five, with any other number."

Blush rose up her neck and she wiped away a tear. "That sounds like an amazing list."

My heart swelled. "Really?" I'd never broached the topic of kids, but prayed she'd want them too.

"Really," she said, pulling me towards her.

I pressed my forehead against hers and exhaled slowly. "I love you."

Her hands circled my ears before easing their way through my hair. "I love you too."

Our smiling lips collided and didn't part until the sun had set, and our eyes mirrored the starry night sky.

We arrived back in Las Vegas by helicopter an hour later, still buzzing.

I pulled Josie toward the Bellagio Fountain in lieu of our hotel, because I didn't want to say goodnight just yet. I booked us separate rooms for the night, because Grandpa told me so, but now I was regretting it.

"So, what should we do with our last night of 'single life'?" I asked, squeezing her hand.

Her eyes sparkled back at me in mischief. "Sky Jump?"

My stomach dropped at the thought and I ran my hands through my hair.

She stifled a giggle. "I'm joking. I never fucking want to do that again."

I hung back my head and laughed. "Thank fucking Christ."

Josie leant back on the handrail, always watching the people around her. Little did she know, I was always watching her. Even on the night we first met. I curiously observed her snapping unsuspecting individuals, and wondered why she'd miss the show to take photos of other people enjoying it.

It didn't take long to figure her out though. Josie was always content to put her happiness aside, to be a bystander of others. Perhaps she didn't believe she had the capacity to be happy again after losing her parents, but I was determined to prove her wrong.

"Wanna hit the clubs?" I asked jokingly, knowing she'd hate the idea.

She smirked. "Or maybe we should go see some strippers?"

I shook my head with a chuckle. "Or get a tattoo…"

Her lazy gaze settled over mine. "I'll settle for a burger and fries?"

I smiled and inwardly fist pumped the air, glancing across the street at the diner where we first met. "I know just the place."

THE END

EXCLUSIVE PAPERBACK CONTENT

Amy

"Professional gamer, eh?" I trailed my new neighbor up the stairs back into the apartment building after watching my best friend leave for the airport.

Reed's cheeks turned pink as he slowly turned. "It's not as lame as it sounds."

"I never said it was lame." I met his exasperated gaze in confusion. "I'm impressed."

His brow furrowed. "You're fucking with me."

"I'm not fucking with you. I think it's really cool."

He stared at me a moment longer before his pretty blue eyes narrowed. "No, you're definitely fucking with me."

"I'm not!"

His left eyebrow rose.

"Fine." I threw up my hands and trudged up the stairs toward Josie's apartment. "I'm fucking with you!"

After slamming the door with a little more force than necessary, I let out a growl that made Luci's ears prick up and proceeded to grumble toward the couch.

I hated not being believed. I prided myself on my honesty, and even though it repelled many from getting too close, I wasn't willing to change. I'd spent years of my life hiding who I really was and masked my unique abilities so well I'd almost convinced myself into not believing them. My mother had done the same until she took her own life when I was only four years old, and that was not going to happen to me.

It was my grandmother who taught me to embrace my powers, to harness my erratic mind to decipher what belonged to my world versus the futures of others. Visions plagued me with almost every human interaction, so I opted for as much solitude as I could find.

Thankfully, I'd found the perfect job at *Maude* with my own quiet office, and when I craved connection, I'd simply dull my senses with alcohol at the local bar. It wasn't the healthiest approach, but I got lonely sometimes.

Josie had always been the exception. She never judged or doubted me, and she embraced my authentic self. For the last six years, she had been my closest friend, but now she was off fulfilling her dreams, which left me a whole lot lonelier.

As I flopped onto the shabby couch, Luci launched into the space beside me as if sensing my grief. He snuggled in, barely leaving enough room for my small frame as I stroked his mass of wiry hair. Animals I could deal with. People, not so much.

After watching a few episodes of *Buffy* on Josie's tiny television, I heaved Luci's enormous head off my lap and headed to the kitchen where I'd left my work laptop. I sat at the counter, turned it on, and logged into my favorite online game. What's so wrong with a little cyber dissociation every now and then? And why did my new neighbor even care what other people thought of his profession? *I'm a fucking psychic!*

Little did Reed know, online gaming was my connection of choice. There was no absorbing unwanted energies or glimpses of the future through a screen full of faceless names, so it was a safe place for me. My day job completely drained my vitality, so I found it rejuvenating to delve into a fantasy world with strangers.

Messages popped up on my screen almost instantly.

EchoWisp: **@PsyPixie Finally! You're back online!**

PsyPixie: **Sorry, guys! I've had a crazy few days.**

BigTed: **We've missed you!**

RippleVex: **@EchoWisp is struggling to win without his lucky charm.**

EchoWisp: **I never lose @RippleVex**

PsyPixie: **Aw, thanks, guys. I've missed you all too.**

Especially *EchoWisp*. We'd been flirting and fighting since our first battle together a year ago.

EchoWisp: **We're about to start a game. You in, Pix?**

My heart always fluttered when he called me that.

PsyPixie: **Of course I'm in. Let's do this!**

I didn't own any fancy gaming equipment, so I had to rely on quick typing to communicate and Josie's internet speed, which was surprisingly fast. Even without high-level gaming experience, I'd become a valuable asset to the squad due to my 'lucky guesses.'

As the next game loaded up, our squad moved around the screen in anticipation. While my avatar looked uncannily similar to my real-life appearance with the addition of vibrant-pink hair and sparkly wings, my team members consisted of a giant teddy bear—*BigTed*, a slimy amphibious creature—*RippleVex*, and a mysterious opaque ghost-like figure called *EchoWisp*. None, I hoped, resembled their true appearance, but I preferred it that way. Remaining anonymous made life a lot easier.

Our team played most nights, but with everything going on with Josie lately, I'd opted to put her first. I was closer to her than my own sister, and since the death of her parents, she had no family left to support her. I filled that void for her, as she did for me.

I barely saw my sister these days. After my mother died and we were taken away from our father by the state, Cassidy took on the mother role, never really having a chance to be a carefree kid herself. I loved and respected her for that, but resentment simmered below the surface, so I kept my distance.

Moments later, our squad was cast off into a fantasy land full of forests, rivers, and waterfalls. The landscape changed every time we played, but this world was one of my favorites. The sounds of birds and babbling brooks floated out of the laptop speakers, and I smiled. It was always so peaceful before the impending massacre.

My message thread pinged.

EchoWisp: **@PsyPixie Your fave!**

My heart lit up. *EchoWisp* remembered.

PsyPixie: **My day just got a whole lot better.**

EchoWisp: **Good to hear. Now, let's go win this thing!**

While the others built our base amongst the trees and collected medicines and weaponry, they also had to protect our *Aetherheart*—a glowing orb that contained powerful magical energy. *EchoWisp* and I were assigned the hunter roles. We had to sneak into enemy territory, capture their orb, and kill anyone who got in our way. Whichever team succeeded in fusing the two *Aetherhearts* inside the hidden crystal cave would ultimately win the game.

It was a game my nephew, Finn, introduced to me to during one of my rare visits upstate, and I'd been hooked ever since. He wasn't allowed to play during the week, so I'd practiced on my own until this squad adopted me. It was nice to feel a part of something outside of work, even if it was considered "lame."

Our team never used audio because *EchoWisp* recorded our games for online content. His videos were funny enough without my chipmunk voice, and his ridiculous commentary clearly made him very popular. Although he never showed his face online, he had millions of people captivated. Perhaps he wanted to protect his identity as much as I wanted to shield my soul from the world.

EchoWisp: **All clear @PsyPixie**

EchoWisp had taken down the other team's defenses, leaving their *Aetherheart* exposed.

PsyPixie: **I'm going in.**

My tiny, unassuming avatar made it easy to slip in and out of places unnoticed, and that was exactly what I did to steal our opponent's orb.

PsyPixie: **Go! Go! Go!**

All we had to do now was avoid or kill the remaining players on the opposing team while running back to base, hoping to get there before our *Aetherheart* was stolen.

A burst of light flashed over the screen, acknowledging the death of one of our teammates—*RippleVex*.

EchoWisp: **F*ck, they must be close to our base.**

Moments later, arrows whooshed past, and I ducked for cover behind a large rock. *EchoWisp* followed.

EchoWisp: **You keep going. I'll hold them off.**

PsyPixie: **No! Take the orb, and you go. You have a much better chance of making it.**

Before I could type another word, *EchoWisp* launched out and attacked the enemy.

"Fuck!" I muttered before taking off into the forest. I scaled up the trees, hoping to make it back to base before the enemy found me.

Two more bursts of light flashed over the screen, and my heart lurched, hoping it wasn't *EchoWisp*. Instead, it was *BigTed* and one of the opposing players. Our base had clearly been exposed.

EchoWisp: **Watch your back, Pix. I'm coming.**

Panning my gaze over the forest floor, waiting for *EchoWisp* to appear, I spotted the remaining opposing player dodging in and out of the trees.

PsyPixie: **He's on the ground, heading to the river.**

EchoWisp: **Roger that.**

Within moments, another flare of light filled the screen, marking the death of our last opponent.

EchoWisp: **I've got our Aetherheart back. Where are you?**

PsyPixie: **Coming in hot!**

I launched out of the tree directly in front of him.

EchoWisp: **Pix! You scared the shit out of me!**

PsyPixie: **My bad.**

EchoWisp: **We're running out of time to find the crystal cave. Any ideas?**

A vision of a waterfall flashed through my mind, and I sniggered. This was my special power, and it had nothing to do with my gaming ability.

PsyPixie: **Follow me!**

EchoWisp chased me through the forest until a waterfall came into view. I dove into the river and swam through the churning water until the crystal cave materialized on the other side.

EchoWisp: **How the f*ck did you know it was here?**

PsyPixie: **Lucky guess?**

I grinned as we merged our *Aetherhearts,* and an explosion of light glittered over the screen, announcing another victory for our squad.

Our avatars teleported back into a holding orb to await the next game, but the rest of our squad had already logged out.

EchoWisp: **Another game? I doubt we need the others to win.**

PsyPixie: **I wish I could, but I have to work tomorrow.**

EchoWisp: **That's too bad. We make a great team.**

I sighed happily. We sure do.

PsyPixie: **I'll try to get on tomorrow night if I'm not too exhausted.**

EchoWisp: **Nite, Pix.**

Warmth filled my belly.

PsyPixie: **Nite, Echo. *pink heart emoji***

EchoWisp had become a constant and pleasant distraction to my nights, and sleep always came easily after our battles. Although he was clearly a professional, he never made me feel inadequate. In fact, he never put anyone down who filled his squad. Perhaps that was why he was so popular online. He was happy to play with anyone, including me—the pink-haired fairy with an uncanny knack for knowing where the crystal cave was. It certainly made up for my internet speed back at my old apartment.

Working at *Maude* was a struggle without Josie, but when she'd called to tell me about her engagement and spur-of-the-moment wedding in Las Vegas, I'd left work with more pep. I'd seen visions of her impending happiness with Grayson, but the speedy timeline surprised me. I guess when you know, you know, and the thought of her happy filled me with joy.

"Luci!" I stomped into the apartment, threw my bag on the kitchen counter, and panned my gaze around for the furry beast. I jumped again, sending vibrations throughout the apartment to alert the almost deaf dog. "Luci! Want to go for a walk?!"

At the sound of the word, Luci bounded out of the bedroom to give me a sloppy greeting. "Oh, you heard that word, didn't you?" I attempted to pat Luci's head, but he proceeded to zoom around the apartment like he was malfunctioning and parkoured over the furniture. "What the fuck?"

As I picked up the leash in an attempt to calm the wild animal, my cell phone rang.

"Hey, Cass," I answered at the first ring. I'd deal with the crazed dog later.

"Hey, Ames, have you finished unpacking?"

"Only five minutes after moving in." I didn't own much. "This apartment is amazing. You and Finn should visit while I'm here."

My sister groaned. "I'm too busy job hunting. There really isn't much work for a *death doula* right now."

"Maybe you should move closer to the city? Plenty of people dying out here."

"To Manhattan?" Cassidy laughed. "God no, plus Finn has school and swimming practice, and Dad has actually been helping out a lot."

I smiled. "So, you've been getting along?"

"Mostly." She paused. "He's trying."

"Good." I was happy with the progress of their strained relationship. "Oh hey, tell Finn my new neighbor is a professional gamer. He'll love that." I smiled. "He's cute too."

"Ames..." Her warning tone echoed through the phone.

"I know, I know." I giggled. "But I have a weird feeling about him."

"Good weird, or serial-killer weird?"

"Just...*weird*." It was a sensation I was unfamiliar with. "But not in a 'he's going to steal my kidneys' or 'wear my skin' kinda way."

Cassidy chuckled. "Well, that's a relief."

"It just feels like I've met him somewhere before."

"Don't complicate things while you're living there, Ames, or you'll be forced to move back into that shitty old apartment with the black mold."

I shuddered. Josie's apartment was heaven compared to my previous accommodations, but it was all I could afford on my wage.

"Are you still paying rent there?" Cassidy continued, being her naturally overprotective self.

"Of course, and the landlord promised he'll do some repairs while I'm gone."

"And you believe him?"

Nope. "Cass... Don't worry about me. Focus on yourself and Finn. What has my nephew been up to lately?"

"Oh, you know Finn. Still gaming, playing basketball, and swimming. He won another race today."

"Another one!" I gushed. "Tell him congrats for me."

"I will. I may even give him some gaming time later."

"On a weeknight?" I gasped dramatically. "Who are you?"

"Ha-ha."

"And what about you, Cass? How are you *really* doing?"

My sister knew exactly what I meant. Her husband had passed away four years before, and she'd been rebuilding her life since.

"I'm doing okay." My heart ached for her. "I'm reading a lot."

"You've got to get out into the real world one day. Maybe even go on a date or two?"

Cassidy scoffed. "And when was the last time *you* went on a date?"

"I don't need a date." I lifted my chin. "I have Gary."

Cassidy's laughter filled my ear. "Your vibrator doesn't count, Amy!"

"He did last night." I loved hearing my sister's laugh. It was rare these days. "You should really get one."

"Oh my god. I'm hanging up now."

I snorted. My sister had no clue what she was missing out on. "Stick to your romance books, then."

"I will." I felt her smile from 150 miles away. "Bye, Ames."

"See ya, Cass. Something will turn up soon, I promise. Love you."

"Love you, too."

Once we'd hung up the phone, I panned my gaze around the eerily quiet apartment. Something felt...off.

"Luci?" I called out again, summoning the demon who'd simply vanished from sight.

A rumbling noise sounded from the bedroom, followed by a growl, dosing me with a shot of adrenaline. *Fuck*. Had an intruder crept their way into the building?

With a racing heart, I tiptoed toward the bedroom as more growls and rustling sheets filled the silence. *Fuck. Fuck. Fuck.*

In a moment of bravery, or possible stupidity, I threw open the bedroom door to reveal Luci rolling on top of the bed, wrestling with what appeared to be a giant purple dog toy. *Phew.*

I momentarily relaxed until the toy buzzed, triggering Luci to attack again. My jaw dropped as the toy came into view. "GARY!"

My trusty vibrator was swung into the air, only to be caught and tossed again. "LUCI! NO!"

Wide, dilated eyes stared back at me, ready for a game. "Please don't do this!"

As if I'd accepted the challenge, Luci scooped up my vibrator and sprinted from the room. I gave chase into the open living space, knocking books and records off shelves and Josie's trusty television onto the floor. "FUCK!" I screamed as the glass cracked in three places.

"LUCI! STOP!" My repeated efforts fell on literal deaf ears as my most faithful companion remained lodged in Luci's jaw, dripping with slobber. "LEAVE GARY ALONE!"

As my shoulders slumped in defeat, the front door swung open, and Reed rushed into the room. "Is everything okay? I heard yelling." He quickly surveyed the damage while my eyes popped out of their sockets. *This isn't happening.*

In Luci's surprise, he dropped Gary to the floor and bolted for his favorite neighbor, giving me a chance to launch onto the floor to hide the evidence. "It's fine! Everything is fine," I cried out, gripping onto Gary and hiding him behind my back. I stood to face Reed with a clenched jaw as drool oozed over my fingers.

"Are you sure?" Reed asked, stepping toward me in obvious concern.

"Completely." With a tight smile and awkward laugh, I backed into the kitchen and discreetly dropped Gary into the trash can. "I, um…forgot Josie gave you a key."

"I knocked, but I doubt you heard over the yelling." His eyebrows elevated as he absorbed the mess Luci and I had made in our wrestle. "What the hell happened here?"

"Luci," I grumbled, washing my hands under the kitchen faucet. "Luci happened."

"Did he eat one of your shoes?"

"I wish."

"And who is Gary?" He dipped his head toward the bedroom. "Your boyfriend?"

I almost laughed. "Not anymore."

"Oh, I'm sorry." He cleared his throat. "Messy breakup?"

Laughter burst from my lips. "Something like that."

Reed shook his head in confusion, clearly catching on to my crazy vibes. *Good.*

As he was about to speak, the trash can vibrated, drawing our attention—and Luci's.

"Fuck." My stomach dropped.

Reed approached curiously. "What is that?"

"Nothing!" I gulped as the trash can bounced toward him.

"Are you sure?"

I kicked it back. "It's just one of Luci's toys. It's malfunctioning."

"Oh, I can fix it," Reed said, about to reach in. "I'm pretty good at—"

"NO!" I snatched Reed's arm away and pulled him toward the door. "I think we should take Luci for a walk." I picked up Luci's leash and attached it to his collar before he launched another attack. "You can show me where the off-leash park is."

With a swift glance over my shoulder, I led Reed out of the apartment with Luci in tow before I completely died from embarrassment.

"So, did you hear the news?" I asked Reed once the fire in my cheeks had simmered down.

He tugged on Luci's leash, slowing him down as we approached the park. "No, what news?"

"Josie and Grayson got hitched in Vegas."

"No fucking way!" His excited grin matched mine. "That's awesome." Reed's smile slowly faded as he let Luci off the leash. "I guess that means she'll be moving out."

"I don't think you need to worry about that. Josie loves that apartment, and they'll be back sooner than expected."

"What makes you say that?"

I shrugged. "Lucky guess."

Reed watched me quizzically.

"What?" My cheeks warmed again.

"You remind me of someone. I'm trying to figure out who."

"Perhaps we've met in a past life."

Reed sniggered. "You believe in that?"

"I believe in everything." I bumped his shoulder. "As *lame* as it sounds."

Reed stopped walking and crossed his surprisingly built arms. "Look, most people think gamers are desperate, obese, child predators. I didn't want to scare you away."

"Scare *me* away?!" That was usually my territory. "I know you're not any of those things."

"And how do you know that?"

"Well, apart from Josie's glowing recommendation"—*here we go*—"I'm a medium."

Reed scrunched up his nose. "Like a psychic?"

I nodded. "And most people think we're all tree-hugging hippies who wear crystals and worship the moon."

"And you *don't* do that?" he asked, eyeing my amethyst earrings.

I smirked. "Not the point."

He scratched his dirty-blond hair. A nervous habit, perhaps. "Does that mean you can read minds?"

"Sometimes." I stared into his bright-blue eyes until his face burned red, then I deliberately raised my eyebrows. "But mostly I get visions, if I'm tuned in enough."

Reed omitted a nervous laugh. "And you do this for work?"

"People email *Maude* with personal questions, and I read cards for them then post the answers online. It's surprisingly popular."

"How do you know if your predications come true or not?"

I shrugged, unfazed by his skepticism. "Some people write back, but mostly I don't find out. It's not my business what they do with what I say. My visions can be interpreted in all different ways."

Reed appeared satisfied with that answer and threw the ball to Luci. "That's intense."

"It can be."

"A gift and a curse, no doubt."

My head spun to Reed, but he was too focused on the dog to see my shock. No one I'd ever met had so willingly believed me. He'd just accepted it without question.

"So, what games do you play?" I asked, eager to continue our conversation before any visions could emerge.

"Oh, I doubt you've heard of them."

"Try me."

As we walked around the dog park, occasionally bumping shoulders, he listed his favorite games. Each touch sent tingles throughout my body until his next word sent an electric bolt.

"*Aetherheart?*" I repeated. "I love that game."

"You play?"

"My nephew got me into it." I smiled up at him. "It helps me relax after work. I need to dissociate for a while before going to bed."

"My entire job is dissociating."

"So, you actually get paid to play video games?"

"Not exactly." Reed threw the ball for Luci. "I have sponsors and get paid for advertising on my videos and live streams."

"You must be doing something right to be living in that apartment building in this part of the city."

"Yeah, I do alright." His bashful smile confessed that he did more than 'alright.' "My family doesn't really get it, but I'm okay with that."

"Most people don't get what I do either."

Luci bounded back to us, seemingly having had enough ball retrieving and butt sniffing for one day. As I grabbed his collar,

Reeds fingertips grazed mine as he attached the leash, and my breath caught.

"Thanks for showing me where to take Luci," I said, hesitant to drag my hand away. "I may need some help until I get strong enough to handle him."

"Anytime." The warmth of Reed's smile reached his eyes. "It's nice to interact with a real-life person every now and then."

Once we reached the top of our apartment entry stairs, I turned to Reed. "Well, I better get going. I have a gaming date with my nephew."

Reed glanced anxiously at his watch. "It's almost time for me to log on too."

"Maybe I'll end up stealing your *Aetherheart*." The words came out more romantic than I'd intended.

"Not unless I steal yours first." His surprise matched mine.

With an awkward-as-fuck goodbye, I rushed upstairs and fell back against the closing door. *Fuck, he is cute.*

After whipping off my bra and grabbing a quick bite to eat, I messaged my nephew to get online and logged into my favorite game.

EchoWisp was already waiting alongside *BigTed*.

BigTed: RippleVex is out. Did anyone find a fourth?

PsyPixie: Sure have. I'm just waiting for him to log in.

EchoWisp: Do they know how to play?

PsyPixie: Since when do you care about their ability, @EchoWisp?

BigTed: Someone sounds a little jealous, @EchoWisp

EchoWisp: Shut up, @BigTed

PsyPixie: He's an amazing player. Perhaps even better than you, @EchoWisp

EchoWisp: We'll see about that.

PsyPixie: Be nice, @EchoWisp. He means a lot to me.

Thankfully, when Finn logged in, he couldn't see our past chat and *EchoWisp's* unusually harsh comments.

PsyPixie: Hey, @SharkFinn. Welcome to the squad.

SharkFinn: **Holy crap! This is your squad?**

PsyPixie: **Only when I'm not playing with you.**

SharkFinn: **I'm a big fan of your live streams, @EchoWisp**

EchoWisp: **Thanks. Are we ready to play?**

Disappointed with *EchoWisp's* curt greeting, we launched into a new game.

Mountains of lava spilled over the volcanic landscape, reflecting *EchoWisp's* crabby vibe. This world was full of fire, ash, and brimstone, and I'd never enjoyed it. Part of me wanted to log out, but I couldn't desert my nephew. Not when *EchoWisp* was in a bad mood.

EchoWisp: **Let's go, Pix.**

PsyPixie: **I think I should stay with @SharkFinn for this game**

BigTed: **Ouch, @EchoWisp**

EchoWisp: **Why? Are you two a couple or something?**

SharkFinn: **Gross, @EchoWisp. She's my aunty.**

BigTed: **Happy now, @EchoWisp? It's her nephew!**

EchoWisp's avatar froze.

SharkFinn: **Is he lagging or what?**

PsyPixie: **@EchoWisp?**

BigTed: **I think he's lost internet. @SharkFinn and I will get the Aetherheart. @PsyPixie, protect your boyfriend until he comes back online.**

As their avatars ran off into a smoky haze, I stared at *EchoWisp*. Still frozen. *Fuck.* There was no movement or sound, except for a quiet tap on my apartment door. Sighing in frustration, I stood and wandered to the door. This game was clearly going nowhere.

The peephole revealed Reed pacing the hallway, scratching his head. *What is he doing here?* He paused and knocked again, louder this time.

I opened the door with a furrowed brow. "Is everything okay, Reed? I'm kind of in the middle of something."

He fell back a step as he panned his gaze over me. "It *is* you."

"And…" I laughed at his awkwardness. *Perhaps he is the crazy one.*

"I fucking knew you reminded me of someone."

"Reed, what are you talking ab—"

"I mean, your hair isn't pink, and you don't have iridescent wings, but you're definitely as cute as the avatar I fight with every night."

"Wait..." My smile faded as my brain caught up with Reed's realization. "You're *EchoWisp?*"

The corner of his mouth curled upward. "Hey, Pix."

With a thundering heart, I glanced at my computer then back at my new neighbor. "That can't be possible. We're playing right now."

Reed grabbed my hand and pulled me toward my laptop just in time to witness both our avatars be slaughtered by the enemy. "Looks like *BigTed* and your nephew are on their own now."

"Fuck," I uttered as our names lit up the screen. "We thought your internet had crashed."

"If my internet crashed, you'd know about it." He chuckled. "You're stealing my Wi-Fi."

I struggled to breathe. "How can this be?"

"So, you're telling me you had no idea? Even with that special gift of yours?"

"I mean, I sensed *something*," I said, sinking against the kitchen counter, urging my heart to slow. "But I refuse to look into my future. It's one of my rules."

His ran his thumb over my hand that was still entwined with his. "That's a shame."

"Why?" I asked, peering into the swirling heat behind Reed's blue eyes. *EchoWisp's eyes.*

"Because we could've cut to this the day we met." With a sudden tug, my chest struck his solid torso, and his lips crashed onto mine.

Momentarily shocked, I almost jerked away before his addictive taste and expert tongue pulled me into full submission. Reed slid his hand around the nape of my neck, deepening the kiss, and had me purring as he took control.

"Oh, wow," I murmured, bathing in our lust-infused auras. There were no visions, only intoxication. "I definitely didn't see that coming."

Reed's finger traced the side of my face, taking in every detail. "What about this?" He shifted his mouth to my earlobe—my weakness—and nibbled while circling his thumb over my visibly bra-less nipple.

"Oh, fuck," I murmured as my head fell back in ecstasy.

Positioning his body between my legs, Reed hitched me onto the countertop so his bulging sweatpants pressed against my core. The gentle grazing and pressure below ignited every nerve ending until I could barely form a thought. "Oh god, that's definitely surprising,"

"Better than Gary?" he rasped out as his hands grasped my thighs, enhancing the force below.

"Oh." My head sprung up. "He's not…"

"A real person?" His chest bounced with his chuckle. "Oh, I know."

"But how?"

The trash can vibrated behind us, and my wide eyes shot to his.

"Let's just call it a 'lucky guess.'" Reed pressed his forehead to mine as his laughter morphed into a sexy chuckle, and with a shit-eating grin, my new neighbor scooped up my ass and carried me to the bedroom, just as our remaining squad members fused the two *Aetherhearts* and won the game.

THE END

If you adored Grayson and Josie's story, you'll be captivated by Melanie's journey next. Keep reading for an excerpt from *Finding Beauty*, book 2 in the Love, Beauty & Soul series

Prologue

Ninety days at New Hope Rehabilitation Center. *Check.*
No alcohol. No drugs. No sex. *Check.*
A newfound sense of confidence. *Fuck.*

I glanced back, waiting for the confidence to Indiana Jones it out the closing doors, but it didn't follow. The brochure lied.

Drawing in a long unsteady breath, I lifted my suitcase and carried it down the stairs. The salty Malibu breeze caressed my face, calming me as I approached my ride. I hadn't seen Grayson since he had brought me here after my self-destructive behavior almost cost him the love of his life. Now, both he and Josie were waiting for me with smiles I didn't deserve.

Although Grayson had kept his distance through my recovery, Josie had called multiple times. After everything I had put her through, she still had the capacity for forgiveness and had turned into an unlikely friend. She is beautiful inside and out, and perfect for Grayson in every way.

My parents hadn't visited once, nor had I expected them to. They were still furious at me for breaking off my *fake* engagement to Grayson and ruining their plans to merge Warren Media with Harlow Corp. I was an embarrassment to the family. A failure. And for the first time in twenty-eight years, I couldn't care less.

With an emotionally and physically absent father and a narcissistic mother, along with years of emotional manipulation, my therapist wasn't surprised my mental health was a shit show. I'd developed depression and a mild dependent personality disorder, and together with my abandonment issues, the anxiety of losing the only person I could truly rely on had sent me spiraling.

Of course, my parents dismissed the diagnosis and refused to support my treatment plan, meaning Grayson had to flip the bill. Ironically, he was the person I was dependent on.

I'd used Grayson as my crutch for so long that I didn't know how to survive without him. I'd done things, terrible things, to keep him beside me, but I'd finally learned to let him go. To let him be happy…without me.

"Do you really expect me to carry my own bags?" I hollered at the two people I cherished the most in the world. Grayson rushed forward to pick up my luggage, but I shoved his hand aside with a laugh. "I got this, Harlow."

Grayson shook his head as he pulled me in for a hug. "Glad to see you haven't lost your sense of humour."

I caught Josie's eye over his shoulder and pushed Grayson off like a sister would a brother. "Hi, Jos," I said, taking a hesitant step toward her.

"Hi, Mel." Josie's mouth curved into a gorgeous smile before she threw her arms around me. "Are you ready to start your new life in the big city?"

Adrenaline filtered through my body. "More than ever."

"Well, jump in the car, or you're going to miss your flight." Grayson snatched my suitcase and threw it into the trunk before opening the door for me.

"I really could've caught a cab," I uttered, sliding into the backseat. I still couldn't believe they had paused their epic honeymoon in Europe just to drive me to the airport.

"Don't be silly," Josie replied, peeking back at me. "We wanted to see you."

Warmth filled my cheeks. "Thank you. It is nice to see some familiar faces."

Grayson caught my eye in the rearview mirror as he started the car. "You still haven't spoken to your parents?"

"No," I said, gazing out the heavily tinted window. "What about you?"

"We're…working on things."

Josie looked across at Grayson with a tight smile before placing her hand over his. "We just need to look forward. We all do."

My heart twinged as I gazed down at their interlocked fingers. I wanted that. Their love was something I never thought possible for people like us, but Grayson had proved me wrong. Their relationship gave me hope. Hope that had gotten me through the last three months.

Apparently, I was a perfect storm of bad parenting and unfortunate experiences. I never realized how damaged I was until I removed all my vices. The drinking, the drugs, and the sex were all my go-to avoidance behaviors. Not even Grayson could fill the inescapable void.

In the downtime I had between therapy sessions, an old love of mine resurfaced—art. I'd studied Art History in college, not to get a job—I didn't need one of those— but to one day fill my house with beauty. I refreshed myself with all the greats... Michelangelo, Van Gough, Monet, Miro, Dali...and researched new artists I believed had the potential to join them.

"Adrian is so excited to have you join their team," Josie said, breaking the silence that lulled over the car.

My stomach somersaulted. "I am too. Thanks, Josie. I owe you."

"Are you kidding? They practically begged me for your number after my exhibition."

I'd attended many exhibitions at AG Galleries throughout America, but Josie's photography show was my first experience behind the scenes. To my delight and the curator's amazement, her incredible work sold out in just one night.

"I hope it works out," I uttered as the devil on my shoulder started dancing.

"You'll be fine," Grayson said, clearly sensing my apprehension. "You're a natural at this stuff."

Josie reached back and squeezed my hand. "You really are."

For the rest of the drive, we chatted about Grayson and Josie's adventures through Europe. Although I was happy for them, the familiar dread of Grayson disappearing again crept up on me. I closed my eyes and repeated several mantras until the unwelcome feelings subsided. I had to do this without him.

Half an hour later, we arrived at the airport to set off in different directions. Grayson and Josie were heading to Spain—

in a private jet, no doubt—while I spent the last of my savings on a commercial flight to New York.

"Now," Josie said, bracing my forearms. "Amy's moving in with her boyfriend in the same building, so you'll have the apartment to yourself."

"And we're not coming home anytime soon," Grayson said, grinning at his wife. "So there's no need to rush things."

"Thank you, but as soon as I have enough saved for a security deposit, I'll be out of there. You guys have already done more than enough for me."

"I'm so proud of you, Mel," Josie said, throwing her arms around my neck. "You have to send me an email once you're all settled, okay? Oh, and give Luci a big hug for me, will you?"

I scrunched up my nose as we parted. "Who's Luci?"

Grayson slipped his arm around his wife's waist with a deep-chested laugh. "Oh, you'll find out."

"C'mon, he's not that bad," Josie said, nudging him away with her elbow. "He's my dog, but he'll be living with Amy and Reed while we're away."

"Are you sure? I don't mind looking after him. I've always wanted a pet."

Grayson chuckled. "He isn't for beginners."

"Fair enough." I was probably more of a cat person anyway.

"Listen," Grayson uttered as all the humour left his face. "I know you won't accept any help from me, so if you need anything, please ask Josie."

The corner of my mouth lifted. "That's a bit of a loophole, isn't it?"

His stern expression didn't falter. "I mean it. Anything at all."

As I nodded my head, Grayson stepped forward and hugged me. "Show them what you're made of, Warren."

I swallowed back tears as I peered up at the man I didn't need anymore and made sure I was the first to let go. "Goodbye, Gray."

With a warm smile, he grabbed Josie's hand and dragged her away. I expected myself to chase them down and plead with them to come with me, but instead, I remained completely still, relishing the moment. In the midst of the crowded airport, I was completely alone, and for the first time, I was okay with that.

Glancing up to the departure screen, I searched for my home for the foreseeable future. New York City. It was time to live on my terms and finally find out what I was capable of. Feeling lighter and happier than I'd ever been, I took my first step forward.

Chapter 1

11 years earlier

"Hold it right there, young lady!"

My hand froze on the doorknob. "Dammit, Grayson," I murmured, ignoring my mother as I stared out the window at the empty driveway. "Where are you?"

"Melanie?!" Her tone grew sterner.

With a low growl, I followed the sound of chopping blades into the kitchen. "Yes?"

"I knew you'd try to sneak out," she said, running her judgmental gaze over my school uniform. "I wanted to see you before your first day back."

Straightening my posture, I stepped cautiously toward my mother. The five food groups lay scattered across the countertop—the ingredients to her latest dieting fad, no doubt.

"Forget something this morning?" she asked, not even wincing as she whizzed the blender.

"I don't think so…" I didn't have chores.

She poured the liquid breakfast into two cups and tapped her lips with her index finger. "What have I taught you?"

"Never leave the house without lipstick," I droned, reaching into my bag to fish out the red lipstick she bought me, which was three shades brighter than necessary.

"You just keep forgetting these simple rules, don't you?" She chortled. "That's why you need to look your best at all times. A scatter-brain like you will need to find a successful man, and successful men appreciate attractive women."

I pressed my lips together into a tight smile but didn't say a word. It was easier to ride out the storm.

"It also wouldn't hurt to hitch that skirt up a little. You may have to wear that horrendous uniform, but you can still flaunt your best assets."

Peering down at my legs, I ran my hands over the gray skirt that already sat just above my knees. "It's fine, Mom."

"Hmm...I guess you're right. You should probably wait until you lose those extra pounds you put on over summer."

I inwardly pleaded for Grayson to arrive, and praise the Lord, a horn blasted outside. "I've got to go. I'm running late."

"I don't know why you don't get Miguel to drive you. You're putting Grayson out, making him come all the way back to Bel Air after swim practice."

The mention of our driver, aka my mother's lover, made my stomach roil. "I'm not making Grayson do anything, but he wouldn't have to if you'd just let me get my license."

Mom's nose turned up at the suggestion. "Women like us don't drive ourselves, Melanie."

"Bye, Mom," I grumbled, spinning on my heel. I'd already lost that fight a thousand times.

"Wait!"

I closed my eyes and blew all the air from my lungs. I'd almost made it.

Mom sauntered over with a sickly sweet grin and handed me an olive-green concoction. "It's the most important meal of the day."

"In a takeaway cup..." I forced a smile. "How thoughtful."

"This should fill you up for the rest of the day, so there'll be no need to eat any of that dreadful cafeteria food."

I grabbed the drink without complaint, just to get the fuck out of there. "Thanks, Mom."

"Anything for my baby," she said, tilting her head as she reached for my face. I was momentarily surprised by the loving gesture until her fingers pinched the ends of my hair. "You're clearly overdue for a trim. I'll book you in."

The horn blasted again.

"I've got to go. Grayson's waiting." I pulled away from her grasp and strode out of the kitchen before she could insult me any further.

"I'll be out late tonight," Mom called out. "So you'll have to organize your own dinner."

"Got it," I yelled before slamming the front door closed.

My smile grew as I jogged down the stairs toward Grayson's car. I threw open the passenger door and jumped in, careful not to spill the disgusting drink on the leather interior.

Grayson's warm laughter filled the car. "Whoa, since when are you so eager to get to school?"

"Since it means I can spend the next eight hours away from my mom."

"Rough morning?"

I shrugged. "Normal morning."

Grayson accelerated down the long winding driveway and through the iron gates. "There's something in the glove box that may cheer you up."

My gaze flew to the compartment in front of me. "A one-way ticket to Paris?"

He grinned. "Better."

Leaving the hideous drink in the cupholder between us, I opened the glove compartment to discover it full of breakfast bars. Full-fat, full-sugar breakfast bars.

"Oh my god." I grabbed the closest one and tore it open. "Have I told you lately how much I love you?"

Grayson chuckled. "Not since I smuggled you that burger last week."

Settling back into the seat, I relished my first bite. "What would I do without you?"

"Waste away to nothing," he grumbled. Grayson hated the way my mother treated me.

"Thanks, Gray."

"Just don't leave *that* in my car," he said, motioning to the drink between us. "It smells like feet."

"But I made it just for you."

"That's fucked up, Mel. I thought we were friends."

I grinned up at him. "The best."

Grayson always had a way of cheering me up. Ever since we were kids, he was the one person I could count on, and my life would've been a nightmare without him. He understood what my parents were like, because his were no better.

"Are you excited about starting our senior year?" Grayson asked as we grew closer to Summerhill Preparatory School.

"I guess," I muttered, eyeing my latest manicure.

"Wow." Grayson's tone oozed sarcasm. "I've never seen you so pumped."

I gazed out the tinted window as we entered the parking lot. "It's just always the same."

"Have we all become too mundane for the most popular girl in school?"

"I'm not the most popular."

Grayson laughed. "All the girls want to be you, and all the boys want to be in you. I'm pretty sure that's the definition of the most popular."

"Not *all* the boys."

He shot me a sideways glance and nudged my shoulder. "You know I don't count."

I smiled sadly. Life would've been so much easier if Grayson and I were more than friends, but it never felt right. "The boys at this school only want what they can see. They don't care about getting to know me."

"You don't exactly make it easy for them."

"Why bother?" I crossed my arms. "It's not like I'd be allowed to date any of them."

"Your parents would let you date me."

"You don't count, *remember*. Plus, there are *20 billion* reasons why they'd let me date you."

Grayson cleared his throat. "You mean *25 billion*."

"Oh right." I rolled my eyes. "My apologies."

"But Summerhill is full of filthy rich kids. I'm sure your parents wouldn't mind you dating someone like…say…Hank?"

"First, ew. And second, the Townsend fortune is leagues behind ours. Just like everyone else's at this school."

"Well, considering our parents have been planning our wedding since we were kids, I doubt either of us will be allowed to start any serious relationships until we've escaped to college."

"I'm counting the days."

Grayson sighed. "Me too."

I scrunched up the breakfast bar wrapper in my hand and chuckled. "They're going to be so upset with us."

"They sure are," he muttered, turning into the empty car space everyone left open for him because he was…well, Grayson. Summerhill's golden boy.

"I think it's our destiny, though."

Grayson's eyebrows rose as he turned to me. "To marry?"

I snorted. "To disappoint our parents."

Thankfully, Grayson and I shared homeroom, otherwise, we only had one subject together. This suited him, but not me. Grayson took school way too seriously and didn't need the distraction, but I only needed to pass. My parents had the right connections and money to get me into any college I wanted—and I wanted whatever college Grayson was going to.

Grayson was adamant about getting there on his own, spending every waking hour studying. He was expected to follow his older brother into the family business, whereas I was simply expected to find a rich husband.

I lowered myself into the seat in the middle of the back row, while Grayson sat in front, spinning around to face me.

"Schedule swap," he said, holding out his hand.

I handed mine over and took his to peruse. "Ouch, you've got Mr. Dawson *and* Ms. Peters."

"And you've got Mr. West," Grayson uttered, turning serious.

"Ugh, I know." Mr. West was more interested in my legs than my grades.

Grayson's stern eyes met mine. "Make sure you sit in the back row."

"Oh, I will," I said with a shudder. "The farther away the better."

"Harlow!" a deep voice boomed across the room.

I groaned as Grayson turned around with a wide grin.

Hank strutted toward our desks and shoved Zach Freeman, the quiet kid, out of his chair so he could sit beside me.

I offered Zach an apologetic smile as he found a new seat before narrowing my eyes at Hank.

"Looking beautiful as always, Mel," he uttered with a sleazy wink.

"Charming as always, Hank," I replied, dripping with sarcasm.

The corner of Zach's mouth twitched, but he didn't look up.

"How was Paris?" Grayson asked, quick to defuse the growing tension.

Hank and I didn't get along. We merely tolerated each other for Grayson's sake.

Hank chuckled. "Let's just say, French women sure know how to fuck."

I groaned and zoned out of their conversation immediately. Grayson wasn't like Hank, but I still didn't want to hear his friend ramble on about his summer conquests.

Staring down at my schedule, trying to memorize it, I was interrupted by growing murmurs echoing through the room. I lifted my head, wondering what the fuss was about, and then I saw him.

Just like a bad 80's rom-com, he strolled into the classroom in slow motion. A shaggy mop of dark hair, a strong jawline, and the prettiest blue eyes I'd ever seen. And tall...not as tall as Grayson, but taller than me. He had my full attention—along with every other girl in the room.

"What's up with you?" Grayson asked, clearly oblivious to the new arrival.

Warmth traveled up my neck and straight down below.

Grayson followed my gaze to where the newbie stood, searching for an empty seat. With a welcoming smile, he lifted his hand and greeted him with a small wave. "Over here!" Grayson called out before pointing to the seat beside him.

"What are you doing?" I hissed.

"Don't be so rude," he muttered with a knowing twinkle in his eye. He turned back and threw out his hand. "Grayson."

The new guy shook it with an uneasy smile. "Scott."

Scott's gaze flickered to mine, but I quickly lowered my eyes, attempting to slow my racing heart.

Grayson chuckled at my response. "This unusually ill-mannered girl is Melanie, and this is Hank."

Hank shook his hand tightly, undoubtedly trying to size him up. "Welcome to Summerhill."

"So, where do you come from, Scott?" Grayson asked, sending me a curious look that I tried to ignore.

Scott tapered his eyes at our weird exchange as he sat down. "Nowhere in particular. We move around a lot."

Hank's eyebrows drew together. "What's your last name?"

My temper spiked as I glared at Hank. "Does it matter?"

Scott's gaze darted to mine, but I lowered my head again. His eyes were entirely too blue.

"I'm just curious," Hank said, leaning back into his chair and crossing his arms.

"Blackwood," Scott answered, but his gaze still burned into the side of my face.

Hank's head tilted. "I'm not familiar with that name."

"That's probably because we've only just met."

I wiped my hand over my mouth to hide my smile, but Grayson erupted into laughter.

"I like you already," Grayson said, turning to face the teacher as she walked in.

Scott's gaze lingered on me until I looked up. "Front of the room is that way," I said, pointing to the teacher.

Hank sniggered. "Oh, burn."

Scott pursed his lips, but his eyes sparkled. With a quick nod, he turned to the teacher as she began the morning roll call.

"Why did you do that?" I asked, nudging Grayson's side as we exited the room.

Grayson laughed and wrapped his arm around my shoulders as we walked down the crowded corridor. "You like him," he whispered in my ear.

My heart lurched, and I pushed him away. "No, I don't."

That only made him laugh harder. "I've never seen you blush over a boy before."

"Shut up!" I glanced back to make sure Scott wasn't nearby.

"Someone has a crush," he sang, continuing the torment.

I ran my hands down my face. "Oh my god, can you stop?"

His rascally smile made girls swoon as they passed us. "I'm right, aren't I?"

"Argh, I'm going to class." I swiveled on my heel in the opposite direction, desperate to end the conversation.

"I knew it," he called after me.

I lifted my hand to wave but raised my middle finger instead. "I'll see you at lunch, Harlow."

―――

As I walked through the cafeteria with my tray of no more than 300 calories, I spotted Grayson at our usual table, but my steps slowed when I discovered he wasn't alone. I took in the faces surrounding him and groaned. Hank. *Idiot.* Lisa. *Moron.* Miranda. *Okay, I guess.* Sarah. *No thanks.* Randy. *Boring.* And the new guy. *Fuck.*

I usually avoided talking to these people, partly because I hated their sense of entitlement, and partly because I was a bitch. I didn't mean to be. I just had no tolerance for people who annoyed me. And most of the people at Summerhill annoyed me.

Summerhill Preparatory School was where you sent your kids if you had money. *Lots* of money. Only Grayson and I were different. While most of these kids were in line to inherit millions, we were set to inherit *billions*. For one reason or another, everyone wanted to be our friend. Grayson let them. I didn't. No one was genuine in our world, and I hated it.

As if he could feel the daggers shooting from my eyes, Grayson looked up as I approached. "Mel," he said, ignoring my death stare. "I saved you a seat." He grinned mischievously as he tapped the chair between him and the new boy.

"I'm fine over here," I grumbled, changing direction and placing my tray at the opposite end of the table.

Grayson shook his head. "Suit yourself."

My entire body heated as Scott watched me, so I picked at my food until the group continued their conversation. I wasn't used to feeling uncomfortable, and it irritated me.

"You play football?" Randy asked Scott. He had the physique for it.

"I've never really been at a school long enough to join a team," he replied before taking a bite of his sandwich.

Hank threw a tater tot in his mouth. "You an Army brat or something?"

Scott's jaw twitched. "Or something."

His response piqued my curiosity. Most of the kids at our school would've reeled off how much their family was worth, where they lived, and what car they drove by now. But Scott didn't utter a word about himself.

"So, where are you all from?" he asked, cleverly turning the question around to avoid further interrogation.

The table lit up with chatter about their family's fortunes, while Grayson and I remained quiet. We didn't announce our wealth.

"What about you two?" Scott asked, panning his gaze from Grayson to me.

Hank laughed. "I'm surprised you don't already know. These guys are Summerhill royalty."

Scott's brows lifted.

"Heir to Harlow Corp," Hank said, pointing at Grayson. "And sole heiress to Warren Media," he added, turning to me with a smirk. "King and Ice Queen of Summerhill Prep."

"Shut up, Hank," I uttered, glaring across at him.

Hank's smug smile grew larger as the girls around him giggled. Grayson cleared his throat, drawing everyone's attention effortlessly. "So, what's happening this weekend?" His eyes caught mine, sending me a silent message to calm down.

"I heard there's a party at Rebecca's," Lisa said, squeezing Grayson's bicep.

I rolled my eyes. "Ugh, no thanks."

Lisa glanced around uncomfortably. "Well, I thought if we all went, it would be kind of fun."

"What's this *we* business?" I stared directly at Lisa without blinking. I'd never liked her.

"Sounds fun. Count me in," Scott interjected.

My eyes snapped to his, and he held my gaze in a silent challenge. Not many people were brave enough to take me on, but I decided to cut the new guy some slack. I turned to Grayson. "You may want to give your new friend some advice on how to avoid an STD...he's going to need it."

Scott's face paled as Grayson chuckled.

Lisa's eyes grew wide. "They're just rumors..."

I smirked. "How's that itch, Hank?"

"What the fu...Gray! You told her?!" Hank lunged at him.

Grayson pushed him away with a laugh. "Sorry, man, you know I can't keep anything from her."

Hank sank back into his chair, shaking his head. "You're a bitch," he hissed at me.

"Thank you." I smiled sweetly. "My mother would be so proud."

Scott's judgmental gaze rolled over me, and all the humour drained from my face. For some reason, his opinion of me seemed to matter, and it irked me.

"So, what do you suggest we do this weekend, Melanie?" Grayson asked, clearly annoyed by my behavior.

"Do whatever the fuck you want," I snapped before leaving the table and the remaining 299 calories behind.

"What was with you at lunch today?" Grayson asked as I climbed into his car that afternoon.

My head fell back against the seat. "You know I'm not great with people."

"Come on, it's our senior year. It can't always be just you and me."

I crossed my arms with a huff. "Why not?"

"Because we're going to miss out on all the fun."

I closed my eyes, knowing he was right. "I'll try to be a little nicer."

Grayson glanced across at me with a sad smile. "You don't have to try. You have a good heart. Stop trying to fight it."

"Just don't make me fake it."

Grayson shook his head with a laugh. "Fake is definitely not a word I'd use to describe you."

"What words would you use?"

He grinned. "Annoying…ly beautiful."

I laughed loudly and sank into the leather seat, wishing it could stay like this forever.

ACKNOWLEDGMENTS

This novel wouldn't have been possible without the love and encouragement of my husband. His belief in me makes me believe in myself. Thank you xox

To my two beautiful boys who think it's hilarious that my book has the f word in it. Love you xox

My beta readers Mal, Sarah and Carmen, you guys are legends. So much wouldn't have happened in this book without you.

To my amazing editors and proof readers, Heather, Jenn & Shae, thank you for making my story shine.

To all my friends who are genuinely interested in my journey as a writer. Thank you. It's such a big part of my life and it means the world that I can share it with you. And to anyone who has read my books, promoted my books via word of mouth or through social media, I truly appreciate it.

Finally, to the incredible Keeperton/Arndell team who are making my dreams come true. THANK YOU!

A x

ABOUT THE AUTHOR

Ann Penny is a contemporary romance author from Melbourne, Australia, known for her emotionally rich storytelling that resonate with readers drawn to tales of passion, resilience, and hope. A two-time finalist for the prestigious Romance Writers of Australia (RWA) Romance Book of the Year Award, Ann Penny is quickly gaining recognition in the romance genre for the exceptional depth and heart in her stories.

Her journey into writing began in childhood, where she often found herself lost in daydreams instead of completing schoolwork—a trait that was later understood to be connected to undiagnosed neurodivergence. These early experiences, where she would immerse herself in imagined worlds and scenarios, ultimately became the foundation for her writing career. Her ability to weave intricate plots and create layered, interconnected stories is a direct result of her imaginative mind and her unique perspective on the world.

Her stories delve into themes of self-discovery, healing from past trauma, and the transformative power of love. Beyond romance, they offer readers tales of post-traumatic growth and personal empowerment, all delivered with a unique voice and a touch of quirky humour.

When Ann Penny isn't writing, she enjoys having a laugh with her husband and sons, cuddling her fur babies, and immersing herself in anything creative. Penny is always striving to craft something beautiful and unexpected while endeavouring to harness her hyperactive mind.

With deep emotional insight, and a huge backlog of untold stories in her head, Ann Penny will continue to embrace her storytelling skills to captivate readers with relatable characters and heartfelt stories—where love and personal growth go hand in hand.

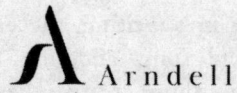

Connect with Arndell

Love this book? Discover your next romance book obsession and stay up to date with the latest releases, exclusive content, and behind-the-scenes news!

Explore More Books

Visit our homepage: keeperton.com/arndell

Follow Us on Social Media

Instagram: @arndellbooks
Facebook: Arndell
TikTok: @arndellbooks

Stay in the Loop

Join our newsletter: keeperton.com/subscribe

Join the Conversation

Use **#Arndell** or **#ArndellBooks** to share your thoughts and connect with fellow romance readers!

Thank you for being part of our book-loving community. We can't wait to share more unforgettable stories with you!